THE EARTH STRIKES BACK

THE EARTH STRIKES BACK

NEW TALES OF ECOLOGICAL HORROR

EDITED BY RICHARD T. CHIZMAR

MARK V. ZIESING BOOKS
SHINGLETOWN, CA   1994

Published by
Mark V. Ziesing
Post Office Box 76
Shingletown, CA 96088

Manufactured in the
United States of America

FIRST EDITION

Interior Design by   *Cover Design & Hand Lettering by*
Robert Frazier   Arnie Fenner

ISBN 0-929480-40-6
LIBRARY OF CONGRESS 94-061244

for a very special person

Andrea Blair Wilson

CONTENTS

THE EARTH
STRIKES BACK

My Copsa Micas

Dan Simmons

1.

I was driving through the mountains of Transylvania in search of the historical Dracula when I encountered Copsa Mica. The town's name is pronounced *Cope-sha Mee-ka* and I had heard of it before coming to Romania—I had even written about it in the short story that had ballooned to a novel and sent me to this cold, remote region to do research—but the impact of the actual place was greater than I had expected.

Copsa Mica had received some small space in the western press as "the most polluted place in the world." The town of some seven thousand people, little more than a village, is dominated by the massive Carbosin plant that makes carbon black for the production of tires. The Carbosin plant and a nearby lead factory employ almost all of the people in Copsa Mica, fill half the valley with their bleak industrial buildings, and rain carbon black on landscape and humans alike. The filth and pollution were the legacy of the late and unlamented Nicolae Ceausescu.

I had not planned to visit Copsa Mica—its role in my story and novel was tangential at most—but our drive from the city of Sibiu to the town of Sighisoara, birthplace of Vlad Dracula, passed through the small industrial town. I say "our drive" because I was traveling with my sister-in-law. She had been born in Germany but had lived in the States since she was sixteen. The theory behind her traveling with me during this research swing through Romania was that although this region of Transylvania had not been a Saxon-dominated area for five centuries or more, the people would still speak German

and we would not require the usual Office of National Tourism "guide" who also served as informer to the Securitate secret police.

The theory worked. We drove the rattling, rental Dacia through the Transylvania Alps for a week, communicating with waiters, officials, museum directors, and ordinary people via our smattering of Romanian and my sister-in-law's German. And then, on a cold, drizzly Monday morning in May, we left the mountain town of Sibiu for the ever-more-mountainous town of Sighisoara and encountered Copsa Mica.

We saw the smoke first. Romania is littered with industrial towns—the air in the refinery city of Pitesti had been so foul that we had rolled up the Dacia's windows and still ended up coughing and wheezing for an hour beyond the city limits—but the smoke above Copsa Mica seemed almost solid, a black fog bank suspended between the hills and above the city like a low ceiling of slowly bubbling asphalt. We were already beneath that black cloud when we came over the last rise and entered Copsa Mica itself.

The kilometer-marker stones were black. One could just make out the town's name on a tombstone-like slab as we entered the edge of the village. The houses were black. The painted wood fences were black. The stones of the sidewalks were covered with an ash-thin film of black; the sheets hanging on the lines to dry were gray. Sheep being driven along the roadside by two young boys were black, although one could catch a glimpse of grayish-white wool in the places where the boys' sticks had touched the backs of the sheep. The boys looked like young Gypsies with black hair, black clothes, and lines of black grime in the creases of their necks and cheeks. Billions of ash-sized carbon particles blew from west to east above the village, the smoke reminding me of the deadly black fog used by the Martian war machines in H.G. Wells' **The War of the Worlds.**

The road swung northeast in the center of Copsa Mica, away from the larger factories and back into the countryside where foothills rose to real mountains swathed in clouds of a cleaner shade of gray. My sister-in-law had brought her camera; I had only a sketchbook. It had begun to rain again. The Dacia's one working wiper smeared black smudge back and forth on the windshield. I drove back down the single paved road of the town again, hunting for a vantage point where we could take a photo. When we stopped to turn around across from the factory entrance near a clutter of empty crates that may have been an

open marketplace, a crowd of Gypsy women and children rushed the car, hands groping for chewing gum that my sister-in-law had offered the first boy to approach. The old woman sitting behind crates, their faces streaked black beneath black hair under black scarves, shoved the grasping children aside in their own eagerness to grab at gum or whatever we would offer.

I turned the Dacia around and headed east again, turning left onto a cinder alley between pre-war factory buildings. Just before the narrow road wound into a maze of slag heaps and brick warehouses, there was a small rise with a view of the town, the smokestacks, and the carbon black factory. I pulled into a cinder turn-out and said, "This should do it. Let's shoot a couple of photos."

It should be understood that I knew that we were breaking the law. All "strategic areas" are off-limits to photography in Romania. Every factory is a strategic area. It didn't matter that this carbon-black factory had been photographed and filmed *ad nauseum* since the fall of the Ceausescu regime as an example of Eastern European pollution at its worst; it did not matter that Ceausescu's police state had been theoretically buried with the man and his wife. This was a factory. Factories were State property. State property was off-limits to all photography, but especially to *foreigners'* photography.

My sister-in-law stepped away from the car and composed the shot with maddening slowness. I didn't want artistry. I wanted one we-were-here, I've-documented-it-for-posterity snapshot of the filthiest town on earth. Then I wanted to get on with finding Dracula's birthplace in Sighisoara, still a three-hour drive through the mountains.

She checked the composition through her viewfinder, found it lacking, moved away from the Dacia, checked it again, frowned, and fiddled with the settings on the long lens.

A heavy truck came up the road out of the slag heaps. I could see three Romanian soldiers in the front seat. There may have been more under the tarp behind the cab.

"Lower the camera," I said through the open window. The drizzle had stopped.

My sister-in-law stood there, camera still raised. The soldiers were pointing at her and talking animatedly.

I said softly, "Lower the camera." It was too late to hide our effort at photography, but there was no need to provoke these clowns. The roll of film in her Minolta held not only the photos I needed of Sibiu, but the documentation of Castle Dracula two

Dan Simmons

hundred miles and a maze of mountains behind us. Those photos were half the reason I had flown to Romania. "Let's go," I said.

She did not lower the camera. The truck had slammed to a stop now and the soldier on the far side swung out on a running board. The driver was waving his hand at her. The soldier on the running board had a small machine-gun, something like the old Sten guns one sees in World War II movies, slung over his shoulder. He shifted it on his hip as he began to shout at us.

My sister-in-law did not lower the camera but she smiled at them. Her theory whenever encountering Romanian officialdom at its most Gestapoish was to give them a big smile.

The soldiers were not beguiled. The one on the running board swung down from the truck. The driver opened his door and shook his fist. A face peered around the canvas at the back of the truck. I had visions of sitting in a security office somewhere down in those slag heaps, waiting while Romanian military bureaucracy ground its peristaltic way toward some decision. Several times in Romania we had been through the process of having our passports taken, scrutinized, frowned over, and argued about by military-types who could obviously barely read. Now I could imagine our film being confiscated in the same methodical, emotionless process.

She continued smiling at them, her eye back at the viewfinder. The soldier was coming around the front of his truck now.

I leaned across the Dacia's front seat, swung the passenger door open, called my sister-in-law by name, and said very quietly but very firmly, *"Lower the fucking camera and get in the fucking car. Now."*

The smile disappeared. She got in the car. The soldier stopped where he was and angrily waved his arm, pointing down the road. I backed the Dacia out, found a wider place to turn around, and left the factory grounds. The truck followed us out.

My passenger brooded the rest of that day and much of the rest of the trip. She would not be party to cowardice. She was an American. She did not back down in front of penny-ante officials. She had a right to photograph whatever she wanted. I might be timid, but she was bold. Her motto was to stand her ground. Never show fear. Smiles are more powerful than guns. They're only human.

I listened for a while and then shut it out when I realized that her bravado was the brittle courage of someone who had

never been in a position of real powerlessness. She had no concept of the depth of Romanian paranoia, no understanding of how real their security mania was...even when it applied to a filthy old carbon black plant.

We reached Sighisoara by mid-afternoon. The birthplace of Vlad Dracula was a medieval mountain town surrounded by stone walls and towers shrouded in gray clouds. The windshield of the Dacia was still streaked with black grime as we parked and climbed the cobblestone alleys of Sighisoara. I found myself looking at the twelfth-century homes and churches but thinking of the black cloud floating above a soot-buried village hundreds of kilometers to the west. I found myself thinking of Copsa Mica.

2.

The anthology request was to write a story of ecological horror. The usual clichés came to mind: mutants wandering a despoiled landscape, roving gangs of thugs in an ozone-blistered desert ala **Bladerunner** or **A Boy and His Dog**, vicious humans drowning in their own filth while the ecosphere gasped its last. *Terence*, A.E. Housman said, *this is stupid stuff.*

I'll wait, I thought. Wait to see what real horror might touch me. If none does, there will be no story.

3.

Madame Bovary may be the most horrific novel I have ever read. I confess I did not read it until the spring of 1991, only weeks before I was to leave for Romania.

I was in New York City for the Nebula Awards: little blocks of Lucite with galaxies of sand in them, given by the Science Fiction Writers of America. I did not belong to the organization. My novel was not destined to win.

The awards ceremony was at the Roosevelt Hotel, a rotting hulk of a place that now catered to large herds of naive foreign and domestic tourists. My room was almost precisely the size of a small storage closet we kept filled with junk in our garage back in Colorado. The walls of the room were waterstained the color of dried blood, the wallpaper was peeling at every corner, the tattered carpet was caked with great gobs of something that may have been semen, the window looked out on an alley and would not close all the way, and there came the sound of in-

sects and rodents scrabbling inside the walls and the equally clear sound of humans mating on the other side of the inhabited walls. All in all, it was about the best one could do for a hundred-dollar room in New York in 1991.

I did not sleep at all that night. The alley outside the sagging window was some sort of central dumping depot for every garbage truck in Manhattan. First would come the grinding of gears, then the wild beeping of their backing-up alert, then a grinding of steel on concrete, then another louder grinding of gears and servomechanisms as trash was mashed, raised, and dumped into what sounded like a bottomless steel tube. This went on from midnight to six A.M. I read **Madame Bovary** until the first April light filtered through the grimy window. I took the paperback with me as I went out into the cold rain to find a coffeeshop open at five-thirty.

I thought as I read of the death of Emma Bovary that this might be the most perfectly horrible scene I had ever read or ever would read. But a few pages further on, there was horror beyond horrors. You probably know the scenes I mean:

"Charles came in, walked over to the bed and slowly drew back the curtains."

"Emma's head was turned toward her right shoulder. The corner of her mouth, which remained open, was like a black hole at the bottom of her face; both thumbs were bent inward toward the palms; her eyelashes were sprinkled with a kind of white dust; and her eyes were beginning to disappear in viscous pallor that was like a fine web, as though spiders had been spinning on her face. The sheet sagged from her breasts to her knees, rising again at the tips of her toes; and it seemed to Charles that an infinite mass, an enormous weight, was pressing down on her."

At six o'clock in the morning, in a Greek coffeeshop in midtown Manhattan, I shoved aside my cup of coffee and leaned against the Formica counter, feeling the cold sweat of revulsion on my forehead and upper lip. This was infinitely worse than anything Skipp and Spector or any of the other so-called splatterpunk horror writers could throw at me. This was pure genius casting a totally unsentimental eye at death. Nor was it just death that rose from the pages like the scent of corruption; it was the absolute death of a character who had been more alive than many living people I knew.

I thought this was the worst. I was wrong. A page later came the worst.

"When Homais came back at nine o'clock (he seemed to have been constantly in the square for the past two days), he was laden with a supply of camphor, benzoin and aromatic herbs. He also brought a vase full of chlorine water, to drive away miasmas. When he arrived, the maid, Madame Lefrançois and the elder Madame Bovary were gathered around Emma, about to finish dressing her; they drew down the long, stiff veil which covered her all the way to her satin shoes.

"Felicité sobbed: 'Oh, my poor mistress! My poor mistress!'"

"'Look at her,' said Madame Lefrançois with a sigh. 'She's still so pretty! You'd swear she was about to get up!'"

"Then they bent over and put on her wreath.

"They had to lift her head a little, and when they did so a flood of black liquid came from her mouth as though she were vomiting.

"'Oh! Look out for the dress!' cried Madame Lefrançois. 'Give us a hand!' she said to the pharmacist. 'You're not afraid by any chance, are you?'"

I don't know about the pharmacist, but I was afraid. I left my breakfast uneaten, my coffee untouched, and went out to walk off the nausea and sickness through the rain-slick streets. There was an apartment-workers' strike. Residents and shop owners had carried out garbage and piled it ten feet high along the curb. The stench was powerful.

It was not the first time I had realized that New York was a corpse, but it was the first time I had seen its face under the veil. The city was like Emma Bovary, its death made all the more terrible by the memory of its vital and vivacious past.

Street workers were flushing something from the sewers near the Roosevelt Hotel. Black liquid gushed from the dark hose and flowed into the garbage-strewn gutters.

4.

Where I live in Colorado, the environment does not seem so badly endangered. When we moved to the Front Range of the Rockies near Boulder in 1974, my wife and I would drive up Flagstaff Mountain and look out at the patchwork of lights running along the base of the foothills: small constellations of towns and villages connected only by the most tenuous of gleams where headlights moved along gossamer webs of highways.

Recently we had dinner with Steve King and his wife Tabitha at a restaurant halfway up Flagstaff Mountain. The carpet of

lights beyond the window was almost solid as far north and south as we could see along the Front Range. Few patches of darkness remained and even those were not absolute.

"It's changed since I lived here in the early 'seventies," said King. "People multiply and spread like cancer cells. It's scary."

I nodded agreement and turned my attention to the chocolate mousse.

5.

I know something about cancer. Both of my parents died of it, each battling it for six months during that final year of their lives.

There is a smell to terminal lung cancer. It may be due to the actual breakdown of lung tissue or to the growth of cancer there like fibrous roots filling up every free space in the sacs of the lungs. I used to sit on the edge of the hospital bed and hold my father's shoulders as he coughed and spat up small, gray pieces of his lungs. The smell was unforgettable. It was not unlike Copsa Mica.

My father's shoulders grew thinner and sharper and more-brittle feeling until I was afraid that I would break bones if I held him too tightly as he coughed. He was only sixty years old. It had been less than two decades since he used to swing me up on his shoulders when I was a toddler; I could not imagine anyone's shoulders being stronger, or broader, or a safer perch to rest on.

During the last weeks of my father's life, my two brothers and I resumed the schedule of watches that we held during the last months of my mother's losing battle with cancer. My older brother would be with Dad from morning until mid-afternoon. My younger brother would spend the afternoon and evening with him. I would stay by the bedside from eleven P.M. until eight in the morning.

A few hours before my father died, at 4:53 in the morning, after two days of what the doctors called coma, Dad sat straight up in bed, opened his eyes, looked at me, said, "Saugus," in a strong voice that seemed to carry some warning, and then lay back, put his hands behind his head the way he used to while dozing off in front of the television, and went back to sleep for the last time.

I didn't know then what Saugus meant. I do not know today. But a few years ago, on a lecture-trip to Boston, I got my

rental car lost on a black, rainy night and found myself wandering through endless streets of rowhouses, then down twisty lanes to darkened suburbs where water dripped from soot-black trees, and finally I stopped near a road sign to find directions back to Highway 1. SAUGUS, the sign read, POP 25,110.

I did not tarry there.

6.

In Copsa Mica almost all of the children suffer from bronchitis and asthma from the carbon black, but it is not the respiratory diseases that will almost certainly kill them at a young age. They will die young from the high concentrations of lead, zinc, and cadmium in the soil.

In Chicago, the air is so rife with lead poisoning from auto emissions that children who live in apartment projects facing the highways test out with a lower I.Q. than children in projects closer to the lake. But even the children living away from the freeway continue to be brain-damaged by eating lead-based paint when they are infants. They will probably not die from lead poisoning; the children of the Chicago projects have a greater than thirty percent chance of dying of gang violence or drug abuse before they are twenty-five.

Saul Bellow once wrote a novel where he championed the hypothesis that lead and other heavy-metal poisoning is making our culture too stupid to survive. The expert quoted in the novel pointed out that Rome began its most precipitous decline after the aqueduct system was lined with lead.

I went to see Saul Bellow at the Miami Book Fair in 1990. So many people showed up for Bellow's reading that they moved it from a university auditorium to a baroque church across the street. The story he read was brilliant and profane; it dealt with a young man's sexual awakening in Chicago around the time of the First World War.

After the reading, I found myself locked out of the church and waiting for a ride in an alley in downtown Miami. Saul Bellow and a small entourage of culture mavens were hustled out by the Book Fair sponsors and for a second we shared the stoop at the back of the church. The car that glided up for him was a new Silhouette Van that looked like one of the photos of the Cars of the Future I used to cut out for my scrapbook when I was seven. Beyond Bellow's wattled neck and porkpie hat, a monorail people-mover glided overhead to the center of Miami.

Farther south, a skyscraper outlined in blue neon pulsed laser beams out toward the bay.

Shit, I thought, *I've finally made it. I'm in the future.*

They bundled Saul Bellow into the Silhouette Van and then I was alone in the alley. There were no cabs, no phone booths, not even a lighted convenience store for blocks in any direction. Beneath the laser pulses and monorail rumbles, the city looked bombed and blasted and as dead as Emma Bovary's eyes. I waited for my ride from the Book Fair for fifteen minutes in that dark alley before going to the locked door of the church and pounding and kicking until someone let me in and arranged to get me back to the hotel.

Future or no, there was no way I was going to walk through downtown Miami at night.

7.

My wife's parents moved to Colorado from their home in Buffalo, New York, about five years ago. We drove back east with our five-year-old daughter to help them move that summer.

On the south side of Buffalo there is an old industrial section called Lackawanna. When the steel industry in this country went belly-up in the late 'seventies and early 'eighties, so did Lackawanna. Now one can drive on a pockmarked and decaying elevated highway through fifteen miles of abandoned steel plants, past weedgrown parking lots designed for five thousand vehicles but now empty except for a single watchman's Pontiac, above slag heaps and scrap metal piles and blackened warehouses with broken windows. It goes on and on and on. The population of Buffalo is now little more than half of what it was twenty years ago. But the detritus remains.

"They should sell it to a movie company," said my wife after ten minutes of driving through the rusting desolation, "and blow it up or something."

"It's been done," I said. The air smelled of old ashes and something darker, more malignant.

8.

Both my parents suffered through radiation treatment: my mother for the brain tumor that killed her, my father for the lung cancer.

The effects of radiation and chemotherapy are—for much of the last months of a terminal patient's life—more devastating than the cancer. We all know the signs: one's hair falls out, blood pools under the skin, nausea and vomiting seem endless.

When I was a sixth-grade teacher, I taught a little girl who was undergoing such treatment. Cybele had been a ballerina before she got sick in fifth grade. She was still beautiful in sixth grade, although her skin was now so pale that it was translucent and she wore a kerchief on her head when she was in the world outside her family at home and her family of friends in the classroom. Her recovery from the brain tumor seemed almost miraculous, and by the summer after our year together she was beginning to dance again.

Cybele died in the spring of her seventh-grade year. The final months were terrible for her; she was in constant pain. She did not complain. Her ballet group specially choreographed **The Nutcracker** so that she could be Clara in the Christmas production and merely sit on the divan and watch the other dancers. When she died, the family did not use the services of a mortuary but held a simple ceremony at home. Cybele's little brother and sister set special toys and photos and snacks in her coffin with her. Every day in sixth grade, my class would have "elevenses"—the British term for mid-morning snack—and every morning Cybele brought out her small brown bag of tortilla chips. Her mother and little brother Sammy set a small brown bag of tortilla chips next to her hand before she was buried.

9.

A friend of mine named Alan is a researcher for the National Center for Atmospheric Research in Boulder, and he was among the first to document the effects of chlorofluorocarbons on the ozone layer. As far back as the late 'seventies he was flying above the arctic and antarctic in pressurized research aircraft, sampling the atmosphere and trying to guess at the extent of the damage.

One winter day not too many months ago, Alan and I were climbing on the Flatirons, a series of giant uptilted rock slabs rising above Boulder, when we climbed out of the Brown Cloud that lay over the Front Ridge like a blanket of airborne filth. Our heads actually came above the smog layer the way a swimmer suddenly rises above the surface of the water.

Eating our sandwiches and chips on a ledge high on the

Flatirons, I asked Alan about his research. He said he had gone on to other things, leaving the ozone problem to satellites and statisticians.

"If I believed in the Gaia theory," said Alan, "I'd say that the living organism that was the Earth is trying to save itself by treating its cancer with heavy doses of radiation."

I swallowed the bit of sandwich I was chewing and raised an eyebrow. "And what's the cancer?"

Alan smiled, leaned back against the warm limestone, and looked out at the Brown Cloud that stretched from Pikes Peak a hundred miles south to the Wyoming border a hundred miles north. "We are," he said softly. "People. Us."

I quit chewing. "And would that radiation treatment be in time?"

Alan shrugged and looked up at the traverse and final bit of climb ahead of us. "We'd better get going," he said. "We don't have too much time left before it gets dark."

10.

Leaving Romania by the Orient Express, my sister-in-law and I spent a day in Budapest and took a hydrofoil up the Danube from there to Vienna. The boat ride was beautiful after the Stalinist nightmares of the train trip.

North of Hungary, between Komarno and the Czech city of Bratislava, those two countries are completing work on one of the largest and most idiotic engineering projects ever undertaken in Europe. A long series of massive dams, reservoirs, and canals are being connected to bypass the slow-moving Danube so that the river can be tapped for hydroelectric power. It will change the Danube and the surrounding countryside forever.

At a bend in the river called the Hungarian Gate, the Danube now irrigates eight nations of Europe, just as it has since before any of those countries existed. Looking at the tree-lined river and rustic valley from the hydrofoil, one can easily imagine the area as the frontier for the Roman Empire, with comfortable patrician dachas along the south bank and nothing but dark forests and barbarians to the north. The Dabcikovo and Dunakiliti Dams and the Gabcikovo Canal will end all that.

To realize a totalitarian fantasy hatched at the height of Stalinist excess, Hungary and Czechoslovakia will—with the help of Austrian bankers—dam the Danube, send the water down the fifteen-mile-long canal, destroy the floodplain habi-

14

tats, silt the reservoirs so that the Danube Delta dies, pour more sewage than ever into the Danube, lower the water table to the point that entire forests far removed from the canal system will die, contaminate drinking water with heavy metals and industrial toxins, finish off the fish population, and drive untold species of wildfowl away from the area or into actual extinction. The Gabcikovo Canal, nearing completion, rises sixty-five feet above the surrounding plain and is built on an active earthquake fault. Any breech in the canal structure—much less in one of the shoddily-built dams—would send a tidal wave of destruction downriver to kill thousands of people and eradicate entire cities.

There is little organized resistance to the project. The Hungarians, who have much to lose and little to gain from the project, finally agreed to it after the energy shortages of the 'seventies.

One additional benefit to the Czech government, and not a small one according to those who know, is that by diverting the Danube River almost a million ethnic Hungarians who now live north of the river in Czechslovakia (and who might someday want to reunite with Hungary) will wake up to find themselves on the south bank of a new moat that has replaced the ancient river. Czechoslovakia will be effectively "de-Magyarized," an outcome which the Czech government has pursued since the days it was shipping Jews to German ovens.

There is little effective international opposition to Gabcikovo. Business is, after all, business. And national sovereignty rules everywhere. A planetary population that merely wrings its hands at the destruction of the rain forests will not focus on something as small as the destruction of the Danube and the life that has fed on it for millennia.

"It's pretty," said my sister-in-law as the hydrofoil skimmed its way past Esztergom and pounded northwest toward the Hungarian Gate.

I looked to the north bank. The forest stretched out to distant hills. The only sign of civilization was a wooden onion-dome church steeple miles to the north. Everything within our view would soon be submerged, dried up, or dead.

"Yes," I said. "It's pretty." I went back to making notes about my Dracula horror-novel.

11.

My daughter's birthday is on February 15. In Colorado, that

date may bring summerlike weather or massive blizzards. When Jane turned six, the day was springlike, the sunlight warm. She wanted to go to the Denver Zoo and we did.

The Denver Zoo is old-fashioned and not terribly exciting, but it takes hours to see all of the sections. By early afternoon we had not made it to the primates yet and the day had turned cloudy and blustery.

"It's getting cold, kiddo," I said. "What do you say we call it a day and come back another time?"

Jane seemed to consider this. She was holding a black balloon with a zebra depicted on it in white stripes. "Can we stay and see the rest?" she said at last. "They might not all be here when we come back."

We stayed and made the complete circuit.

12.

"How would you kill the cancer of humanity?" I asked my friend Bill. We were having lunch at the National Oceanic and Atmospheric Research Center in Boulder where Bill worked as an astrophysics instructor.

"If I were Gaia?" he asked around a mouthful of salad.

"Yeah."

Bill looked at his fork. "I don't much like the Gaia business," he said. "It's too limited. Too parochial."

I gave him a quizzical look.

Bill sipped his iced tea and lifted the salad fork like a baton. "Why limit the self-regulation organism to just this planet?" he said.

"It's the only one that has a biosphere," I said.

He shrugged. "That's like saying that the heart is the only muscle that pumps blood so that it's the most important. Why not look at the system as the total self-regulating organism?"

I frowned. "The solar system?"

Bill picked a tomato out of the salad and ate it thoughtfully. "Why stop there? Assuming that superstrings actually connect the galaxies on some level that we can't understand and that the Taoist physicists are right that a cause here creates an effect *there*, why not designate the entire universe as Gaia?"

"All right," I said. "Assuming that everything is Gaia and Gaia is everything, how would you go about eliminating the cancer of humanity?"

Bill focused on the blank cafeteria wall across from him.

"Well, assuming that Gaia was just the earth," he began, ignoring the premise we had just created, "she'd have the usual self-regulating mechanisms for decreasing or eliminating the population: famine, disease…can't say predators because we've eliminated almost all the other species that have traditionally preyed on us…except ourselves, of course." He ran a hand through his mane of gray hair. "Ice ages, ozone depletion with its commensurate radiation rise, volcanic activity with its associated temperature drop, greenhouse effect with just the opposite effect…" He shook his head and looked at me. "Nope, none of them are radical enough to count as cancer surgery. Some might have the desired effect, but it takes too long. Like cancer, humanity metastasizes too quickly."

"What if Gaia was the whole thing?" I said, gesturing feebly toward the ceiling.

Bill cleared his throat and adjusted his glasses. "Are we talking about Noah here?"

"No. Natural causes and believable effects."

He rubbed his cheek. "Well, radiation is elegant. But it's hard to get the desired amount from the sun. It's too stable. Plus half the planet is shielded by the planet itself half the time."

"Nova?" I said.

He shook his head. "Our sun can't go nova. Too small by about a factor of ten."

"A nearby sun then?" I persisted. "Supernova?"

Bill smiled as if I had finally said something interesting. "Most of my colleagues would get a hard-on if a nearby sun went supernova. Hasn't happened in our galaxy since sixteen oh-four and the recording instruments weren't too sophisticated then. Watching that sort of event in another galaxy's sort of like kissing your sister…"

"But would it sterilize the cancer?" I said, realizing that I was perseverating.

Bill blinked and seemed to bring me in focus. "Kill all of us human germs?" he said. He pursed his lips for a minute and said, "Uh-uh."

"Why not?"

He sighed the way any specialist sighs when he or she is talking to a not-especially-bright lay person. "Look, let's say the nearest star to the earth…other than our own, of course…were to go supernova…"

"Alpha Centauri," I said, trying to show him that I was not a total ignoramus.

Bill twitched a smile. "Proxima Centauri, yes. Let's say it goes nova."

"Supernova you mean."

"No, just a plain nova to start with." Bill looked down at the table and moved his fingers as if tapping invisible calculator keys. "It'd reach an absolute magnitude of about...mmm, nine...so that would give an apparent magnitude of...ah, thirteen point five let's say. Pretty bright. About the same as a full moon. Of course, you couldn't see it unless you were near the equator or in the southern hemisphere..."

"What about the radiation?" I asked calmly. I was determined not to show any impatience.

"You mean other than the visible radiation I just mentioned?" said Bill, matching my patience with his. "Hard radiation wouldn't pose any problem, although there'd be some electromagnetic interference in communications bands using..."

"What about a supernova?" I interrupted.

Bill tapped the table again. "Okay. Not likely with the Centauri system, but let's pretend...Mmmm, an absolute magnitude of twenty-one point five. Pretty bright. About four thousand full moons. You'd definitely cast a shadow. It'd be like a second, smaller sun in the sky for a couple of months. Like the end of that movie sequel, whatsitsname...**Two Thousand Ten**."

I smiled a bit. "And it would wipe out humans? All the higher life forms?"

Bill matched my smile with a slight frown. "Did I say that? Uh-uh, the actual energy increase above what our sun puts out would be...oh, six tenths of a percent. Not insignificant, to be sure. It'd create havoc with our weather, wipe out satellite communication and keep the Concorde at lower altitudes for a few weeks, but wipe us out? No way."

I must have looked disappointed, because Bill said, "But there is a way Gaia could eradicate us. Other than massive comet or meteor strikes, I mean...which seems like rather radical surgery since you'd have to wipe out all life down to the level of phytoplankton..."

"What?" I prompted after a moment of silence had passed.

"Triggering a supernova chain reaction," he said, spearing at a radish in his salad.

I waited.

"Galaxy M-Eighty-two blew itself to shit about twelve million years ago," said Bill. "There's no reason ours couldn't do it." He pointed his fork at me. "You see, a lot of stars are al-

ready in the pre-supernova condition. A nearby supernova— this'd have to be near the Core obviously..."

"Obviously," I said.

"A nearby supernova warms its pre-supernova neighbor that's already on the brink of supernovadom and the radiation it absorbs shortens its already-short lifespan...say, from a thousand years before blowing to just a few months. Then star number two goes supernova and the energy of both blown stars travels a few light years—remember, this is in the Core—to a third pre-supernova sun and...well, it's obvious..."

"Yes," I said.

"A chain reaction like M Eighty-two," he said, nodding.

I nodded with him.

"The release was equivalent to five or six million normal stars," mused Bill, looking at the wall again. "We got pictures of the remnant of a hydrogen jet at least a thousand light-years long flashing out from the galaxy's core. Like a giant blowtorch. Anything in the way of that torch got crisped. Then the entire galaxy blew like a kid's balloon."

I stared at him a moment. "So you're saying that Gaia could get rid of humanity...the cancer...by blowing our entire galaxy to bits? Isn't that a little extreme for a cure?"

Bill turned toward me. "Have you even seen the effects of a double mastectomy?"

I had. My mother had battled breast cancer before the brain tumor killed her. I remember standing in the upstairs hallway as a child of ten and seeing the light shining through her nightgown and thinking, *Oh, Jesus.*

"Besides," said Bill, "there are over a hundred billion galaxies and each of them contain a couple of hundred billion stars on average. Don't think of Earth...or even of our galaxy...as an organ in Gaia's body. More of a cell." He finished his iced tea, rose, and picked up his tray. "But then, I don't buy this Gaia stuff anyway. See you around."

I watched Bill amble away with his tray. There were no windows in the cafeteria. I had no idea if the sun was still out.

13.

Today, driving north along Interstate 25 toward Cheyenne, Wyoming, I count six cars with anti-nuclear bumper stickers. Our only nuclear power plant in Colorado is the St. Vrain Nuclear Power Station less than ten miles from my home. Designed as a

high-temperature gas-cooled reactor for regions with little water for coolant, the device was touted as infinitely safer than even the standard American water-cooled reactor, much less the type of insane, half-assed design that led to Chernobyl. But the St. Vrain reactor was a prototype and as expensive and cantankerous as a handbuilt Maserati. It was down for repairs more than it was on line. So the utility company cut its losses, shut the plant, and arranged to ship the radioactive core, the contaminated reactor vessel parts, and the tons of radioactive debris to the national storage center that had been planned for twenty years.

Only there is no national storage center. All of our western states refuse to accept nuclear waste, or the sites are not yet certified, or the political debate has stymied action. The waste sits there at St. Vrain Nuclear Power Station. Last summer two tornados ripped through the area, four miles from us, precisely between the reactor storage fields and our home.

Another car passes me. This bumper sticker says **Split Wood, Not Atoms**. Our area has over two hundred high-risk, pollution-alert, non-burn days a year. The mountain towns are worse. Vail and Aspen are literally strangling on their own wood smog.

The mountains seem to recede now and high prairie stretches miles to the west and a seemingly infinite distance to the east. Just before I reach the Wyoming border I see the Rawhide Energy Project in the middle of sagebrush and desolation. Its smokestacks seem taller than the mountains behind it. Rail lines cross the sagebrush-strewn prairie to deliver the mountains of coal the plant needs. There is little visible pollution today, but I know that the emissions from this plant follow the low area of the old Platte River and sometimes blanket the empty hearts of three western states with airborne particulates.

We are lucky here. In some areas, the high arsenic content of the coal being burned dumps over a ton and a half of arsenic *a day* on the surrounding countryside. School children in such areas test for almost lethal levels of arsenic in their hair, blood, and urine. Most do not immediately die from it. Many will die of cancer in years to come. Some of the children will receive radiation treatment, but that rarely works with a cancer that is sufficiently far along. I know. I have seen it.

The radio tells me that the President has again vetoed the findings of the international science committees that recommended immediate action to deal with the ozone depletion and

the greenhouse effect. New committees will be convened to seek further data.

A green Ford Taurus passes me with a bumper sticker I have never seen before. It reads—*CREATIVITY IS MORE IMPORTANT THAN KNOWLEDGE*—**Albert Einstein**.

14.

Richard T. Chizmar is the guy who invited me to do an "ecological horror story." I call him and tell him to forget it, that I have none to write.

15.

A group of us go backpacking into the Roosevelt National Forest along the Continental Divide. One of the guys has been foolish enough to pack two sixpacks of beers onto the eleven-thousand foot high sub-alpine plateau and we drink them all that first night.

I find myself telling my disjointed thoughts about Gaia. A friend of ours, a very smart but very New-Ageish woman named Niki, says, "You've got it all screwed up."

I just look at her across the fire.

"We're the cancer, all right," she says, her dark eyes reflecting the flames, "but not because of all the overpopulation and pollution."

"What then?" I say, mildly irritated. It was *my* theory.

"We're the cancer because of all the emotional and psychic poisons we're pouring into the world."

I roll my eyes slightly and sip my beer. Niki has been to Sedona to tap into the power center there. If she and I have any common basis for conversation, we have not found it yet.

"I'm serious," she says.

"You mean like bad vibes?" I say, trying not to let the derision be too audible.

She does not blink. "No," she says. "I mean like hatred, like lust for power, like racism and anti-Semitism and the thousand other prejudices we pour into our surroundings every day of every year for thousands of years. If Gaia is real, then we're destroying her mind and nervous system more surely than her other systems."

"Mental illness," says Connie.

"Madness," says Tom.

"Didn't the mercury in the tanning process used to drive hatters crazy?" says Karen from her place by the fallen tree.

"Yep," says Ed. "Thus the phrase 'mad as a hatter.'"

Niki rests her elbows on her knees, laces her fingers, and stares into the campfire. "And what do people often do when they get crazy enough?"

"Kill themselves," says Connie.

"Or other people first and then themselves," says Tom.

A log comes apart and tumbles into the embers below, sending sparks rising toward the black sky.

16.

Distraught, ashamed, too deeply in debt to ever escape it, Emma Bovary went to the pharmacist's house and gobbled arsenic. She vomited what looked like gravel into her basin at home. Then the pain began in earnest. She died horribly.

"Her chest immediately began to heave rapidly. Her whole tongue emerged from her mouth; her eyes rolled and grew dim, like the globes of two lamps about to go out, and she would have seemed dead already if it had not been for the frightful movement of her ribs, shaken by the furious, constantly quickening gasps, as though her soul were struggling to break away...

"Suddenly, from outside, came the sound of heavy wooden shoes and the scraping of a stick on the sidewalk, then a voice rose up, a raucous voice singing:

"The heat of the sun on a summer day

"Warms a young girl in an amorous way.

"Emma sat up like a galvanized corpse, her hair hanging loosely, her eyes fixed and gaping.

"To gather up the golden stalks

"After the scythe has cut the wheat,

"Nanette bends down and slowly walks

"Along the furrows at her feet.

"'The blind man!' she cried.

"And she began to laugh, a horrible, frenzied, desperate laugh, imagining that she could see the wretched beggar's hideous features looming in the shadows of eternity like the face of terror itself.

"The wind was blowing hard that day

"And Nanette's petticoat flew away.

"A convulsion threw her back down on the mattress. Everyone moved toward her. She had ceased to exit."

17.

In my dream, Mother's funeral is set among the slagheaps of Copsa Mica. The sky hangs low above us like black crepe. There are other mourners there. I see my brothers in the black-garbed throng, but I also see others whom I had not known were part of the family until today.

Mother is laid out on a black bier which itself lies upon a rusted mass of metal which may have once been a machine. When it is my turn, I step closer to pay my last respects. Her face is not as I remember it. For a second I think I have come to the wrong funeral or that they have replaced my mother's body with a stranger's, but then I see the familiar planes of the face and recognize the family resemblance. We all, in our silent rows, standing amidst the silent ashfall, we all resemble her.

Her mouth is open and is little more than a black hole at the bottom of her face. Her hands are contorted as if still fighting death. Her thumbs are bent inward. Her eyelids are congealed with faint granules, like spider eggs. Her eyes, which no one has closed, are beginning to disappear in a viscous pallor that is like a fine web.

I bend over to kiss her goodbye.

Mother's eyes widen, air rushes from the hole of her mouth as if someone had leaned on a bellows, and her contorted fingers grasp my shoulders hard enough to snap bone and gristle. She pulls me toward her.

I think she is going to whisper something to me. I allow my ear and cheek to be drawn to her face.

A flood of black liquid vomits from her. Drenched in it, I try to pull away, but although her fingers have relinquished their grip on my shoulders, the black fluid is as sticky as tar. It connects me to the corpse like viscous strands of licorice-black muscle.

I can see the others inundated, struggling, webs of blackness connecting them to me, to her, and to each other. The ash is now falling so heavily that I cannot see faces, only black forms struggling in the ever-dimming gloom.

The voice, when it comes, is old and not kind. There is an offhand, almost taunting quality to it which belies the terrible struggle for existence going on in the sticky darkness all around me.

"Oh," says the voice. "Look out for her dress!"

And then. "Give us a hand!"

The black fluid has covered my mouth and eyes by this time. I am holding my breath but know that in a second I must inhale the dark, gelatinous poison. It smells of oil and camphor and sulfur and arsenic and vomit. The voice when it comes an instant before I breathe in the blackness, is all but inaudible.

"You're not afraid, by any chance, are you?"

Harvest

Norman Partridge

'Arboles de la ladera porque no han reverdecido
Por eso calandrias cantan o las apachurra el nido...'
—Las Amarillas (Traditional Folk Song)

Raphael Baca split the skin, weeping as he uncovered the skull beneath. He slipped his fingers under a fleshy flap and tugged. The skin peeled off in one piece and he dropped it to the floor, a limp, bloody husk.

He threw the skull into a corner and kicked the skin after it. How many times would it happen? How many seasons would pass before he peeled an orange and found only fruit?

Through the winter, through the spring, he had prayed that things would be different this year. And just this morning his hopes had swelled when he discovered the first orange of the new season, for the fruit had not screamed when he chopped it from the dead branch with his machete.

But in the end it had all been the same as the year before.

Raphael sat at the kitchen table and sharpened his machete. He listened to the wind, heard the woman wailing above it as she wandered the empty streets of C-Town. Raphael prayed that he would look up from his work, through the kitchen window, and see the *bruja* leading the children's ghosts through the deserted streets and away. But Raphael did not bother to look up, because the kitchen window was dirty.

It didn't matter. He had never seen the woman—not even once.

Norman Partridge

He had only heard her cries.

And then, suddenly, he could not hear her at all. The music of the flies was much too loud.

They came, fat and black, squeezing through chinks in the window, buzzing around the bloody fruitskull, ignoring the other skulls that had been picked clean during the previous season.

A stray fly danced over Raphael's bloodstained fingers. He listened to its music and did not move. The fly was hungry, and he would not disturb it. He would not raise his hand against even the most disgusting of God's creatures.

He stared at the dirty window and imagined the woman out there, somewhere, weeping for an audience of ghosts.

The afternoon waned. The flies had gone, their bellies full. Raphael left the shanty. He checked the mailbox at the end of the road, hoping for a reply from the government, but there was nothing waiting for him. There hadn't been any mail in more than a year. He started along the border of the grove, avoiding the *bruja's* domain.

Not far from the mailboxes, a car was parked on the shoulder of the dirt road. Dead trees blanketed it with feeble fingers of shade, printing strange cracks on the white hood and hardtop. Raphael looked inside. He saw keys hanging from the ignition and a wallet tucked haphazardly beneath the front seat. He glanced into the grove but saw no one there.

He hurried away. The wind was rising, and he could almost hear the evil woman weeping again.

This was not the first abandoned car that Raphael had discovered. He imagined the *bruja* falling upon the driver, an innocent who took a wrong turn off the highway. An innocent who had no protection. These days, people didn't believe in creatures like the one that haunted C-Town. They had no faith to protect them.

Raphael wished that he could do something to protect the people who came here, but he could do nothing. Gripping his machete, he walked to the west side of the grove, almost to the highway. The sunlight was still strong there. He skirted the dead trees and was happy at their nakedness, pleased by the spindly shadows that were much too feeble to frighten him.

He sat down and thought about the bewitched fruit. The *bruja's* bugs had killed the trees when the farmers stopped spraying. Raphael imagined that the insects made her witchcraft possible, even though the trees were long dead. He wished he could

find a spray that would kill the cursed bugs, and he decided that tonight he would write another letter to the government and ask if they knew of such a spray.

The sun drifted slowly from the sky. Raphael's shadow stretched before him, as long and gray as a rich man's gravestone.

None of Raphael's children had gravestones. Not Ramona, not Alicia, not Pablo or Paulo. Before his wife left him, Raphael had promised her that he would buy stones as soon as he had enough money to fix the old car. They had to do that first, he said, because they needed the car to visit the cemetery. It was too far away, otherwise.

But it never worked out. His wife left him, and he never had any money. He didn't have the car anymore, either, and the only time he visited the *camposanto* was when nobody came for the cars that he found near the grove.

When that happened, he would drive to the *camposanto* and park nearby. Then he would visit his children. He always found their graves, even though they had no headstones.

Except when the long shadows fell.

And when the shadows turned to darkness and the gravestones disappeared, he walked back to C-Town.

Alone. Crying.

Shadows fell across the grove, thickening, stretching toward him. Raphael moved on and found a rabbit trapped in one of his snares. He took it back to the shanty, where he built a fire beneath a dead oak tree.

Sometimes he worried about eating the rabbits. If the lawyers were right, the animals could be sick with the same disease that killed the children.

The idea frightened him. He looked at the rabbit, suddenly afraid of it. But he was hungry, and he knew that the lawyers were wrong. He had eaten many rabbits in the last two years, and he was not sick.

Still, he was afraid, because he knew that C-Town was bewitched. He hung the rabbit and skinned it, his hands unsteady, his face dripping sweat. And then he laughed and laughed, because it was only a dead rabbit, after all, and there was only good meat in the places where he had imagined that he might find sticky fruit.

That night Raphael lay still and listened to the *bruja's* weeping.

He had heard of her as a boy in Mexico. The story had come from the lips of his grandmother. "You must be a very good little *nino*, Raphael," she had said. "If you are not, La Llorona will come for you."

"Who is she, grandma?"

"She is a very bad *bruja*. Long ago, someone stole her babies. Now she steals children who are bad, because she knows that their parents will not miss them."

Raphael wasn't the only one who knew the story. As the children of C-Town fell ill and the doctors failed to help them, more and more people remembered the tale. Raphael's neighbors had not spoken La Llorona's name in years, except in jest. But death made things different, especially the deaths of so many. The priest at the little chapel near the highway tried to stop the talk. He said that it was all superstitious nonsense. But the priest only came to the chapel once a week, and soon it seemed that the stories were more than just rumors.

Epifanio Garcia said that he saw La Llorona in the grove one evening, spying on his shanty. Epifanio and his wife had two babies, and he was determined to protect them. He chased La Llorona through the grove, but he could not catch her. He said that every tree which the *bruja* touched was instantly blighted, its fruit suddenly heavy with huge black bugs.

Rosita Valdez said that she was walking to Mass when she came upon La Llorona drinking from an irrigation ditch. Rosita was so frightened by the evil one's muddy leer that she ran home without stopping, and that was something, because Rosita was barely five feet tall and weighed nearly two hundred pounds.

Epifanio's babies fell ill and died. Rosita's daughter died, too.

Not everyone who lost children saw the weeping woman. Raphael never saw her. But everyone heard her, even over the children's cries. Each night her wails haunted the camp, sawing through the dead trees along with the summer wind. The poor little ones feared La Llorona so much that they could not sleep at night for the terror of her. They shivered and wept and begged for God's mercy. But God did not help them. He did not heal the sickness that stole their appetites but somehow left them as fat and bloated and bald as giant babies. And He did nothing to stop La Llorona.

The lawyers said that the sickness came from the water,

but Raphael did not believe them. He knew that La Llorona was making the children sick so that they could not escape when she came for them.

She came for Raphael's children over the space of a month. Poor little Paulo was the last to go. His final days were spent in agony. He cried and cried, promising his father that he was a good little boy and that La Llorona would not take him. Raphael wiped his son's tears and said that he would stay with Paulo always.

Paulo was the youngest. Raphael sent him to school whenever the family was going to be at one *colonias* for a long time. When Paulo fell ill, Raphael brought him books to read, and Paulo taught his father how to read them, too. They slept together, holding each other close in the tiny bed.

Night after night, Raphael listened to his son weeping.

He listened to the wind weeping.

He listened to La Llorona's cries as she walked the dirt streets of C-Town. Each night she came closer, her sobs louder in the tiny room. One night Raphael felt her breath on his face, her tears on his cheeks, and then he heard Paulo take his last breath.

Raphael awoke to the sound of a plane overhead. It came in low and shook the shanty. He ran outside, naked, and watched it fly over the dead grove.

It flew on, releasing no spray, silver wings gleaming in the morning sunlight. The roar of its engines became a hum, then the sound of an insect, then faded away to silence.

Raphael dressed, grabbed his machete and the letter he had written the night before, and headed for the chapel, where there was a mailbox.

He walked through the empty streets, listening to the silence. Everyone but Raphael was gone now. Many left when the sickness started. More left after Epifanio and Rosita encountered La Llorona. The rest abandoned their homes after the lawyers came.

One of the lawyers had talked to Raphael. He was a polite man, but he had bad ideas in his head, and Raphael had refused to sign the papers that so many of his neighbors had signed.

"Mr. Baca," the lawyer said, "I know money cannot replace the loss of your children, and I know that appearing in a courtroom can be a frightening thing. But unless we fight them, the people that did this to you will do the same thing to other people,

as well."

Raphael didn't know how to explain it to the man. C-Town had been a good *colonias* before La Llorna came. The fruit was delicious and the water was plentiful, and his family had made the most of both resources. They had worked in C-Town every season for the past ten years, and they had never fallen ill before.

C-Town was not the real name of the place, of course. That was the name the lawyers used—Cancer Town, the place that killed little children by poisoning their blood.

Raphael tried to explain that La Llorona was taking the children, but the lawyer could not understand. He was too intent on explaining things to Raphael. He said that the corporation that owned the land was attempting to declare bankruptcy to avoid his lawsuit. He said that there would be no more work in C-Town, and that Raphael should not stay, because C-Town was a very dangerous place to live, even for adults.

Raphael agreed. C-Town was dangerous because La Llorona was there. But he would not leave. He had nowhere else to go.

One day, long after Raphael's neighbors had moved on, a man came from the corporation that owned the land. The man told Raphael that he would have to move. Raphael tried to tell him about La Llorona, but the man was just like the lawyer and wouldn't listen.

Raphael asked if the man knew of anyone who would listen to his story. The man thought about it for a long time. Finally, he gave Raphael the address of the Department of Agriculture. Raphael thanked him very sincerely. The man must have been pleased with that, because his smile became very broad, indeed.

Raphael wrote many letters to the Department of Agriculture. He never received an answer. He thought that it must be his fault. He was a good reader, but he had trouble writing. His printing was not nearly as neat as that of his teacher, Paulo, and sometimes he did not know the right words to use.

Still, he thought that his latest letter was the best yet. In it, he told the Department people not to listen to any lawyers. He promised that he would tell them all about La Llorona and the dead children if they would only come to C-Town.

The afternoon was cloudy, the sky the color of a wet stone. Raphael cut across the grove, hurrying to mail his letter before a summer shower hit. It was very still among the trees. Raphael's boots crunched over dead twigs. His steps came faster

and faster, and he found that his throat had gone very dry.

"Thirsty, Raphael? My fruit is so goooood. Sweet and juicy, Raphael. Come and taaaste..."

The *bruja* seemed to be standing next to him. Raphael's gaze darted through the grove. He saw nothing, but heard everything. A ripping sound, flesh being rended from bone. A scream. And then another sound, a moan of pleasure as La Llorona sucked at the horrid fruit.

Raphael ran. The sky was darker now. Above him, dead branches creaked against a rising wind. One broke loose and crashed to the ground in front of him. He tripped and fell, his hands skidding over wood that was pitted and hollow with the efforts of many insects.

The weeping sounds washed over him as he lay there. Not just the cries of La Llorona. A dozen tiny sobs rang in his ears, each choking with pain and fear. Raphael rolled away, eyes closed.

He felt something grabbing him, holding him still.

The branches. The grove was coming *alive*...

He opened his eyes. The fruit loomed above him, suspended from a dead branch by a net of shadows. Its pink lips moved around white teeth.

"Raphael..." it said. "Raphael Baca..."

Raphael lashed out with his machete, severing the fruit. It dropped and rolled against a tree trunk, and a great shard of bark came loose and fell on it. Raphael ran to the shanty, hands over his ears, but he could not escape the ghostly weeping or the anguished cries that poured from his own lips.

Morning brought the sun, and silence.

Raphael went outside, into the light.

A truck was parked in front of the shanty.

There were words on the door of the truck. Big gold letters. DEPARTMENT OF AGRICULTURE. But there was no one inside the truck, and no one on the streets of C-Town.

Raphael walked to the edge of the grove. Nothing moved there. No fruit hung from the naked branches. No sounds drifted on the warming breeze. Not the weeping of La Llorona. Not the cries of the dead children.

Raphael knelt down. He prayed that the person from the Department of Agriculture had not entered La Llorona's grove.

He waited for someone to appear, thinking how best to explain things.

He waited a long time.

When no one came, he got his machete and went into the grove, searching for another orange.

Toxic Wastrels

Poppy Z. Brite

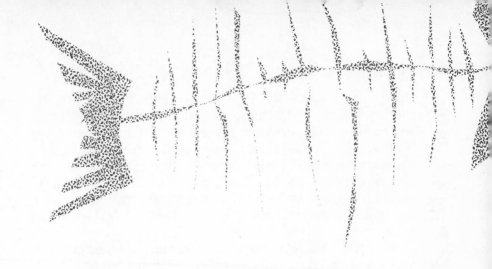

Monday, May 20
Cuttacaloosa, Louisiana

In the swelter of the swamp—in the fresh batch of springtime muck just beginning to steam with the accumulated heat of long Louisiana days—in the roots of the oak and cypress and in every ashen frond of their Spanish-moss beards, in the jewelled red eyes of gators and the million iridescent wings of gnat-swarms that hung like glittering spirits over pools of stagnant water—in all of those, a fertile world of poison waited to be born.

The swamp was lush and fertile and always wet; it spread itself wide and welcomed all comers into the softness of its dark night-scented mud. The swamp was the egg, and the factory with its giant nozzles and gargantuan hoses, the factory with its great fat black smokestack jutting up into the humid sky, the factory held the seed and could manufacture it a billion times over if necessary.

But only one was needed.

Puss Robicheaux left the cold stone comfort of Charity Hospital late in the afternoon and hurried down Tulane Avenue in the direction of the French Quarter. At Carondelet he turned left and crossed the gaudy thoroughfare of Canal Street, then ducked down Bourbon and was soon in the heart of the Quarter.

At this time of year, New Orleans was balmy, almost tropical; the days were long and warm and steamy, with intervals of rain and sunshine in quick succession. Puss wore a light jacket made of some synthetic fabric that shimmered with iridescent colors. It was an expensive piece of clothing, but it hung on him awkwardly, his thin wrists jutting from the sleeves like chicken bones. His sparse, longish fair hair blew about in the breeze off the river, despite the print scarf he had tied over it. As he walked, he trailed one bony, beringed hand along the ornate spikes of a wrought iron railing, then along the timeworn texture of old brick.

The afternoon light was very clear, with an almost greenish cast, when Puss reached Jackson Square. He rendezvoused with a tall, leather-clad, deathly beautiful boy at the western corner of the square, near the cathedral. Puss knew the boy only slightly—he was of a newer breed than Puss' old crowd—but the boy obviously knew who *he* was; he palmed the two crisp hundred-dollar bills Puss offered with no flicker of surprise, then slipped Puss a sealed, unmarked manila envelope.

"It's real clean," the boy murmured through rouged lips. "Something called 'Nuke,' from California I think. You won't need to do more than one at a time—two tops."

"In that case, we're stocked up." Puss tucked the envelope into the fuschia silk lining of his jacket. "Would you care to join us tonight?"

"Sorry. Big party at Pasko's—it's Drag Night, you should come." The boy turned and walked quickly down one of the cobblestone alleys that led away from the square. The spires of the cathedral loomed oppressively overhead. The boy's refusal had been too fast, and Puss caught a glimmer of something distasteful—pity, revulsion?—in the elegantly shadowed recesses of his eyes.

It was humiliating to be brushed off by these goddamn brats of nineteen or twenty. But through his shame Puss still felt a flicker of desire. He wished he could have brought the boy home with him, brought him to meet The Artist. The Artist would have known what to do with those insouciant lips, those slyly condescending eyes.

The children of the French Quarter fringe scene didn't trust Puss, though they allowed him into their circle because he bought them vast quantities of drinks and drugs without batting an eye. As long as he was willing to pay for the pleasure of their company, they were willing to sell. And surely he was something of a curiosity to them. Once, he believed, he could have been more. If he had shaken off the clutches of his family

and given up the ancestral home he loved. If no one knew his last name.

He had been called Puss since he could remember, but always wrote out his full legal name—Christopher Lance Robicheaux—whenever he had to sign something, because people tended to read his nickname as "Pus," a seeping bodily fluid, rather than "Puss," a luxuriant, furred pet. He had signed Christopher Lance on the guest register at the hospital before going up to see his pain-besotted mother, with her shrivelling, collapsing face and her rotting brain behind it. When the cancer was discovered marbling her temporal lobes like the fat on a particularly tender cut of meat, Puss had installed her in Charity Hospital rather than the posh private place where his father and older brother Carmen had died of the same cancer, ten and five years earlier respectively. He put her there because he knew the reporters and ravening environmentalists would never expect to find a Robicheaux dying in the hands of Charity. He put her there because the family was no longer as rich as anyone believed, and he refused to give up the house to the tolls of sickness and rot. But most of all he put her there because she had not wanted to go, because she was afraid of the place, and so Puss knew she would die faster in Charity. It was an act of mercy, a small evil for a greater good.

He decided to catch a trolley back to the hospital where he had parked his car, a rusting Cadillac that guzzled gasoline like champagne. But as he passed the Cafe du Monde on the way to the trolley stop, someone recognized him.

Three clean-cut little terrorists, to be exact, two moonfaced girls in Earth First! T-shirts and a lovely boy with a fashionable asymmetrical haircut and striking, Nazi-blue eyes. The boy jumped up, almost upsetting his cafe au lait and plate of beignets. "Robicheaux!" he howled. "POISONER! MURDERER!" He vaulted over the iron railing of the cafe and ran toward Puss. The girls scrambled over the railing after him. "Shut it DOWN!" they began to chant.

The Cafe du Monde tourists gaped, and some raised their cameras to snap pictures. But a few street performers and assorted Quarter freaks around the cafe took up the chant. They all knew what it was about. "Shut it DOWN! Shut it DOWN!"

Puss kept walking. Behind him, he heard the boy's voice raised in righteous anger. "We know who you are, Robicheaux! You *look* different, but you're a murderer, just like the rest of your family!"

"People in Cuttacaloosa die of cancer at EIGHT TIMES the normal rate and their blood is on YOUR HANDS!" added one of the girls.

"Shut it DOWN...Shut it DOWN..." The chant followed Puss all the way to the top of the levee. He didn't want to listen to it until the next trolley came; instead he just started walking back along the river. The sky was just beginning to darken, and the air seemed thinner up here, suffused with a pre-sunset light. Puss stared down at the surging, glowing river as he walked. It was so mighty and so polluted; doubtless it had been the carrier and deliverer of more poisons than one insignificant factory could ever be. But no one ever called the Mississippi a murderer.

He reached inside his jacket and touched the manila envelope. *Nuke*, the deather boy had told him. One hundred doses of top-grade LSD; Puss tried to buy a sheet whenever he was in New Orleans. Psychedelics were difficult to come by in the swamp.

The drugs, at least, were a comfort.

Claude Augustine Robicheaux, Puss' father, had built the factory thirty years ago. Land on the edge of the swamp was cheap, and the earth was just firm enough to support heavy machinery. Now the Robicheaux money was gone and the family business acumen had died with Puss' older brother Carmen, but some parts of Robicheaux Chemicals were still used for production. There were cauldrons of molten plastic and vats of seething, gnawing solvent. There were carefully contained pockets of hellfire that could incinerate ten tons of poison a day. In these parts of the squat and sprawling complex of buildings, everything seemed in syncopated motion, churning and thrusting and letting out little colored puffs of steam, as if at any moment the factory might segue into genuine, animated life.

But most parts of the complex were no longer in use. There were tall boxlike rooms where the ceilings could not be seen overhead, so shrouded were they in cobwebs and shadow. There were vats still glazed with the residue of chemicals long drained or evaporated. There were spigots that trailed long drips of plastic frozen in the moment of falling; there was machinery mottled with strange patterns of rust. There were warrens of offices where the plaster on the walls seemed to echo with a faint moaning voice, as if something were forever lost in the maze of tiny fissures.

In Claude Robicheaux's old office, a writhing, marbled pattern had spread over the walls, a growth that no amount of disinfectant could remove for very long. Eventually the office had been locked and abandoned. Now the growth ran rampant over the walls and floor and ceiling, twisting itself into a thousand patterns that almost formed a whole: an intricate web of nerves and capillaries, a jagged line of brainwaves, a screaming, sobbing mouth.

Puss left New Orleans by way of Interstate 10, then turned onto U.S. 90, which corkscrewed down into the swamp. The twinkling cityscape receded behind him; before him was only darkness pierced by the wavering twin needles of the Caddy's headlights. He turned on the tape player, and a frenetic, over-amplified voice blared out at him. "THEY WERE WOMEN WHO LOVED OTHER WOMEN…AND THEY LOST THEIR HEADS OVER ONE ANOTHER…LITERALLY!" The only tape in the car was a collection of movie trailers Ivor had spliced together; that one, if Puss remembered correctly, was a softcore-porn costume drama about aristocratic lesbians during the French Revolution. Puss remembered how the camera had focussed in on the shimmering razor-edge of the guillotine, then on the ragged neck-stumps, the blood spurting in sexual rhythm.

He had tried to get Ivor to come into the city with him today, thinking Ivor ought to see Mother once more before she died, not that Mother would benefit from it. But Ivor could have been an ally against the self-righteous brats at the Cafe du Monde. Perhaps he and Puss could even have stopped on Magazine Street and had a cocktail in some festive little bar. Puss had once liked the bars in and around the Quarter, with their air of year-round Carnival, but he hated drinking alone.

And Ivor would not go into the city any more, though he had spent most of his teenage years trying to pass for a hoodlum in the seedier parts of the Quarter. Carmen had been the oldest Robicheaux son, expected to follow in his father's wake; he had done so all too well. Ivor was the youngest, and he had always done exactly as he liked, taking pleasure in horrifying his parents, sucking up their money and their love.

Puss was the middle son, and it had never seemed to matter what he did; no one ever noticed.

An hour out of New Orleans, he left the highway and turned onto a narrow hardtop road that twisted through miles of teeming swampland. Water lapped at the road on both sides; reeds

and cattails hushed in his wake. Ghostly white cranes stalked the silent pools on jackstraw legs. Puss had seen gators on this stretch of road. The last part of the drive always seemed to go on forever. At last he swung to the right, coasted down a long, cypress-shrouded, mud-rutted driveway, and parked in front of a huge, spectral, mouldy wedding cake of a house.

The Robicheaux plantation was Puss' birthright, even if no one in his family had wanted him to have it. It was the ancestral stronghold, with grounds that had once been home to acres of rice and sugarcane and—as Claude Robicheaux had always proudly pointed out—more than a thousand slaves.

But building a plantation house in the swamp was a little like sinking toothpicks into Jell-O and then trying to balance a lead weight on the toothpicks. For the past hundred years the ancestral stronghold had been slowly sinking into the morass. Now foul black mud covered most of the first floor windows and the house listed like a giant white-columned shipwreck. Ivor and Puss lived upstairs now; the first floor was damp and rotten, with evil-smelling water seeping through the fine Indian carpets and mould blossoming on the golden flocked wallpaper.

The house was surely Puss' birthright, for he was the only one who could love it anymore.

Blue light flickered in a single upstairs window. Ivor's skinny frame would be immobile in front of the television, his bird-sharp face bathed in its phosphor glow. Puss walked up the overgrown alley of cypress and ascended the sloping steps of the porch. The front door was still clear of the encroaching mud, but only just. When that was covered, Puss supposed, they would go in and out the windows. Or rather, *he* would; Ivor never went out.

Above the front door was a fanlight of opalescent glass Puss had always particularly loved. He tried to imagine the mud oozing over it, sucking out its subtle colors. Instead a more disquieting image rose unbidden. He had dreamed about Ivor last night. In the dream, as they watched a kung fu film, Puss had moved closer to Ivor on the floor. Ivor kept watching the movie as Puss touched his thigh, then his crotch. At last Puss had unzipped Ivor's ragged jeans and cupped his brother's flaccid penis in his hand. He masturbated Ivor to erection, then to unprotesting orgasm. Ivor's breath sobbed in and out as he came, but his eyes remained fixed on the TV, the camera panning in on a handful of something raw and twitching held up to the

screen. In the way of dreams, Puss had felt a sudden, terrible empathy with the film: a red-hot pain flared between his legs.

But that was wrong. He must never touch Ivor like that. He must do his best to take care of Ivor, even if that meant letting him sit in front of his beloved TV and watch bad films until his brain fried like an egg in hot grease. This Is Your Brain On Movies: any questions? Who knew; perhaps the radioactive waves that were supposed to come out of TV screens would burn away nascent tumors in Ivor's head.

Puss shivered, then glanced over his shoulder. The swamp seemed still tonight. Usually it was noisy, the shrilling insects and tree frogs, the night bird's chorus, the occasional cough and hum of a boat engine over by Cuttacaloosa. Tonight it was so quiet that he imagined he could hear the sinister chuff of his father's factory across the swamp, the slow seepage of its toxins.

He shook his head and let himself in.

In some of the forgotten chambers of Robicheaux Chemicals, enormous pyramids had been built, like monuments erected to the memory of poison.

These pyramids were made of metal, towering stacks of fifty-gallon steel drums slapped with a dozen different colors of dull industrial paint, sloshing with the chemical leftovers of thirty years. Some of the drums were stencilled DANGER in bright red letters, or bore skulls and crossbones as if they might be forgotten caches of Lafitte's treasure. Some were unmarked.

And some, like the shade of Elvis, had left the building.

For years the factory foreman, a distant, increasingly alcoholic cousin of Claude's wife, had paid various teams of "waste disposal experts" to haul the drums away, shunting them off to the lowest bidder and breathing a prayer of relief as the trucks disappeared down the winding swamp road. No one had any idea what became of the drums after that, and no one was required to know.

But those were the good old days, and long gone. Now there was not even enough money to pay the "waste disposal experts," and most of the drums simply stacked up in the unused parts of the factory, pyramids housing death as surely as the great tombs of Egypt ever did. But the factory, though vast, had a finite amount of space that could be filled with drums full of poison.

And so a great many of the drums ended up in the swamp. The colorful, new ones sank slowly into the welcoming mud

and came to rest on the rusting hulks of others, for of course many of the "waste disposal experts" had been using the swamp all along. Fresh poisons mingled with ones that had been brewing for years; molecules broke apart and re-coalesced in deadlier formation. Clusters of fern and swampgrass withered, then grew back a seething, animate shade of green, a noxious but somehow lush color, greener than nature; silent coves and twisted knots of water-oak roots became caked with a thick orange foam, like whipped cream gone bad in the can. An oily purple sheen laced the surface of the water; at night the swamp's natural phosphor made this sheen swarm with a thousand iridescent colors.

The industrial poisons mingled with pesticides and herbicides blowing in from the bayou ten miles away, where they were sprayed on the rice crops. The toxic soup was diluted with rain whose acidity often matched that of vinegar. The whole mess ate endless runnels and rivulets through the soft springtime mud, and the high Louisiana groundwater soaked it up like manna.

Perhaps a billion toxic seeds found a billion mutagenic eggs; perhaps, like the first life conceived on Earth, it began with a single meeting of slimes.

But on this hot spring morning, the swamp stretched its shimmering surface and began to breathe.

At the ruin of the Robicheaux plantation, poisons of a different sort held sway over the night.

Each tiny square of acid was patterned with two intersecting ovals, and at their center, a black dot: symbol of the atom. Puss placed three squares on his own tongue and three on Ivor's. Never mind what the boy in the Quarter had said; he and his crowd were lightweights, inexperienced as children. No doubt they wanted to see through the drugs, to cling to some shred of their personality, some reminder of who they were supposed to be, who they thought themselves to be. That was exactly what Puss wanted to forget.

They spent the next two hours watching zombies shred chunks of quivering muscle fiber between rotting teeth and stuff iridescent gobs of intestine into hungry, gore-rouged mouths. Puss had never known the human eye could distinguish so many different shades of red, or that the play of light on meat could create such intricate mandala-like patterns. But when the film ended, he only stretched, sat up, and took a long swallow from

the pitcher of heavily sweetened iced tea Ivor kept beside him at all times. He hated the taste of Ivor's tea, but his throat was parched.

"One more movie," Ivor said hoarsely. "It's a good one." Without taking his eyes off the static on the screen, Ivor extended a skinny arm and took a big slug of tea. Ivor's diet consisted largely of sugar and caffeine, speed and hallucinogens, with an occasional handful of Flintstones chewable vitamins for fiber. With a little effort Puss could visualize the vibrant red-brown stream of liquid flowing down Ivor's throat and into his stomach, staining his guts as rich a crimson as any zombie's gourmet meal.

"What *good one*?" Puss asked. Last night it had been some badly shot docudrama about African puberty initiations. The juicy-voiced announcer said the technical term for one such process was a "clitorectomy"; his voice had sounded approving. Puss remembered the girl's skinny thighs being wrenched apart like a wishbone, the white-hot knife flashing down. Then the camera focussed straight in on the raw new wound, shockingly red against dull ebony skin, closer and closer until the pulpy mutilated folds filled the entire giant screen of the TV, like a decapitated alien, like a bloodied, sobbing mouth.

Ivor grinned. It was an expression too wise for his tender years, and too depraved. Ivor was smart, all right; he had always been smart, but had never seemed remotely tempted to use his intelligence for anything other than scamming money and memorizing bad film trivia. "Sorry. No erotica tonight." He held up a video cassette in its brightly colored storybox. TOXIC WASTE MUTANTS VS. THE VAMPIRE SLUTS. "And they say we Robicheauxs are politically incorrect! We watch this stuff, don't we? Now this is the very worst work of one of the world's worst directors, Samuel 'Lip' Fraydon, Jr., who died penniless in a tarpaper shack somewhere in Georgia..."

"A Yankee?"

"Fuck you, Puss. You think anybody north of Shreveport is a godamn Yankee."

This was true, but Puss couldn't help it. That was how the family had been. Steeped in the sodden Louisiana heat, in the genteelly decaying monstrosity of a house, surrounded by yellowed photographs and portraits of his ancestors with their lace shawls and peacock-feather fans and faces powdered to a ghostly perfection, he had grown up with a craving for that sort of elegance. He wished he could have been born a hundred and

fifty years ago, the quintessential antebellum sweetheart, the perfect hothouse flower. He wished for seed pearls and crinolines. And while he was at it, he wished he could have been born without three useless scraps of flesh dangling from his crotch.

"What was the 'Lip' for?" he asked as Ivor fed the tape into the VCR.

Ivor looked up. The bleachy nimbus of his hair was backlit by the TV screen, making an electric bluish halo around his head. In the hectic, giant-pupilled eyes that met his own, Puss thought he glimpsed Ivor's sanity skipping gaily away down some back road into the acid-swirled recesses of his brain.

"Fraydon had a harelip," Ivor explained. "He couldn't talk to anyone without drenching them in spit. Look close when we watch the movie—in a couple of shots you can see saliva droplets on the actors' faces, or flecks of foam if they're wearing dark clothes."

Puss looked askance at him. But Ivor had an angelic smile on his face and was gazing raptly into the Cyclopean eye of the television as the opening credits began.

The vampire sluts of the title did not hold Puss' attention as the African girl's freshly scarred vulva had. None of them looked as if they had tasted anything as nourishing as blood in a long time. Their breasts were loose pouches of meat gone gray with age or overuse, and they all had elaborate crumbling hairdos that looked like dimestore wigs frosted with the dust of too many years on the shelf. What a waste, Puss thought, of bodies that could have been beautiful.

The toxic waste mutants were another matter entirely, though they were more like weird works of art than monsters. Like the unholy marriage of a brain, an octopus, and an oil slick they rippled across the wide screen, wreathed in a million iridescent colors, dissolving flesh as they went. Puss tried to imagine the subtle toxins of the creatures coming into contact with his own hapless, abused cells, eating up his boredom and the discontent he had always felt with his own body, changing them into something more alien and therefore more free.

Changing...alien...free. The words touched a familiar chord in his mind, something half pleasurable, half born of dread.

Ivor was engrossed in the adventures of the junkie scientist who was the film's ostensible hero. The actor resembled Henry Spencer from **Eraserhead**—the same livery lips, the same shellshocked glaze in the eyes—but instead of Henry's famous

Toxic Wastrels

fuzzy-mushroom-cloud hairdo, the scientist had a bald head covered with very realistic-looking, very wet festering sores. Apparently he had lived through some kind of toxic takeover and was trying to warn the world about it before it devoured him entirely. Every now and then the vampire sluts would come lurching through in one of their hideous interpretive-dance numbers that bore no relationship to the plot.

Ivor reached up and gingerly scratched the top of his head, as if his cranium too might be veined with trickling pus. Puss knew Ivor was living out the film; for an hour or two it would be his only reality. He wouldn't even notice if Puss left the room.

Puss stood up. His neck was already beginning to ache from the minute quantity of strychnine present in even the purest blotter acid. He had been reclining on a rose velvet love seat, one of his mother's most prized antiques; now the rich finish of the wood was scuffed and gouged, the sumptuous fabric stained with wine and sweat. Ivor lay sprawled on the floor, his head propped against the sofa, his pitcher of tea within easy reach. His eyes never left the TV screen.

Puss began going through the deep pockets of his jacket. He carried all manner of things around with him: tubes of rouge, tissues, an Exacto knife and several spare blades, a long hatpin tipped with a two-caret diamond. The hatpin poked him as he felt in his pocket, and he absently put his finger in his mouth, half-tasting the blood.

At last he found what he wanted: the key to a room on the first floor, heavy and ornate, tarnished by his own sweat. His fingers closed around it and he pulled it out of his pocket.

Earlier, after dosing himself and Ivor, Puss had tucked the rest of the acid into one of his pockets. Six hits gone, ninety-four left. Then he had forgotten about it.

He did not notice when it fluttered from his pocket as he pulled out the key.

As Puss left the room, the sheet of acid wafted gently down, landed in Ivor's tea pitcher, and began to dissolve.

Puss descended the long curving staircase, placing his bare feet carefully on the marble risers. The stairs rippled and billowed before his eyes; the red lacquer on his toenails looked almost black against the paleness of his long, hairless feet. The acid was kicking in hard. The shadows of the first floor landing swarmed with dots of color and points of light. He reached the door of his room and slid the sweat-tarnished key into the wait-

47

ing mouth of the lock.

The rusty tumblers slid back with a faint grating sound, but the heavy wooden door did not swing open. All the doors down here were warped in their frames; some would no longer open at all. Puss heard a low moan from inside the room. He twisted the knob viciously and threw his shoulder against the swollen wood.

The door shifted on its hinges, then creaked open. Puss stepped into the room.

The junkie scientist died screaming, and the credits began to roll over an extreme closeup of his swollen, agonized, already mutating face. Ivor didn't need to read the cast list— "Lip" Fraydon always worked with the same stable of actors, since he couldn't get better ones and they couldn't get work anywhere else—so luckily it didn't matter that all the credits seemed to be written in squirming Hindi.

He looked around for Puss, but his brother was nowhere to be found. Probably off reapplying his lipstick or something. Ivor scanned a towering stack of video cassettes, wondering what to watch next. His Japanese snuff films? His collection of amputee pornography? Or perhaps just a comfortable old favorite like SLAVERING MEATHOLES OF THE PUTRESCENT DEAD, final masterpiece of Will O'Dobbs, the only director who could rival Fraydon's exquisite badness?

He tugged at the neck of his T-shirt and his fingers came away wet. The heat and dampness of the swamp rose from the first floor, permeating every corner of the steamy old house. And decisions made him thirsty. Ivor hoisted his pitcher of tea and took a deep swallow, then another. The icy, sugary brew was like balm on his acid-parched throat. He peered into the depths of the pitcher. Almost gone. Well, what the hell; he'd make another one before the next movie. The tea came in a can, ready to mix—all he had to do was add water from the faucet. Ivor tipped the pitcher and drained it.

Puss felt in his pockets again, just missed slicing his finger open on one of the Exacto blades, and finally found what he wanted: a gaily colored folder of matches from Brennan's in the Quarter, where he and Ivor had once eaten a hundred-dollar breakfast and then, in the bonecrushing grip of a bourbon hangover, promptly thrown it all up. Now he tore out a match and moved around the room lighting thick black candles in ornate

wrought iron wall-sconces. The wall of mud on the other side of the tall windowpanes sparkled with oily colors. Puss watched it for a moment. This acid was strong, all right—the mud almost seemed to *writhe* against the window, as if it were trying to push the glass in.

Puss stood in the center of the room, letting his drug-dazzled eyes resolve themselves to the candlelight. Gradually the outline of another form became visible, thin and pale, bound cruciform to a long table by the windows. Then all at once it was as if a caul of sanity was lifted from his eyes, and his vision became clear.

The boy had been fresh off a Greyhound bus when Puss found him in the French Quarter, a punk rock refugee from the cornfed complacency of the Midwest, with the fuck-you attitude and the fine-boned, heartbreaking beauty that seldom lasted much past eighteen. This boy might have had as long as five years left to be bratty and beautiful. Now he was in the process of becoming something stranger and far finer.

As Puss stood trembling in the center of the room, he felt something detach itself from him and go to the foot of the long table, a shadowy persona he thought of only as "The Artist." *He*, Puss, could never do things like this. But The Artist knew how to do all sorts of things. His medium was flesh, and the boy stretched out on the table was both his palette and his canvas.

First of all, right after Puss brought the boy home and got him drunk on red wine laced with sleeping pills, The Artist had used heavy black nylon thread to sew the boy's lips shut. There was only a small opening at one corner so Puss could administer a few drops of water each day. Puss remembered the glaze of terror in the boy's dark eyes as he woke up and tried to speak, the sight of those soft swollen lips straining at the blood-crusted stitches that sealed them.

Now the canvas was almost complete. Thrust through the boy's nipples were two knitting needles The Artist had sharpened on a whetstone from the kitchen. Strong wire filament wound around these needles ran to a pair of hooks on the ceiling. Each day The Artist pulled the filament a little tighter, stretching the skin a little more—but carefully, so that the needles would never quite rip through the delicate tissue. So far the wire had been shortened by about five inches.

Just above the sweet concavity of the boy's hipbones, The Artist had fastened a stiff leather belt perhaps four inches wide

and fourteen inches in diameter. The belt was fastened snug below the ribs so that the boy's already flat stomach was cinched in absurdly tight, and the graceful arc of the ribcage was clearly visible. The Artist had used two larger belts before this one, gradually decreasing the size—the first twenty inches long, the second sixteen, both with heavy iron clasps that could not be burst apart by the boy's constant struggle for breath.

The Artist looked down at the youthful face, once so clear and innocent despite its attempts at worldweariness, now smeared with blood and makeup, tear-streaked, ill-used by fatigue and pain. The boy's eyes were rolled up to meet his own and The Artist was struck by the hopelessness he saw there. The boy was ill, ready to give in to the limitations of his body; he wouldn't last much longer. The canvas would have to be finished tonight.

It was more than just a work of art; it was a work of *creation*. One need not be confined to one's own dull flesh; one could manipulate it, force it to change. The Artist was sure of it. Tonight he would prove that his talent was equal to such a task; after this practice run, he could begin work on poor Puss at his leisure.

Puss would be The Artist's masterpiece.

Beneath the wasp-waist belt, the boy's abdomen was crisscrossed with long shallow incisions that had been stitched up with the same coarse black thread The Artist had used to sew the boy's mouth shut. These incisions served no real purpose; he had made them to test the malleability of the flesh, to see what was beneath the skin. Most of them had been done with Puss' Exacto knife, which The Artist ran through the candle flame before each use; still the cuts had become infected. The fresh ones were puffy, limned in angry-looking red; the older ones had begun to suppurate and give off a smell like swamp gas, strong but not unpleasant.

But the final incision was ever so important. The Artist reached into Puss' pocket and fingered the Exacto, then shook his head. For the master stroke, a larger brush was required.

He crossed the room, opened the center drawer of a fine oak credenza whose surface was crawling with mildew, and took out an electric carving knife.

"MMMMNNN!" said the boy when he saw The Artist coming back toward him holding the knife. His head whipped from side to side. The Artist ignored him and knelt to plug in the power cord. The sockets in these buried rooms could no longer

be depended upon; luckily Puss had had a generator hauled in to ensure a power supply for Ivor's TV. With enough extension cords, The Artist could bring the current down here too.

He flicked the knife on. Immediately the blades began chewing the air; the whine of the tiny motor was very loud in the hot, still room. He cupped the boy's shrivelled penis and scrotum, gathered them up in his hand. "MMMNN!" insisted the boy. "MNN! MMMMMM!"

"Yes, yes…" The Artist sighed. "Life is difficult. How we all must suffer." He lowered the carving knife to the soft juncture of thigh and groin. A fine spray of blood misted the air.

The meat beneath the thin skin beneath was soft as jelly. Blades jittered harsh against bone. The Artist withdrew the knife, then ran it in one magnificent crimson stroke down the other side of the boy's groin. The pulpy, useless wedge of flesh came away in his hand. *Done!* His canvas successfully manipulated, a work of art, a work of creation!

He picked up a bottle of hydrogen peroxide and upended it over the beautiful wound. The foaming, blood-streaked liquid struck The Artist as festive. Champagne of the body, Mardi Gras of mutilation.

He began to laugh, and Puss Robicheaux stared haplessly out of his joyful, crazy eyes.

SLAVERING MEATHOLES OF THE PUTRESCENT DEAD was just not as good as Ivor remembered. The plot had never made a whole lot of sense, but when had all of the actors been skinned alive and become gut-packed, vein-strung skeletons? This in itself would not have been bad, but their dialogue sounded as if it were being forced through mouthfuls of liquefying flesh. And the dialogue was usually the best part.

Worst of all, the toxic waste mutants from the last movie seemed to be making a surprise guest appearance in this one, too. Every few minutes, just when Ivor glanced away from the TV, one of their amorphous smashed-centipede shapes would ripple across the screen and be gone before he could fully see it.

He was still horribly thirsty even though he had drunk another full pitcher of tea. There had been a dark, glistening sludge at the bottom of the last one, but Ivor hadn't bothered to wash it out, figuring that the caffeine was concentrated there. Instead he had just added tap water, and if he noticed how that water fizzed and sparkled when he stirred in the tea, he assumed it was the drugs.

Now the TV screen looked like nothing but a glowing mass of colored dots. He had to look away from it. Maybe this was just a very *bright* movie. Maybe he should watch something darker: DUNGEON OF THE TOOLBOX MANIAC, perhaps, by "Leg" Clarke, the world's only triple-amputee horror-film director…

But for once in his life, he didn't really want to watch a movie. His eyes hurt. In fact, his whole head hurt, a steady throb, then a stabbing pain. It felt as if something were alive in there. Ivor thought of a fetal bird in its shell, its tiny, razor-sharp eggtooth slowly chipping away at the fragile dome that has cradled and nurtured it…cracking…cracking.

A salty drop stung his eye. He must be dripping with sweat. He wished Puss would buy an air conditioner to hook up to the generator. He wished Puss would come back from wherever he sometimes went to.

Ivor reached up and felt the top of his head. His fingers sank into a deep fissure, and came away coated with thick, viscid blood.

As Puss came up the stairs, he saw a gray and jellied mass go bounding past the door. It was about the size of a small cat, but infinitely more fluid in form, seeming to have neither limb nor facial features. The whorled texture of the thing was vaguely familiar, but it had been moving too fast for Puss to identify it.

Puss poked his head around the doorframe and saw the thing disappearing through the open window at the end of the hall. He could just make out the bloody smudges it had left in its wake—they reminded him of some spongeprint art Ivor had brought home from school once.

He ran to the window, but the thing was gone; he could not tell whether it had crawled down the side of the house or simply hurled itself into the waiting swamp. But something was wrong outside. This was more vivid than any hallucination: the whole world was alive, seething. Puddles of scummy water boiled like thick, scalding soup. The wall of mud was more than halfway up the side of the house now. As Puss watched, it advanced another inch. And the plants were trying to get out of the ground. The overgrown rose bushes in the front yard ripped themselves free like hair being pulled from a scalp. There was a tremendous wet sucking sound as a fifty-year-old water oak toppled. Newly exposed roots whipped the air, raw and shocking as innards.

Now the early morning sky was full of a flat, dead-looking light. Puss could see all the way to the road that ran south past the house a hundred yards away. There were people on the road. But none of the people were walking. They were being dragged.

Cuttacaloosa, the fishing and trapping village a mile north of here, had always had a higher cancer rate than normal. Some, like the activist brats who had tried to terrorize Puss today, blamed it on the Robicheaux plant. They had been trying to get the place shut down for more than ten years. Claude Robicheaux had refused to believe a word of it; he claimed that the cancer surely came from the villagers' steady diet of seafood, and furthermore that many of them died not of cancer, but of rampant venereal disease. Such things, Claude told his boys, were bound to happen to uncivilized people.

The people on the road were all coming from the direction of the village; even from this distance Puss could make out the black hair and thickset, sturdy bodies common to the villagers, who were mostly Cajun. But their bodies were dwarfed by the lumpy, fleshy things attached to them, seeming to *grow* out of them, shading from raw pink to coarse, fibrous gray, humping along toward the swamp and dragging their hosts with them. There was a man with a huge mass of shapeless flesh sprouting from his mouth, and he being pulled prone behind it: his lungs, his larynx? Here was a woman whose left breast had swollen to elephantine size, half again as large as her body; she clung to it as if trying to ride it. Venereal disease gone wild? Or chemically induced cancers, going to meet their maker?

Ivor.

Puss turned away from the window and rushed into the TV room. Ivor's tea pitcher lay overturned on the floor. The TV screen was a mass of squirming iridescence, shapeless and multi-hued as a slick of oil on water. In front of it, stretched out as if crucified, was Ivor. The top of his skull littered the floor in pieces, matted with hair on one side, slick and fresh on the other like some grisly Easter egg; his cranium was a nightmare of blood and thin yolky fluids. Deep in the glistening well, Puss thought he saw the frayed end of Ivor's brainstem protruding like the stump of a severed tongue.

What had gone through the window?

Below, Puss heard glass bursting, then a slow, implacable slithering sound as of a giant worm turning restlessly beneath the jellied foundations of the house. The windows of the first floor had finally given way, and the swamp was claiming its

Poppy Z. Brite

new domain.

Puss turned to run, but there was nowhere to go. So he lay down beside his brother's vacated body and stared at the writhing, flickering screen, and he waited. Soon the screen became a long swirling tunnel, and Puss thought he could see a blinding light at the end.

When he finally got used to it, the factory wasn't a bad place at all.

He could never love it as he had loved the house. But he did grow accustomed to it. He could not leave, but he could go anywhere in the complex; with his new, malleable form he could melt through any crack, slide through any pipe or ventilator shaft.

Most of the factory was underground now. Teams of "waste disposal experts" had come in and poured concrete over the rest of it, men in moon boots and unwieldy plastic suits that were supposed to protect them. He knew the suits hadn't worked. He had been in the mud that oozed over the tops of their heavy shoes; he had been in the air that filtered through the respirators on their masks. Ten or twenty years from now, he would visit them again.

He missed Ivor, it was true. And his own death had been bad. But the memory of his brother's scooped-out skull, the memory of foul black mud sucking at his body, filling his nose and mouth and dissolving his soft tissues, these were almost gone. At last, the identity of Puss Robicheaux was nearly dissipated. He would need the help of no more drugs, no more Artists.

He could go anywhere now, be anything. He was both the egg and the seed.

At night, he liked to curl up and rest among the pyramids of poison, in one of the thousands of steel drums that had been entombed in the empty chambers of the factory.

If he concentrated, he could feel himself becoming one with the wastes and poisons contained in the drums.

Soon, he thought, he would be able to eat through the metal.

The Forest Is Crying

Charles De Lint

There are seven million homeless children on the streets of Brazil. Are vanishing trees being re-born as unwanted children?
—*Gary Snyder, from* **The Practice of the Wild**

The real problem is, people think life is a lad-der, and it's really a wheel.
—*Pat Cadigan, from "Johnny Come Home"*

Two pairs of footsteps, leather soles on marble floors. Listening to the sound they made, Dennison felt himself wondering, What was the last thing that Ronnie Egan heard before he died? The squeal of tires on wet pavement? Some hooker or an old wino shouting, "Look out!" Or was there no warning, no warning at all? Just the sudden impact of the car as it hit him and flung his body ten feet in the air before it was smeared up against the plate glass window of the pawn shop?

"You don't have to do this," Stone said as they paused at the door. "One of the neighbours already IDed the body."

"I know."

Looking through the small window, glass reinforced with metal mesh, Dennison watched the morgue attendant approach to let them in. Like the detective at Dennison's side, the attendant was wearing a sidearm. Was the security to keep people out or keep them in? he wondered morbidly.

"So why—" Stone began, then he shook his head. "Never mind."

It wasn't long before they were standing on either side of a metal tray that the attendant had pulled out from the wall at Stone's request. It could easily hold a grown man, twice the hundred and seventy pounds Dennison carried on his own six-one frame. The small body laid out upon the metal surface was dwarfed by the expanse of stainless steel that surrounded it.

"His mother's a heavy user," Dennison said. "She peddles her ass to feed the habit. Sometimes she brings the man home—she's got a room at the Claymore. If the guy didn't like having a kid around, she'd get one of the neighbours to look after him. We've had her in twice for putting him outside to play in the middle of the night when she couldn't find anybody to take him in. Trouble is, she always put on such a good show for the judge that we couldn't make the neglect charges stick."

He delivered the brief summary in a monotone. It didn't seem real. Just like Ronnie Egan's dead body didn't seem real. The skin so ashen, the bruises so dark against its pallor.

"I read the file," Stone said.

Dennison looked up from the corpse of the four-year-old boy.

"Did you bring her in?" he asked.

Stone shook his head. "Can't track her down. We've got an APB out on her, but…" He sighed. "Who're we kidding, Chris? Even when we do bring her in, we're not going to be able to find a charge that'll stick. She'll just tell the judge what she's told them before."

Dennison nodded heavily. I'm sorry, your honour, but I was asleep and I never even heard him go out. He's a good boy, but he doesn't always listen to his momma. He likes to wander. If social services could give her enough to raise him in a decent neighbourhood, this kind of thing would never happen…

"I should've tried harder," he said.

"Yeah, like your caseload's any lighter than mine," Stone said. "Where the fuck would you find the time?"

"I still should've…"

Done something, Dennison thought. Made a difference.

Stone nodded to the attendant who zipped up the heavy plastic bag, then slid the drawer back into the wall. Dennison watched until the drawer closed with a metal click, then he finally turned away.

"You're taking this too personally," Stone said.

"It's always personal."

Stone put his arm around Dennison's shoulders and steered him towards the door.

"It gets worse every time something like this happens," Dennison went on. "For every one I help, I lose a dozen. It's like pissing in the wind."

"I know," Stone said heavily.

The bright daylight stung Dennison's eyes when he stepped outside. He hadn't had breakfast yet, but he had no appetite. His pager beeped, but he didn't bother to check the number he was supposed to call. He just shut off the annoying sound. He couldn't deal with whatever the call was about. Not today. He couldn't face going into the office either, couldn't face all those hopeless faces of people he wanted to help, there just wasn't enough time in a day, enough money in the budget, enough of anything to make a real difference.

Ronnie Egan's dead features floated up in his mind.

He shook his head and started to walk. Aimlessly, but at a fast pace. Shoe leather on pavement now, but he couldn't hear it for the sound of the traffic, vehicular and pedestrian. Half an hour after leaving the morgue he found himself on the waterfront, staring out over the lake.

He didn't think he could take it anymore. He'd put in seven years as a caseworker for social services, but it seemed as though he'd finally burned out. Ronnie Egan's stupid, senseless death was just too much to bear. If he went into the office right now, it would only be to type up a letter of resignation. He decided to get drunk instead.

Turning, he almost bumped into the attractive woman who was approaching him. She might be younger, but he put her at his own twenty-nine; she just wore the years better. A soft fall of light brown hair spilled down to her shoulders in untidy tangles. Her eyes were a little too large for the rest of her features, but they were such an astonishing grey-green that it didn't matter. She was wearing jeans and a "Save the Rainforests" T-shirt, a black cotton jacket overtop.

"Hi there," she said.

She offered him a pamphlet that he automatically reached for before he realized what he was doing. He dropped his hand and stuck it in his pocket, leaving her with the pamphlet still proffered.

"I don't think so," he said.

"It's a serious issue," she began.

"I've got my own problems."

She tapped the pamphlet. "This is everybody's problem."

Dennison sighed. "Look, lady," he said. "I'm more interested in helping people than trees. Sorry."

"But without the rainforests—"

"Trees don't have feelings," he said, cutting her off. "Trees don't cry. Kids do."

"Maybe you just can't hear them."

Her gaze held his. He turned away, unable to face her disappointed look. But what was he supposed to do? If he couldn't even be there for Ronnie Egan when the kid had needed help the most, what the hell did she expect him to do about a bunch of trees? There were other people, far better equipped, to deal with that kind of problem.

"You caught me on a bad day," he said. "Sorry."

He walked away before she could reply.

Dennison wasn't much of a drinker. A beer after work a couple of times a week. Wine with a meal even more occasionally. A few brews with the guys after one of their weekend softball games—that was just saying his pager left him alone long enough to get through all the innings. His clients' needs didn't fit into a tidy nine-to-five schedule with weekends off. Crises could arise at any time of the day or night—usually when it was most inconvenient. But Dennison had never really minded. He'd bitch and complain about it like everybody else he worked with, but he'd always be there for whoever needed the help.

Why didn't Sandy Egan call him last night? He'd told her to phone him, instead of just putting Ronnie outside again. He'd promised her, no questions. He wouldn't use the incident as pressure to take the boy away from her. Ronnie was the first priority, plain and simple.

But she hadn't called. She hadn't trusted him, hadn't wanted to chance losing the extra money social services gave her to raise the boy. And now he was dead.

Halfway through his fourth beer, Dennison started ordering shots of whiskey on the side. By the time the dinner hour rolled around, he was too drunk to know where he was anymore. He'd started out in a run-down bar somewhere on Palm Street; he could be anywhere now.

The smoky interior of the bar looked like every other place he'd been in this afternoon. Dirty wooden floors, their polish

scratched and worn beyond all redemption. Tables in little better condition, chairs with long wooden legs that wobbled when you sat on them, leaving you unsure if it was all the booze you'd been putting away that made your seat feel so precarious, or the rickety furniture that the owner was too cheap to replace until it actually fell apart under someone. A TV set up in a corner of the bar where game shows and soap operas took turns until they finally gave way to the six o'clock news.

And then there was the clientele.

The thin afternoon crowd was invariably composed of far too many lost and hopeless faces. He recognized them from his job. Today, as he staggered away from the urinal to blink at the reflection looking back at him from the mirror, he realized that he looked about the same. He couldn't tell himself apart from them if he tried, except that maybe they could hold their drink better.

Because he felt sick. Unable to face the squalor of one of the cubicles, he stumbled out of the bar, hoping to clear his head. The street didn't look familiar, and the air didn't help. It was filled with exhaust fumes and the tail end of rush hour noise. His stomach roiled and he made his slow way along the pavement in front of the bar, one hand on the wall to keep his balance.

When he reached the alleyway, it was all he could do to take a few floundering steps inside before he fell to his hands and knees and threw up. Vomiting brought no relief. He still felt the world doing a slow spin and the stink just made his nausea worse.

Pushing himself away from the noxious puddle, the most he could manage was to fall back against the brick wall on this side of the alley. He brought his knees slowly up, wrapped his arms around them and leaned his head on top. He must have inadvertently turned his pager back on at some point in the afternoon, because it suddenly went off, its insistent beep piercing his aching head.

He unclipped it from his belt and threw it against the far wall. The sound of it smashing was only slightly more satisfying than the blessed relief from its shrill beeping.

"You don't look so good."

He lifted his head at the familiar voice, half-expecting that one of his clients had found him in this condition, or worse, one of his co-workers. Instead he met the grey-green gaze of the woman he'd briefly run into by the lakefront earlier in the day.

"Jesus," he said. "You...you're like a bad penny."

He lowered his head back onto his knees again and just hoped she'd go away. He could feel her standing there, looking down at him for a long time before she finally went down on one knee beside him and gave his arm a tug.

"C'mon," she said. "You can't stay here."

"Lemme alone."

"I don't just care about trees either," she said.

"Who gives a fuck."

But it was easier to let her drag him to his feet than to fight her offer of help. She slung his arm over her shoulder and walked him back to the street where she flagged down a cab. He heard her give his address to the cabbie and wondered how she knew it, but soon gave up that train of thought as he concentrated on not getting sick in the back of the cab.

He retained the rest of the night in brief flashes. At some point they were in the stairwell of his building, what felt like a month later he was propped up beside the door to his apartment while she worked the key in the lock. Then he was lying on his bed while she removed his shoes.

"Who...who are you?" he remembered asking her.

"Debra Eisenstadt."

The name meant nothing to him. The bed seemed to move under him. I don't have a water bed, he remembered thinking, and then he threw up again. Debra caught it in his wastepaper basket.

A little later still, he came round again to find her sitting in one of his kitchen chairs that she'd brought into the bedroom and placed by the head of the bed. He remembered thinking that this was an awful lot to go through just for a donation to some rainforest fund.

He started to sit up, but the room spun dangerously, so he just let his head fall back against the pillow. She wiped his brown with a cool, damp washcloth.

"What do you want from me?" he managed to ask.

"I just wanted to see what you were like when you were my age," she said.

That made so little sense that he passed out again trying to work it out.

62

She was still there when he woke up the next morning. If anything, he thought he actually felt worse than he had the night before. Debra came into the room when he stirred and

gave him a glass of Eno that helped settle his stomach. A couple of Tylenol started to work on the pounding behind his eyes.

"Someone from your office called and I told her you were sick," she said. "I hope that was okay."

"You stayed all night?"

She nodded, but Dennison didn't think she had the look of someone who'd been up all night. She had a fresh-scented glow to her complexion and her head seemed to catch the sun, spinning it off into strands of light that mingled with the natural highlights already present in her light brown hair. Her hair looked damp.

"I used your shower," she said. "I hope you don't mind."

"No, no. Help yourself."

He started to get up, but she put a palm against his chest to keep him lying down.

"Give the pills a chance to work." she said. "Meanwhile I'll get you some coffee. Do you feel up to some breakfast?"

The very thought of eating made his stomach churn.

"Never mind," she said, taking in the look on his face. "I'll just bring the coffee."

Dennison watched her leave, then straightened his head and stared at the ceiling. After meeting her, he thought maybe he believed in angels for the first time since Sunday school.

It was past ten before he finally dragged himself out of bed and into the shower. The sting of hot water helped to clear his head; being clean and putting on fresh clothes helped some more. He regarded himself in the bathroom mirror. His features were still puffy from alcohol poisoning and his cheeks looked dirty with twenty-four hours worth of dark stubble. His hands were unsteady, but he shaved all the same. Neither mouthwash nor brushing his teeth could quite get rid of the sour taste in his mouth.

Debra had toast and more coffee waiting for him in the kitchen.

"I don't get it," he said as he slid into a chair across the table from her. "I could be anyone—some maniac for all you know. Why're you being so nice to me?"

She just shrugged.

"C'mon. It's not like I could have been a pretty sight when you found me in the alley, so it can't be that you were attracted to me."

"Were you serious about what you said last night?" she

Charles De Lint

asked by way of response. "About quitting your job?"

Dennison paused before answering to consider what she'd asked. He couldn't remember telling her that, but then there was a lot about yesterday he couldn't remember. The day was mostly a blur except for one thing. Ronnie Egan's features swam up in his mind until he squeezed his eyes shut and forced the image away.

Serious about quitting his job?

"Yeah," he said with a slow nod. "I guess I was. I mean, I am. I don't think I can even face going into the office. I'll just send them the letter of resignation and have somebody pick up my stuff from my desk."

"You do make a difference," she said. "It might not seem so at a time like this, but you've got to concentrate on all the people you have helped. That's got to count for something, doesn't it?"

"How would you know?" Dennison asked her. No sooner did the question leave his mouth, than it was followed by a flood of others. "Where did you come from? What are you doing here? It's got to be more than trying to convince me to keep my job so that I can afford to donate some money to your cause."

"You don't believe in good Samaritans?"

Dennison shook his head. "Nor Santa Claus."

But maybe angels, he added to himself. She was so fresh and pretty—light years different from the people who came into his office, their worn and desperate features eventually all bleeding one into the other.

"I appreciate your looking after me the way you did," he said. "Really I do. And I don't mean to sound ungrateful. But it just doesn't make a lot of sense."

"You help people all the time."

"That's my job—*was* my job." He looked away from her steady gaze. "Christ, I don't know anymore."

"And that's all it was?" she asked.

"No. It's just...I'm tired, I guess. Tired of seeing it all turn to shit on me. This little kid who died yesterday...I could've tried harder. If I'd tried harder, maybe he'd still be alive."

"That's the way I feel about the environment, sometimes," she said. "There are times when it just feels so hopeless, I can't go on."

"So why do you?"

"Because the bottom line is I believe I can make a difference. Not a big one. What I do is just a small ripple, but I know

it helps. And if enough little people like me make our little differences, one day we're going to wake up to find that we really did manage to change the world."

"There's a big distinction between some trees getting cut down and a kid dying," Dennison said.

"From our perspective, sure," she agreed. "But maybe not from a global view. We have to remember that everything's connected. The real world's not something that can be divided into convenient little compartments, like we'll label this, 'the child abuse problem,' this'll go under 'depletion of the ozone layer.' If you help some homeless child on these city streets, it has repercussions that touch every part of the world."

"I don't get it."

"It's like a vibe," she said. "If enough people think positively, take positive action, then it snowballs all of its own accord and the world can't help but get a little better."

Dennison couldn't stop from voicing the cynical retort that immediately came into his mind.

"How retro," he said.

"What do you mean?"

"It sounds so sixties. All this talk about vibes and positive mumbo-jumbo."

"Positive thinking brought down the Berlin Wall," she said.

"Yeah, and I'm sure some fortune teller predicted it in the pages of a supermarket tabloid, although she probably got the decade wrong. Look, I'm sorry, but I don't buy it. If the world really worked on 'vibes' I think it'd be in even worse shape than it already is."

"Maybe that's what *is* wrong with it: too much negative energy. So we've got to counteract it with positive energy."

"Oh please."

She got a sad look on her face. "I believe it," she said. "I learned that from a man that I came to love very much. I didn't believe him when he told me, either, but now I know it's true."

"*How* can you know it's true?"

Debra sighed. She put her hand in the back pocket of her jeans and pulled out a piece of paper.

"Talk to these people," she said. "They can explain it a whole lot better than I can."

Dennison looked at the scrap of paper she'd handed him. "Elder's Council" was written in ball point. The address given was city hall's.

"Who are they?"

Charles De Lint

"Elders from the Kickaha Reservation."

"They've got an office at city hall?"

Debra nodded. "It's part of a program to integrate alternative methods of dealing with problems with the ones we would traditionally use."

"What? People go to these old guys and ask them for advice?"

"They're not just men," she said. "In fact, among the Kickaha—as with many native peoples—there are more women then men sitting on an elders' council. They're the grandfathers of the tribe who hold and remember all the wisdoms. The Kickaha call them 'the Aunts.'"

Dennison started to shake his head. "I know you mean well, Debra, but—"

"Just go talk to them—please? Before you make your decision."

"But nothing they say is going to—"

"Promise me you will. You asked me why I helped you last night, well let's say this is what I want in return: for you to just talk to them."

"I..."

The last thing Dennison wanted was to involve himself with some nut case situation like this, but he liked the woman, despite her flaky beliefs, and he did owe her something. He remembered throwing up last night and her catching the vault in his garbage can. How many people would do that for a stranger?

"Okay," he said. "I promise."

The smile that she gave him seemed to make her whole face glow.

"Good," she said. "Make sure you bring a present. A package of tobacco would be good."

"Tobacco."

She nodded. "I've got to go now," she added. She stood up and shook his hand. "I'm really glad I got the chance to meet you."

"Wait a minute," Dennison said as she left the kitchen.

He followed her into the living room where she was putting on her jacket.

"Am I going to see you again?" he asked.

"I hope so."

"What's your number?"

"Do you have a pen?"

He went back into the kitchen and returned with a pencil

and the scrap of paper she'd given him. She took it from him and quickly scribbled a phone number and address on it. She handed it back to him, gave him a quick kiss on the cheek, and then she was out the door and gone.

Dennison stood staring at the door after it had closed behind her. The apartment had never seemed so empty before.

Definitely flaky, he thought as he returned to the kitchen. But he thought maybe he'd fallen in love with her, if that was something you were allowed to do with angels.

He finished his coffee and cleaned up the dishes, dawdling over the job. He didn't know anything about the Kickaha except for those that he saw in his office, applying for welfare, and what he'd seen on the news a couple of years ago when the more militant braves from the reservation had blockaded Highway 14 to protest logging on their land. So he had only two images of them: down and out, or dressed in khaki, carrying an assault rifle. Wait, make that three. There were also the pictures in the history books of them standing around in ceremonial garb.

He didn't want to go to this Elder's Council. Nothing they could tell him was going to make him look at the world any differently, so why bother? But finally he put on a lightweight sportsjacket and went out to flag a cab to take him to city hall because whatever else he believed or didn't believe, the one thing he'd never done yet was break a promise.

He wasn't about to start now—especially with a promise made to an angel.

Dennison left the elevator and walked down a carpeted hallway on the third floor of city hall. He stopped at the door with the neatly-lettered sign that read "Elders' Council." He felt surreal, as though he'd taken a misstep somewhere along the way yesterday and had ended up in a Fellini film. Being here was odd enough, in and of itself. But if he was going to meet a native elder, he felt it should be under pine trees with the smell of wood smoke in the air, not cloistered away in city hall, surrounded by miles of concrete and steel.

Really, he shouldn't be here at all. What he should be doing was getting his affairs in order. Resigning from his job, getting in touch with his cousin Pete who asked Dennison at least every three or four months if he wanted to go into business with him. Pete worked for a small shipping firm, but he wanted to start his own company. "I've got the know-how and the money,"

he'd tell Dennison, "but frankly, when it comes to dealing with people, I stink. That's where you'd come in."

Dennison hesitated for a long moment, staring at the door and the sign affixed to its plain wooden surface. He knew what he should be doing, but he'd made that promise, so he knocked on the door. An old native woman answered it as he was about to lift his hand to rap a second time.

Her face was wrinkled, her complexion dark; her braided hair almost grey. She wore a long brown skirt, flat-soled shoes and a plain white blouse that was decorated with a tracing of brightly-coloured beadwork on its collar points and buttoned placket. The gaze that looked up to meet his was friendly, the eyes such a dark brown that it was hard to differentiate between pupil and iris.

"Hello," she said and ushered him in.

It was strange inside. He found himself standing in a conference room overlooking the parking garage behind city hall. The walls were unadorned and there was no table, just thick wall-to-wall on the floor and a ring of chairs set in a wide circle, close to the walls. At the far side of the room, he spied a closed door that might lead into another room or a storage closet.

"Uh…"

Suddenly at a loss for words, he put his hand in his pocket, pulled out the package of cigarette tobacco that he'd bought in the way over and handed it to her.

"Thank you," the woman said. She steered him to a chair, then sat down beside him. "My name is Dorothy. How can I help you?"

"Dorothy?" Dennison replied, unable to hide his surprise.

The woman nodded. "Dorothy Born. You were expecting something more exotic such as Woman-Who-Speaks-With-One-Hand-Rising?"

"I didn't know what to expect."

"That was my mother's name actually—in the old language. She was called that because she'd raise her hand as she spoke, ready to slap the head of those braves who wouldn't listen to her advice."

"Oh."

She smiled. "That's a joke. My mother's name was Ruth."

"Uh…"

What a great conversationalist he was proving to be today. Good thing Pete couldn't hear him at this moment. But he just didn't know where to begin.

"Why don't you just tell me why you've come," Dorothy said.

"Actually, I feel a little foolish."

Her smile broadened. "Good. That is the first step on the road to wisdom." She put a hand on his knee, dark gaze locking with his. "What is your name?"

"Chris—Chris Dennison."

"Speak to me, Chris. I am here to listen."

So Dennison told her about his job, about Ronnie Egan's death, about getting drunk, about Debra Eisenstadt and how she'd come to send him here. Once he started, his awkwardness fled.

"Nothing seems worth it anymore," he said in conclusion.

Dorothy nodded. "I understand. When the spirit despairs, it becomes difficult to see clearly. Your friend's words require too much faith for you to accept them."

"I guess. I'm not sure I even understand them."

"Perhaps I can help you there."

She fell silent for a moment, her gaze still on him, but she no longer seemed to see him. It was as though she saw beyond him, or had turned to look inward.

"The Kickaha way to see the world," she finally said, "is to understand that is everything is on a wheel: Day turns to night. The moon waxes and wanes. Summer turns to autumn. A man is born, he lives, he dies. But no wheel turns by itself. Each affects the other so that when the wheel of the seasons turns to winter, the wheel of the day grows shorter. When the day grows shorter, the sweetgrass is covered with snow and the deer must forage for bark and twigs rather than feast on its delicate blades. The hunter must travel farther afield to find the deer, but perhaps the wolf finds her first."

She paused, sitting back in her chair. "Do you see?"

Dennison nodded slowly. "I see the connection in what you're saying, but not with what Debra was trying to tell me. It was so vague—all this talk about positive energy."

"But the energy we produce is very powerful medicine," Dorothy said. "It can work great good or ill."

"You make it sound like voodoo."

She frowned for a moment as though she needed to think that through.

"Perhaps it is," she said. "From the little I know of it, *voudoun* is a very basic application of the use of one's will. The results one gains from its medicine become positive or negative only depending upon one's intention."

Charles De Lint

"You're saying we make bad things happen to ourselves?"

Dorothy nodded. "And to our sacred trust, the earth."

"I still don't see how a person can be so sure he's really making a difference."

"What if the child you save grows up to be the scientist that will cure AIDS?"

"What if the child I don't get to in time was supposed to be that scientist and so she never gets the chance to find the cure?"

Dorothy lifted her hand and tapped it against his chest. "You carry so much pain in here. It wasn't always so, was it?"

Dennison thought about how he'd been when he first got into social work. He'd been like Debra then, so sure he knew exactly what to do. He'd believed utterly in his ability to save the world. That had changed. Not because of Ronnie Egan, but slowly, over the years. He'd had to make compromises, his trust had been abused not once, or twice, but almost every day. What had happened to Ronnie had forced him to see that he fought a losing battle.

Perhaps it was worse than that. What he felt now was that the battle had been lost long ago and he was only just now realizing the futility of continuing to man the frontlines.

"If you were to see what I have to work with every day," he said, "you'd get depressed, too."

Dorothy shook her head. "That is not our way."

"So what is your way?"

"You must learn to let it go. The wheel must always turn. If you take upon yourself the sadness and despair from those you would help, you must also learn how to let it go. Otherwise it will settle inside you like a cancer."

"I don't know if I can anymore."

She nodded slowly. "That is something that only you can decide. But remember this: You have given a great deal of yourself. You have no reason to feel shamed if you must now turn away."

She had just put her finger on what was making the decision so hard for him. Futile though he'd come to realize his efforts were, he still felt guilty at the idea of turning his back on those who needed his help. It wasn't like Debra had been saying: the difference he made didn't have far-reaching effects. It didn't change what was happening in the Amazon, or make the hole in the ozone layer any smaller. All it did was make one or two persons' misery a little easier to bear, but only in the short term. It seemed cruel to give them hope when it would just be

taken away from them again.

If only there really was something to Debra's domino theory. While the people he helped wouldn't go on to save the environment, or find that cure for AIDS, they might help somebody else a little worse off than themselves. That seemed worthwhile, except what do you do when you've reached inside yourself and you can't find anything left to give?

Dorothy was watching him with her dark gaze. Oddly enough her steady regard didn't make him feel self-conscious. She had such a strong personality that he could feel its warmth as though he was holding his hands out to a fire. It made him yearn to find something to fill the cold that had lodged inside him since he'd looked down at Ronnie Egan's corpse.

"Maybe I should get into environmental work instead," he said. "You know, how they say that a change is as good as a rest?"

"Who says that you aren't already doing environmental work?" Dorothy asked.

"What do you mean?"

"What if the dying trees of the rainforest are being reborn as unwanted children?" she asked.

"C'mon. You can't expect me to believe—"

"Why not? If a spirit is taken from its wheel before its time, it must go somewhere."

Dennison had a sudden vision of a tenement building filled with green-skinned children, each of them struggling to reach the roof of the building to get their nourishment from the sun, except when they finally got up there, the smog cover was so thick that there was nothing for them. They got a paler and paler green until finally they just withered away. Died like so many weeds.

"Imagine living in a world with no more trees," Dorothy said.

Dennison had been in a clear-cut forest once, it was while he was visiting a friend in Oregon. He'd stood there on a hilltop and for so far as the eye could see, there were only tree stumps. It was a heartbreaking sight.

His friend had become an environmentalist after a trip to China. "There are almost no trees left there at all now," he'd told Dennison. "They've just used them all up. Trees clean the environment by absorbing the toxins from carbon dioxide and acid rain. Without them, the water and air became too toxic and people start to die off from liver cancer. China has an incredibly high mortality rate due to liver cancer."

"That's going to happen here, Chris. That's what's going to happen in the Amazon. It's going to happen all over the world."

Dennison had felt bad, enough so that he contributed some money to a couple of relevant causes, but his concern hadn't lasted. His work with social services took too much out of him to leave much energy for other concerns, no matter how worthy.

As though reading his mind, Dorothy said, "And now imagine a world with no more children."

Dennison thought they might be halfway there. So many of the children he dealt with were more like miniature adults than the kids he remembered growing up with. But then he and his peers hadn't had to try to survive on the streets, foraging out of trashcans, maybe taking care of a junkie parent.

"I have a great concern for mother earth," Dorothy said. "We have gravely mistreated her. But when we speak of the environment and the depletion of resources, we sometimes forget that our greatest resource is our children.

"My people have a word to describe the moment when all is in harmony—we call it Beauty. But Beauty can find no foothold in despair. If we mean to reclaim our mother earth from the ills that plague her, we must not forget our own children. We must work on many levels, walk many wheels, that lives may be spared—the lives of people, and the lives of all those other species with whom we share the world. Our contributions, no matter how small they might appear, carry an equal importance, for they will all contribute to the harmony that allows the world to walk the wheel of Beauty."

She closed her eyes and fell silent. Dennison sat quietly beside her for a time.

"What...what advice would you give me?" he asked finally.

Dorothy shrugged. Her eyes remained closed.

"You must do what you believe is right," she said. "We have inside of each of us a spirit, and that spirit alone knows what it is that we should or should not do."

"I've got to think about all of this," Dennison said.

"That would be a good thing," Dorothy told him. She opened her eyes suddenly, piercing him with her gaze. "But hold onto your feelings of foolishness," she added. "Wisdom never comes to those who believe they having nothing left to learn."

Dennison found an empty bench when he left city hall. He sat down and cradled his face in his hands. His headache had

returned, but that wasn't what was disturbing him. He'd found himself agreeing with the Kickaha elder. He also thought he understood what Debra had been telling him. The concepts weren't suspect—only the part he had to play in them.

He felt like one of those Biblical prophets, requiring the proof of a burning bush or some other miracle before they'd go on with the task required of them. If he could just have the proof that he'd made a real and lasting difference for only one person, that would be enough. But it wasn't going to come.

The people he helped continued to live hand to mouth because there was no other way for them to live. Caught up in a recession that showed no sign of letting up, they considered themselves lucky to just be surviving.

And that was why his decision was going to have to stand. He'd given of himself, above and beyond what the job required, for years. The empty cold feeling inside told him that he had nothing left to give. It was time to call Pete and see about that shipping business. He wasn't sure he could bring Pete's enthusiasm to it, but he'd do his best.

But first he owed Debra a call: Yeah, I went and saw the elder, she was a wonderful woman, I understand what you were saying, but I haven't changed my mind. He knew he'd be closing the door on the possibility of a relationship with her, but then he didn't feel he had even that much of himself to give someone anyway.

He dug a quarter out of his pocket and went to the payphone on the corner. But when he dialed the number she'd given him, he got a recorded message: "I'm sorry but the number you have dialed is no longer in service."

"Shit," he said, stepping back from the phone.

An older woman, laden down with shopping bags, gave him a disapproving glare.

"Sorry," he muttered.

Flagging down a cab, he gave the drive the address that Debra had written down to accompany her bogus phone number, then settled back in his seat.

The building was a worn, brownstone tenement, indistinguishable from every other one on the block. They all had the same tired face to turn to the world. Refuse collected against their steps, graffiti on the walls, cheap curtains in the windows when there were any at all. Walking up the steps, the smell of urine and body odor was strong in the air. A drunk lay sleeping

just inside the small foyer.

Dennison stepped over him and went up to the second floor. He knocked on the door that had a number matching the one Debra had written down for him. After a moment or two, the door opened to the length of its chain and a woman as worn down as the building itself was looking at him.

"What do you want?"

Dennison had been expecting an utter stranger, but the woman had enough of a family resemblance to Debra that he thought maybe his rescuing angel really did live here. Looking past the lines that worry and despair had left on the woman's face, he realized that she was about his own age. Too young to be Debra's mother. Maybe her sister?

"Are you...uh, Mrs. Eisenstadt?" he asked, trying the only name he had.

"Who wants to know?"

"My name's Chris Dennison. I'm here to see Debra."

The woman's eyes narrowed with suspicion. "What'd she do now?"

"Nothing. That is, she gave me some help yesterday and I just wanted to thank her."

The suspicion didn't leave the woman's features. "Debra!" she shouted over her shoulder. Turning back to Dennison, she added, "I've got lots of neighbours. You try anything funny, I'll give a scream that'll have them down here so fast you won't know if you're coming or going."

Dennison doubted that. In a place like this, people would just mind their own business. It wouldn't matter if somebody was getting murdered next door.

"I'm not here to cause trouble," he said.

"Deb-*ra*!" the woman hollered again.

She shut the door and Dennison could hear her unfastening the chain. When she opened the door once more, it swung open to its full width. Dennison looked down the hall behind the woman and saw a little girl of perhaps nine coming slowly down the hallway, head lowered, gaze on the floor.

"I thought you told me you were in school yesterday," the woman said to her.

The girl's gaze never lifted. "I was."

She spoke barely above a whisper.

"Man here says you were helping him—doing what, I'd like to know." She turned from her daughter back to Dennison. "Maybe you want to tell me, mister?"

The girl looked at him then. He saw the grey-green eyes first, the features that might one day grow into ones similar to those of the woman he'd met yesterday, though this couldn't be her. The discrepancy of years was too vast. Then he saw the bruises. One eye blackened. The right side of her jaw swollen. She seemed to favour one leg as well.

His training kept him silent. If he said something too soon, he wouldn't learn a thing. First he had to give the woman enough room to hang herself.

"This is Debra Eisenstadt?" he asked.

"What, you need to see her birth certificate?"

Dennison turned to the woman and saw then what he hadn't noticed before. The day was warm, but she was wearing slacks, long sleeves, her blouse buttoned all the way up to the top. But he could see a discoloration in the hollow of her throat that the collar couldn't quite hide. Abrasive or not, she was a victim, too, he realized.

"Where is your husband, Mrs. Eisenstadt?" he asked gently.

"So now you're a cop?"

Dennison pulled out his ID. "No. I'm with social services. I can help you, Mrs. Eisenstadt. Has your husband been beating you?"

She crossed her arms protectively. "Look, it's not like what you're thinking. We had an argument, that's all."

"And your daughter—was he having an argument with her as well?"

"No. She…she just fell. Isn't that right, honey?"

Dennison glanced at the girl. She was staring at the floor again. Slowly she nodded in agreement. Dennison went down on one knee until his head was level with the girl's.

"You can tell me the truth," he said. "I can help you, but you've got to help me. Tell me how you got hurt and I promise you I won't let it happen to you again."

What the hell are you doing? he asked himself. You're supposed to be quitting this job.

But he hadn't turned in his resignation yet.

And then he remembered an odd thing that the other Debra had said to him last night.

I just wanted to see what you were like when you were my age.

He remembered puzzling over that before he finally passed out. And then there was the way she'd looked at him the next morning, admiring, then sad, then disappointed. As though she

already knew him. As though he wasn't matching up to her expectations.

Though of course she couldn't have any expectations because they'd never met before. But what if this girl grew up to be the woman who'd helped him last night? What if her being here, in need of help, was his prophetic sign, his burning bush?

Yeah, right. And it was space aliens who brought her back from the future to see him.

"Look," the girl's mother said. "You've got no right, barging in here—"

"No right?" Dennison said, standing up to face her. "Look at your daughter, for Christ's sake, and then tell me that I've got no right to intervene."

"It's not like what you think. It's just that times are hard, you know, and what with Sam's losing his job, well he gets a little crazy sometimes. He doesn't mean any real harm..."

Dennison tuned her out. He looked back at the little girl. It didn't matter if she was a sign or not, if she'd grow up to be the woman who'd somehow come back in time to help him when his faith was flagging the most. What was important right now that he get the girl some help.

"Which of your neighbours has a working phone?" he asked.

"Why? What're you going to do? Sam's going to—"

"Not do a damned thing," Dennison said. "It's my professional opinion that this child will be in danger so long as she remains in this environment. You can either come with us, or I'll see that she's made a ward of the court, but I'm not leaving her here."

"You can't–"

"I think we'll leave that for a judge to decide."

He ignored her then. Crouching down beside the little girl, he said, "I'm here to help you—do you understand? No one's going to hurt you anymore."

"If I...he said if I tell—"

"Debra!"

Dennison shot the mother an angry look. "I'm losing my patience with you, lady. Look at your daughter. Look at those bruises. Is that the kind of childhood you meant for your child?"

Her defiance crumbled under his glare and she slowly shook her head.

"Go pack a bag," he told the woman. "For both of you."

As she slowly walked down the hall, Dennison returned his attention to the little girl. This could all go to hell in a hand

basket if he wasn't careful. There were certain standard procedures to deal with this kind of a situation and badgering the girl's mother the way he had been wasn't one of them. But he was damned if he wasn't going to give it his best shot.

"Do you understand what's happening?" he asked the girl. "I'm going to take you and your mother someplace where you'll be safe."

She looked up at him, those so familiar grey-green eyes wide and teary. "I'm scared."

Dennison nodded. "It's a scary situation. But tell you what. On the way to the shelter, maybe we get you a treat. What would you like?"

For one long moment the girl's gaze settled on his. She seemed to be considering whether she could trust him or not. He must have come up positive, because after that moment's hesitation, she opened right up.

"For there still to be trees when I grow up," she said. "I want to be a forest ranger. Sometimes when I'm sleeping, I wake up and I hear the trees crying because their daddies are being mean to them, I guess, and are hurting them and I just want to help stop it."

Dennison remembered himself saying to the older Debra, *Trees don't cry. Kids do.* And then Debra's response.

Maybe you just can't hear them.

Jesus, it wasn't possible, was it? But then how could they look so similar, the differences caused by the passage of years, not genetics. And the eyes—the eyes were exactly the same. And how could the old Debra have known the address, the phone number—

He got up and went over to the phone he could see sitting on a TV tray beside the battered sofa. The number was the same as on the the scrap of paper in his pocket. He lifted the receiver, but there was no dial tone.

"I…I've packed a…bag."

Debra's mother stood in the hallway beside her daughter, looking as lost as the little girl did. But there was something they both had—there was a glimmer of hope in their eyes. He'd put that there. Now all he had to do was figure out a way to keep it there.

"Whose phone can we use to call a cab?" he asked.

"Laurie—she's down the hall in number six. She'd let us use her phone."

"Well, let's get going."

As he ushered them into the hall, he was no longer thinking about tendering his resignation. He had no doubt the feeling that he had to quit would rise again, but when that happened he was going to remember a girl with grey-green eyes and the woman she might grow up to be. He was going to remember the wheels that connect everything, cogs interlocked and turning to create a harmonious whole. He was going to remember the power of good vibes.

He was going to learn to believe.

I believe it. I learned that from a man that I came to love very much. I didn't believe him when he told me, either, but now I know it's true.

But most of all he was going to make sure that he earned the respect of the angel that had come to visit him from the days still to come.

Dennison knew there was probably a more rational explanation for it all, but right then, he wanted to believe in angels.

I Remember Me

Me

Thomas Tessier

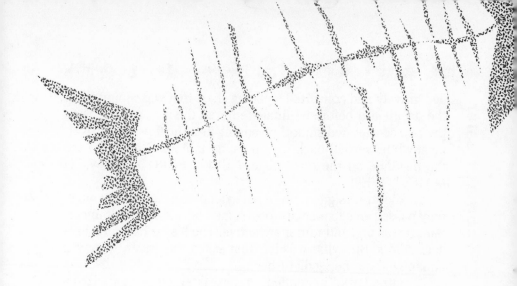

Glen came out of the building on Park Avenue South and stood on the sidewalk. He wasn't sure what to do. A couple of men out by the curb noticed him, and exchanged words. One of them walked briskly toward Glen. Ah yes, he would be a pointer.

"Cab, sir?" the man asked politely. "Or directions?"

"Yes," Glen replied. "A cab, please."

The pointer raced to the curb and waved at the passing river of traffic. The other man stood by with an approving look on his face. He would be the pointer's pointer. No doubt the pointer's pointer's pointer was on patrol nearby. They did an amazing job, moving twelve million people around Manhattan every day. But now the man came back, visibly upset with himself.

"What was it again, sir?" he asked sheepishly.

Glen looked at the piece of paper he discovered in his hand. "A taxi," he read aloud.

"Gotcha this time."

The pointer turned back to the road and resumed his attempts to flag down a vacant cab. A few moments later, he had one.

"Thank you," Glen said as he got into the vehicle.

"You do have your destination, sir?"

"Yes, thanks."

"Thank you."

The pointer closed the door and bustled away. Such a polite man, Glen reflected. He handed his piece of paper to the driver, who nod-

ded gravely and consulted a plastic chart that was mounted on the dashboard before he finally entered the destination. Then the taxi accelerated smoothly, edging into the flow. The driver, meanwhile, settled back with a gaudy tabloid. Glen could see the headline on the open page: I EVEN FORGOT HOW TO MAKE LOVE!!!

As the street signs went by, Glen recognized them. But when they passed an expanse of wooded land he suddenly felt uncertain. It was big, and rather attractive. The leaves had such brilliant colors. But what was it? Glen asked the driver, who was unhappy about being disturbed.

"Central Park," he replied a minute later, when he spotted a sign that said Central Park West.

I thought so, Glen told himself. A park that big could only be Central Park. He had known all along—you can know a thing, even if the name for it slips your grasp. It was nothing to fret about, it didn't mean you were stupid or sick. Everyone has such lapses from time to time. It was—but Glen was too tired right now to think about it.

Just past 99th Street, the taxi swung around boldly and came to a stop in front of a large apartment building. The driver sat up and looked around.

"Here you are."

"Thanks."

Glen paid the fare. Money was still fairly easy, because it had numbers on it. Numbers went deep. Money went deeper. Money would last until the end, no doubt about that. He put his wallet back into his jacket pocket, and caught sight of two words penned in blue ink on the inside of his wrist:

GLEN BARNES

"And you are?" the doorman asked.

"Glen Barnes," Glen announced calmly.

The doorman checked Glen's face against the house photo bank on the desk terminal. Apparently everything was in order, as the doorman soon looked up and smiled.

"Yes sir, Mr. Barnes. You're in apartment eleven-twenty, as I'm sure you know."

"Yes, of course. Thank you." Glen hesitated, searching the wide lobby with anxious eyes. "The, uh—"

"The elevators are around there, to your right," the doorman supplied helpfully.

"You haven't moved them since this morning," Glen said in an attempt to make a joke.

"Couldn't be bothered," the doorman shot back, breaking into self-appreciative laughter. "Nice to see you again, Mr.—"

"And you, Jimmy."

"George."

"George, yes. What happened to Jimmy?"

"Jimmy? There's no Jimmy here, Mr. Glen."

"Really? I am sorry. My mistake."

"You're thinking of another place," the doorman named George suggested considerately. "Where you work, maybe."

"Yes, yes, that must be it."

What a strange man, Glen thought as he stepped into the open elevator. Eleven-twenty, wasn't it? He noticed he was sweating. It would help if everybody wore name tags. But there were others who said that would only make matters worse. Glen didn't see how that was possible.

He found a card-key in his wallet and tried it on the door. It worked. He went inside. It was a pleasant-looking apartment. It was his. And hers. She smiled at Glen, came and gave him a kiss on the cheek.

"Hi, Glen," she said sweetly.

"Hello...dear."

A lot had changed with the coming of The Flu.

Glen sat and watched the news on television. The main story of the day was the announced closing of all the dinosaur exhibits at the Museum of Natural History. It was claimed that scientists had now debunked the theory that dinosaurs had ever existed. But there were also reports that too many people had complained about the dinosaur displays on the grounds of bad taste. The same sort of thing was happening in other cities at home and abroad. There seemed to be a great deal of debate about it.

Glen's wife was in the kitchen, doing something. Glen had a small notebook in his hand. He flipped through it discreetly and found the page he was looking for. Her name was Marion— but he knew that, of course!

"Marion," he called out.

"Yes?"

"How are you, Marion?"

"Fine...dear," she called back to him.

Glen quickly scanned the rest of the page, and saw much that was immediately familiar to him. You see, he thought, it's still all there. She

- has a mild case of high blood pressure
- is a lapsed Catholic
- works at a shelter for teenage girls
- likes icky French pop singers
- but does not speak or give French
- and is generally lazy in bed
- reads historicals
- likes microwave cuisine
- drinks one spritzer at night
- hates smoke
- except her father's pipe
- (her father is Phil, mother invalid)

Glen slipped the notebook back into his briefcase and looked at the television again. The economic news was very good. There was virtually no unemployment now, thanks to the pointer program. There was a dark cloud attached to the silver lining, however, as it seemed that the demand for pointers would continue to grow for the foreseeable future, the need far outstripping the supply. It didn't take a genius to see what was coming. Eventually everyone would be a pointer.

There was also news about The Flu. The news was that there was no news, just a new statement to the effect that its symptoms were still believed to be transient in nature, and not permanent, deteriorating alterations. A doctor told the newsperson that six years was not too long a time for symptoms to persist. Good God, Glen thought. Don't tell me we've had The Flu for six years now. That is a bit much. He got up and went into the kitchen to raise this point with—his wife.

She hastily closed a notebook she was studying and shoved it into her handbag.

Glen emerged from his apartment building and stood there. A pointer soon appeared to help him, but had trouble finding a cab. You could try to flag one down yourself if you knew that was what you needed, but the drivers gave preference to the pointers. The thing to do was to cooperate. Everyone had to change and adjust, otherwise nothing would work anymore. As he waited, Glen heard a loud metallic voice coming from the park.

When the light changed, and there was still no taxi, he went to see what was going on. A crowd had gathered around a bald man who stood on a red plastic crate. He had a megaphone.

"The Flu is not a virus," he shouted. "The Flu is not just a

bunch of bacteria. The Flu is a single organism. The biggest, most vicious creature alive on this planet. It sweeps across the continents and oceans as if they were nothing, and it feeds on us like locusts on a field of corn. It decimates us, and with every new feeding season the disaster grows far greater. Soon the dark process will be complete, the final changes wrought, and—"

"How do you know all this?" a heckler cut in.

"I know, because I worked for the government. I learned the awful truth they're trying to keep from you. I—"

"Yeah, but how do you remember it?"

This produced gales of raucous laughter. Glen smiled. What was he supposed to be doing? He had a piece of paper in his hand and he was wearing his suit for work. He made his way out of the crowd and headed toward the street. A young man approached.

"Need a cab, sir?"

"Yes. Are you a pointer?"

"Yes sir."

"Don't you have a badge?" Glen asked. "Or a uniform?"

"They abandoned that idea, sir," the young man said gently, as if speaking to an idiot. "Negative psychology. Where are you going?" He took the destination chit from Glen's hand and peered at it briefly. "Downtown. You're in luck, sir. I've got a taxi here with a couple of other downtown passengers, and there's room for one more. Hurry up, they're ready to go."

"I don't want to share a ride."

"We've all got to cooperate, sir," the man said sternly. "I hope you're not one of those selfish people who refuses to pitch in and make sacrifices like the rest of us,"

"Well, no..."

"That's the spirit. Here you go."

Glen slid into the back seat of the taxi. There was a burly fellow already there, and another soon followed, sandwiching Glen in the middle. No one said anything. The taxi moved away, and a short while later it swung onto a road that ran through the park. The dying leaves had wonderful color now—it was that season of the year. Glen wished he had a window.

The man on his right suddenly hit him in the face. The man on his left began hitting him in the stomach. They kept hitting, and Glen never had a chance to say anything or resist. His mouth was full of loose teeth and blood, his vision was blurred, and he couldn't breathe. Then something hit him on the head, and he

Thomas Tessier

had only the vaguest sensation left in his body. He was being moved, he flew in the air—landed, fast and hard.

His briefcase was gone. His pockets were empty. His hands were empty—and bleeding; Glen must have landed on them when he hit the pavement. He wandered about for a while after coming to, and now he was sitting beside a pool of water. His head and body ached tremendously. He took off his tie, dipped it in the water, and cautiously touched his face with it. His skin stung, he knew his lips were swollen, and his teeth felt wobbly. The usual host of people moving about; they ignored him. He lowered a hand into the water and then began to pat it with a dry patch of tie. Glen sponged off some of the grit and gravel. Where the skin was only blood-stained, not torn, he rubbed harder to get clean.

Then he saw the faint ink marks swirling off with the blood, vanishing in the water—and he froze. My name was there, Glen realized too late. A few traces of ink remained, but they formed nothing. Not even a single complete letter.

This could be very bad, he told himself, but don't panic too soon. He knew a lot about himself. He had a job, he had a wife, he had an apartment. His job was downtown—that phony pointer had said so. These simple facts were hardly conclusive, but they were good to know and Glen was determined to hang on to them.

A little later he saw a policeman, who listened patiently to his story. The policeman explained that such muggings were quite common nowadays, and that the streets were full of people who had more or less lost their identities this way. Glen wondered if he had heard about it on the news and then forgotten it.

"What can I do?" he asked.

"You don't remember your name, not even your first name?"

"Not at the moment," Glen said. "I hit my head, and…"

"Yeah," the policeman said, nodding sadly. "Same thing with your address and place of work?"

"Yes."

"Okay, here's what you do. There's an Identification Center in the Plaza Hotel. That's the nearest one to here. If you ever had your fingerprints taken, or if you have any kind of criminal record, they'll have it on the computer and then they can confirm who you are."

"Otherwise?"

"Otherwise, you got a problem. There's talk about creating

a national identity program but that's probably a couple of years away. In the meantime..." The policeman shrugged.

"This is terrible," Glen murmured.

"Makes you wish you knocked over a gas station when you were a teenager, don't it? Hey, cheer up. Maybe you did."

"Why didn't they tell us it was this bad?"

"They been telling us for the last few years," the policeman said after consulting a fact sheet. "You just keep on forgetting about it. That's how this thing works."

"God, it's fiendish."

"Damn right it is. You don't notice until something happens so you get pushed off your spot, and you can't get back."

The policeman pointed Glen in the right direction and wished him luck. As he walked along he became aware of the large number of people who seemed to be wandering about aimlessly. Perhaps he was just imagining it as a result of his current state, but where was the sense of purpose in their stride, the glimmer of focus in their eyes? Glen was also disturbed by the presence of so many bodies on the ground. They were lying everywhere, on the benches and the grass, some even sprawled on the sidewalk. Some of them almost looked dead, but surely the situation hadn't reached that point yet. Dead bodies rot, they smell, they cause disease. But he had to admit that the signs were not good.

The line of people outside the hotel was enormous. It would be hours before he got inside. The line didn't seem to be moving at all. He might have to come back tomorrow or the next day. As far as he knew, he'd never broken the law or been fingerprinted, but it was apparently his only chance. Glen moved along, looking for the end of the line. Then a short man took him by the elbow and leaned close.

"Looking for an I.D.?"

"I'm looking for mine, yes," Glen answered.

"I got just what you need," the man went on. "Credit cards, keys, Social Security, addresses, phone numbers, everything a guy needs to get going again. The whole package."

"But is it mine?"

"You gotta start somewhere, pal."

"I don't have any money."

"Then what're you wasting my time for?"

The little man disappeared into the throng. It took a while for Glen to realize how unsettling that exchange was. Identities

for sale. But what good would it do? You couldn't just take the contents of someone's wallet and pockets, and gain the benefit of their identity. An interloper was bound to be exposed at home or at work. No, this was a scam, pure and simple. First you robbed some unfortunate person, and then you sold their useless personal papers to someone desperate enough to try anything.

There was one more aspect to this that particularly worried Glen. What if you walked into another person's home and the wife didn't recognize you as an imposter? She had forgotten what her husband looked like, and she had no photographs—or she thought they were photographs of someone else. You had the key, you were acting as if you belonged there. Would she accept the wrong man? Was anything like that possible? No, of course not. But when he tried to form a mental picture of his wife's face, Glen could not fill in any details.

Late in the afternoon the air turned very cold, a nasty wind set in and the sky was grey with wintry menace. Glen was in line but had advanced only a few yards, or so it seemed. If he had to come back tomorrow, where would he spend the night? He felt weak and sluggish, and it occurred to him that he was hungry. But how could he get anything to eat without money? If he had somebody's credit card at least he could get a meal in a restaurant. If the card still worked. But if he had cash to buy a card he could buy food more easily. The grave implications of his predicament were pressing in on his mind.

"This is all because of The Flu?" he asked the man tottering vacantly beside him in the line.

"What flu?"

"The Flu," Glen repeated sharply. "You know."

"If you say so."

Glen said nothing more. He had to think. Perhaps he could find a corner in the bus station, or the train station, a doorway sheltered from the wind. Something like that. People lived that way, and survived. What shocked him to the core was how suddenly it had happened to him. One minute he was being driven to work, the next he was literally thrown away like garbage. And from the moment he came to in the park he could feel the awful change that was taking place. Terrible new facts assailed his brain. He was loosing the will to resist, he could almost feel it leaching away. Helplessness was rooting itself in him.

"Mike?"

The breathless voice of a plain young woman. Glen had seen her approaching, studying the faces in the line. Now she stared at him with frantic eyes.

"Oh my God, it *is* you," she exclaimed. "Mike, oh Mike."

The woman threw her arms around Glen. She hugged and kissed him, and told him how she had searched and searched for him. She had almost given up hope of ever finding him.

"This just happened to me today," he told her.

"That's what you think," she replied with an understanding smile. "But how do you know that the way you remember it is more accurate than what you've forgotten? Besides, don't you think I know my own husband?"

"Tell me your name," Glen said.

"Roberta. Roberta Stone, and you're Mike Stone." She shook her head with amused delight, and laughed. "I bought that shirt for you at the Smartfellas shop."

Mike. Stone. Surely it would come ringing back to mind, if that was his name. But maybe it was symptomatic to draw a blank. There were no rules in this new situation, you had to play it by ear all the time. Mike was a short and simple name, and in that respect it did feel right.

"What should I do?" Glen asked her.

"What do you think you should do, silly?" She put her arm through his and pulled him out of the line. "You should go home. Where you live. Now. With me."

"Should we get a taxi?" Glen heard himself asking.

"What're you, made of money?"

"I don't have any money," he had to admit.

"So what else is new?"

Home was a rather drab basement apartment on West 54th, near Eleventh Avenue. Roberta had the address tattooed to the back of her left hand. She had her name on the heels of her feet. There were hot dogs for supper, and a warm bed later. The next morning she took him around to Skinpainter, who made sure that MIKE STONE would never lose track of his life again.

"What can I do?" Mike Stone asked Roberta Stone.

"You were unemployed before you got lost."

"What about you?"

"I don't work."

"How do we pay the rent and buy things?"

"Interest from the sale of my mother's house."

"You mean we don't have to do anything?"

"Neat, huh?"

Thomas Tessier

Until the French-cut stringbean fiasco. There was big news about a shipment of frozen French-cut stringbeans into Manhattan. Food had become a problem. Either the farmers forgot to plant it or harvest it, or the middlemen forgot to process and deliver it. Something was always going wrong, it seemed. But then a few tons of French-cut stringbeans arrived. The government had found them in a freezer. Roberta bought as many packages as she could grab. So did Mike Stone.

He was watching the news on television. The news was about how no one had heard from Europe in a long time. Well, they said it was a long time—but how could they be sure? Perhaps it was just the day before yesterday.

There was also news about The Flu. The news was that there was no news, but a doctor explained that the symptoms "continued to persist." He said that was not very unusual, even after eight years. Good God, Mike Stone thought. Have we had The Flu for as long as that? Eight years.

He got up and went into the kitchen to raise this point with Roberta (whose name was tattooed along the right side of his left index finger).

She had a wrapper in her hand. There were a couple of green blocks on the counter. Frozen French-cut stringbeans, glistening with moisture. She looked very unhappy, at a loss. He knew that something was wrong, so he didn't mention The Flu.

"What's happening?"

"I don't understand," she complained.

"What?"

"What do you do to get this stuff ready?"

"It's right there on the wrapper," Mike Stone said. He took the foil-paper from her hand and studied it. There was a picture of piping hot stringbeans with butter melting over them. "That's how you do it. Like that."

"That's how you eat them," she said. "But how do you get to where they're like that?"

He looked at the directions. "Put them in a pot with a half inch of water. Heat to a boil. Cover, turn down the heat. Then let simmer until tender. That means test them after five minutes or so, to see if they're done. Okay?"

She nodded, but a while later he discovered that she had put the covered pot in the oven and baked it. The handle melted, and then began to burn. The beans were a dead loss.

The next day he took her out for a walk. A very long walk.

I Remember Me

He lost her in the crowd. There were crowds everywhere now. But he wasn't worried. She could find her way home if she could read her tattoos, or get someone to read them for her and give her the right directions. There were so many pointers available.

Of course, if she forgot to read the tattoos, or forgot what they meant, that would be a different matter.

Roberta failed to return. After a few days it seemed likely that she would never come back. Which was more or less what he, Mike Stone, had expected. He managed quite well without her, and the time soon came when he stopped thinking about her at all. He had more important things to worry about by then.

Some other people moved into the apartment with him. A gang of young women, and a couple of tough men, one of whom claimed to be the actual owner of the building. He had no documentation but that was not surprising because paperwork had been in decline for a while now. Mike was allowed to sleep in the tiny front hallway every night, as long as he brought back food or firewood. It was a fair compromise, he decided.

This arrangement worked for a short while. One of the young women began to show an unusual interest in him. This was quickly discouraged by the two men, who spent most of their time each day herding the women about on mysterious missions to unknown places. When they went out, Mike had to leave too. Once, when he forgot to bring any food or firewood, they made him sleep outside in the stairwell.

That was the day he came across a storefront office that had been converted into a branch of the Federal Identity Network. It was dark and empty inside, but a great many people stood about on the street as if expecting it to open for business again.

"What's the problem?" he asked someone.

"I don't know."

Mike waited a while. Nothing happened. Then a car sped by, drawing considerable attention since there was hardly any traffic anymore. Nothing else happened, so Mike left.

The next day he saw a man hanging by the neck from an awning pipe. Pinned to his chest was a piece of cardboard, on which the letters ADR had been hand-printed.

"What does that mean?" Mike asked someone.

"He was a doctor."

"How did they know?"

"I don't know."

Some little while later, on a similar day, Mike did not find his way back to the apartment. There was never a pointer around when you needed one. But then, there seemed to be less people on the streets, so the pointer program might have been discontinued. The warm weather had arrived, fortunately; shelter was no longer a problem.

He was sitting on the curb, eating peanuts, when a woman sat down next to him. She was about his age. He offered her some of the peanuts. She took them, watched what he did and then did the same thing. They smiled at each other.

"What's your name?" she asked.

He looked at his finger. "Roberta."

She looked at her hand. "I'm Carl."

"Hi, Carl."

"Hi, Roberta."

They shook hands. They spent that night in an empty office. They hugged and kissed and did it, and he felt better than he had in a long time. But when he woke up in the morning she was gone, and so were his shoes. Why had she taken them, he wondered. You could find shoes easier than food. Besides, he was sure that she had her own shoes. He tried to picture her, and he concentrated on her feet. Well, maybe she didn't have any. Shoes.

He watched a man standing by the curb. The man swayed as if he were caught in a windstorm, though the air was calm. The man looked up the street, then down. Then up again, and down. There was no traffic to worry about, but the man stayed on the curb. A minute later, the man fell to the sidewalk.

This park overlooked the water. The big buildings were back behind him. He liked the place. There were only a few people on the ground. A nice breeze, the taste of salt in the air. A very high blue sky, some puffy white clouds, a warm sun. He bent over and snatched a stalk of tall grass. It was like a miniature tree with leaves and branches sprouting from the top of it. He placed it between his teeth—not because he was hungry, but because it was a naturally irresistible thing to do. He found that he could twirl it around easily, without opening his lips. You must have done this before, he told himself.

It was more pleasant to sit down than stand. Just for a few minutes. Then he would have to get up and do something. He knew he had something to do, somewhere to go. It had slipped

his mind just what, but it would come round again. The sun felt wonderful on his skin. He hoped it would fade the peculiar markings on his hands. He studied his fingers, as if he were seeing them for the first time.

"Remarkable," he said aloud.

He stretched out on his back and twirled the stalk of grass, imagining that it was a tree growing out of his mouth. The earth was warm beneath him. Sooner or later it would rain. He thought of the rain washing him into the ground. Yes. Warm rain, sun, a deep blue sky far above. While I melt away like snow.

"Time to stand up," he says, but he does not stand up.
"Time to get up and go."
He does not.

Ground Water

James Kisner

The earth beneath my feet is swollen, puffy, like a pregnant beast. There's a smell in the air you can't quite identify, yet you know you should recognize it by instinct.

I'm not quite used to the smell. I don't want to get used to it.

The man from the Water Company is coming today. I have my rubber boots on, so I'm ready.

It's a very hot day here in the Midwest. And, of course, there's the humidity that makes the air thick and hard to breathe. It's best to inhale carefully, measuring each intake of air before you suck it into your lungs.

There are no flies today.

No June bugs, either.

I don't even see a grasshopper.

I eat cold pork and beans for lunch—right out of the can, using a plastic spoon. I drink a can of cold Pepsi with my meal. I don't use dishes any more.

About one o'clock, I see the plain, municipal-duty Plymouth drive up from my mailbox out at the main road along my gravel drive. Puffs of dust whir out behind the tires until the car is about twenty yards away. Then there is no dust, and the tires sound like they're sucking their way through slush. The earth all around the house is like that: mud, slush, slime. Whatever you want to call it.

The Plymouth pulls up in front of the house, parking next to my pitted, but still beloved, Ford pickup which doesn't run very well any

more.

I don't wait for the guy getting out of the sliver-gray car to come up and knock on my door. I go out to meet him. I note the Public Water Works insignia on the side of the Plymouth.

The man is a typical office grunt with the pained set of a professional clerk on his face, the look that is frozen forever in a grimace meant to be a greeting, supposed to be a smile, but is in reality, a warning that you are dealing with someone in public service who doesn't *have* to give a damn about you. All he cares about—all any of his type cares about—is that you pay your bill on time and don't present him with any problems that are beyond his abilities and upset the relative peace of his tidy little world.

I don't ever pay water bills myself.

He wears a cheap suit, a summer weight polyester that's supposed to be seersucker but doesn't quite make it because of the sheen of petroleum in the fiber. I can always see that. Some people can smell it too. There's a badge clipped to the left lapel with a miniature of his face, and I can just barely read the name on it, "Oscar Worth."

He presents his official face to me: the practiced grimace, the pretended courtesy. He obviously considers me an inferior. I'm wearing only a white cotton T-shirt and jeans; I'm about half a head taller than he is, my hair is thick and starting to gray in places, and I haven't shaved or bathed in a week. I don't look like much to the little man, Mr. Worth; I can read that in his eyes. To him, I'm one of those problems he shouldn't have to deal with. He'd prefer to be sitting in his air-conditioned office, downtown, stamping things or maybe calling up people to tell them he's going to cut off their water and make them squirm. I can tell he'd probably get off on that sort of duty. He's too small to be intimidating; without his credentials, his claim to petty officialdom, he'd be an absolute zero in this world.

I'm standing in the shade of the porch, so he has to stare up at me through his glasses. He holds a clipboard in front of him, and I have a fleeting impression of a country parson about to deliver a sermon.

"Hot day," I say.

He ignores my remark and doesn't bother to greet me in any civil way, not even introducing himself. The clipboard is meant to command my attention. The badge is intended to quelch any inquiries regarding his status.

I sigh inwardly.

"Now, Mr. Riggs," he says, wrinkling his nose as the scent in the air tickles it, "what exactly is the nature of your complaint?" He glances up and the sun bounces off his lenses briefly.

I squint, taking note of his patronizing tone. He assumes, as everyone does, that just because I dress down and live in what is considered by most a very modest house I must be ignorant and meek, that I won't understand the big words he will lay on me to put me in my place. I am used to dealing with that. I sit down on the porch and carefully let my legs dangle over the edge.

"You know what it is," I tell him. "It should be written there somewhere—in duplicate, or triplicated, or some exponent of copies only a computer can handle."

He blinks. He's under forty, maybe six years or so younger than I am, but because of his mind-set and his way of making a living he will age quickly, his face collapsing into premature wrinkles. Already his brown hair is thinning, and the dark eyes behind the glasses are moister than they should be. He blinks again, processing my reply in his mind slowly. I see him mouth the word *exponent* under his breath; the word intrigues him.

"I want city water," I say. "I've been asking for years."

He bends his face to the clipboard, ruffles a few sheets of paper. "I see now. You've filed a petition for city water over twenty-five times."

"Twenty-seven, to be exact."

"And each one has been rejected."

"That's my complaint."

He blinks again and flips a sheet over the end of the clipboard. He reads something and looks up at me again, a smug expression temporarily displacing his mask of officialdom.

"You can't have city water. You are over three miles from the nearest main, and two miles from any public sewage facilities. Besides, according to what's recorded here, you have your own private well. You don't really need..."

As usual, his information is not up to date. You'd think these guys would pick up a newspaper every now and then to see what's going on in the outside world.

"What about all the construction that's been going on the last year or so? The new housing developments? You're piping city water to them."

He checks another paper and his brow wrinkles; he doesn't like the idea that I know more than he does. "You'll still be over a mile and a half away. It would cost us thousands of dollars to

run a line to your house alone, and it would never pay out."

"I'll pay to have the water put in. I always said I would."

"That's not the issue. We have no obligation to run a line to an isolated house."

"But the housing developments..."

"That's different. Those are *communities*."

"So I don't count."

"No, sir, that's not it. Of course you count. But it's a matter of what's practical."

"My well isn't any good, any more."

"According to our records, you have an efficient water treatment system."

"My well water has always been bad. Sulphur. Sand. Calcium. God-knows-what-else. That's why I've been sending in the petitions so long."

"But a good water treatment system..."

"Things have changed," I say. "A lot."

"Surely..."

"In just the last few weeks," I say, "I've written the Public Service Commission, the E.P.A., the Board of Health..."

"Yes, I know. That's why I'm here, to resolve this once and for all. You simply can *not* go on petitioning us and bothering people, Mr. Riggs. As you can see, it's gotten you nowhere."

"Can I show you something?"

He hesitates. He licks his lips and he can taste the smell that's in the air and he doesn't like it a bit.

But he's determined to settle this thing, even though it's pretty evident he's decided I'm crazy.

In a way, I am.

The wind shifts slightly, disturbing the fine wisps of hair above Worth's forehead. I ask him inside the house. He enters, regarding my small living room with distaste. The air is so damp that mold and mildew are growing on the furniture.

"Come on," I say, leading him into the kitchen.

He tiptoes across the molded carpet as if it is an expanse of manure. The kitchen is nicer. It's easier to keep the mold off the slick surfaces in there and when Worth enters, I can see relief on his face. I just recently scrubbed the floor, cabinets and table with disinfectant. A cabinet door is open next to the refrigerator, and, spying the cans of Alpo, sharp-eyed Worth says, "Where's your dog?"

"Dead," I say with no feeling. I open the refrigerator and

take out two cold cans of Pepsi, leaving the door ajar a few seconds so Worth can see the gallons of bottled water inside.

"Sit down a minute."

"I don't..."

We're on my turf now. The space between us has lessened; he has to show some degree of courtesy, no matter how phony. He sits reluctantly on one of the dinette chairs, after inspecting it carefully.

"It's clean," I say.

He nods.

"Have a drink." I sit down and slide a can of Pepsi across to him. It's so hot he doesn't think of refusing. He snaps open the pop-top and sips. He doesn't even know how to say, "Thank you."

"It's strange how the dog died," I say.

He eyes me warily with an air of anticipated boredom. I don't blame him. It's not exactly a great conversational gambit.

"Do you want to hear about it?"

"Mr. Riggs, I don't see what that has to do with your complaint."

"A lot. You see all that construction around us—around my place—well, it's disturbed the ground water."

He takes another sip of Pepsi and glances secretly at his watch.

"So?" he says at last.

"The ground water is important. That's what a well taps into—like mine. And when you stir it up, even a couple of miles away, it can make a big difference in the quality..."

"Has your well run dry?"

"No." I take a long swallow of Pepsi myself now. "I wish it did. Or it had."

"Get to the point, Mr. Riggs. I have other appointments."

"You're an impatient man, Mr. Worth. That causes stress, heart attacks at a young age."

"I don't need you to tell me..."

"I know. Forget it." I sit back in my chair. "Well, the dog, he died about two weeks ago. He was poisoned."

Worth doesn't know how to say, "I'm sorry," either. His face doesn't even twitch.

"Not by a dog hater, but by the water in the well."

"Then I suppose you'll have to dig another well."

"A logical solution." I set my can of pop down on the table. "A neat and tidy solution. But it wouldn't make any difference,

because the ground water itself is poisoned. Maybe even toxic—for yards in every direction. Maybe it's poisoned for miles. The water tables have just been totally screwed up."

"That's not our department. Our water comes from the river."

"So, you're not responsible."

"No."

"Didn't you give that factory across the way a permit to dump waste in a pit—that dumps into the river?"

"That waste is treated."

"Not enough. It's in the ground water too. I kind of hold you responsible for that. Maybe there's even some graft involved, though I suppose *you* don't get a cut of it."

He started to get up.

"Sit down!" I said firmly. "I'm not done with my story."

He sighed. I was making him really uncomfortable now. Without thinking, I scratch at the spot on top of my right hand. It turned iridescent green only yesterday. Flecks of skin crumble under my fingernails. Worth doesn't seem to notice. He probably thinks I have scaly skin from not bathing.

"Normally, if a dog gets poisoned, he just dies. My dog didn't just die. One minute there was my dog; another minute there was a pool of something that used to be my dog. Like a puddle of some kind of primordial stuff—bubbling and stinking. Do you understand?"

"No, I don't."

"My dog *dissolved*."

Worth ponders my last statement a long time. He doesn't know how he's supposed to react.

"From the water," I continue. "He drank the water and it just ate him up. I found him on the kitchen floor over there. The only thing that wasn't dissolved—immediately—was his license tag."

"That's impossible."

"You think so?"

"I know so."

"You don't know much of anything, Mister. You can't drink our water, you can't wash with it, and you can't even bathe in it. I have to use bottled water for everything—even to flush the toilet."

He gave me a look that said he was surprised I had indoor plumbing.

"It can't be as bad as that."

"Still need convincing?" I'm growing tired of this man, but I have to continue. I have only so many hopes left. "Get up."

His face is drawn, and there's confusion evident in his features. He no doubt wonders how I am suddenly in control of the situation. He rises as ordered.

I take him to the bathroom.

It's also very small. There's barely room for the toilet, the basin and the shower-tub combination. The shower curtain, with its pink-flowered design fading rapidly in this sunless room, is drawn.

"I was gone in town the next day—gone several hours, taking care of some business. I didn't know what was happening. I didn't realize it was the water yet. I stopped off at the vet to ask him how a dog might just dissolve and, of course, he regarded me as a nut case. I can't blame him, you know. Anyhow, I'd left my wife and children alone."

He nods, as if he understands. I know the reports he has told him I had a family. If he wonders where they are, he doesn't say so. Worth would never die of curiosity.

"I was worried as I drove home. Worried about the dog, and how maybe he'd gotten hold of some fertilizer or something, though I'd never heard of it having that effect on anything."

"Of course not," Worth mumbles.

"When I got home, I called for my wife and kids and nobody answered. I walked through the house. I heard the shower running. I came in here and yanked back the curtain..."

I pause, reliving that moment the thousandth time.

"...just like this!"

He glances in the tub. A partially dissolved woman's body, holding a partially dissolved baby sits there in a congealed pool of unidentifiable muck that is now a dark brownish-red. Some putrid flesh remains on the two corpses, adding its spice to the overall smell of decay and mold. There are no maggots, thank God, and I doubt there will be.

Worth starts heaving; he doesn't even reach the toilet.

He's lucky. When I found them, they were still half-alive, Cindy unable to save the baby because the muscles on her forearms were gone and she could only clutch him as his face and the upper part of his body were washed away. That's how I got the spot on my hand, reaching in to turn the water off. I didn't bother to inquire if my wife was all right. A fleshless head doesn't answer questions.

Worth is still heaving. I wonder if I should offer him a glass of water.

Worth backs into the corner, clutching his clipboard like a shield. His eyes shift back and forth. Then I know what he thinks—that I killed my wife and baby this horrible way. Momentarily I'm angry, but then I realize that's all he *can* think. He has no imagination, either.

I do have his attention now. I step out of the bathroom. "Come out here, I say, and I'll show you the worst of it."

His face is ashen. I can see he wants to make a run for it, but he isn't sure how fast I am. I don't know what goes on in the tick-tock brains of clerks and civil servants, but clearly it's not abstract thought. The fact is that all he has to do is hightail it for his car and I will do nothing to stop him.

He chooses to join me in the kitchen.

"You..." he begins, starting to accuse me, then thinking better of it. I wasn't someone who was late on a water bill.

"Outside," I say.

"I don't...want..."

I'm already out the back door, down the stoop, heading towards a spot in the yard.

"Come out here," I demand, "and just stand by me." Then, in a lower tone of voice, I say, "just stand next to me, here, and let me show you why I got to have city water."

Worth's mind is ticking faster now. There is no distance between us. He can turn and run, maybe make it to the car.

Maybe. That's what separates the courageous from the cowardly, the inability to grab on to that "Maybe" and make it a "for sure."

I stare at him, waiting.

Maybe he could make it.

But maybe not, so he comes out the door, comes down the stoop and approaches me.

"What do you want me to do?"

"I told you—just stand by me." The song "Stand By Me" occurs to me. What would Worth do if I sang a few lyrics to him?

He walks across the yard slowly.

Perhaps "Lean On Me" would be more appropriate. I can't help but smile.

He regards me curiously. The smile is upsetting him, so I let it go.

He comes up and deliberately stands a couple of arms' length away from me. That's fine.

"Now what?" he asks breathlessly.

"Just stand." We're on the backmost edge of my land. A culvert behind us lets off the odor that permeates air. At the moment it is dry; only a greenish residue remains in it, enough to generate the smell. I point to the culvert. "Ground water seeps into that ditch sometimes. It runs towards the city, I think. Right now, it's not much more than a piss in the ocean, but if you just let things go, I'm sure it will start having the same effect on the river."

"We treat the water very efficiently."

"Maybe there's something in the ground water you can't treat! Did you ever think of that?"

He's mute.

"Of course not. You're not paid to think about anything but what the boys upstairs tell you to think."

He glances over his shoulder at the culvert. Then he looks back to me. He frowns. He's awaiting the climax. Maybe he's thinking he could hit me with the clipboard.

"You know," I said quietly, "my other child—my six-year-old girl, was standing right where you are when she..."

Worth doesn't have rubber boots. In seconds the acid in the ground eats through the leather soles of his polished official shoes.

"...started sinking. She was barefoot. She was screaming for me, but I couldn't get close enough in time."

Then Worth feels the cold dampness leeching into his socks, biting at his skin.

"Wha the hell?" He looks down.

"The ground water, Mr. Worth. It's like acid."

I take a couple of steps away from him, to make sure he can't reach me at all.

The acid is eating faster now. His feet are dissolving into the earth. Skin is blistering on his calves. I can probably save him now; he wouldn't have any feet, but he'd be alive.

My daughter had sunk up to her navel by the time I reached her. I tried to pull her out, but I was immobilized by the "maybe." Maybe it wouldn't do any good.

Then she was gone—absorbed into the soil, liquified into the strata of ground water coursing beneath the earth.

"That's the problem," I say. "I told you my well is no good at all now."

He screams as the ground gobbles him up, stripping his clothes, then his flesh as he sinks into the hungry earth. There is no one around to hear him, of course, not even a chipmunk or a rabbit. Only the dead trees surrounding my land.

I listen to him dispassionately. Without guilt.

Only his head sticks out now, staring with eyes devoid of life. I go over and place my foot on it and jam it into the ground. His glasses pop off. Then only his clipboard remains.

I shake my head. He just didn't want to listen to me, I guess.

There is a slightly acrid aroma in the air, perhaps the smell of Mr. Worth mixing with the soil and the water in it. Or maybe it's the smell carried on the wind of the factory that is dumping chemicals in a pit north of me, or the smell of diesel equipment operating a mile away, gouging the earth, disturbing the ground water. It does not matter.

I talked to the E.P.A. man.

I talked to the township committee man.

Now I have talked to the Water Company man.

No one understands my problem. No one wants to act. So I have to.

The Public Relations man from one of the housing developments will be out here tomorrow. And then the man from the Public Service Commission is coming.

Maybe one of them will listen.

Coughing, I wrap a kerchief around my face, and I go into the house to be with my family.

Cages

Ed Gorman

He knows the bad thing will happen, the way it always happens, his father coming home late and all dreamdusted up and his mother shrieking and screaming how he spent all the money on the dreamdust and then the—

He knows when to put the pillow over his head so he will not hear when his father slams his mother into the wall and starts hitting her.

Sometimes he tries to stop it but it never does any good. He is three foot six and has only the one arm and is no match at all for his father.

Then in the room next to his, in the darkness, after the hitting and the screaming, there are other sounds now on the bed, grunts and sighs and whimpers and then

Sleep.

A dream.

His mother and father and himself in a new car riding down the street. People pointing at them. Envious. Such a nice family. The envious people do not even seem to notice his bald head or his lone shriveled arm or the way the sticky stuff runs from his ear and

Awake.

Late night.

Sirens.

Laser blasts.

Coppers hunting down dreamduster gangs.

He wants to kill the man who invented dreamdust. All the misery it causes. Mrs. Caruso's daughter letting all those men stick themselves up the slit between her legs. Mr. Feinmann smashing his wife's head in with a bottle because she wouldn't give him the tips from her waitress job. Little Betty Malloy being killed by the dreamduster who put a broomhandle up her backside and then cut her up with a butcher knife.

Night.

Hot.

Goes out on the fire escape.

Tomorrow it will just start again. The argument about you fucking cunt where'd all the money go? and her shrieking you dreamdust fucker you dreamdust fucker!

Always: money money money.

And then he remembers the commercial on the vid. Seen that commercial a lot the last five six weeks. And always has the same thought.

$

$

$

flashing on the screen and this real loud guy telling you how you can collect them.

All you gotta do see is

Be so easy.

So fucking easy.

And then they'd have plenty of $.

No more fights.

No more hitting.

He lies out on the fire escape thinking about tomorrow morning. His mother will be gone to work and so will he.

No trouble going in the closet where

And getting a sack

And

Going down to the place it says in the commercial

And

He can see all those fuckers who pick on him and hit him and call him faggot and mutant and all that shit

He can see them standing enviously on the corner when he cruises by in the back seat of his parents' new car

Fuck you

You're the faggot

You're the mutant

Not me

Fuckers

And yes yes yes won't they be sorry & yes yes won't they be envious

He wishes it was tomorrow morning already

...

Bitch can't even fix me any fuckin breakfast? you know how fuckin hard I work on that fuckin dock you cunt?

Early morning battle

Father slamming out heading for the choppy dark waters on this muggy overcast day

Mother not long behind him

Coming in and leaning down to his bed and giving him this wet perfume kiss and still crying from the early morning battle and because she got clipped a good one on the right cheekbone even a little bruise there

And him going fitfully back to sleep

And dreaming the car dream again

And dreaming about going to see this doctor who fixes him up so he looks just like the fuckers who pick on him all the time

Hey Quasimodo they say sometimes

Hey hunchbacka Notre Dame you little faggot

And is awake now

And in the bathroom taking down the underwear his mother always washes out at night him only having the one pair but no amount of washing taking the brown stains from the back or the yellow from the front

And then moving fast

Afraid one of them might pop back in and see what he's doing and

With his sack he hurries from the apartment

Horns and exhaust fumes and perfume and farts and fat people and skinny people and people talking to themselves and dreamdusters and gangs and whores and faggots and

And he's hurrying fast as he can down his little street carrying his little sack and he makes it no more than half a block when he sees Ernie that fucking Ernie wouldn't you know

And nigger Ernie steps in front of him and says, What shit you got there in that sack?

Is scared. Isn't sure what to say. Ernie is real real tall with gold teeth and knuckles that feel like sharp rocks when they hit your skull.

Takin back some popsies. You know get the refund.

Popsies shit. That ain't popsies in that sack, you little fuckin

mutant.

Then Gil then Bob then Mike are all there friends of Ernie two of them be white but no matter they're every bit as mean as Ernie hisself

And Mike grabs for the sack and says gimme it you little faggot

Hunchbacka Notre Dame Bob says

You heard him Ernie says give it to him

Just a plain brown sack but you can see stains on the sides of it now damned thing leaking from inside

Thinks he's gonna get a clear run for it starts to weave and wobble between them

But then Gil and Mike grab him by the shoulders and throw him up against the building and

Ernie grabs the sack from him

And smiles with his gold teeth

And holds the sack teasing up real high

And says you can have it faggot if you can jump this high

And he starts to cry but stops himself knowing that will only make it worse

Fuckin Ernie anyway

Nigger Ernie

Hey asshole Mike says look inside

So Ernie does

Turns away

And holds the sack down

And opens it up

Holy shit

What's wrong?

Man, you gotta see what's in this sack, man.

So Gil takes a look. And he makes the same kinda sick face that Ernie did. Aw God. I wanna puke.

He's afraid they'll do something to it. He keeps thinking of the place he saw on the commercial. He wants to be there now. Getting his money.

You just bring 'em right down here for more cash $$$$ than you ever seen in your life. You just ask for Smilin Bob. That's me.

And reaches out to snatch the sack back.

And gets hit fullfist by Mike.

Please c'mon you guys please.

Doesn't want to start crying.

And then they start throwing the sack back and forth over

their heads.

Fuckers you fuckers he cries running back and forth between them.

And then he sees the cop, an android, not a real person, android coppers being the only kind they'll send to a shithole like this one

And the android senses something wrong so he comes over

And of course Ernie and the others split because androids always want to ask a lot of questions being programmed to do just that and all, and people like Ernie and Gil always having something to hide and never wanting to answer questions

They drop his sack on the ground and take off running

He bends and picks it up and then he starts running, too. He doesn't like androids any better than Ernie does.

He keeps his sack pulled tight.

By the time he gets to Smilin' Bob's, the rain has started, dirty hot city rain summer rain dirty summer rain, and he's drenched.

And there's a line all the way out the front door and all the way down the block.

People of all ages and descriptions holding boxes and sacks and bags. And the things inside them making all kinds of squeals and groans and moans and grunts and cries. And smelling so bad sometimes he thinks he's gonna puke or pass out.

And then this guy dressed all in yellow with this big-ass laser gun dangling from the same hand bearing the fat sparkly pinkie ring, he keeps walking up and down the long line saying, If you got somethin' dangerous, you let us know in advance, folks, cause otherwise we'll just have to kill the thing right on the spot unless you warn us about it. He says this in both English and Spanish. And then just keeps walking up and down up and down saying it over and over and over again.

All the time raining its ass off.

All the time getting bumped and pushed and kicked because he's so little.

All the time his sack wiggling and wriggling trying to get free suddenly.

There's a lot of talk on line:

How this one guy heard about this other guy who brought this little sack to Smilin' Bob's and two days later the fucker was a millionaire.

How this one guy heard about this other guy he's waitin' in line here just like now ('cept it ain't rainin' in this here particu-

lar story) and this fuckin' thing comes right up outta this other guy's sack and kills the first guy right on the spot, goes right for his throat and tears it right out.

How this one guy heard about this other guy said that he had two of them once that ate each other—just like cannibals you know what I'm sayin'—but then they'd puke each other back up whole and start all over again. No shit. I swear onna stack of Bibles and my pappy's grave. True facts. Puked each other up and started all over again...

Finally finally finally the rain still raining and the thing in his sack still crying, he reaches the head of the line and goes inside.

First one this fat girl, they say no.

What you do inside is stand in another line and when you're first up they take your sack or your box from you and carry it inside this room that's bright with a special kind of lighting and they half-close the door and they talk among themselves except Smilin' Bob himself who stands at the head of the line sayin You folks jes relax we're getting to ya fast as we can. He's got up just like on TV big-ass ten-gallon hat and western-style shirt and string tie and downhome accent.

And when they're done with the fat girl's bag this tall pale guy comes out and shakes his head and says sorry ma'am just won't do us no good.

Fucker you fucker you know how bad I need this money? she shrieks.

But Smilin' Bob jes kinda leans back and says No call for talkin' that way to Butch here no call at all.

And the fat girl goes away

And a black kid steps up and they take his box and they go inside the blinding bright room and lights flash and male voices mutter and they come back out and hand him the box and the tall pale one is wiggling and waggling his hand sayin that little fucker bit me you want me to I'll kill him for you kid. We got an easy way of doin it kid won't hurt the little fucker at all.

But the kid snatches the box back and takes off all huffy and pissed because there's no money in it for him.

And next and next and next and next and finally
his turn.
Is scared.
Knows they're not going to take it.
Knows he won't get no money.

Knows that his dad'll beat the shit out of his mom tonight soon as they start arguin' about money and dreamdust and shit like that.

Smilin' Bob takes the sack and peeks inside and makes the same face Ernie did and says Well well well and my my my and I'll be jiggered I'll just be jiggered and then hands the sack over to the tall pale assistant

Who takes it inside the bright room and starts all the usual stuff lights flashing meters clicking voices mumbling and muttering and

Holy shit

That's what the guy inside says:

Holy shit. Lookit that friggin meter.

Smilin' Bob he hears it too and he looks back over his shoulder and then back at him and winks.

Maybe you dun brung Smilin' Bob somethin special.

I sure hope so Smilin' Bob.

And Smilin' Bob smiles and says: I give you a lotta money, what y'all gonna do with it anyways?

Give it to my dad and mom.

Well ain't that sweet.

He's a dreamduster and they fight all the time and I'm scared some night he's gonna kill her and maybe if I get enough money and give it to my Mom they won't have to argue any more and

The door opens

Tall pale guy comes out

Walks right over to Smilin' Bob and whispers something in his ear

And Smilin' Bob real solemn like nods and then comes over and puts his hand on his shoulder and leads him away from the line

You know how much we're gonna give you? Smilin' Bob asks.

He's excited: How much?

$500!

$$$$$$$$$

Just like on the commercial.

That's all he can think of

$$$$$$$$$

How happy his Mom will be

How proud his Mom will be

No more arguments

No more beatings for anybody

$$$$$$$$
Oh thank you Smilin' Bob thank you

One hour and twenty-eight minutes later he's on his way home. No sweat with Ernie and those fuckers. Rainin too hard. They're inside.

Wants to beat Mom home.

Wants to be sittin there this big grin on his face

And all this money sittin right on the table

And wants to see her face

See her smile

And say oh honey oh honey now me'n your dad we won't have to argue no more

Oh honey

Which is just where he is when she comes through the door

Right at the table

And which is just what he's doing

Counting out the money so she's sure to see it

$$$$$$

And at first she's so tired she don't even notice it

Just comes in all weary and all sighs and says think I gotta lay down hon I'm just bushed

And starts draggin herself past him into the little living room with all the smashed-up furniture from the last couple of fights

And then she notices

Out of the corner of her eye

Says: Hey, what's that?

Money

Aw shit honey them cops they'll beat you sure as shit they catch you stealin like that

Didn't steal it Ma honest

Comes closer to the table and sees just how much is there: Aw honey where'd you ever get this much money?

And he tells her

And she says: You what?

Sold it

Sold it! It ain't an "it" for one thing it's your sister

Ain't my sister he says (but already he's feeling hot and panicky and kinda sick; not turning out the way he planned not at all) ain't nobody's sister she's just this little—

And she slaps him

And he can't believe how terrible and rotten everything has turned out

Where's her smile?
Where's her sayin they won't argue no more?
Where's her sayin what a good boy he is?
She fuckin slaps him
Slaps him the way the old man always slaps him
And after he did so good too
Gettin the money and all
Slaps him!
Then she's really on him
Shakin him and slappin him even harder
Where is she? Where is she?
Smilin Bob's got her he says
Who's Smilin Bob
He's this guy on TV ma
SHE'S YOUR SISTER YOU STUPID LITTLE BASTARD!
CAN'T YOU UNDERSTAND THAT SHE'S YOUR OWN FLESH
AND BLOOD! Now you take me to this Smilin' Bob
Never seen her like this
Not even when the old man beats her
All crazy screamin and fidgetin and cryin
Grabs him and pulls him up from the chair and says: Take
me to this Smilin Bob and right now
And so they stumble out into the early night
And on the way she explains things again even though he
can't seem to understand them: sixty years ago bad people put
bad things into the river and ever since then some of the babies
have been strange and sad and sometimes even frightening creatures, some babies (like his sister) being born so ugly that they
had to hide them from the government, which is why they kept
his little sister in the spare room because word would get around
the neighborhood and government agents might find out and
would kill the little girl
But she isn't a little girl he says she doesn't even look like a
little girl
(His mother hurrying down the streets now, hurrying and
jerking him along)
And these Smilin' Bob fuckers (she says) what they do is
they take in these babies and the ones they think are telepathic
(or something else worth study) they sell to the government or
private labs to study. They wouldn'ta paid you no $500 unless
they thought she was gonna bring em a lot back.
The rain has stopped. Night has come. A chill night. The
neon streets shine blue and yellow and green with neons. The

freaks and the geeks are back panhandling.

As she hurries hurries

And (she says) You was lucky and don't you ever forget it. You was lucky, the way you was born I mean, you wasn't normal but you wasn't like your sister. Nobody wouldn'ta taken you away like they woulda her.

And then she starts crying again

Which is the weird thing as they hurry along

How she keeps shifting in and out of sobbing and tears and curses

One minute she'll be all right talking to him and then she just goes crazy again

You shouldnt'a fuckin done it you shouldnt'a fuckin done it over and over and over again

Without the long lines (and in the night) Smilin' Bob's looks very different, long shadows and soft street light hiding the worst of the graffiti

And

You show me the door you went in

Right there ma

And she goes up and peers inside

And then goes crazy again

Banging and kicking on the door

And screaming you gimme my little girl back you fuckers you gimme my little girl back

And is crying again of course ·

Sobbing screaming keening

And banging and kicking and banging and kicking and

Just the darkness inside

Just the silence

You gimme my little girl back

And then

She runs around back and all he can do is follow

Alley very dark smelling awful as they pass a dumpster

She opens the dumpster lid and peeks inside and

Screams

Freaks and geeks of every kind inside the rejects that they thought they could sell but couldn't

half-cat half-baby things things with one cyclopean eye in the middle of their forehead things with a flipper-like little arm sticking out of their sternums things that are doll-like little replicas of human beings except in the open eyes (even dead)

you can see their stone madness

And every one of them had been hidden by their mothers till some stupid family member decided to earn some extra money by coming down to Smilin' Bob's or some place just like it and sell off the family shame

And you didn't have to be legal age because the Smilin' Bobs all got to together in Washington and had a bill passed sayin' any family member at all of any age could bring in these mutants and

They lay like fish piled high in a net these dumpster mutants moonlight glistening on their bloody faces and limbs and the stench

Then she runs to the back door which doesn't even have a window to peer in and starts banging and kicking again

You fuckers you fuckers

And him going up to her now and sayin

Ma I'm sorry ma please don't be like this it scares me when you get like this

And she turns on him and shrieks

She's your little sister! Can't you understand that!

And then she turns back to the doors and starts banging and kicking again

And then something startling happens

Door opens

And Smilin' Bob is standing there and

Evenin ma'am he says (in his Texas way) help you ma'am?

You bought my little girl today. You give my boy here $500. I wanna give it back to you and take my little girl home.

And Smilin' Bob takin off his white ten-gallon hat and scratchin' his head says Well now, lemme get a better look at this young 'un here

And he opens the door and looks down and says 'fraid not ma'am 'fraid I never did see this here kid before and I'd certainly remember if I had, givin him $500 Yankee cash and all like you said

Tell him (she says) tell him

And so he tells him

How he waited so long in line

How everybody ahead of him got turned down

How he got $500

But Smilin' Bob he just looks down at him and nods his head and says Oh yeah, now I remember you. You brung that teeny-tiny girl with three eyes.

Ed Gorman

She pushes the money at him.

Please take it.

'fraid I can't ma'am. Deal's a deal, least where I come from.

I just want her back

'fraid she's gone ma'am.

Gone?

Lab guy, he just happened to pop by and we showed her to him and—Well, he took her.

You liar.

No call for that kinda language, ma'am.

You fuckin *fuckin* liar is what you are. She's in there ain't she?

And suddenly hurls herself at Smilin' Bob and tries to get past him

And he flings himself at her trying to get her off Smilin' Bob but as he grabs out he feels Smilin' Bob's arm and

Smilin' Bob is an android!

But Smilin' Bob is also somethin else besides—a very pissed off citizen hitting an alarm button to the right of the door

She just keeps trying to get inside

Kickin scratchin hittin even bitin (but with android flesh bitin don't matter much)

And then footfalls in the night

Jackboots

Two three four of them maybe

Comin real fast

And then surrounding them there in the alley

Four android coppers, lasers pulled and ready to blast and

Two of the coppers go up and pull her off Smilin' Bob

Sure glad you boys got here

She hurt you Smilin' Bob?

Little lady like that? Not likely (Smilin' Bob smilin about it all) But sure would appreciate it if you'd get her out of here so I could get some work done

You bet we will Smilin' Bob (and some kind of look exchanged some kind of murky android look that no human could ever understand) and the coppers pull her even further away from the door as Smilin' Bob goes back inside

She your ma? (one of the coppers says)

Uh-huh.

Then we're gonna put her in your custody. You understand?

Yessir.

We're gonna give you a pill.

120

A pill?

(Android nods) She gets all crazy again, you give her this. You understand?

Yessir.

'cause if there's any more trouble she's gonna be in deep shit.

Yessir.

You think you can handle this?

Yessir.

We already gave her a little juice with a stun needle.

Yessir.

So she's calmer now. But if she should happen to get—

Yessir. This here pill.

The coppers nod and leave.

Halfway home the rain starts up again but this time it's just a mist and the black streets shine with blue neon and red neon and yellow neon and in the shabby little rooms and holes and hallways you can hear the human music of conversation and laughter and crying and sex.

His mother walks in silence

The stun needle having curbed her tongue

Her fingers touching her stomach

Remembering what it was like to have the little girl in her womb

And not until it is too late does he realize that as they've been walking

His mother has been letting the filthy useless money fly from her hands

And leave a trail of dollars behind them

In the long sad night

The long sad night.

Where It's

Safe

John Shirley

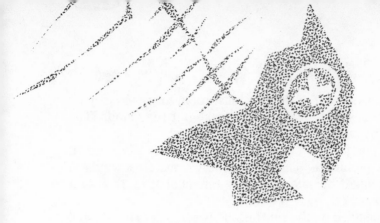

Nephilim set the charge and stood well back. Crowel chuckled, with his tongue caught between his teeth in that yokel way he had, and said, "Don't need to worry about blast. It don't work that way."

"I know," Nephilim said. "It's—I'm used to non-directional explosives."

"Me'n Crispin, we lucked onto some beauties at th' armory raid—"

A muffled *whump* as the explosion, directed precisely from the blast plate they'd attached to the airlock of the smog shield, punched out the locking mechanism. The mechanism fell away with the slight reverberation of the controlled blast, leaving a perfect oval cut through the six-inch door around the lock, the cut's edges giving out only wisps of gray smoke.

"Very nice indeed," Nephilim said. He reached through the gap with the battery-charged alligator clamps, and sparked the electronic tumblers. The door hummed, and gave a click. For Nephilim that sound was an affirmation of life; it was a tiny little sound that was all hope and meaning. It was an affirmation of death, too.

Crowel pushed the airlock open as Nephilim turned and signaled the Pack.

The Dow Jones Industrial had dropped two and a half. Secondary and Tertiary markets were suffering a -3.1. But AkInc's own Montana Chemicals was up. That cheered Akwiss a little.

He looked up from the morning financial print-outs, squinting

through the glass roof of the breakfast room to try to see past the gray smog shield. He couldn't make out the clouds. The shield was too smudgy. Better have it cleaned.

He was planning to copter to New York that afternoon, if the weather permitted. They got some vicious crosswinds in July, and it might be safer to take a tunnel shuttle, though it was a longer trip.

Akwiss decided on the shuttle, and went back to his stewed prunes and print-out. The prunes were execrable. Sometimes he thought the doctor was giving him this pain-in-the-ass diet out of personal animosity. He had only the doctor's word; for all he knew he could be eating eggs and bacon with abandon. Hell, he could always take a cholesterol sweeper.

Lunch was the one meal he was permitted to enjoy a little. A lean-meat sandwich, a piece of Jorge's very realistic apple pie—it was something to look forward to.

He scowled at the prunes and cereal and orange juice. A man could starve on this diet.

Akwiss looked around in annoyance, hearing the whine of the MadeMaid rolling into the room, its electric engine complaining for lubrication. The robot was a metal box with complicatedly jointed hydraulic arms and whirring graspers and a rotating camera. It reached up clumsily to clear the dishes onto its tray and promptly swept them onto the floor instead. "Whoopsi!" said the female voice from its speakers. Its voice was the thing that worked best about it. He ought to use it to answer phones instead of cleaning up. Normally he didn't use it at all.

Akwiss thumbed the intercom button. "Murieta! Get in here!"

His Mexican butler came in with startling immediacy, smiling. Irritatingly chummy, Akwiss thought. "Murieta—what the hell is this? Where's Dunket? This clunker is supposed to be in a closet somewhere. It never did work and I find these things offensive. People should be served by people. This company is all about providing good work for good people, Murieta. We make an example, here."

Murieta smiled and nodded just as if he bought into Akwiss's reflexive company-slogan populism. "I know, I know that, I told Dunket we need you, he say chure he come back this afternoon, until then we use the ma-cheen, he said—"

"Come back this afternoon? I didn't give him any time off."

"He said you give him time to go to the doctor. Chure."

"Well. I don't remember it. I suppose if he needs to see a doctor...Well. Well uh—clean up this mess, this damn thing can't manage it."

"Chure."

Akwiss exhaled windily through his nose. Dunket should have called for a temporary from Chicago Central. The damn fool should have known better, anyway. He'd served Akwiss for years.

He hit the intercom again. "Finch? Yo, Finch!" He looked expectantly at the video monitor flush with the table top, expecting to see his Security Supervisor appear. The screen stayed blank.

Murieta was busily picking up chunks of crockery with his bare hands. The MadeMaid was whirring confusedly back and forth at his side, getting in the way. Akwiss watched him for a moment, then quietly asked, "Murieta—did Finch have a doctor's appointment too?"

"I don't know, Mr Atch-wiss." He didn't look up from the dish fragments. "I deedn't see him."

That one, Nephilim thought, is probably Finch. Lean guy with receding blond hair. Definite I.D. or not, he had to go down: he had a gun on his hip.

Finch was just rounding the corner, coming down the Eastern corridor to check on the breach in the mansion's Eastern airlock. Looking bored, probably expecting to find it was another false alarm triggered by acid corrosion. Then he saw the Pack and froze in his tracks. Nephilim expected him to go for the gun but he just gaped in surprise. He'd never had anything to do here but scare off salesmen.

Crowel was raising his gun, but it was Nephilim's practice to take responsibility for these things when he could. If the Feds pulled off a swoop some of the Pack might get off with twenty years if they weren't tied to killings. He pushed Crowel's gun-muzzle down and said, "Mine." His autopistol hissed as he swept a four-shot burst across Finch's chest and the guy went spinning down. Finch had been pretty complacent, as expected: He hadn't bothered with armor.

Akwiss was waiting for the elevator. It was taking too long. Another glitch. The whole estate needed a tightening-up from top to bottom. Maybe one of the girls he'd brought over last night was monopolizing the elevator, on her way home. He cer-

tainly hoped Finch had sent them back to town. They got on his nerves when they hung around.

He glanced at the out-conditions indicator, for something to do as he waited. Air Quality for the morning of July 18, 2007, was pretty good outside. One could walk about freely.

It wasn't as bad as people made it out, any time, of course. Only when the rare Black Wind came along was a respirator necessary. Most of the time, the smog shield's importance was security and not bad air. He'd explained that pretty handily to the reporter from UNO, last week. The media ate out of his hand; always had.

He could hear the elevator moving now. It was about time. Maybe he ought to have a new elevator put in. But most of the time he was the only one who used them—

The doors opened and the elevator was filled with strangers.

Nephilim didn't bother to chase the fat guy down the glass hall. He knew he wouldn't get past the breakfast room.

Crowel laughed, watching Akwiss wheezing along.

"So that's Akwiss," Holovitz said, coming out of the elevator behind Nephilim. "Well anyway it's his butt. Fat as his cred-account."

Nephilim said, "Holovitz, wait here for the others. Bring 'em straight along this tube after us. Crowel, Crispin—come along."

In no particular hurry, Nephilim strode along after Akwiss. Crispin, who carried the tools and the bags, gave a yellow, snaggly grin, and fell into step beside him.

The nearest general alarm button was in the breakfast room. Akwiss thought his heart would hammer its way out of his chest before he got there. It was stupid, fucking stupid. There should be an alarm every forty feet or so. Where the bloody hell was Finch?

Maybe they were a work crew or something. Maybe that had been a lube gun in his hand...

Murieta was standing over the console on the breakfast table, working busily with a cutting torch. Akwiss skidded to a stop in front of him, wheezing, sweat tickling his neck, staring.

Murieta was humming to himself as he melted away the inside of the console. A few sparks spat through the crater in the plastic hull, smoke curled up. No alarms went off. He'd burned through those circuits. He switched off the cutting tool and smiled up at Akwiss. "You're back surprisingly early, boss. Surely you didn't forget your briefcase."

Akwiss tried to swallow, but his throat was too dry. It felt like there was something obstructing it. He could just barely breathe. "You...you're not..."

"My accent? Oh chure. I forgot." His eyes were as bright as the flame of his cutting torch.

"You fucking traitor." Akwiss was thinking about trying to run past Murieta. But the way the man was tensed...the way he held that torch..."How'd you get through the screening?"

"Your personnel-screening database is more porous than you think, boss."

Akwiss heard the others coming up behind them. He tried to compose himself as he turned to face them. Thinking, *Anything can be negotiated. Just stay cool.*

The short, stocky one with the dark eyes and the cryptic symbols cut into the black hair on the side of his head: That would be their leader. The other two were most definitely followers, Akwiss thought, but they were hungry looking men who seemed hardly in check. All three of them wore fatigues tucked into military boots, iridescent anti-UV ponchos, respirators slung around their necks. They were all a bit grimy, unshaven. Thin, ravenous men. Those weren't lube guns in their hands. And one of them was training a videocam on him.

"Oliver Akwiss," the dark-eyed man said, "CEO, president and owner of Akwiss Incorporated, a multinational corporation also known as AkInc, I arrest you for the Citizen's Reclamation Troop on a charge of mass murder."

"'Citizen's Reclamation Troop'! You're a *Pack*, is what you are," Akwiss snorted. "You can dress it up any way you want." *Careful*, he told himself: *You should be pacifying them. They have the guns.* But his pride demanded some rebuke to this outrage.

"We are, yes, what you call a 'Pack'," the man said, shrugging. He went on smoothly, with a characteristic glibness that Akwiss found increasingly irritating. "And a Citizen's Reclamation Troop. Your Congressional lobbyists push the buttons on the official laws so the public's own justice has to be enforced by a pack of outlaws. It's a damn shame but there it is. You can call me Nephilim, Mr Akwiss..."

Akwiss thought, *Stall them.* He glanced past Nephilim through the glass of the corridor, hoping to see a security team moving up, outside it. No one yet.

Nephilim read Akwiss' glance. "The outdoor guards are all getting loaded on Hot Morph at the South gate, Mr Akwiss. We've been selling it to them on the cheap for weeks. They've been using more and more heavily. Not Finch, of course. Him we had to kill."

Akwiss decided to fake admiration. He glanced at Murieta. "And this one you planted inside. Ingenious."

"No it's not. You and your security got sloppy and complacent. The price of living so long where it's 'safe'." Four more of the Pack were trotting up behind Nephilim. Well armed.

There would be no escape. It was all up to negotiation now, Akwiss thought. Well. That was his strength, after all.

Nephilim nodded toward the corridor leading into the living room. "Let's go in there."

Akwiss licked his lips. Have to calm down. He was dangerously close to hyperventilation, maybe heart attack. He nodded, and made himself breathe slowly, as he turned and walked between the man who called himself Murieta, and Nephilim, to the barn-sized living room of the main house.

"Whew!" the skinny one said, looking around. Adding mockingly: "This is, like, so tasteful. And yet so elegant."

The others laughed. Akwiss felt his face go hot.

"You got the disk, Crowel?" Nephilim said, to the skinny one.

Crowel took a sealed videodisk from a pouch on his flak vest, and went to the player. Murieta was smiling mysteriously up at the big beams thirty feet overhead; they were genuine wood, retrofitted from a 20th Century yacht. Near the fake-log fireplace was a big grand piano that had once belonged to Leonard Bernstein. The other furnishings were expensive designer antiques, which Akwiss had once thought a contradiction in terms. But his decorator had insisted it was all a matter of style, not materials or chronology. And Akwiss had to agree: Surfaces are all.

Some of the men seemed a little in awe of the vast room, the *faux* antique furniture, the gently segueing videopaintings, the yellowing impressionist oils, the platinum lamps.

Prompted by Crowel, the video screen rose from the floor: Ten feet by fifteen, high-rez and state of the art. "Have a seat, Mr Akwiss," Nephilim said, gesturing at the blue velvet sofa.

"Thanks, I prefer to stand," Akwiss said, trying to create an atmosphere of equality.

"I said sit the fuck down," Nephilim said quietly, as Crowel handed him the video remote control.

Akwiss sank onto the sofa,.

Crowel went about setting up a small video camera on a thin aluminum tripod, and a recording deck. It was trained on Akwiss, Nephilim and Akwiss's video screen.

"What's the camera for?" Akwiss asked. "Proof to my company for the hostage money?"

Nephilim shook his head grimly. "For the trial. We're making a whole set of them to mail out to select media. Last week we videotaped your good friend George Pourneven. The video deck belonged to him, in fact."

"George? There was no report of anything unusual with—"

"You didn't look at anything but the financial news today, evidently." He stepped a little closer to the small microphone attached to the videocam. "Now, I'm going to have to hold forth a bit on certain subjects—things you know about but the public doesn't. You and your cronies having done very well at keeping them in the dark…" He tapped the remote, and the disk began play. "You're on trial, Akwiss. Kindly review the evidence with us."

Akwiss looked at the images rezzing up on the videoscreen. It was as he'd expected. Pictures of starving children. The bleeding hearts were always trying to intimidate him with starving children. As if he were one of the parents, the people really responsible for those kids.

"This is today," Nephilim was saying. "The Great American Famine. Ten to twenty thousand children die every week in our America the Beautiful, of famine or famine-related disease. It's going to get worse before it gets better…"

Akwiss blew out his cheeks and looked at his shoes. They needed a shine, he decided.

He felt a small cold circle pressing into his left temple: A gun muzzle. He looked at Crowel from the corners of his eyes; Crowel, his cheek twitching, was saying, "*Look at the fucking screen.*"

Akwiss looked at the screen. The gun muzzle was withdrawn. But he thought he could feel it watching him.

On the screen: Rows of emaciated children lying on cots in some school gymnasium. Small children of every color. But there were lots of white ones in particular. It must be around Des Moines or Salt Lake City. Children who couldn't hold their heads up on their shrunken necks; whose skin seemed shrink-wrapped over their bones. Whose bellies were horribly distended from

Where It's Safe

131

famine bloat. Their bugging eyes listless, wandering. Only a few of them with strength to cry. Most of them would die, of course.

"In 1990," Nephilim was saying, "children were dying in the so-called Third World at a rate of about 40,000 a day, from hunger."

"'Or hunger-related disease,'" Akwiss heard himself say, dryly. *Don't sneer at them*, he warned himself. Suppress your pride. He went on hastily, "Oh, I know! And AkInc gave a fortune to famine relief for Ethiopia in the 90s."

"Actually you gave exactly as much as you needed for the tax break you required, and not a penny more," Nephilim said, casually. He was maddeningly casual about it all. At first. "Anyway—40,000 children dying every day globally was acceptable to people in the U.S. because it wasn't their kids. They didn't feel responsible. Now the famine is *here*, in the USA, and people at last are looking at some of the causes, at least the causes in this country. Let's rewind a little…" The disk zipped back to its beginning. Shots of AkInc factories and similar outfits—Dow, Union Carbide, Exxon, Arco, Georgia Pacific, others. Chemicals plants, oil refineries, paper mills, heavy industry of all kinds.

But they kept coming back to AkInc plants: AkInc sluicing toxic fluids into rivers, gouting toxic waste into the sky, burying cheap barrels of toxins; dumping barrels of toxins into the sea. "It started even before the CFCs began to chew away at the ozone. You are a chemicals octopus, Akwiss. You have a tentacle in every chemicals product. Foam packaging. Plastics of all kinds. Pesticides and herbicides particularly, in the early years. Between the years 1960 and 1990 the rate of stomach cancer quadrupled; the rate of brain cancer increased five hundred per cent. A lot of people think it was pesticides in our foods." Footage now of children and old people dying in cancer wards. Sickening stuff. Akwiss tried to let his eyes go out of focus. Nephilim went on: "Pesticides in the air, too. They evaporate from fields and lawns, so eventually we even inhale them. Some pesticides run off into the streams, into the oceans. We eat pesticide-tainted fish, pesticide-poisoned produce. It builds up and up in us—and in the environment. Dolphins and seals begin to wash dead from obscure viruses because the toxins undermine their immune systems. The dead dolphins were just a symptom of what was coming: *all* the fish dying, sea creatures of every kind."

"And all this from my pesticides? I hardly think you can pin it all on me, personally," Akwiss said, as politely as he could manage.

"You and a few hundred others at the top of the pyramids of big business—you are the most culpable. But the rest of us too. We didn't vote out the Congressmen who buckled under to your lobbies and campaign-contribution bribes..."

The bathroom, Akwiss thought. If I could get into the bathroom. There's a phone there, one they may not notice in the cabinet by the toilet. Let them burn off a little of their self righteousness with the lecture and then if I can talk Nephilim into letting me use the toilet...

"The pesticides contributed to the great famine in half a dozen ways," Nephilim went on, his professorial tone weirdly incongruous with the gun and fatigues. "They destroyed beneficial bacteria and threw the ecological balance in the insect world completely out of whack. The side effects got worse and worse. The airborne pesticides merged into the clouds of toxins altered by UV light—and synergistically combined with the other factory toxins to make the Black Winds."

"You've obviously had the opportunity to memorize your accusations," Akwiss pointed out. "I haven't had a chance to memorize a defense."

"You've made your excuses and your defenses for years," Nephilim said calmly. "You defended yourself with your P.R. firms, your Congressional lobbies, your doctored environmental impact studies. It's our turn now."

Akwiss licked his dry lips, and nodded. *Let him get through it. Then...*

Nephilim picked up his rote speech where he'd left off. "The killer clouds they call Black Winds kill not only people—also wheat and orchards and cattle and sheep and chickens. And of course the UV burn was worse than ever because of the CFCs that companies like AkInc were mass producing. Chlorofluorocarbons that nibbled endlessly at the ozone layer—the huge growth in the incidence of skin cancer was the least of it. In 2002...where's that shot...Here it is..." He'd fast forwarded to a long sweeping shot of a dust bowl field. "Looks like Oklahoma in the early 20th century. But it's good old Iowa. Here's another in Kansas. This one is Oregon: The Willamette Valley, one big dust bowl...The unchecked ultraviolets killed the plants and small organisms that held the topsoil down. They killed crops and they—"

"Now really, CFCs—they were used by virtually everyone," Akwiss protested coolly. He glanced toward the door to the

bathroom. Should he try for it now? Not quite yet, he decided. Damn, he wanted a drink. "Probably you used them yourself when you were young. Spray cans and such."

"Your company—at your instigation—spent millions suppressing the evidence, paying off research scientists, giving campaign contributions to Congressmen in exchange for slowing the ban on CFCs."

Startled by the range of Nephilim's inside information, Akwiss blurted automatically, "Nonsense, we did no such thing—!"

"We have all the documentation, Akwiss. You weren't picked arbitrarily. We don't go about executing innocent people, you know."

Akwiss's throat constricted. *Executing.*

Get to the bathroom. The phone. Fast. "Listen I need to—"

Nephilim over-rode him, going on, "I almost admire the subtlety of your favorite strategies. Your industry-sponsored 'environmental initiatives'—which did nothing but cancel out the real initiatives, if you read the fine print. And your bunk 'studies'. You—and the other big companies did the same, of course—you'd fund 'independent' researchers, push them into churning out studies that seemed to show that pesticides were safe for consumption, that CFCs weren't necessarily the agent in depleting the ozone layer, that low-level radiation from nuclear power plants was no danger, that the toxins you were spewing by the thousands of tons into the air wouldn't cause cancer and birth defects. And so on. There were always contradictory studies by responsible people, but a great many of the newspapers—usually owned by one of your conglomerates—cited only *your* studies, strangely enough..." The men around him laughed.

"Look—the country needed jobs—"

"Dead men are unemployable, Akwiss," Nephilim went on relentlessly. "And it's not as if you couldn't have had your factories without polluting—that whole line is a lie. *You could have!* The technology to clean all emissions and convert waste—*it exists.* Has for decades. But it was costly. And you didn't want to spend the money, you and your cronies. You were too greedy. And that's what this is all about. *Greed.* Greed is the reason for this..." He gestured at the screen. "Here we have a lovely shot of some birth defects traceable to emissions from your chemicals factories—this child born with his brain hanging outside his head died, of course, but his brother, the imbecile with the flippers and the missing jaw you see now, survived to crawl through his own shit the rest of his life…"

Akwiss had to look away. Crowel started toward him but then Akwiss turned desperately to Nephilim. "Please—I have to go to the bathroom." The others laughed. Controlling his resentment, Akwiss went on, "You're trying to conduct this in a civilized way, aren't you?"

"Yes yes, we don't want to have to clean up after you *again*," Nephilim said with heavy sarcasm.

It took Akwiss a moment to get it. Then he smiled weakly, "Yes. Well. The bathroom's just over there…"

"Take this man to the bathroom, Crowel. But look around in there for alarms or telephones."

Akwiss thought he was close to a heart attack as Crowel searched the bathroom. But Crowel didn't find the phone. He evidently expected to see it attached to the wall. It was a cellular phone, in a drawer.

Left alone in the bathroom, Akwiss did his best to use the toilet; Crowel was just outside the door. Akwiss didn't want him to get suspicious. But his bowels didn't want to work, at first.

At last, as the toilet flushed, Akwiss tapped the code into the little touchtone keypad on the cellular phone. He didn't dare use the phone vocally. Crowel would hear him. But the code should set up a buzzing in the guard house, at the checkpoint, and in their jeeps. The alarm buzzing meant, *Come to the main house at once.*

A thumping on the door made him nearly fall off the toilet. "Get out *now* or I'm comin' in!" Crowel yelled.

Hands shaking, trying to make no sound at it, Akwiss replace the phone in the drawer and closed it.

"The…the other men…?" Akwiss asked, looking around as he and Crowel returned to the main room. Only Nephilim, Crowel, and this odd, eager fellow Crispin remained. Murieta had gone too. That might make things easier for Akwiss…

"The other men aren't here as soldiers, in particular," Nephilim said distractedly, fast forwarding through the video disk. He seemed tense and impatient. Soon, it'd be over, one way or another. "They came along to move out your food supplies and anything that'll help us buy more food on the black market." He stopped the disk and turned a cold, onyx glare at

John Shirley

Akwiss. "Your people—your class, if that's what they are—monopolize the available food, of course. After destroying most of North America's capacity to grow food, they hoard what's left. A lot of real charmers, you and your cartel buddies. My own kid died of diarrhea, Akwiss. My boy Derrick. Diarrhea's the leading cause of death for children, globally. Has been for decades. Did you know that…Akwiss?"

"Yes. Yes I—I'd heard that." Try to show them you care, that you know about these things. "The, ah, hunger weakens their immunity, so they get a diarrhea which dehydrates them and they die of, ah—"

"My wife and I," Nephilim interrupted, looking abstractedly at his gun, "got stuck out in the new dust bowl, looking for water, and the car ran out of charge…" Hardly audible, he finished: "And I couldn't get Derrick to water in time…"

He turned to gaze emptily at Akwiss. And Akwiss thought Nephilim was going to shoot him on the spot. He held his breath.

And then let it out slowly when Nephilim visibly regained control and turned to gesture at the video screen. "Cancer patients downstream from AkInc factories in Louisiana. The link between your dioxins and their cancer was very clear but the whole thing was suppressed—"

"Now wait a moment," Akwiss broke in. Thinking, now's the time to really stall them till my men get here. "Honestly—if that's what happened I really did not know about it. I mean—maybe some of what you were saying is true. But like every man in a high position, I'm surrounded by yes-men." He tried not to look at the archway behind Crowel, through which his outdoor security men would be coming. "My subordinates tell me what they think I want to hear. About the environment. About our…our impact on it. I'm sure no one told me about the Dioxin link to cancer in Louisiana and I doubt I ever got honest information from my people about CFCs and the dangers of famine—"

"First of all, yes you did," Nephilim snapped. "Your attorneys gave you an extensive briefing about all these issues when they were trying to protect you from lawsuits. We have a tape of that briefing, from *fourteen years ago*. You understood, all right. Second—even if you hadn't been briefed, the information was out there. You were responsible for finding out on your own, Akwiss, what your company was doing to the world. But that's a red herring—you ordered the suppression of the truth. 'Smokescreen it' you said, on one occasion. You had a lot to do with weakening the various Clean Air Acts, you and your lobbies—and you knew exactly what you were doing." He looked into Akwiss' eyes, and spoke with a certain formal finality: "*You knew people were dying because of what you'd done.*"

"No, truly, I—"

"*You knew!*" Nephilim roared, leaning over Akwiss, who shrank back on the sofa, glancing at the archway. *Where were they? Stoned or not they had to come.* Nephilim turned away, pacing now, shouting, "You knew damn well! And you didn't give one rat's ass about the children dying of cancer, about the birth defects, about the emphysema, about the destruction of the sea, the destruction of the farmlands, the famines that would have to come. The *millions of Americans* dying from famines! You son of a bitch, you're the biggest mass murderer since Hitler!" He stopped pacing, his back turned, his voice breaking, sounding far away as he admitted, "But we all practiced denial. And none of us wanted to admit that criminals were running the country. We just didn't want to believe that it was murder. That it was mass homicide. Just a kind of carelessness, we thought. Or ignorance. When it was nothing of the kind..."

Crowel nodded, put in hoarsely, "It was murder. Pre-fuckin'-meditated."

And then Brightson and Margolis stepped into the archway, guns in hand. Brightson a young, heavy-set black guard with an elaborate silvery coif, and Margolis the potbellied, gray haired white guard. Where were the others? Were these all that would come? The drugs, damn the drugs!

Crowel and Crispin vaulted over the sofa and crouched back of Akwiss; Crowel looped his wiry arm around Akwiss's throat, nearly crushing his windpipe, holding him in place on the sofa.

Nephilim stepped behind the piano, loosing a sloppy burst of autofire at Margolis. Missing. Nephilim's rounds traced a crooked line of holes across the walls of the corridor as Margolis and Brightson jumped back beyond the edge of the archway, out of the line of fire. "Jesus fucking Christ!" Brightson muttered.

"You men stand firm!" Akwiss yelled hoarsely. "Get the police! Get the other men!"

"We can't find the others!" Margolis yelled. "Outside phone lines are down!"

"Mr Akwiss!" Brightson shouted, from around the corner of the archway. "We'd better go and try to get help, these fellas got us outgunned!"

"No! No, don't leave—"

Crowel tightened his choke-hold around Akwiss's throat. "Shut up, asshole."

Nephilim yelled out, "You men out there—you want some Hot Morph? It's pharmaceutical! We got it on a pharm-industry raid and it's the same good stuff you been getting! I'll give you an ounce if you go away and forget about this! Just tell em we got past ol' Finch and there was nothing you could do!"

Hesitation. Then Margolis yelled, "Hell yeah! Toss it over and I'm gone!"

They could hear Brightson hissing at Margolis. "Goddamn it that ain't no way to treat the man, he employed you ten years!"

"He underpaid everybody ever worked for him, Brighty! Fuck him and fuck you too!"

Another traitorous bastard, Akwiss thought.

Nephilim tossed over a sandwich bag full of yellow powder. It slid past the archway, into the corridor. They could hear Margolis scoop it up and run. His bootsteps receding down the hall. Gone.

Nephilim shouted, "Throw down your gun, 'Brighty', cause I'm coming over there and if you're armed—"

Brightson, bless him, responded with two gunshots that rang out dissonant, hysterical notes as the bullets stuck the piano. Nephilim ducked back, cursing under his breath. There was a burst from another automatic weapon, out of sight in the hallway. A cry of pain. The sound of someone falling. Footsteps. "Hold your fire!" Murieta called, as he stepped into view. He was grinning, carrying a small machine pistol. "Brighty's gone down, Nephilim. Let's get back to the trial."

Crowel released Akwiss, Gagging, trying his best to look pitiful, Akwiss turned to Nephilim. "Look, let's negotiate this. I can offer you a fortune. You—you have to give me a chance to—"

"You had your chance." Nephilim moved out from behind the piano, and pointed to the video screen. The image was frozen on the face of a starving child. "He had none. Your guilt is clear. The penalty…"

"You're not going to torture me," Akwiss broke in, losing control. "You're not that kind of person. I know that. You're not!"

"Torture you? You mean force you to die slowly—of cancer? Of starvation? No. We're not barbarians, Akwiss."

They aren't really going to do it, Akwiss thought. He was standing on a chair, with a neatly-tied hangman's noose around his neck, the knot behind his left ear. The rope running up to loop over his beautiful real-wood rafters. *They're trying to scare me into signing something, giving them money.*

"I can sign over a great deal of money to you," Akwiss said.

"You could stop it getting to us, too," Nephilim said. "If you were alive. You've given us your account numbers. That'll help. We'll feed a lot of kids before your Swiss banks figure it out. You got any last words?"

Now even Akwiss' knees threatened to betray him. They were going gelatinous. "Please...I didn't know..."

"You keep saying that," Nephilim said. "But I keep saying: Oh but you most certainly *did* know. Ackwiss—haven't you wondered why I know so much about the inner workings of your outfit?" His voice broke, but he went on. "I worked for you, Ackwiss. We never met—but I was one of the two hundred some lawyers AckInc employed. That's how I got my hands on the tapes of your briefing. And that's when I resigned. When I realized what we were doing. I could hear it on the tape: *You just didn't care.* I have a theory, Akwiss—that you have to be a real sociopath to get to the top of American Industry. And a sociopath feels nothing for anyone but himself. So it didn't matter that you knew your company was helping launch a famine in which millions would die. You felt nothing. *You* were living where it was safe, after all..."

They were both crying now: Akwiss and Nephilim. For different reasons. Nephilim said hoarsely: "I was a damn good lawyer. I defended you people—I ought to be up there with you, with a rope around my neck. And someday I will be, when all this is done. Now. This is for Derrick."

And then he kicked over the chair.

This time, and for the last time, Akwiss' bowels worked very well.

The others were back; the trucks were loaded with tons of stashed food. No sign of Federal troops or police. It was going smoothly. Just one thing left to attend to, Nephilim thought: the very last of the liberated food.

That was nearly ready, too. Nephilim saw that Crispin was almost done cutting the meat off Akwiss's body, and putting it in the bags.

The kids wouldn't know the difference. It might save a life

or two.

"What kind of meat you going to tell them it is?" Crowel asked, smiling. "Pig?"

"No," Nephilim said. "No if I told them that, they might guess what it really is."

Expiration Date

William Relling Jr.

Michael Moyle got up from the sofa unsteadily. For a moment, as he came to his feet, the living room whirled. *Whoa*, he said to himself, blinking his eyes. *I'm tipsier than I thought.* He looked at the empty cocktail glass in his hand. *Maybe that's enough for tonight, m'lad. Let's see if we can't find you something a little less potent.*

Heading toward the kitchen, he wove his way through the other party guests. He passed a knot of people gathered around the host, who was playing the piano. The host was leading the group surrounding him in a song, "…I'm a joker, I'm a smoker, I'm a midnight toker…" The host smiled at Moyle, who raised his empty glass and smiled back.

I wonder if he remembers my name, Moyle said to himself. He had come to the party at the behest of a mutual friend whom he'd left behind on the sofa, engaged in conversation with the host's wife. Listening to the singers gathered around the piano, Moyle was struck by a sensation of *deja vu*. He recalled another occasion when another group was gathered around another piano singing that exact same song: New Year's Eve, twenty years ago, in the company of a different friend with whom he'd split a tab of Orange Sunshine while they were driving to the party. Moyle was a junior in college at the time. LSD was the drug of choice on that particular night; tonight, eighteen-year-old single malt scotch. *I guess that means I'm a grown-up now*, Moyle thought, smiling wistfully at the irony. A respectable adult with a respectable job and a respectable life—one among many respectable adults at this party tonight.

...People keep talkin' about me, baby...

Moyle made a face. *Come to think of it,* he told himself, *I've never been much of a Steve Miller fan.*

...They say I'm doin' you wrong, doin' you wrong...

The kitchen doors swung open at his touch. Immediately he smelled the aroma of freshly-brewed coffee. The overhead fluorescent lights in the room were harsh and bright, and he had to squint to adjust his eyes. He saw the girl, sitting at the small, white table in the breakfast nook off to one side of the kitchen. She was looking at him expressionlessly, without pleasure or malice or concern. "Hello," he said, trying to recall her name. "You're the daughter, right?"

"Laura," she answered. She motioned in the direction of the counter behind him. "I was just having a cup of coffee. There's more if you'd like some."

"Thanks." Moyle stepped to the counter and set down his cocktail glass. A line of mugs hung on wooden pegs above the sink. To the right of the sink was a Mr. Coffee machine. He pulled down a mug and filled it with steaming coffee. Replacing the carafe on its warming plate, he turned around and lifted the mug in a graceful salute. The girl smiled hesitantly. He sipped. The coffee seared his tongue.

Crossing to the breakfast nook, he eased himself to a seat opposite the girl. A textbook was open on the table in front of her. "Homework?" he asked.

She nodded. "Sociology."

"Hmph," he acknowledged. "Do you mind if I ask you what grade you're in?

"I'm a senior."

"So you're how old? Seventeen? Eighteen—?"

"Seventeen."

"Ah." He studied her more closely. She was barefoot, wearing jeans and a sweatshirt that was baggy and ill-fitting, with the word "Stanford" printed across the chest. She sat with her legs curled beneath her. He decided that she was pretty, in a vague, coltish way; she had wide, brown eyes and high cheekbones, and smooth, creamy skin. Her sandy-colored hair was braided into a pigtailed queue that draped over her left shoulder. She looked very young to him. He blew on his coffee and sipped again.

She gestured in the direction of the living room. "It sounds to me like you're missing a good party," she said without long-

ing.

He shrugged. "It's not bad. I'm surprised you're trying to do your homework down here. It must be difficult to concentrate."

"It's not much better upstairs. You can still hear everything. I don't mind the noise, really. Besides, I felt like a cup of coffee."

He grinned. "Funny, you don't look like one."

She looked at him with puzzlement. His grin became sheepish. "Sorry," he said. "Old joke. Before your time."

"Oh."

An uncomfortable silence settled upon them. Moyle shifted in his seat, lifted his mug of coffee, swallowed. He rested the mug on the table and sighed. She looked up from her book. "Don't you like parties?"

"Not as much as I used to, I guess." The silence settled again, briefly. He nodded toward the textbook. "What are you working on?"

"It's research," she replied. "I'm supposed to be writing a paper on the future of the world." She frowned. "That sounds like a dumb topic, doesn't it?"

He shook his head. "As a matter of fact, that's pretty much the subject of conversation out there." He motioned toward the living room. "That's the reason I came in here."

Moyle could read by her expression that she doubted he was telling her the whole truth. *Perceptive girl*, he thought. He said quickly, "So what do you think about the future?" He grimaced inwardly, feeling as though he were on the sofa once more.

"I don't think there's going to be much of one," she said flatly. "Judging from the way things are these days."

Her reply surprised him. "That's kind of depressing, isn't it? Somebody your age feeling so cynical? When I was seventeen, the only thing girls had on their mind was guys. And the only thing us guys thought about was girls."

"But isn't that the problem?"

"I'm not sure I follow you."

Her lips drew into a tight line, then she said, "Most of my friends…the people my age…that's the way they are, too. Only thinking about partying all the time."

He smiled again. "'Things have never been more like the way they are today in history.'" Her look queried him. "Dwight Eisenhower," he said.

"The president?"

Score one for you, young lady, he thought.

She said, "I don't get it."

"I think what I was trying to say is the more things change, the more they stay the same. You know, my generation and yours, we're not really very much different, when you get right down to it."

She nodded. "That's what I meant. We—my friends, people my age—we tend to blame you—people your age, like my parents—for the shape the world's in. When it's just as much our fault as it is yours. We're just as greedy and selfish and irresponsible as you…" She paused, and he could see that she was reading the scowl that had crept across his face. "Sorry," she said. "I didn't mean anything personal."

He was shaking his head. "It's not that. It's just…I don't disagree with you." He smiled wanly. "Now I *am* depressed."

Silence descended once again. She motioned toward his empty mug. "Would you like some more coffee?"

"Please."

She got up and carried their mugs to the coffee machine. As she was pouring from the carafe, she said, "A couple of nights ago, I had a very strange dream. I was flying with my father— he owns his own plane, you know. We were going over a big patch of woods, like some kind of forest. A whole huge section of it had been stripped away—by loggers or something—so there was a big, bare space of open ground in the middle of the trees, like a wound. 'Look down there, Daddy,' I said. In the bare space, both of us could see the words 'Expiration Date' carved right into the ground. The words and a date."

She was carrying their refilled mugs back to the table. She set his down in front of Moyle, then returned to her seat. His expression queried her. "You know," she explained. "Like they put on food and milk cartons and stuff. The expiration date."

"You mean, like, the date the *earth's* going to expire?"

She nodded. "The date when we'll have used everything up. Exploited every resource there is to exploit, poisoned the last breath of air, the last drop of water."

He sipped his coffee, watching her thoughtfully. "So what was it?" he asked. "The date, I mean."

She hesitated for a moment. "Today," she said.

"Today?"

She nodded again.

He was taken aback. "And how's it supposed to happen?

How's the world going to end?"

She shook her head. "I don't know."

He smiled, looked around the kitchen, then pointed to a clock that hung on the wall beside the refrigerator. It was a few minutes past 10:00 PM. "If it is going to happen, it'd better be soon. In less than two hours today'll be over."

She returned the smile. "I didn't say I believed it, did I? After all, I *am* doing my homework—"

She was interrupted by the opening of the kitchen doors. Moyle turned and saw the host peering at him. "Say, what's going on here?" the host asked.

"We were having a conversation," Moyle replied, still wearing his smile. "About the future."

The host snorted knowingly. "A conversation with Little Miss Gloom-and-Doom?"

"She seems awfully sincere," said Moyle.

The host rolled his eyes. "I think you need to re-join a happier group."

"To tell you the truth," said Moyle as he rose from the table, "it's probably time I hit the road. Now that I've had a chance to sober up a little."

"So soon?"

"I've got an early morning tomorrow." He turned to the girl. "Nice to've met you, Laura. Thank you for the coffee."

She nodded farewell. "You're welcome."

Moyle accompanied the host back to the living room. While the host went to a closet to retrieve his coat, he said goodbye to the host's wife and to the friend who had invited him along. The host walked him outside to his car. They shook hands. The host asked him if he felt well enough to drive. "No problem." Moyle assured the man. "I feel fine."

Watching the host walk back into the house, Moyle reached into a pocket for his car keys and unlocked the driver's side door. He wobbled slightly as he was grasping the handle to pull the door open, losing his balance when the ground began to tremble. At first Moyle thought that perhaps he wasn't entirely sober after all.

— *In Memory of Shirley Jackson*

The Dreaded Hobblobs:
A Heavy-Handed Fable For Short-Sighted Times

Gary A. Braunbeck

"There is a reason in Nature why something should exist rather than not."
—*Gottfried Wilhelm von Leibniz*

As far as Daniel Campbell could remember, the dreaded Hobblobs had always been part of his life.

He'd first been introduced to them (in a way) when he was five years old and being scolded by his mom because his room was such a mess.

"Aren't you embarrassed?" she'd said, shaking her head and making that awful *tsk*ing sound with her tongue. "What do you suppose people would think if they came in and saw this place? It looks like the Hobblobs live here."

And that was it. There had been no explanation about who or what the Hobblobs were, where they came from, or why any of them would want to live in a five-year-old boy's messy room. But from that day on, whenever either of his parents thought the house was getting too messy (and one dirty dish in the sink constituted a messy house, God forbid someone should forget to take out the trash or allow the laundry hamper to get a little too full), then it was with the *tsk*ing and the head shaking and the "It looks like the Hobblobs live here!" or "People'll think we had those Hobblobs over!" or—the worst of them all, the one that struck absolute, head-to-toe, spine-chilling, nuts-freezing terror into a young boy's heart—"We might as well call the Hobblobs and invite them to move in!"

Oh the horror, the horror.

By the time Daniel turned seven, his imagination aided by a steady diet of reading **Famous Monsters of Filmland**, he had a pretty good picture in his mind of what the dreaded Hobblobs looked like and how they lived.

They had big balloon faces on fat, waddly-pig bodies and were all scuzz-ugly and smelled bad and had crooked yellow fangs and never washed their clothes because they couldn't peel them off their stinky scaly skin and they never used knives or forks, just threw the food down on the floor in a pile and got on their hands and knees and shoved their faces in and gobbled up yukky-chunk mouthfuls and when they chewed they looked like big dumb cows and all of them had globby buggers hanging from their noses and that crusty stuff around their eyes and cooties and foot-long dirty fingernails that always cut their butts when they scratched back there because a true Hobblob liked to scratch their butt all day long and then smell their fingers.

Oh, yeah—and their house was filled to the ceiling with mountains of dripping, oozing, steamy, fly-covered, crinkly, smelly, slime-infested garbage. And if you weren't careful and they got their hands on you, they'd bury you underneath that mountain of garbage and leave you there until you got all puffy-gas purple and your body started to hiss, then they'd take you out and have you for dinner.

That's who the dreaded Hobblobs were, and that's why no one ever had to tell Daniel a second time to get in there and clean that room, or help with the dishes, or take out that garbage.

He never, ever wanted the Hobblobs to come to his house.

They did, however, move in next door to him on the morning of his thirty-third birthday.

He was in the kitchen fixing breakfast for his wife, Lauren (who was still recovering from recent surgery) when he heard his five-year-old daughter squeal in the front room.

"Daddy! Come look! The Pig People are moving in next door!"

He put the breakfast fixings aside and went to see what she was so excited about. "Keep your voice down, Sharon. You know Mommy's not feeling well."

"Oops. I'm sorry, Daddy. But look—it's the Pig People!"

The actual Pig People were characters from one of Sharon's favorite storybooks, a family of mischievous porkers who made life on the farm a real adventure for Farmer Jones and his dim-

witted sidekick, Eustice. They also always beat the rooster at cards, which made him so irate he often failed to crow at dawn just out of spite.

Daniel joined his daughter at the window, pulling back the curtain to get a better look at the massive moving van parked on the street.

"Somebody's moving into the old Keyser house," he said.

"It's the Pig People!"

"What did I tell you about calling people names?"

"...that it's not nice."

"So?"

She gave him a puzzled look, then shrugged her shoulders. Daniel sighed. *"So that's why you shouldn't do it."*

"Oh. I'm sorry."

"Well, don't do it again." He watched as someone came out of the back of the moving van carrying a large barrel.

Sharon tugged on his sleeve.

"What?"

"That's just one of the men who drove the truck. The Pi— uh, the people who're moving in there drove up in a big car."

"Thank you. Now, why don't we leave them alone and go fix break—"

"—there's one, Daddy! There's one!"

Now, Daniel was not a judgmental person—at least, he tried not to be—and he hated derogatory terms like 'fat,' but at that moment he was hard-pressed to come up with any nice word to describe the man who erupted through the front door like pus from a really juicy pimple.

He was...*grotesque.* Corpulent, plump, enormous, pudgy, and stout didn't even come close. He was dressed only in a pair of summer shorts. Bread-dough pilings of bleached flesh drooped at every angle, pulled into pendant bags by pesky gravity. His jowls would have put any basset hound to shame and his belly hung so low Daniel wondered how the man managed to find his dick to go to the bathroom. His lumpy, dimpled thighs jiggled like Jell-O even when he stood still. His neck was a wonder of layered turkey wattles and when he turned around to go back in the house, the sight of his butt shifting in his shorts, struggling to spring free, straining against the material, one cheek undulating clockwise, the other counterclockwise, was an image that would haunt Daniel until his dying day.

Daniel thought: *Richard Simmons, where are you when you're needed?*

Gary A. Braunbeck

"He seems...well—"

"He's *fat*, Daddy. They're all fat!"

"That's not a nice word."

"But *they are*! Fat fatties!"

"They're just...*large*. Large people."

"And they eat garbage."

Daniel turned toward his daughter. "I would imagine part of the weight problem stems from a bad diet, yes, but I wouldn't say they eat *garbage*."

"Oh, Daddy," said Sharon, giggling. "I *know* the difference. But I saw the little boy go over to the garbage can in the alley and take out a empty milk carton, a *plastic* one. He ate it."

"He did not."

"Did too."

"Did not!"

"Did too!"

"You're goofy."

"No, *you're* goofy."

"Only goofy people make up stories like that."

"You're the goof! Goofy Daddy! Goof, goof, goof!"

"If you ask me," came a voice from the stairway, "you're both a couple of goofs—and annoying ones, to boot."

"*Mommy!*" shouted Sharon, running across the room and throwing her arms around Lauren's waist.

Daniel was right behind her. "Should you be up? I thought you were feeling weak."

Lauren patted the back of Sharon's head. "I did feel kind of bad but—ow! Hon, don't squeeze Mommy so hard down there, all right?"

"Sorry," said Sharon, pulling away and rolling her eyes dramatically. "Jeez, I just wanted to give you a hug."

"Well, you have, and it was a wonderful hug—I mean, as wonderful as a goofy girl can make it."

"Yeah? Well at least I don't eat milk cartons out of the garbage."

Lauren looked up at Daniel, arching one eyebrow and smiling. "Oh, I have just *got* to hear about this one."

"Later," said Daniel, genuinely worried about her. "I want you to sit down and rest."

"I've been doing nothing *but* resting for the last ten days."

"Please?"

"I—oh no you don't. Don't give me that lost puppy dog look. It won't work."

"I'm making waffles."

"On the other hand, those kitchen chairs are pretty comfy."

Thirty minutes later, breakfast a happy memory at the pit of their stomachs, Daniel, Lauren, and Sharon moved to the front room and surreptitiously watched as the new neighbors moved in.

There was a husband and a wife and two children—a boy and a girl—and they looked like your typical middle-class family, not particularly distinguished in their appearance, but no so plain as to vanish in a crowd. They looked tired from the move yet happy and healthy, nonetheless—

—but the thing which confused both Daniel and Sharon was that all four of these people combined wouldn't outweigh the great, gross pale whale who'd been out on the porch a little while ago.

Sharon tugged on her father's shirt sleeve, then gestured for him to bring his ear close. When he did she cupped a hand around her mouth and murmured, "Those aren't the people I saw. The people I saw where like that other man, all fat and piggy."

"What about the little boy? Is he the same one you saw going through the garbage?"

"I don't think so. That boy's skinny."

"It does you no good to whisper," said Lauren from the couch. "My hearing's too good."

So Daniel and Sharon told Lauren about the mysterious disappearing Pig People. When Daniel finished describing the human dirigible in summer shorts, Lauren pressed a hand against her mouth and snickered.

"See, Daddy?" said Sharon. "Mommy's laughing. Fat people are funny."

"That's not why I'm laughing," replied Lauren, trying to keep the smile off her face and failing miserably. "It's not nice to laugh at people. Why don't you go upstairs and find a couple of storybooks and you can read them to me."

"You're only saying that 'cause you want me to leave the room."

"Then leave the room."

"'Kay." And she was off; up the stairs and into her room to find some storybooks.

"What's so funny?" asked Daniel, sitting on the floor near the head of the couch.

"Didn't the way you described that man sound familiar to

Gary A. Braunbeck

you?"

He thought about it for a moment, then shook his head. "Can't say that it rings any bells. Why?"

"You just described one of the Hobblobs."

"The *Hobblo*—oh, my god." Stunned into momentary silence, he stared at his wife. "You're right. The Hobblobs were fat."

"And lived on garbage."

Daniel released a long, low whistle. "You know, I hadn't thought about it in that way. When I said they lived on it, I meant that they ate it, not actually, physically lived on top of it." Then he laughed.

The community in which Daniel and his family lived was called Clear Lake Estates, an experimental development that had been built on top of one of Central Ohio's largest landfills. When Daniel and Lauren had originally bought their house six months before Sharon's birth, the project and the area was still shrouded in fear and suspicion and paranoia whose fires were constantly stoked by concerned environmental groups. The initial barrage of negative publicity had insured that prices would be low—and they were. Outrageously, miraculously low. Lauren and Daniel bought in right away, becoming one of the first ten families to purchase a CLE home.

Nowadays, the houses were going for six to nine times the price Daniel and Lauren had paid. The population of Central Ohio was growing at a rapid rate, developers were buying up land faster than God could manufacture it, and—if the economists and developers and so-called "futurists" were to be believed—communities like Clear Lake were the Next Big Thing.

Sort of gave a whole new meaning to the phrase *He could land in shit and come up smelling like a rose.*

Except that sometime in the last ten months Lauren had developed ovarian cysts. Four of them. Three had been benign but the fourth was a progeny of the big C. All of the doctors swore that it had been caught in time and there was next to no chance of a recurrence but, hey, let's do that kee-mo thang just to make sure and keep that insurance policy working for you.

She'd had the operation two weeks ago. First thing next week they'd go back to the doctor for a few prelims, and the kee-mo thang would start by the end of next month. Lauren had already bought three different wigs for the baldy stage, and often joked that she might as well pig out on chocolate and pizza and cheesecake because she was about to go on the best

fucking diet in the world.

More than once recently Daniel wondered if her condition had somehow been caused by living on a landfill. God knew this place had had its share of problems; even now there was a section property in a field ten miles away that had erupted. That was one of the drawbacks to living here; every so often the tectonic plates had this habit of shifting—nothing like the quakes that had been hitting California in the last ten years but enough to rattle some of the china—and the waste beneath the ground would sort of...*pop up*. A section of road here, a parcel of parking lot there, but thus far no one's living room had been at the epicenter when a trash zit popped, and according to the management company that could never ever *ever* happen because the place had been designed too well. Blow-holes usually happened well outside the residential areas.

"...to Daniel. Earth to Daniel—"

"Sorry," he said, turning toward Lauren and taking hold of her hands, then kissing them.

"What's wrong, hon?" she asked.

"You're gonna be all right, baby."

"Oh, Lord—*of course* I will."

"I'm sorry that our baby-makin' days are over. And I am so, so sorry that you got sick."

"I know. Me, too." She cupped his head in her hands and looked into his eyes; directly, intensely, unblinkingly. "I need to ask you something—seriously, Danny. It's been bothering me since..."

"Ask."

'You don't think I'm unclean, do you?"

"What the hell kind of—"

"I feel like a leper, Danny.

"Look, by the time she was my age, my mother had so many scars on her body from various surgeries that she didn't even look like a human being anymore, let alone a woman. She used to resent that I was always so healthy, that I'd never needed any kind of operation that left a scar behind. She used to tell me that all women had their bodies taken away from them eventually, either all at once or in small pieces; child by child, stitch by stitch, scar by scar. I was always so glad that that was never going to happen to me.

"But what if it does? What if it *is*, right now? What if this is only the start and you have to spend the rest of our lives hauling me in and out of the hospital like my dad did with my

mother—"

"—don't do this to yourself, baby—"

"—and watch as my body gets cut up and old and mangled and wrinkled and scarred—"

"—doctor said you can't upset yourself—"

"—until finally you stop seeing me as a woman and just think of me as some sexless thing called a wife that you can't stand the thought of touching, let alone making love to? What if—oh hell, *tell me* that's not going to happen."

"It's not going to happen."

"And you'll still love me even if I'm still sick."

"I'll still love even if you're still sick—which you are not."

"And you'll still want to tear off my clothes in a passionate frenzy and hump my brains out after I'm bald."

Silence.

"*Danny…?*"

"I'm thinking."

"That explains the burning smell."

Daniel tried to come up with something to say to that but couldn't and by that time it didn't matter anyway because Sharon was back downstairs with a Pig People book and soon they were laughing about Eustice and the rooster and Daniel forgot all about the new neighbors.

Until he got home from work the next evening and found the mother and son in the living room with Lauren. When he'd seen them on the porch yesterday, at a distance, he'd thought their appearance was nothing special; now that he saw two of them close up, his original impression was validated.

"Hi, honey," said Lauren as he came into the room. "I'd like you to meet Jean Sanderson. And this is her son, Tommy."

"How do you do, Mr. Campbell," said Jean, extending a thin and elegant hand that seemed to Daniel out of proportion with the rest of her body. He shook her hand and they exchanged pleasantries for a few minutes while Sharon dragged Tommy into the front room and the two of them compared their favorite Pig People stories.

"Jean's a nurse," said Lauren. "And her husband, Bernard, is a doctor."

"Really," said Daniel. "Do you both work over at Memorial or—"

"Oh dear me, no," replied Jean, brushing a strand of impossibly black hair from her eyes. "We were hired by Lake Management for the new community clinic. Bernie and I are going

to be your resident health-care professionals. We'll even make housecalls."

Daniel was suddenly tense. "Is that what this is? Lauren—are you all right? Should I get the car and—"

Lauren tilted her head toward her husband as she spoke to Jean. "See what I mean? If I were to get a hangnail, he'd be right there."

"You're lucky to have such a concerned husband," said Jean.

"And a nurse and doctor living right next door." She turned toward Daniel. "I gave them Doctor Maines's name and number and signed an authorization form."

"For what?"

"So he'll send them a copy of my records."

"Bernie will call Maines first thing Monday morning and arrange a meeting," said Jean, a concerned but reassuring tone in her voice. "Don't you worry, Daniel, your wife isn't switching doctors, she's simply making sure that we've permission—and the necessary information on her medical background—to treat her in case an emergency should arise."

She went on to explain a few other specifics—such as Lake Management was providing these medical services to the residents on a 24-hour, 7-days a week, 365-days per year basis, free of charge. As Daniel listened to her he knew he should ask her about these services because there was nothing in this world that was free—

–but he didn't because it finally occurred to him why something about her seemed different from yesterday.

She was heavier. And it wasn't just the typical It's-two-days-before-my-period-and-my-water's-heavy weight gain; Jean Sanderson had, in the course of twenty-four hours, put on what looked like fifteen or twenty pounds, all of it in her face and midsection. No wonder something about her seemed odd.

They talked for a few more minutes, then Jean excused herself and took everyone's coffee cups into the kitchen ("I absolutely insist, you two just stay there.").

"Isn't this great?" whispered Lauren. "A doctor and a nurse right next door—and *for free!*"

"Yeah," said Daniel. "It's, uh…it's great. Great."

"Why don't I believe you?"

"I, uh—" He looked at his wife's face and saw there a certain measure of relief that hadn't been present in months and knew he couldn't say anything to spoil it for her. "I'm sorry, hon. Yes! Yes, it's absolutely terrific. Looks like we really fell in

it this time."

"Hallelujah," replied Lauren.

"Well," announced Jean Sanderson as she came back into the room, "I've taken up enough of your time. I should get back to the house and help with the unpacking, there's just *tons* to do."

"Let me know if I can help in any way," said Daniel.

"Oh, you already have. Just by being good neighbors."

Jean shook Lauren's hand, then called for Tommy, then shook Daniel's hand before leaving. Daniel held her grip for a beat longer than was necessary, thinking that her hand felt thicker than it had before, and was it his imagination or was she even heavier now than when he'd gotten home?

"Somethin' smells," said Sharon, crinkling her nose.

"Oh, I wouldn't worry about it, hon," said Jean, kneeling in front of her and brushing back Sharon's hair. "Probably just the garbage disposal. You know how some things smell worse in warm weather. My, aren't you a pretty thing?"

Tommy came over to shake Daniel's hand and tell him it was nice meeting everyone. The kid seemed heavier, as well. And Sharon was right—something smelled terrible.

Jean and Tommy left. After a quick but enjoyable dinner of warmed leftovers, Daniel put Sharon to bed, then stopped in the bathroom to get some aspirin from the cabinet. The old container was empty, so he removed the new one from its box and turned to throw the box into the small plastic trash container—

—which had been fairly full this morning but was empty now. Strange; whenever Sharon performed a chore without having to be told to, she usually pointed it out to him.

He took two aspirin and started back downstairs, then stopped, considered something, and went back to his daughter's room. He knocked twice on the door, then stepped in and said, "Hon, did you empty the trash can in the bathroom?"

"Huh-uh. Tommy said he'd do it for me. I think he likes me."

"Tommy? He emptied it before I got home?"

"No. Just before his mom said it was time for them to go home."

Right. So why hadn't he been carrying anything? Was he some little smartass who thought it'd be funny to hide the trash somewhere up here? Wonderful, just what the area needed, a Dennis the Menace wannabe.

"Well, that was nice of him, I guess."

"He was nice, even if he smelled a little icky. G'night, Daddy."

Back downstairs, Lauren was trying to get up from the couch.

"Whoa," said Daniel, putting a hand on her shoulder and gently but firmly pushing her back down. "What do you need? I'll get it."

"You know, Danny, I really love you, but sometimes this Mother Hen routine gets on my nerves."

"Jean thought you were lucky to have a husband like me."

"She hasn't gotten to know you yet."

"Oh stop it with this effusive praise. I'll get a big head. Now what did you want from the kitchen?"

"Chocolate ice cream."

"Consider it done."

It was only as he was putting the ice cream container back in the freezer that he chanced to look over at the trash receptacle—

—which was empty.

He peered inside and saw that its interior was spotless—as if it was brand-new and not three years old. No stains from coffee ground that hadn't quite hit the garbage bag, no stray bits of orange peel or dust or even a hint of that funky, ripe smell that a lot of plastic receptacles got after a while.

He raised his head and looked out one of the kitchen windows at the Keyser—make that Sanderson—house.

"Okay, folks," he whispered to himself. "I give up. What happened to our trash? Did it just disappear or did you—" He stopped himself before the words *eat it* completed the question. Because if he actually asked the question he might be tempted to answer *yes* and that would mean that the dreaded Hobblobs had changed their name to Sanderson and acquired better grooming habits and medical training and had moved in right next door and that was just a little too weird for him right now, thank you very much.

Then, as he turned off the lights and plunged the kitchen into darkness, the light in the Sanderson's kitchen came on and Daniel saw the giant sluglike man from yesterday lumber into the kitchen and lay flat on the large wooden cutting block in the center of the room. Then Jean and Tommy, followed by Bernard and the little girl, came in and gathered around Slugman.

"Hey," called Lauren from the front room. "Where's my ice-cream?"

"It's coming," said Daniel, more harshly than he would have

Gary A. Braunbeck

liked.

Tommy Sanderson broke away from the group and went over to the refrigerator and opened the door to reveal rows upon rows of small vials filled with liquids of various colors and consistency. He reached in and took out one, then pulled a small case from a nearby drawer.

There was a small flurry of activity when he came back, and just as Bernard Sanderson turned to lower the window blinds Daniel caught sight of three things that happened simultaneously: Tommy plunged some kind of needle into his mother's arm, Jean climbed up on top of Slugman, and Slugman opened his mouth so wide it looked as if his jaw actually wrenched away from the rest of his skull.

Then down came the blinds, leaving Daniel in the darkness with a lot of questions.

The events of the next several days did nothing to ease Daniel's anxiety about the Sandersons.

The day after Jean and Tommy's visit, flyers were distributed among all the Clear Lake residents requesting them to deposit all their recyclable items in the four large steel dumpsters located behind the Sanderson home. This included any old tires, batteries, styrofoam containers, plastic bags, aluminum cans, foil, glass, household chemical containers, aerosol cans, cardboard, and anything else that people wanted to get rid of, even old broken furniture and televisions, radios, toys, and—one of the most curious items—used disposable diapers. Anytime, day or night, and any amount.

The parade was practically nonstop. Some mornings Daniel found it almost amusing as he watched the people walk or drive up (sometimes in rented trucks, trailers stuffed to overflowing) with their items.

Then came the notice asking everyone to please begin setting their trash cans in front of their homes on Tuesday night. Everyone did, and come Wednesday morning, the trash was gone. No one was ever awakened by the noise of garbage trucks.

Jean and Tommy, their weight changing on what seemed an hourly basis, visited with Lauren three more times that week, each time beating a hasty retreat when Daniel got home from work. When he questioned Lauren about it, she became increasingly more hostile and defensive until, after the third visit, she told him it was none of his fucking business what she talked about with her friends and oh by the way she wasn't going to

be seeing Dr. Maines next week. Daniel decided to let that one go for a few days, chalking her mood swing up to worry.

She would not let him make love to her.

Another flyer appeared, this one asking the residents to put their trash in front on a nightly basis, this way everyone could start each day trash-free.

The blinds in the Sanderson home stayed down all the time now, and Daniel was starting to get anxious.

Later, he would wonder why the rest of the events hadn't set all the Gothic bells ringing, and curse himself for not having caught on sooner.

Here are some of those events, in no particular order:

The residents of Clear Lake began gaining and losing weight with alarming regularity—and not just a little weight; like Jean Sanderson and the rest of her clan, every person Daniel saw seemed to put on a minimum of twenty-five to thirty pounds each day, only to have that excess weight vanish by the time he got home at night.

Garbage pickup ceased altogether; no one bothered to set their trash cans by the curb anymore, yet there was none of the aftereffects that usually result when waste builds up—no stray paper cups littering the streets or fields or yards, no coffee-grounds finding their way into the gutters, no remains of rotten food being scavenged by dogs, not even so much as the occasional torn paper bag: for all appearances, Clear Lake Estates had stopped throwing anything away.

Lauren began cooking again, something she hadn't done since having the cysts diagnosed. And the dishes that she prepared—casseroles, souffles, meat loaf, et cetera—looked all right but tasted...odd to Daniel, as if they were synthetic imitations of the foods rather than the foods themselves. But he ate them, and he only got sick three times as a result but was damned if he'd let his wife know about it—cooking made her so happy and relaxed, he couldn't bring himself to taint her bliss.

Then they began eating on paper plates.

"Special occasion?" he asked.

Lauren smiled and said, "I just want to get rid of all these awful paper plates. They take up room in the pantry and just add to the landfills."

"When did you develop an environmental conscience?"

Lauren cocked her head to the side—was her neck thicker than it was yesterday?—and said, "Don't you want to make a better world for Sharon?"

"Yeah," said his daughter. "Don't 'cha want me to have a better world?"

"Of course," replied Daniel, and silently added, *But don't you think if we could have made it a better world, we'd have gone and done it for ourselves?*

There was never any sign of the paper plates later.

And something connected with dinner always disappeared: "Did you see my plastic fork?" "Wasn't the empty margarine tub right there a minute ago?" "What happened to the box that the macaroni came in?" "Damn, we go through a lot of aluminum foil." "Where'd all the chicken bones go?"

And it seemed most people were spending a lot of time at the sight of the eruption.

The Gothic bells were sounding.

Daniel Campbell just didn't hear them until (as it always must go in stories of this kind) It Was Too Late.

Then came the night when he was a little late getting home and found the house empty. He went from room to room, calling for Lauren and Sharon, not finding them anywhere. The sound of a car door slamming out front drew him to the upstairs window, and he pulled back the curtain in time to see his wife and daughter climb into the Sanderson's car along with Jean. He bolted down the stairs and out the front door in time to see them drive off.

"Goddammit!" he shouted to no one in particular. As he turned to go back inside he saw three figures standing at the large bay window in the front of the Sanderson house. Bernard, Slugman, and the Sanderson's daughter—whose name Daniel still didn't know.

It was time to introduce himself to the rest of the family.

He stormed over to their yard and started toward the porch when it hit him that all three of them were bare-ass naked. Not only that, but they were embracing one another quite tightly.

Almost too tightly.

Then they stepped forward and Daniel saw, as clearly as he'd ever seen anything in his life, that the three of them weren't embracing one another, they were *connected* to each other, via flesh-colored and -textured membranes hanging from their hips, like some fantastic set of Siamese triplets. Only the membranes seemed to be breathing, and with every breath it looked as if Bernard and the little girl were being absorbed by Slugman like victims drowning in quicksand.

"Jesus!"

Slugman leaned forward, pressing his corpulent face against the window, and opened his mouth, dislodging his jaw. It dropped down, farther and farther, his jowls stretching like fresh taffy until his chin actually touched the windowsill.

Daniel was frozen to the spot.

Slugman's teeth were long, yellow, jagged fangs.

Frothy saliva dribbled over his bottom lip, pooling against the glass.

Time to go.

Drawing on some inner reserve of strength he'd never suspected he possessed, Daniel turned to run back to his house—

—and almost knocked over his daughter, who smiled at him and said, "I told you they were a bunch of fat fatties!"

Then someone clobbered his skull from behind.

The first thing that registered before he could even open his eyes was the unbelievable stench. Take the worst August afternoon you can think of, oppressive with heat and so humid that sweat will evaporate as soon as it breaks the surface of your skin, and imagine that someone has dropped a dozen eggs on the scalding sidewalk. The glob of yolks and shells lays there, turning rancid, drawing flies. Then a dog happens by and pisses into the mix, sniffs it to make sure it picked up its marking scent, and vomits on top of it. Someone in a passing car heaves the contents of their ashtray out the window and the ashes and old cigarette butts land right on tip of the congealing puddle. Add the remains of a five-day-old hamburger (its dull brown color now mostly green), a healthy does of liquified baby shit, several blackened banana peels, top it all off with gelid chunks of sour milk, and let it bake under direct, ninety-degree sunlight.

Now intensify that stink about twenty thousand times.

Take a deep breath.

Mm-mm-*good*.

That's roughly the smell Daniel found searing his nostrils and clogging his lungs when he regained consciousness.

He was lying on his back near the foot of the erupted mound. The vapors rising from the landfill were so thick they looked like serpents dancing to some charm music only they could hear. After a few moments, his nostrils gave up the ghost and his sense of smell died, for which he was almost grateful,

Then the figure of Jean Sanderson rose up before him, naked and sweating, her skin stained with filth.

She had to weigh at least four hundred pounds.

Gary A. Braunbeck

"I hadn't planned on having to deal with someone like you so soon," she said. "But that doesn't make me any less grateful to have found you."

"Where the fuck are my wife and daughter?"

"Right over here. Sit up and take a look."

Lauren and Sharon, also naked, were scrabbling around on their hands and knees with most of the rest of the Sanderson clan and several other people who Daniel recognized as residents of Clear Lake Estates. Someone or something had crawled down into the opening of the eruption and was tossing out all manner of foulness and trash. One man grabbed a pile of aluminum cans and stuffed them into his mouth one by one, his cheeks puffing out like a blowfish as he chewed. Lauren and Sharon, slobbering out repulsive, semi-human sounds, sucked up lumpy puddles of sewage while, next to them, an elderly couple, holding hands, belly-flopped into a small but deep pond of something that looked like glazed fat; in a matter of moments the pond was drained, absorbed into their bodies like water into sponges. This obscene orgy continued for several minutes more, until Tommy emerged from the mound pushing a large metal barrel clearly marked **HAZARDOUS WASTE**.

"You were right, Mother!" he called down. "There're hundreds, maybe thousands of these down there,"

"Wonderful," said Jean, smiling. "Tommy, pop off the cork. Let's celebrate."

Tommy opened his mouth, revealing dozens of multi-rowed needlelike teeth, and bit into the lip of the barrel, ripping the top off with a long, loud, protracted groan that sounded to Daniel like an automobile being crushed under a press.

Everyone ran to the base of the mound as Tommy upended the barrel and the first slopping trail of radioactive waste streamed downward. Hands cupped the liquid and brought it toward hungry mouths, and Daniel could see now that everyone—Lauren and Sharon included—were growing fatter by the second.

"Ohgod," he managed to get out.

"No, not God…not exactly," said Jean.

Two bright headlight beams bled across the field, accompanied by the sounds from a powerful truck engine. Daniel whirled around and saw the wrecker pull up, something huge dangling from its crane in back.

A steel net.

And inside that net, lying on his back like a bleached whale,

blubber jiggling, was Slugman.

The crane bucked, then screeched and groaned as it lowered him to the ground.

Slowly, everyone gathered around him. At one point Lauren and Sharon stumbled by Daniel, their eyes glassy as if drunk. They looked like a couple of albino ticks that had gorged themselves to the point of bursting. Neither of them looked when he screamed their name.

"Won't do you any good," said Jean. "The only thing they can hear is the pulsing of the Earth."

"The what?"

Jean heaved her great bulk around, straddling Daniel's waist and crushing one of his hips. He threw back his head and screamed. "OHGOD! GOD! Who the hell are you? What in God's name is that...that *man* over there?"

"I was human once, so was the rest of my family, human just like you. We got over it. Hold that thought. I want you to see something."

She waved at Tommy, who came running down from the mound, grabbing a small black medical bag setting at the base. He ran over to the group, who parted right down the center, allowing Daniel a clear view of Slugman, Lauren straddling his waist.

"Ohgod," choked Daniel.

Tommy opened the case and removed two small vials of liquid; one red, the other clear, and filled a hypodermic with equal measures of both.

"Don't worry," said Jean. "One of those is just a small sample of Lauren's own blood that I drew from her on one of my visits. I've coded a few basic changes into it, nothing her system can't handle.

"The other vial is some rather potent growth hormones. She and your daughter have each been getting four shots a day for the last week. Lauren didn't tell you because she didn't want you to worry. You see, they didn't get all of the cancer. In fact, there's a malignancy in her uterus the size of a quarter. It wasn't too hard to convince her that she was taking part in a radical cancer cure experiment.

"Sharon, on the other hand, took a little doing. Did you know that your daughter thinks she's ugly? Yes, she does. So Tommy went to work on her. She thought that the shots would make her beautiful. In a way, she's right."

Tommy inserted the needle in Lauren's arm, then sunk the

plunger. As soon as he removed it, Lauren threw back her head and released an orgasmic cry of ecstasy that brought tears of rage, helplessness, and jealousy to Daniel's eyes.

Then she reached down with one of her hands and began kneading the flab around her center, working her hand in deeper and deeper, then her forearm, and even part of her elbow. As she went deeper into herself a thick transparent liquid gushed out of her.

She paused a moment, her eyes closed, and began to moan.

"What the fuck is—"

"Shut up and pay attention, Daniel Campbell, because I am about to tell you a story, and you'll *want* to hear it, believe me.

"When this planet awoke to sing its First Song, there was only one Being living on its surface. This creature breathed and dreamed just as you do today. But it had no definitive form. And it was lonely. Here was this magnificent Earth, filled with beauty, and it had no one and nothing with which to share it.

"The Being took a deep breath and began to swell in size, rearranging itself within, then split into two identical halves. The halves mated, creating a third, a hybrid of themselves which in turn mated with them, producing other hybrids. They continued to mate and produce, as did the progenies, giving birth to everything from the Manticore and Sphinx down to the ants and maggots—that is how the Earth became populated.

"Even after that, the birthing continued. Single cells fused together, creating metazoans that eventually culminated in the invention of roses and elephants and dew-glistened leaves and even human beings. All life on this planet—past, present, and what there is of the future—sprang from the same single organism. Jesus, if everyone only knew what it is we're throwing away. If they could just see the joining of organisms into communities, those communities into ecosystems, those ecosystems into the biosphere...

"Do you have any idea how unique each single living creature is? Everything alive at this moment is one in three billion of its kind. Each is a self-contained, free-standing individual labeled by specific, genuinely unique protein configurations at the surface of its cells. You'd think we'd never stop dancing.

"But somewhere along the line the dancing *did* stop and the world became a trash can. Its system became poisoned, and that poison continued to spread. And the Earth has had enough. She's tired, and she's sick. And like any good mother, she doesn't want to hurt her children or see them suffer too much for their

mistakes.

"So she's ridding herself of the poison in her system by giving birth to one last new species, born from disease and poison and filth, that can only subsist on poison and waste and garbage. All of the bugs haven't been worked out yet, but who said the next step of evolution was going to be easy?

"Take a look, quick, and see what we have to become in order to save ourselves and this planet."

Lauren was removing her arm from inside herself, pulling a long, thin, viscera-drenched tube that looked more like a tentacle of intestine. Groaning and squealing in unbridled sexual climax, she pushed the end of the tube into Slugman's mouth, then took a deep breath and lurched forward.

A sound like the liquid-groan of swelled bowels blowing their contents into a toilet erupted from inside Lauren as the tube expanded and Slugman sucked hungrily on what she fed to him, the waste pumping out until, after a few more seconds, Lauren had shrunk back down to her regular size and Slugman had doubled in weight and bulk. Lauren fell to the ground, drenched in sweat and wailing as the seizure struck. She bucked and shuddered and slammed her head up and down until she lost consciousness.

"She'll live," said Jean. "The creation of a new species is not a painless thing."

"Why her?" said Daniel, crying. "Why my wife and daughter?"

"People with certain cell configurations adapt more quickly to the process than others. Especially people with cancer."

"Ohgod! Do you mean t-that Sharon—"

"—and yourself, as well. And most of the people living here. You've been exposed to a slow radioactive leak for years. The tumors are ripe. It's only a matter of reprogramming genetic codes, of redirecting an infection, strengthening your blood's defenses and combining it with...well, I called it a growth hormone but that's a bit of an oversimplification. When the initial Being divided itself for the first time, some of it in its original form, drained into the Earth, and the Earth stored it away for safekeeping. Call it the primordial soup, if you want. Anyway, once everything is released into the system, there's no undoing it."

Now others were straddling Slugman and feeding him and he kept eating it and eating it and eating it.

Jean was the last one to feed him, then she returned to

Daniel, her body svelte and firm.

"What is he?" croaked Daniel.

"I honestly don't know. My husband and I found him in northern Uganda, outside of an Ik village. We were part of a Peace Corps medical team. We'd gone into the village because there'd been reports of severe mass birth defects among the women of the tribe. There was so much shit in the water supply I was surprised everyone wasn't dead. Methyl-mercury, poly-chlorinated biphenyls, dioxins, phenol, acetone…none of us had ever seen so much toxic waste concentrated in such a small area.

"Nostromo there—that's what we decided to name him, he never gave us a name—was wandering the only road into the village. He collapsed in front of our truck as we were driving out with six dead, deformed infants in the bed. We picked him up and put him back there and drove to the hospital…he somehow absorbed the infants while we were driving along. Because when we went to pull everyone out, he was in the process of…digesting them back into the world. Alive, with normal bodes, and disease-free. It took us years to understand what was happening, what is still happening.

"He is what the human race must evolve into. A combination garbage disposal/system purifier."

"What's happening now?" asked Daniel. "What are you going to do with me?"

"Nothing, yet. Nostromo has to process what's been fed to him, then he'll excrete more of the…growth hormone–"

"Which you, in turn, use to create more…more…"

"Think of them as a human recycling plant. They consume the material in its solid form, break it down into a semi-liquid state, then feed it to Nostromo. Nature is nothing if not cyclic."

"What do you want with me?"

"Nostromo is very old, and he can't do it all by himself anymore. You're the youngest of the infected men. You're the perfect candidate to become the second host." She snapped her fingers and gestured for some of the people to come over and pick up Daniel. Lauren was among them, but she gave no sign that she recognized her husband.

Jean stroked Daniel's brow and said, "While you were unconscious I pumped your system full of Nostromo's DNA, among other things. You'll have to ask him to tell you the First Being story sometime. He tells it much better than I do. In fact, by the time he's finished, he'll have you thinking he was there when it

Gary A. Braunbeck

 170

went down."

They began carrying Daniel up the side of the mound, toward the opening of the landfill. He tried to struggle against them but found his limbs were numb.

"I'm not stupid, Danny," said Jean. "I also gave you a slow-release sedative/muscle relaxant right before you came to. Can't afford to have you digging yourself out."

"D-digging myself—"

"One thing Nostromo did manage to get across to us was that he'd spent time hibernating under a hill. He led us to that hill. Turned out to be toxic dump, not unlike here. We've tried this at least twenty times with other subjects. Poor Bernie can't do it anymore, so we agreed this time it would be my responsibility."

"...please, please no, please don't do it, I just, god, ohgod—" He was over the opening now and they were lowering him. "—pleasegod NO DON'T DO THIS *OHGOD NO, NO NOOOOO!!!*"

He felt them release him, felt himself flying down into steamy darkness, felt his body land on something spongy and thick.

He looked up through the whorls of fumes and saw Jean looking down.

"It'll only be a few days before we'll know if you'll work or not. If you haven't climbed out of here on your own by Saturday, we'll come dig you out. I promise that I'll give you something to kill you quickly if that happens.

"Believe me, you won't want to live if this doesn't work.

"Sleep well, Danny."

And then a wide, thick, heavy tarpaulin was stretched across the opening and Daniel felt himself sinking into the muck and the last thing he heard before submerging into the waste was the sound of his mother's voice yelling *Will you look at this mess! Looks like the Hobblobs have moved in.*

God, had she been right.

Something long and slimy swam onto his face and wriggled up into his left nostril.

Then he lost consciousness.

Two days later, a little after midnight on Friday, the being called Nostromo lurched and waddled through the back door of the Sanderson house. Something that looked like a giant maggot with sinewy-muscled human legs followed him inside.

A large pile of rotten food, speckled here and there by rusty

Gary A. Braunbeck

tin cans and acid-encrusted batteries, sat in the center of the kitchen floor.

Which was fortuitous, because Daniel Campbell had worked up quite an appetite with his little climb.

"Looks like the Hobblobs have been here," he said through the small, puckered slit that was now his mouth.

Time to take out the trash.

And on some nights, if you happen by the sight of the eruption, you will find Daniel and Nostromo surrounded by their followers, who listen with rapt attention at the tales their Hosts tell.

Here is one of Daniel's favorites:

"A very foolish bird waited too long to fly South for the winter. By the time he took off the temperatures were well below zero. It didn't take long before his wings froze solid and he plummeted to the ground, landing in the middle of an ice-covered field.

"The bird lay there, slowly freezing to death. Then a cow came along and took a massive shit right on top of the bird.

"It was warm underneath. It smelled a little, but the bird didn't mind it—after all, the warmth melted the ice on his wings and kept him from dying of exposure to the cold. 'I think I'll just stay here for a little while,' thought the bird to himself. 'The weather will get better soon enough, then I'll be on my way.'

"So he stayed there, doing nothing, all warm and smelly and comfortable.

"Then a cat came along and saw the tip of one of the bird's wings sticking out. It pounced on top of the cowpie, dug the bird out, and ate it.

"And the moral of this story is: Not everyone who shits on you is your enemy, and not everyone who digs you out is your friend."

Everyone agrees that such wisdom is sorely needed in these nervous times.

To date, property values at Clear Lake Estates have increased 124.87% over what they were last year at this time. People don't much complain about how expensive it is. There's no crime, flawless security, smooth roads, easy access to the interstate, and a sentient sense of community among the residents. The only drawback, some say, is that every so often there

will be this funky smell in the air for a few days. But no one much minds that.

Because Clear Lake is one of the *cleanest* places you're ever likely to live.

> *— for Joe R. Lansdale, and in memory of*
> *Joseph Payne Brennan and Avram Davidson*

Kancer Alley

Alley

Nancy A. Collins

The volunteer stood in the meager shade provided by the tar-paper shack's front porch and rapped her knuckles once more on the screen door's wooden frame.

"Hello? Hello, Mr. Marsalis? Is anyone home? *Hello!*"

The volunteer scanned the front yard while waiting a response. A handful of rumpled chickens scratched near the dirt road, while a slat-thin hound slumbered under a partially demolished Buick. She frowned and cupped her free hand over her brow, pressing her nose to the rusty screen, and peered inside. The interior of the Marsalis home was dark and redolent of countless meals of fatback and mustard greens.

"Can I help you, young lady?"

The volunteer jumped, startled by the appearance of a small, wrinkled negro man standing at the corner of the house.

"Oh! Sorry about that! You surprised me!"

"That's awright, honey. Didn't mean to scare you none." The old man pulled a clean white handkerchief from his back pocket and mopped at his brow.

"Are you Mr. Marsalis? Mr. Homer Marsalis?"

"Have been for the past sixty-five years. You with Parish Services?"

"No, sir! I'm a volunteer worker for the Louisiana Chapter of Ecology Now. We're an environmental group trying to control pollution by America's big corporations...Maybe you got one of our flyers in the mail?"

Marsalis shrugged. His face was broad and expansive, the color of teak. The sweat beading on his brow and cheeks made him look he'd recently been polished. "Wouldn't do me much good if I did, ma'am! I can't read except to make out m'own name."

"Oh. Well. Uh, the reason I'm here is to tell you about a meeting we're having in the town hall this evening. I'm sure you're very much aware of Redeemer Parish's high cancer rate, and that research has tied it to the chemical dumped into the Mississippi by the companies up-river and from contaminants seeping into the groundwater from supposedly 'safe' toxic waste dumps in the area…"

The old man nodded, his eyes unreadable. "Yeah. I know something about it."

"Well, together we're having a meeting and representatives from Arcadia Petrochemicals are going to be there. They're the largest—and most notorious—polluter in the whole state…"

"I know about Arcadia. I worked for 'em for close to thirty years." The hostility in the old man's voice was unmistakable.

"Oh. Well, uh, we'd really appreciate it if everyone who can make it would come to the meeting…There'll be reporters from both the Baton Rouge and the New Orleans dailies, plus a camera crew from Channel Four."

The old man nodded slowly. "I'll be there. Don't you worry 'bout that, ma'am."

The volunteer smiled nervously. There was something about the way the old man's eyes gleamed that made her antsy. "That's good to hear, Mr. Marsalis…Be sure to bring your family and friends with you. We'll need all the local support we can get."

Homer Marsalis stood in his front yard and watched as the activist climbed into her little compact car and headed down the dirt road, leaving a pall of yellowish dust in her wake.

Be sure to bring your family and friends with you.

Funny how everything was so green; how everything looked so alive. Homer Marsalis paused to stare at the field of sugar cane flanking the road. In the distance he could hear the roar and rumble of the diesel harvesters. The smell of fresh-cut sugar cane drifted on the humid breeze.

He remembered how, decades ago, he and his brothers used to steal sugar cane; chopping it open with their pa's machete to get at the stuff inside. He could still recall how it was made even more delicious by the knowledge he would be beaten

should the overseer discover the theft.

Back then life was sweet. As sweet as the syrup from stolen sugar cane. As sweet as the words that dripped from the tongue of the Father of Lies.

But that had been long ago. Homer wasn't fooled. The lush fertility of the Mississippi Delta hid many dangers; cane rattlers, water moccasins, alligators…cancer.

Homer closed his eyes as the pain resurfaced once again, blotting out his surroundings. He'd become adept at riding it, like a veteran bronco buster. His one regret was that the pain would never be enough to kill him.

Despite what the songs and movies said, no one had yet to die from terminal grief.

"Sorry I'm late, folks, but I got hung up at the house."

If Homer Marsalis' family and friends noticed his tardiness, they kept it to themselves.

"There was this li'l white gal talkin' bout a meeting down at the town hall. It's about Arcadia."

Homer paused to let the words sink in for effect. He'd always had a flair for the dramatic. He pointed a finger at his brother Nestor's headstone.

"You recall that time you woke up and found that orange dust all over the yard? That stuff that looked like rust an' smelt like rotten eggs? I tole you to move then, that it weren't healthy to be livin' downwind of Arcadia! But would you listen to me? No! Just cause yore my big brother don't mean you'll always know more'n me, Nestor!"

Nestor said nothing. He never did.

Homer pulled his handkerchief out of his back pocket and wiped the tears from his face. He shuffled over to a badly listing grave stone and leaned against it.

He knew he must look a sight; a small, banty rooster of an old fool dressed in his Sunday best, chattering away at the Dead like a washerwoman gossiping at the fence.

Not that he was in any danger of being seen. To Homer's knowledge, he was the only one who still bothered to visit the boneyard. Most of the others who had loved ones planted in its dark ground were either lying directly underfoot or had moved on.

Move on. That's what his son-in-law had told him. That he ought to move on.

That was well and good if you were young and still had

some life left in you. But there was no way Homer could bring himself to leave Redeemer Parish. After all, his whole family was here.

Over to his left were the headstones that marked his parents' final resting place. His daddy had died when Homer was twelve, killed in a farming accident. His mama had lived another twenty years without her man, dying during the winter of 1957 from double pneumonia. Homer remembered how old she'd seemed at the time, then realized—with a start—that at her death she'd been eight years younger than he was now.

Flanking his parents' graves were those of his brother Calvin and his sister Esther. Calvin had died of pancreatic cancer back in '83. He'd been sixty-one at the time. No one really thought anything about it. Same with Esther, the oldest of his brothers and sisters, who developed cancer of the colon the next year. Folks didn't grow very old in Redeemer Parish. Least ways, not the poor ones. The best someone like Homer could shoot for was seventy. Maybe seventy-two, if his luck held.

By the time Nestor died of leukemia in '86, Homer knew that whatever was carrying off his family wasn't natural. As bad as losing his big brother had been, what came next had been a thousand times worse.

It started with Ernestine. His baby.

She'd got herself married to a fellow up in Detroit back in '83. When she finally got herself pregnant she came back down to be with her mama. She'd been so excited. Gussie, Homer's wife, had been tickled to death by the idea of having a baby round the house again.

Ernestine hadn't been home a week before the well-water started stinking. They kept on drinking it, of course. What other choice did they have? It had happened before, but it usually went away on its own.

Then the baby came. Early. Way too early.

Homer stared at his daughter's head stone. His grandchild's name was also on there, although it had never really been alive. Homer wasn't even really sure if it had even been a baby. What Ernestine had birthed that cold winter night in '87 looked more like a tumor with a head on it.

For form's sake, they'd given it a boy's name.

Ernestine died a week later in Charity Hospital. They'd cut out her womb trying to save her.

Her husband took the first bus from Detroit he could find, but he was too late. By the time he reached New Orleans, she

was gone. Homer could still see the emptiness in his son-in-law as he watched his wife's coffin be lowered into the delta's rich dirt.

Shortly after the funeral a couple of white folks dressed in suits came out to the house and asked his permission to take samples from his well. They wore plastic gloves and were real careful not to get anything on their clothes. A couple of weeks later the same two men came back out and told Homer he needed to move his well. They showed him some papers and said that his well was contaminated. Then they left.

Homer might have been illiterate, but he'd worked for Arcadia Petrochemicals long enough to recognize the corporate logo on the papers. He showed the report to his son Nolan to see what he could make of it. Nolan had graduated from the vo-tech school and worked out on the oil rigs as a mechanic.

Nolan said the reports talked about stuff called Phenols and HHCs and Benzene Hexachloride and Cadmium. There was also stuff about carcinogenics and other words Homer did not fully understand. After he'd finished reading the report aloud, Nolan had looked his father in the eye and said: "Daddy, they're saying the water's poisoned."

"How can that be? That well's been there since my daddy was a boy! It's a good well! With good water! How can they say it's poison?"

"Cause they're the ones that poisoned it, daddy. They knew exactly what they were looking for, and they found it."

"But—but—It'll cost *money* to dig a new well!" Homer had never felt so stupid and helpless before in his life. The knowledge that the water that his family had relied on for more than seventy years was no longer safe had hurt him like a blow. For how long? For how long had it been like that? Weeks? Months? Years? The realization that Ernestine had drunk from the well, not to mention Nestor, Calvin and Esther, made his soul knot up inside him.

He'd been so proud of himself. Of his job. He'd been working as a janitor at the main Arcadia plant since it opened in 1959. Decent jobs were scarce in Redeemer Parish. Most men either busted their backs working in the cane fields or they didn't work at all. A lucky handful landed jobs in the oil fields or at the chemical plants that lined the last fifty miles of the Mississippi River before it emptied into the Gulf of Mexico. Homer had counted himself amongst the lucky. He brought home enough pay to keep a roof over his family's heads and put his

son through school. He didn't see any reason to question the source of his good fortune.

Oh, he'd heard the rumors about illegal dumping procedures. You couldn't work at the Arcadia plant and *not* hear something. Back during the Sixties, the papers had taken to calling the stretch of river the Chemical Ditch. But in the last ten years the name had changed to Cancer Alley. But he'd paid it no mind. It had nothing to do with him.

And now the company he'd worked for the better part of thirty years was telling him he couldn't drink from his well anymore. That it was poison.

He went to the man in charge of public relations at the plant and demanded to talk with the president. He told the public relations director about the poison in his well and how his sister and brothers had died of cancer; of how the poison made his daughter miscarry.

The p.r. director gave Homer a hard, cold stare and said: "Look, it ain't our fault if you people have sex all the time! That's what causes miscarriages. You people are always trying to blame us for your mistakes! Now get back to work!"

Two days later Homer lost his job.

Six months after that Nolan started losing weight. By Christmas he was diagnosed as having leukemia. He managed to hang on until the spring of '89. Homer thought he'd never feel a greater sorrow than that of burying his only son. But six months later Gussie, his wife and help-mate for the past forty years, followed her son into the ground.

Gone. They were all gone. Everyone he'd ever loved or cared for lay beneath his feet. The last three years had been busy ones for the tiny graveyard. The mortal remains of Bordelons, Tanners, Watsons, and Johnstons lay cheek by jowl; good Baptists all, and each laid low by cancer of some kind.

Homer turned to stare at the towering twin chimneys of the Arcadia plant, looming over the landscape like an industrial volcano. Yellowish-brown smoke billowed from the funnels. Gussie's monument was not yet a year and a half old, but already the inscription was unreadable, the limestone badly pitted.

The pain blossomed again and Homer gasped. There was no pretending what he felt was simple grief. Not now. Not here. He needed no doctors to tell him the agony in his stomach was cancer. He leaned heavily on the tilting headstone and fumbled with his breast pocket.

"Forgive me, darlin'," he whispered under his breath. "But I can't let what they did go unpunished."

The flute was made from bone and it was very, very old. Older than Homer. Older than his mother, who had given it to him on her death bed. It had come from Africa, and it was carved from the thigh-bone of a powerful wizard-king. Homer did not know if these stories were true. It did not matter. The flute held power, that much he *did* now know.

His mother's family had been witchy as long as anyone could remember. His grandmother, dead these fifty years, had claimed to be descended from a powerful *obeah* man and that, as a young woman, she had once ruled as New Orleans' reigning *voudou* queen. Homer had inherited his mama's witchy ways, just as she'd gotten hers from granny.

When he met Augusta Timms, everything changed for Homer. Gussie was a devout Baptist. For him to win her love, he had to put aside what she called "heathen ways". And, because he loved her, he'd done as she asked. He never really developed a taste for church or preachers, but he agreed to their children being raised Baptist and never mentioned the old ways to them. Not that it mattered. Both Ernestine and Nolan seemed to be more their mother's children than his. Homer had not glimpsed the gleam that burned in his mother's eyes. The same that touched his own. He'd prayed that one of his grandchildren might carry on, but even that hope had been destroyed.

"I know I promised you," Homer told his wife's grave. "And you know I wouldn't go back on my word less it was important! They don't know. None of them! None of them knows what it's like to suffer and die the way you and the young'uns did! There's no way the Livin' can know the sorrow of the Dead. They don't want to know. And they never will. Unless they're shown. It's time for the Dead to speak their piece! It's the only way those fools will ever learn!"

Homer placed the bone flute in his mouth and closed his eyes, squeezing tears onto his seamed cheeks. And he began to play.

The music was the sound of grief. The notes pierced the late-afternoon air, carried high and far by the wind. Men toiling in the cane fields paused in their labors, their eyes burning with sudden, unexplained tears. A truck driver carrying a load of gypsum to the Arcadia treatment plant found his vision abruptly blurred and was forced to pull over to the side of the road as great, wracking sobs shook his body.

And the thick green carpet that covered the graves of Homer Marsalis' friends and loved ones rippled like an uneasy sea. Tombstones toppled and cracked as the earth split itself asunder. First there was a smell of freshly turned dirt; then a far more pungent reek.

Nestor was the first to rise, the powder-blue polyester leisure suit he'd been buried in looking little worse for the wear, despite occasional clumps of grave mold. Esther clawed her way free, one skeletal hand clutching the tattered remains of her burial gown. Esther had always been modest. Beetles dropped from her wig as Nestor helped her to stand.

Calvin pushed his way through the top soil like a plant eager to meet the sun, scattering dirt with a mighty shrug of his shoulders. Although death and decay had whittled him down, he was still a big man.

Ernestine cradled her misshapen son to her worm-eaten breast, staring at the sun with withered eyes. Nolan, his gaunt frame made even more so by two years underground, teetered uncertainly in the afternoon light, looking like a dreamer awakened from a deep sleep.

Gussie wore the same green dress he'd last seen her in, her sweet face ravaged by worms and decay, but Homer could not find it in him to be repulsed by the sight of her. Anyone else would be frightened by the things that stood before him, but to Homer Marsalis, they were his family. It felt good to see them again.

The graveyard continued to surrender its dead, as more and more of its occupants—all of them familiar, all of them friends or family—stood up to be counted. Homer nodded his appreciation as each new recruit moved to join the others. While he had provided the power to reanimate the Dead, it was up to each individual whether or not to rise. Homer did not believe in forced solidarity.

When they were fifty strong, and the afternoon shadows had lengthened, Homer motioned for them to follow him. And they did, swaying on unsteady limbs. Those who were too decayed to walk alone were aided by the more recent dead.

Homer reached out and took Gussie's hand in his own. It was cold and its texture reminded him of soft soap, but he didn't really mind. He'd missed her so much. It was as if they'd buried a part of him along with her. And now it was back. At least for awhile.

It would take them an hour or two to make it into town. The

meeting would already be under way by the time they got there. Homer hoped the fat-faced fool from Arcadia's public relations department would be there. Homer had a lot to say to that man. And this time he'd listen.

Binary

Roman A. Ranieri

David Webber had just finished checking the air regulator on his scuba tank when Sergeant Cheney climbed into the rear of the van.

"Are you ready, Dave?"

"Almost. Go ahead, fill me in."

"You're going after a ten-year-old Caucasian boy named Joey Potter. He was playing hockey with about a dozen other kids when the ice broke. Four kids went into the water. The rest of the boys were able to pull three of them back out, but Joey went under too fast. He was playing goalie and apparently his pads got waterlogged before he could get them off."

"How long's he been in the water?"

"About fifteen minutes."

Webber glanced down at his partner who was methodically checking the thick rubber seams of the insulated diving suit. "How much time do we have left?"

"I think sixty-five minutes is the current record for a successful resuscitation," replied Swenson. "The water's only about eighteen feet deep in this area. If the currents haven't swept him downriver, you should find the kid somewhere near the hole in the ice."

"Okay, let's go," said Webber.

Police and other emergency vehicles were still arriving along Delaware Avenue as the three men carefully made their way down the snow-covered bank to the edge of the frozen river. Up on the pier, a squad of uniformed officers tried to contain several unruly camera

crews from the local news media before they could disrupt the rescue operation.

Swenson and Cheney stopped at the edge of the ice.

"Why couldn't it have been *your* turn to be the hero?" joked Webber, trying to relieve some of the tension knotted in his stomach.

"Because *you're* more photogenic," replied Swenson, patting him on the shoulder.

After slipping on his flippers, Webber took the powerful underwater flashlight from Sergeant Cheney. A moment later, he stepped off the edge of the ice and plunged into the Delaware River.

Although his wet suit and face mask were designed for arctic temperatures, Webber shuddered involuntarily as the water engulfed him. He seemed to sense, rather than actually feel the numbing frigidity. When he approached the silt of the riverbed, Webber switched on the light and began searching.

Ordinary objects cast distorted alien shadows as the police diver urgently explored the watery dumping grounds of a large industrial city. Everything was covered in a thick, oily scum, making it nearly impossible to distinguish rusting automobile parts from jagged chunks of broken concrete.

After about four minutes, Webber began to panic. Where was Joey Potter? Even with the amazing advancements in the field of medical resuscitation, if he didn't find the boy quickly, there would be no hope of recovery.

Suddenly, the light glinted off a piece of shiny steel. He swung the beam of light back again and saw the blade of an ice skate protruding from the twisted hulk of an old pickup truck. Webber's heartbeat pounded in his ears as his muscular legs propelled him toward the drowned child.

He grabbed hold of the boy's thickly-padded coat, then pulled upwards. The child's head unexpectedly jerked down, causing Webber to lose his grip.

Just stay calm, he mentally cautioned himself as he reached down and gently turned Joey onto his side. In the beam of his flashlight he saw a long strand of copper wire stretching from the boy's open mouth to a tangled mass of electrical wiring beneath the dashboard of the truck. Webber grasped the strand and gave it an exploratory tug. Joey's head gently bumped against his hand, but the wire did not come out.

He aimed the light into the boy's mouth and instantly saw the problem: the end of the copper wire had become hooked in

the top half of Joey's dental braces. Webber then tried to pull the opposite end of the wire out of the dashboard, but it hardly budged. He looked down again and examined the point where the wire was snagged. It was directly behind the third molar, too far back for him to reach while wearing such bulky rubber gloves.

The icy water burned like acid as he pulled the insulated glove off his right hand. The fingers were already growing numb as he carefully slid them into Joey's mouth. Webber silently prayed as he awkwardly fumbled with the wire. He couldn't stand the pain much longer. His fingers were probably already frostbitten.

Just then, as he was about to give up, the wire came loose.

Webber hastily thrust his tingling fingers back into the glove, then clutched a fistful of the boy's coat, and kicked powerfully toward the surface.

"May I help you?" asked the nurse at the Emergency Room desk.

"Yes. What's the status of the Potter boy?"

"I'm afraid I don't have any new information. He's still in the O.R. There's a lounge around the corner if you'd like to wait."

The lounge appeared empty as he entered, then he saw a young couple huddled anxiously in the far corner. He was about to turn around and leave when Sergeant Cheney appeared in the doorway with two cups of steaming coffee.

"Mr. and Mrs. Potter, this is Officer Webber, the diver who rescued your son."

At that moment, he would have enjoyed punching Cheney in the mouth.

Mr. Potter, a thin and wiry man, jumped up and rushed at Webber with outstretched hands. "How can we ever thank you, Officer Webber?" he said.

"I certainly appreciate your gratitude, but I really only did what I was trained to do."

"You risked your own life to save Joey. I'd say that's the definition of a hero," replied Potter as he coaxed Webber toward his wife.

Although she was surely no older than thirty, at this moment Mrs. Potter looked haggard and frail. Webber reached out to shake the woman's hand, but she only clutched feebly at his wrist and wept.

"I'm afraid all this has hit my wife rather hard, Officer

Webber. She's still a bit out of it," Potter apologized.

"I understand. I'll be down in the cafeteria. Sergeant Cheney can come for me when something happens."

"No. Please don't go. Joey wouldn't have any chance at all if it weren't for you. We'd like you to be here when the doctors come out of the Operating Room."

Webber nodded reluctantly. This was exactly the type of situation he dreaded. If the doctors were unable to save their son, then all his supposedly-heroic efforts had done nothing more than give these two desperate people a false sense of hope. And their pain would be all the more torturous when that hope was shattered.

It was nearly two in the morning when a tall, middle-aged doctor dressed in hospital greens entered the lounge.

The Potters and the police officers stood up and met him in the center of the room.

The doctor introduced himself as Joshua Avram, Chief of Internal Medicine. After a short pause, he began. "I'm not quite sure how to explain this to you. We have a very unusual situation here. Although we did manage to successfully resuscitate Joey, while we were working on him our monitors detected a high concentration of an incredibly toxic chemical in his bloodstream."

"Toxic chemical?" asked Potter in amazement. "How could there be a toxic chemical in his bloodstream?"

"At this point, we're not certain, but the most probably conclusion is that the chemical was in the water where Joey drowned."

"Well, that's not life-threatening, is it? Surely there must be some type of antidote you can give him," said Mrs. Potter, her eyes pleading for the answer she desperately wanted to hear.

"We don't know yet. It's an extremely rare compound. We had a hell of a time just trying to identify it. We should know more by this afternoon."

"Where did it come from?" asked Cheney. "It's illegal to dump toxic chemicals in the river. You tell me where it came from, and I'll have somebody's ass in jail by noon."

"It's going to be very difficult to trace, Sergeant. You see, it's a binary compound made up of two chemicals which are individually quite harmless. There's no way of telling whether both chemicals even came from the same source."

"Yeah? Well, we'll find the asshole responsible for this. Don't you worry about *that*," fumed Cheney.

"We'll give you all the help we can, Sergeant."

"Can we see Joey now?" Mrs. Potter asked timidly.

"All right, but just as a precaution, we've placed him in an isolation room until we learn more about this toxin. You'll be able to see him through the window, but that's all for now."

They followed Dr. Avram out of the lounge. The long white corridor was silent except for Mrs. Potter's gentle sobbing.

The next morning, Dr. Avram suggested that Webber be given a blood test since he had also been exposed to the toxin when he went in the water to get Joey. Webber didn't feel it was necessary, but Cheney had all but made it an order.

"You'll be relieved to know that the preliminary results of your blood test have come back negative," said Avram as he sat down behind his massive walnut desk.

"I'm not surprised," replied Webber. "You said the toxin got into Joey through the water he inhaled. My diving mask covers my entire face."

"That's partially true, but the more we learn about this compound, the deadlier it becomes. This toxin could enter your bloodstream through a cut, or even a tiny scratch. I've never seen anything like it."

"What about Joey?"

The doctor shook his head sadly. "I'm afraid we've tried everything we can think of. Nothing seems to have any effect."

"He's just a little kid!" Webber exploded. "How much of this shit could he have swallowed?"

"As I said before; this is a very rare compound. We've never dealt with it before. Chemically, the toxin is almost identical to hemoglobin. In some way we don't yet understand, this substance is able to trick the body into manufacturing *it* instead of hemoglobin. Within a short time, the blood becomes saturated with toxin and can no longer carry oxygen to the tissues."

"How long does he have?"

"Three, four days. Possibly five."

Webber silently walked to the large picture window and gazed out at the crisp winter morning. A boisterous group of children were throwing snowballs at one another and sledding down the gently sloping hills in the park across from the hospital. "I want to see Joey," he said without turning around.

"The toxin also happens to be extremely contagious. We've had to keep Joey in insolation. The doctors and nurses who are caring for him are all volunteers."

"Then I'm volunteering."

Avram studied the hard, determined expression on the policeman's face for a moment, then nodded. "You'll have to sign a waiver absolving the hospital of culpability if you become infected, and you'll have to put on protective clothing before entering the room."

"Let's do it."

Webber zipped up the green cotton coveralls the nurse had given him. From the neck down, he was now fully encased in a protective layer of antiseptic garments. A string-tied cotton cap and a surgical mask completed the outfit.

Joey appeared to be sleeping when Webber entered the room. He stood for a moment, gazing at the intimidating assortment of monitoring equipment and intravenous tubing surrounding the solitary bed. The boy's skin had an unnatural bluish coloring, and his breathing was shallow and slightly labored. As Webber reached the side of the bed, Joey opened his eyes.

"Are you a new doctor?" asked the child, his small voice raspy with mucus.

"No. I'm Dave Webber. I'm the police officer who pulled you out of the river."

"Oh, yeah. My Mom and Dad told me about you," he said, slowly raising himself to a sitting position. "Are you *really* a rescue diver?"

"Yes. I learned how to dive while I was in the Navy."

"When you go underwater, does it really look like it does on those TV shows?"

"It depends. The waters of the Caribbean and the South Pacific are very beautiful, just like on TV, but the Delaware River is sort of dirty and ugly."

They talked for hours, moving easily from one subject to the next like old friends. They both seemed genuinely surprised when a nurse softly tapped on the window, then pointed to the clock on the wall above her desk.

"Will you come back?" asked Joey.

"You bet. I'll be back tomorrow around noon."

A combination of sadness and puzzlement suddenly clouded the boy's face. "You know? It really isn't very fair," he murmured.

"What isn't fair?"

"Well, I remember falling into the water. And I think I kinda remember drowning too. The water was real cold at first, but

after a minute or two, it wasn't so bad anymore. I mean, it really didn't hurt or anything. I felt like I was just going to sleep. You know?"

A lump formed in Webber's throat, and tears welled up in his eyes.

"If God wanted me to be with Him, why didn't He just let me stay drowned? Why did He want me to die this way? *This way hurts.*"

Webber reached down and gently pulled the boy into his arms. "I'm sorry, Joey," he said, choking back his emotions. "But I don't know how to answer that."

The next few days passed quickly. Webber requested a personal leave from the police department and spent as much time as he could with Joey. They watched television, played games, read stories, and discussed a thousand different topics.

Joey valiantly tried to ignore the pain while Webber was around, but it slowly worsened until the doctors were forced to prescribe an intravenous drip of morphine. The powerful narcotic rapidly sedated the small boy to the point where he could hardly move, and only barely recognized his family and friends, including Webber.

The hospital staff tried every treatment imaginable. Nothing had even the slightest effect on the relentless poison. All they could do now was try to make the young boy's final hours as comfortable as possible.

Sergeant Cheney approached Webber as he came out of the isolation room. "Morning, Dave. How's Joey today?"

"It's almost over," he replied softly.

"We think we may have found where the chemicals came from."

"Who was responsible for this?" asked Webber, his voice low and menacing.

"We don't have anything definite yet. We're still investigating. The governor even called in the EPA guys a few days ago to give us a hand."

"What you really mean is; you know who did it, but you don't have enough evidence to prosecute the bastards."

"I never said that. I know how you feel, Dave, but don't go putting words in my mouth. Okay?"

"Okay. I'm sorry. Just tell me what you've got up to this point."

"A company called United Chemicals International manu-

Binary

195

factures both chemicals at a subsidiary plant about a half-mile up Delaware Avenue from where the kid went into the river."

"So what's the problem? Can't the D.A. subpoena their records?"

"Sure he could, but it isn't necessary. So far the company's been extremely cooperative. They've let us inspect the separate storage tanks for each chemical, which are located in fenced-off areas at opposite ends of the plant, and there's no record of a spill. They can account for every drop they've manufactured in the last two years."

"That's all bullshit!" Webber shouted. "You know records can be altered, and people can be bribed to say anything you want them to."

"Calm down, Dave. We're not giving up on this. We intend to cover every angle, and look under every rock. If we can find a way to nail them, we will."

"I'm sorry. I don't mean to take it out on you. I know you'll give it your best shot."

"No need to apologize. I know how hard this has been for you."

Webber smiled sadly. "You don't know the half of it."

"There's one more thing. But before I tell you, you've got to promise not to freak out on me. Okay?"

"Okay. What is it?"

"Although they aren't acknowledging any responsibility for the toxin spill, the board of directors at United Chemicals International want to make an endowment to Drexel University to set up a **Joseph Potter Memorial Scholarship Fund**."

"Are you serious?" gasped Webber incredulously. "Man, those bastards really have some *huge* brass balls. Don't they?"

"That's what it takes to run a multimillion-dollar corporation nowadays, Dave. They've scheduled a press conference for tomorrow afternoon to make the announcement."

"You mean the Potters *agreed* to go along with this farce?"

"They said they'd allow it as long as there was no stipulations which would hinder the current investigation. Also, I think the Potters just really want Joey to be remembered, and this scholarship fund is something they could never afford to do on their own."

"I know I'll remember him."

Cheney was silent for a moment, then he continued. "The board of directors have also requested that *you* attend the news conference. They'd like you to make the presentation to the

university."

Webber shook his head disgustedly. "Leave it to a bunch of businessmen to turn a human tragedy into a public relations spectacle. Tell them I won't be there."

"Well, the police commissioner sort of already accepted on your behalf. He thought it would make the department look good."

"Then FUCK HIM!" Webber shouted. "I'm *not* going to be there."

"I know how you feel, Dave, but think about your career. You feel Joey deserves better than this. Right? Well, so do I, but this is all we can do for him now."

Both men stood in silence for several minutes, then Webber patted Cheney on the shoulder.

"All right. Tell the commissioner and the board of directors that I'll do it."

The press conference was in the Constitution Ballroom of the Adam's Mark Hotel. When Webber arrived, a public relations assistant escorted him to one of the chairs on the raised platform at the front of the room.

The area facing the platform was crowded with reporters and video cameras from all the local news stations. As a few latecomers were shown to their seats, a junior executive in an impeccably-tailored business suit stepped up to the microphone.

"Ladies and gentlemen. Please allow me to introduce Mr. Benjamin Sheldon, the chairman and chief executive officer of United Chemicals International."

Amid polite applause, a balding, middle-aged man came forward and replaced the younger man behind the podium.

"First, I'd like to thank all of you for coming here this afternoon. I only wish that our reason for being here could have been a more pleasant one.

"We are here to acknowledge the enormous bravery and inner strength of Joseph Potter, a young boy whose recent tragic accident has profoundly touched the hearts of the people of Philadelphia. We at United Chemicals International wanted to honor this courageous youngster, and also demonstrate our serious concern for the ecological welfare of the Delaware Valley, by establishing **The Joseph Potter Memorial Scholarship Fund** at Drexel University.

"At this time, I take great pride in introducing Officer David Webber of the Philadelphia Police Department, the heroic diver

who risked his own life to rescue Joey from the icy depths of the Delaware River. Officer Webber has graciously agreed to present the endowment check to Doctor Harold Elder, the Dean of Drexel University."

There was an immediate eruption of applause, then as Webber approached the podium, people began rising to their feet. The reluctant hero gave an embarrassed smile, and motioned for the crowd to sit back down.

"I want to begin by thinking Mr. Sheldon for inviting me here today. Like him, I also feel that Joey Potter deserves to be honored. But not only for his amazing courage in the face of such devastating misfortune. Joey should also be a reminder to all of us that the time has come for us to begin accepting the responsibility for our actions.

"As a people, we can no longer idly stand by and allow our industrial and government leaders to place profits and personal interests above the welfare of future generations. Our world is rapidly being poisoned. Very soon, the damage will be irreversible.

"Many changes have already begun, but we must move faster, and with much greater commitment. We have such precious little time left.

"I'm truly honored to be a part of this generous tribute to Joey Potter. And I'd especially like to thank Mr. Sheldon for making it all possible."

Webber abruptly turned to the wealthy businessman and extended his hand.

Sheldon was momentarily caught off guard. He was slightly confused by Webber's comments, which at best, had sounded like a backhanded compliment. But he was far too expert in the art of public relations to ignore the proffered hand of a local hero in front of a battery of television cameras. He fixed a deceptively sincere smile on his face, and stretched toward the policeman.

Webber solemnly gazed at his reflection in the bathroom mirror. He had stopped at the hospital on his way home from the news conference. The nurse in charge of the isolation section told him Joey had died at 9:15 that morning.

He turned on the faucet and began washing his hands. As the warm water dissolved the coating of theatrical make-up, his right hand became an unnatural bluish color.

It must have happened when he reached into Joey's mouth

to unhook the copper wire. His hand had been so numbed by the freezing water, he hadn't even realized that his index finger had been cut.

He wondered if he should tell Dr. Avram about it taking longer for the toxin to appear in the bloodstream if it entered the body through an incision.

No. The well-meaning doctor would only force him into the hospital, and that was the *last* place he wanted to be. What good would it do anyway? They hadn't been able to do anything for Joey, had they?

Webber intended to spend his few remaining days at home. Now he'd finally have time to read some of those novels he'd been collecting for the last several years. He would endure the pain as long as he could, then, he'd take his service revolver from the dresser and...

As he shut off the water, Webber glanced down and noticed the tiny clumps of dead skin under the front edges of his fingernails. Skin which he had gently scraped from Mr. Sheldon's wrist when they shook hands.

The chairman of United Chemicals International had probably never even considered the fact that he was at least partially responsible for Joey's horribly premature death. Throughout his privileged life, he had probably kept himself well-insulated from the consequences of his actions. Now, Mr. Sheldon was about to learn the irrefutable truth that life is more precious than money. That revelation would undoubtedly come as quite a shock.

Tyrophex-fourteen

Ronald Kelly

*J*asper Horne knew something was wrong when he heard the cows screaming.

He was halfway through his breakfast of bacon, eggs, and scorched toast, when he heard their agonized bellows coming from the north pasture. At first he couldn't figure out what had happened. He had done his milking around five o'clock that morning and herded them into the open field at six. It was now only half past seven, and his twelve Jersey heifers sounded as if they were simultaneously being skinned alive.

Jasper left his meal and, grabbing a twelve-gauge shotgun from behind the kitchen door, left the house. He checked the double-ought loads, then ran across the barnyard and climbed over the bobwire fence. It was a chilly October morning and a light fog clung low to the ground. Through the mist he could see the two-toned forms of the Jerseys next to the clearwater stream that ran east-to-west on the Horne property. As he made his way across the brown grass and approached the creekbed, Jasper could see that only a few cows were still standing. Most were on their sides, howling like hoarse banshees, while others staggered about drunkenly.

Good God Almighty! thought Jasper. *What's happening here?*

A moment later, he reached the pasture stream. He watched in horror as his livestock stumbled around in a blind panic. Their eyes were wild with pain and their throats emitted thunderous cries, the likes of which Jasper Horne had never heard during sixty years of Tennessee farming.

The tableau that he witnessed that morning was hideous. One cow after another dropped to the ground and was caught in the grip of a terrible seizure. Their tortured screams ended abruptly with an ugly sizzling noise and they laid upon the withered autumn grass, twitching and shuddering in a palsy of intense agony. Then the sizzling became widespread and the inner structures of the Jerseys seemed to collapse, as if their internal organs and skeletal systems were dissolving. A strange, yellowish vapor drifted from the bodily orifices of the milk cows, quickly mingling with the crisp morning air. Then the black and white skins of the heifers slowly folded inward with a hissing sigh, leaving flattened bags of cowhide lying limply along the shallow banks of the rural stream.

Numbly, Jasper approached the creek. He walked up to one of the dead cows and almost prodded it with the toe of his workboot, but thought better of it. He couldn't understand what had happened to his prime milking herd. They had been at the peak of health an hour and a half ago, but now they were all gone, having suffered some horrible mass death. Jasper thought of the stream and crouched next to the trickling current. He nearly had his fingertips in the water when he noticed the nasty yellow tint of it. And it had peculiar smell to it too, like a combination of urine and formaldehyde.

The farmer withdrew his hand quickly, afraid to explore the stream any further. He stood up and puzzled over the dozen cow-shaped silhouettes that laid around the pasture spring. Then he headed back to the house to make a couple of phone calls.

"I don't know what to tell you, Jasper," said Bud Fulton. "I can't make heads or tails of what happened here." The Bedloe County veterinarian knelt beside one of the dead animals and poked it with a branch from a nearby sourgum tree. The deflated hide unleashed a noxious fart, then settled even further, until the loose skin—now entirely black and gummy in texture—was scarcely an inch in thickness.

"Whatever did it wasn't natural, that's for sure," said Jasper glumly.

The local sheriff, Sam Biggs, lifted his hat and scratched his balding head. "That goes without saying," he said, frowning at the closest victim, which resembled a cow-shaped pool of wet road tar more than anything else. "Do you think it could have been some kind of odd disease or something like that, Doc?"

"I don't believe so," said Bud. "The state agricultural bu-

reau would have contacted me about something as deadly as this. No, I agree with Jasper. I think it must be something in the stream. The cows must have ingested some sort of chemical that literally dissolved them from the inside out."

"Looks like it rotted away everything; muscle, tissue, and bone," said Jasper. "What could do something like that?"

"Some type of corrosive acid maybe," replied the vet. He squatted next to the stream and studied the yellowish color of the water for a moment. Then he stuck the tip of the sourgum branch into the creek. A wisp of bright yellow smoke drifted off the surface of the water and, when Bud withdrew the stick, the first four inches of it were gone.

"Well, I'll be damned!" said Sheriff Biggs. "That water just gobbled it right up, didn't it?" He took a wary step back from the stream.

Bud nodded absently and tossed the entire stick into the creek. They watched as it dissolved completely and the ashy dregs washed further downstream. "I'm going to take a sample of this with me," said the vet.

The doctor opened his medical bag and took out a small glass jar that he used for collecting urine and sperm samples from the area livestock. He lowered the mouth of the container to the surface of the stream, but dropped it the moment the glass began to smolder and liquify. "What the hell have we got here?" he wondered aloud as the vial melted and mingled with the jaundiced currents, becoming as free and flowing as the water itself.

The three exchanged uneasy glances. Jasper Horne reached into the side pocket of his overalls and withdrew a small engraved tin that he kept his smokeless tobacco in. He opened it, shook the snuff out of it, and handed it to the veterinarian. "Here, try this."

Bud Fulton stuck the edge of the circular container into the creek and, finding that the chemical had no effect on the metal, dipped a quantity of the tainted water out and closed the lid. He then took a roll of medical tape, wrapped it securely around the sides of the tobacco tin, and carefully placed it in his bag. "I'll need another water sample," he told Jasper. "From your well."

Jasper's eyes widened behind his spectacles. "Lordy Mercy! You mean to say that confounded stuff might've gotten into my water supply?" He paled at the thought of taking an innocent drink from the kitchen tap and ending up like one of his unfor-

tunate heifers.

"Could be, if this chemical has seeped into an underground stream," said Bud. "I'm going to make a special trip up to Nashville today and see what the boys at the state lab can come up with. If I were you, Jasper, I wouldn't use a drop of water from that well until I get the test results."

"I'll run into town later on and buy me some bottled water," agreed Jasper. "But where could this stuff have come from?" The elderly farmer wracked his brain for a moment, then looked toward the east with sudden suspicion in his eyes. "Sheriff, you don't think—??"

Sam Biggs had already come to the same conclusion. "The county landfill. This stream runs right by it."

"Dammit!" cussed Jasper. "I knew that it would come to something like this when they voted to put that confounded dump near my place! Always feared that this creek would get polluted and poison my animals, and now it's done gone and happened!"

"Now, just calm down, Jasper," said the sheriff. "If you want, we can drive over to the landfill and talk to the fellow in charge. Maybe we can find out something. But you've got to promise to behave yourself and not go flying off the handle."

"I won't give you cause to worry," said Jasper, although anger still flared in his rheumy eyes. "You coming with us, Doc?"

"No, I think I'll go on and take these water samples to Nashville," said Bud. "I'm kind of anxious to find out what those state chemists have to say. I'm afraid there might be more at stake here than a few cows. The contamination could be more widespread than we know."

"What are you trying to say, Mr. Horne?" asked Alan Becket, the caretaker of the Bedloe County landfill. "That I deliberately let somebody dump chemical waste in this place?"

Jasper Horne jutted his jaw defiantly. "Well, *did* you? I've heard tell that some folks look the other way for a few bucks. Maybe you've got some customers from Nashville that grease your palm for dumping God-knows-what in one of those big ditches over yonder."

Sheriff Biggs laid a hand on the farmer's shoulder. "Now, you can't go making accusations before all the facts are known, Jasper. Alan has lived her in Bedloe County all his life. We've known him since he was knee-high to a grasshopper. That's why we gave him the job in the first place; because he can be trusted to do the right thing."

"But what about that stuff in my stream?" asked the old man. "If it didn't come from here, then where the hell did it come from?"

"I don't know," admitted Sam Biggs. He turned to the caretaker. "Can you think of anything out of the ordinary that might've been dumped here, Alan? Maybe some drums with strange markings, or no markings at all?"

"No, sir," declared Becket. "I'm careful about what I let folks dump in here. I check everything when it comes through the gate. And if someone had come around wanting to get rid of some chemicals on the sly, I'd have called you on the spot, Sheriff."

Biggs nodded. "I figured as much, Alan, and I'm sorry I doubted you." The lawman stared off across the dusty hundred acre landfill. A couple of bulldozers could be seen in the distance, shoveling mounds of garbage into deep furrows. "You don't mind if we take a look around, do you? Just to satisfy our curiosity?"

"Go ahead if you want," said the caretaker. "I doubt if you'll find anything, though."

Sheriff Biggs and Jasper Horne took a leisurely stroll around the dusty expanse of the county landfill. They returned to the caretaker's shack a half hour later, having found nothing of interest. "I told you I run things legitimately around here, Sheriff," Alan said as he came out of the office.

"Still could be something out there," grumbled Jasper, not so convinced. "A man can't look underground, you know."

"We can't go blaming Alan for what happened to your cows," Biggs told the elderly farmer. "That creek runs under the state highway at one point. Somebody from out of town might have dumped that chemical off the bridge. We can ride out and take a quick look."

"You can if you want," said Jasper. "I've pert near wasted half a day already. I've got some chores to do around the farm and then I've gotta run into town for some supplies." He cast a parting glance at the barren acreage of the landfill. Although he didn't mention it openly, Jasper could swear that the lay of the land was different somehow, that it had changed since the last time he had brought his garbage in. The land looked *wrong* somehow. It seemed *lower*, as if the earth had sunk in places.

Alan Becket accepted the sheriff's thanks for his cooperation, then watched as the two men climbed back into the Bedloe

County patrol car and headed along the two-lane stretch of Highway 70.

After the car had vanished from sight, a worried look crossed the caretaker's face and he stared at the raw earth of the landfill. But where there was only confusion and suspicion in the farmer's aged eyes, an expression of dawning realization shown in the younger man's expression. He watched the bulldozers work for a moment, then went inside his office. Alan sat behind his desk and, taking his wallet out of his hip pocket, fished a business card out of it.

The information on the card was simple and cryptic. There were only two lines of printing. The first read TYROPHEX-14, while the second gave a single toll-free phone number.

Alan Becket stared at the card for a moment, then picked up the phone on his desk and dialed the number, not knowing exactly what he was going to say when he reached his contact on the other end of the line.

It was about six o'clock that evening when Jasper Horne left the county seat of Coleman and returned to his farm. After catching up on his chores that afternoon, Jasper had driven his rattletrap Ford pickup to town to pick up a few groceries and several gallon jugs of distilled water. He felt nervous and cagey during the drive home. He had stopped by the veterinary clinic, but Bud's wife—who was also his assistant—told him that the animal doctor hadn't returned from Nashville yet and hadn't called in any important news. He had checked with Sheriff Biggs too, but the constable assured him that he hadn't learned anything either. He had also told Jasper that he and his deputies had been unable to find any trace of illegal dumping near the highway bridge.

However, that didn't ease Jasper's mind any. He could picture himself forgetting the grisly events of that day, maybe stepping sleepily into the shower tomorrow morning and melting away beneath a yellowish cascade of deadly well water. He forced the disturbing image from his mind and drove on down the highway.

He was approaching the driveway of his property, when he noticed that a South Central Bell van was parked smack-dab in the middle of the gravel turn-off. Jasper craned his neck and spotted a single repairman standing next to a telephone pole a few yards away, looking as though he had just shimmied down after working on the lines.

Jasper tooted his horn impatiently and glared through his bug-speckled windshield. Then man lifted a friendly hand and nodded, walking around to the rear of the van to put his tools away. The old farmer drummed his fingers on the steering wheel and glanced in his rearview mirror to see if there were any vehicles behind him. There weren't. The rural road was deserted in both directions.

When Jasper turned his eyes back to the road ahead, he was startled to see that the telephone repairman was standing directly in front of his truck, no more than twelve feet away. The tall, dark-haired man with the gray coveralls and the sunglasses smiled humorlessly at him and lifted something into view. At first, Jasper was certain that the object was a jackhammer. It had the appearance and bulk of one. But on second glance, he knew that it was a much stranger contraption that the man held. It had the twin handles of a jackhammer, but the lower part of the tool resembled some oversized gun more than anything else. There was a loading breech halfway down and, beneath that, a long barrel with a muzzle so large that a grown man could have stuck his fist inside of it.

"What in tarnation—?" began Jasper. Then his question lapsed into shocked silence as the repairman aimed the massive barrel square at the truck and fired once.

Jasper ducked as the windshield imploded. The projectile smashed through the safety glass and lost its force upon entering the truck cab, bouncing off one of the padded cradles of the gun rack in the rear window. Jasper looked up just as the cylindrical object of titanium steel landed on the seat next to him. He stared at it for a moment, not knowing what to make of the repairman's attack or the thing that he had fired into the truck. Then the old man's confusion turned into panic as the projectile popped into two halves and began to emit a billowing cloud of yellow smoke. He knew what it was the moment he smelled the cloying scent. It was the same rancid odor he had gotten a whiff of that morning at the creek.

Jasper Horne wanted to open the truck door and escape, but it was already too late. He was engulfed by the dense vapor and was suddenly swallowed in a smothering cocoon of unbearable agony. That sizzling noise sounded in his ears, but this time it came from his own body. He felt his clothing fall away like blackened cinders and his skin begin to dissolve, followed by the stringy muscle and hard bone underneath. He recalled the screams of his Jersey cows, and soon surpassed their howls

of pain…at least until he no longer had a throat with which to vent his terror.

The following morning, Bud Fulton received an urgent call from Sheriff Biggs, wanting him to come to Jasper Horne's place as soon as possible.

Bud didn't expect to find what he did when he arrived. A county patrol car and a Lincoln sedan with federal plates were parked on the shoulder of the highway. Only a few yards from Jasper's driveway was a blackened hull that looked as if it might have once been a Ford pickup truck. It contained no glass in its windows and no tires on the rims of its wheels. A knot of cold dread sat heavily in the vet's stomach as he parked his jeep behind the police car and climbed out. Slowly, he walked over to where three men stood a safe distance from the body of the vehicle. One was Sam Biggs, while the other two were well-groomed strangers wearing tailored suits and tan raincoats.

The sheriff introduced them. "Bud, these gentlemen are Agents Richard Forsyth and Lou Deckard from the FBI." Forsyth was a heavy-set man in his mid-forties, while Deckard was a lean black man with round eyeglasses.

Bud shook hands with the two, then turned his eyes back to the truck. "What happened here?" he asked Biggs. "Damn, this is old Jasper's truck, isn't it? Did it burn up on him?"

"No," said Deckard. "The truck body hasn't been scorched. The black you see on the metal is oxidation. Something ravaged both the exterior and interior of this vehicle, but it wasn't fire. No, it was nothing as simple as that."

The veterinarian stared at the federal agent, then at the sheriff. "It was that damned chemical, wasn't it, Sam? But how did it get in Jasper's truck?" He peered through the glassless windows of the truck, but saw no sign of a body inside. "Where the hell is Jasper? Don't tell me he's—"

"I'm afraid so," replied the sheriff, looking pale and shaken. "Take a look inside, but be careful not to touch anything. Agent Deckard is a chemist and he thinks the black residue on the truck might still be dangerous."

Cautiously, Bud stepped forward and peeked into the cab of the truck. Like the rubber of the tires and the glass of the headlights and windows, the vinyl of the dashboard and the cushions of the truck seat had strangely dissolved, leaving only oxidized metal. Amid the black coils of the naked springs lay a pile of gummy sludge that resembled the remains of the dead

cows. In the center of the refuse were a number of shiny objects, all metal; a couple of gold teeth, a pocket watch, the buttons off a pair of Liberty overalls, and the steel frames of a pair of eyeglasses, minus the lenses.

Bud stumbled backward, knowing that the bits of tarnished metal was all that was left of his friend and fishing buddy, Jasper Horne.

"We appreciate you bringing this to our attention, Mr. Fulton," said Agent Forsyth. "I know you must have been frustrated yesterday when the state lab refused to give you the test results of the two samples you brought in, but we thought it best to have Agent Deckard analyze them before we released any information to local law enforcement or civilians in the area. We had to be certain that they matched up with the other samples we have in our possession."

The veterinarian looked at the FBI agent. "Do you mean to tell me that this has happened before?"

"Yes," said Deckard. "Three times in the past six months. We've done our best to keep it under wraps and out of the news media. You see, this is a very delicate investigation we have going. And the chemical involved is a very dangerous and unpredictable substance."

"Do you know what it is?" Bud asked him. "This stuff that was in the creek…and in Jasper's truck here?"

"It is a very sophisticated and potent type of acid. More precisely, a super enzyme. From the tests we've ran on the previous samples, it is not biological in nature, but completely synthetic. It can digest almost anything; organic matter, paper, plastic, wood, and glass. The only thing that it has no destructive effect on is metal and stone. We believe that it was produced under very strict and secretive conditions. In fact, its development might well have been federally funded."

"You mean the government might be responsible for this awful chemical?" asked Bud incredulously.

Agent Forsyth looked a little uncomfortable. "We haven't been able to trace its origin as of yet. That's what Agent Deckard and I are here to find out. You must understand, Mr. Fulton, the United States government funds thousands of medical, agricultural, and military projects every year. It is possible that one of these projects accidently or intentionally developed this particular enzyme and that it somehow got into the wrong hands, or has been unscrupulously implemented by its manufacturer."

"Do you have any leads in the case?" asked the sheriff.

"We have several that are promising," said Deckard. "The previous incidents concerning this chemical took place in Nebraska, Texas, and Maryland. There seems to be only one solid connection between those incidents and the ones here in Tennessee."

"And what is that?"

"Municipal and rural landfills. There has always been one within a few miles of the reported incidents."

Sam Biggs and Bud Fulton exchanged knowing glances. "So old Jasper was on the right track after all," said the veterinarian. "Do you think Alan Becket might have something to do with this?"

The sheriff shook his head. "I don't know. I was sure that Alan was a straight-shooter, but maybe he isn't as kosher as we thought."

"I suggest we pick up this Becket fellow for questioning," said Forsyth. "He might just have the information necessary to wrap up this case."

The four climbed into their vehicles and headed east for the county landfill. None of them noticed that a van was following them at an inconspicuous distance. A telephone company van driven by a tall man wearing dark sunglasses.

It was seven o'clock that night when Alan Becket finally decided to come clean and tell them what they wanted to know.

Sam Biggs brought Becket from the cell he had been confined to most of the day and led him to the sheriff's office on the ground floor of the Bedloe County courthouse. Alan took a seat, eyeing the men in the room with the nervous air of a caged animal. Agent Forsyth was perched on the corner of a desk, looking weary and impatient, while Agent Deckard and Bud Fulton leaned against a far wall. Despite his veterinary business, Bud had decided to stick around and see how the investigation turned out. Jasper Horne had been a close friend of Bud's and he wanted to see that justice was done, as far as the elderly farmer's death—or murder—was concerned.

"So, are you ready to level with us, Mr. Becket?" asked Forsyth.

"Yes, I am," said the man. "I've been thinking it over and I think it would be in my best interest to tell you everything. But, believe me, I had no idea that what I did was illegal or unethical. And I certainly didn't think that it would end up killing anyone."

"Why don't you tell it from the beginning," urged the FBI man. "And take your time."

With a scared look in his eyes, Alan Becket took a deep breath and began to talk. "It happened a couple of months ago. A man came to the landfill office. He claimed to be a salesman for a chemical firm called Tyrophex-14. At first, I thought it was a pretty peculiar name for a corporation, but after he made his sales pitch, it didn't seem so odd after all. He said that his company manufactured a chemical called Tyrophex-14, and that the chemical digested non-biodegradable waste...you know, like plastic and glass. It also sped up the decomposition process of paper, fabric and wood. He said that one treatment per month in six calculated spots in the landfill would keep the volume of garbage to a minimal level. You see, after a month's worth of garbage was buried and covered over, a representive would arrive with a weird-looking contraption and inject this chemical, this Tyrophex-14, six feet into the earth. The capsule that held the chemical unleashed a gaseous cloud of the stuff, which wormed it way through the air pockets of the buried garbage and digested it."

"Let me tell you, it was a strange process. Minutes after the chemical was injected, the trash underneath seemed to simply disappear. The earth would sink, leaving empty ditches that were ready to be refilled and covered over again. In my eyes, it was a miraculous procedure and the cost was surprisingly affordable. I signed a one-year contract with the guy, sincerely thinking that I was doing it for the benefit of the community. I mean, just think of it. A perpetual landfill that digests its own garbage; a dumping ground that will never reach its projected capacity. I thought it was some sort of incredible environmental breakthrough, one that would do away with the need to find new landfill sites. The old ones could be used over and over again."

"But this miracle of modern science didn't turn out to be such a blessing after all, did it?" asked Forsyth. "At least not for Jasper Horne, and a dozen other victims that we know of."

"I'm sorry," said Becket. "I know I should have checked it out, or at least okayed it with the county commission before I signed that contract. It was just that I didn't see any need to. The monthly treatments were only a few hundred dollars, and the county allots me twice that amount for supplies and maintenance."

"How do you get in touch with this corporation?" asked

Ronald Kelly

Forsyth. "Did they leave an address or the name of the sales representative?"

"No, just a card with a phone number on it," said the caretaker. "It's in my wallet."

Agent Forsyth exchanged a triumphant glance with his partner Deckard, then turned to the county constable. "Sheriff, could you please get me Mr. Becket's wallet? I'll call the phone number into the bureau office in Nashville and have them trace it. It shouldn't be long before we know exactly who has been distributing this synthetic enzyme across the country."

Sheriff Biggs was about to open the side drawer of his desk and get Becket's personal property, when the upper pane of the office's single window shattered. "Get down!" yelled Forsyth, drawing his gun and hugging the floor. The others followed suit—all except Alan Becket. The caretaker of the county landfill merely sat frozen in his chair as a cylindrical projectile of shiny steel spun through the hole in the window and landed squarely in his lap.

"Oh God, *no!*" he screamed, recognizing the capsule for what it was. He grabbed it and was about to toss it away, when the pod snapped in half, engulfing him in a dense cloud of corrosive gas.

"Everybody out!" called Sheriff Biggs. "This way!" The other three obeyed, crawling across the room in the general direction of the office door. They could hear the crash of broken glass as two more projectiles were shot through the window. When they reached the temporary safety of the outer hallway, they got to their feet and looked back into the room. They watched in horror as the screaming, thrashing form of Alan Becket dissolved before their eyes, along with the wooden furnishings and paperwork of the sheriff's office.

Two hissing pops signaled the activation of the second and third projectiles. "Let's get out of here!" said Deckard. By the time they reached the front door of the courthouse, they could hear the creaking and crackling of the wall supports dissolving away and collapsing beneath the weight of the upper floor. They glanced back only once before escaping to the open space of town square, and the sight they witnessed was truely a horrifying one. A rolling cloud of the yellow gas was snaking its way down the hallway, leaving a trail of structural damage in its wake.

"The one who shot that stuff through the window!" Bud suddenly said. "Where is he?"

214

He was answered by the brittle report of a gunshot. He and Sam Biggs turned to see Agents Forsyth and Deckard rushing to a dark form that laid beneath a oak tree. They joined the FBI men just as they were holstering their guns and cuffing the man's hands behind his back. The tall, dark-haired man in the gray coveralls had been hit once in the calf of his right leg. Next to him laid the injection tool that the late Alan Becket had described. No one went near the thing or picked it up, afraid that they might accidently trigger another lethal dose of Tyrophex-14.

A moment later a thunderous crash sounded from behind them and they turned. The Bedloe County courthouse had completely collapsed, its lower supports chemically eradicated by the spreading cloud of vaporous enzyme. All that was left were bricks and blackened file cabinets. As for the destructive mist that had reeked the havoc, it drifted skyward and dissipated in the cool night air, soon becoming diluted and harmless.

"Well, we finally got the story," called the voice of Richard Forsyth. "And, believe me, it turned out to be a lot worse than we first suspected."

Sam Biggs and Bud Fulton looked up from their coffee cups as the two FBI agents entered the lounge of the federal building. It was almost midnight and the pair had been at it for hours, interrogating the man who been responsible for the deaths of Jasper Horne and Alan Becket. From the weary, but satisfied expressions on their faces, the county sheriff and the rural vet could tell that they had finally cracked the killer's shell and gotten the information they wanted.

Forsyth and Deckard got themselves some coffee and sat down at the table. "First of all, the killer's name is Vincent Carvell," said Forsyth. "He's a white-collar hitman; a trouble-shooter that hires out to major corporations and takes care of their dirty business. And it seems that his latest client paid him very generously to help keep Tyrophex-14 a big secret."

"Exactly who was this client?" asked Bud.

"A major corporation whose name you would instantly recognize. We would reveal it, but unfortunately we can't, due to security risks," said Forsyth apologetically. "You see, this corporation manufactures some very well-known products. In fact, it is responsible for thirty percent of this country's pharmaceutical and household goods. What the public doesn't know, is that its research and development department also does some government work on the side. Mostly classified projects for the

Tyrophex-Fourteen

215

military." The older agent sipped his coffee and looked to Deckard, passing the ball to him.

"Although we can't give you the intimate details," continued Deckard, "we can give you the jist of what Tyrophex-14 is all about. You see, this corporation was doing some work for the Defense Department. Their scientists were attempting to develop an enzymatic gas to be implemented by the armed forces. It was originally intended to be used for chemical warfare. The President gave his okay for the project during the crisis in the Middle East, mostly in response to Saddam Hussein's willingness to use chemical gas against our troops. But the Defense Department pulled the plug on the project when the corporation's scientists perfected a gas that dissolved any type of matter, organic or otherwise, with the exception of metal and stone. Tests showed that it was very unstable and difficult to control, so the project was quickly terminated and hushed up."

"But what the Defense Department didn't know," said Forsyth, "was that this corporation had already produced quite a large quantity of this destructive chemical, which had been named Tyrophex-14. They did a battery of tests, unbeknownst to the federal government, to see if it had any practical commercial use. And, obviously, they believed they had found it. Maybe their intentions were good at first. Maybe they actually believed that they had discovered a solution to the earth's garbage problem. But, ultimately, they failed to seek the proper approval and chose to market it covertly. That was when the unstable properties of Tyrophex-14 got out of control…and began to kill innocent people."

"And they hired this hitman to hush things up?" asked Sheriff Biggs. "He killed Jasper Horne and Alan Becket, just to cover this corporation's tracks?"

"Yes, and he would have killed us too, if we hadn't escaped from the courthouse. Carvell figured he could erase the threat of discovery if the investigators and the evidence vanished in a cloud of Tyrophex-14."

The thought of having come so close to death cast an uneasy silence over the four men. They thought of the blackened hull of Jasper's pickup truck and the rubble of the Bedloe County courthouse, and thanked God that they hadn't fallen victim to that corrosive monstrosity that had been conjured from the union of raw elements and complex chemical equations.

A couple of nights after the collapse of the county court-

house, Bud Fulton sat alone in his den, stretched out in his recliner and sipping on a beer. The room was dark and the nightly news was playing on the television, but he wasn't really paying very much attention to what transpired on the 25-inch screen. Instead, he thought of the phone call he had received at the clinic that day. It had been Sheriff Biggs, filling him in on the results of the FBI's midnight raid on the shadowy corporation responsible for manufacturing the deadly chemical gas known as Tyrophex-14.

Sam had told him that the raid had taken place discreetly and that it would remain a secret matter, solely between the federal government and their unscrupulous employee. The FBI had failed to say what sort of steps would be taken to see that the project was buried and that experimentation in that particular area was never explored again. But Agent Forsyth had volunteered one last bit of information, albeit disturbing, to repay Biggs and Fulton for keeping silent on the delicate matter.

Forsyth had said that the records of the corporation had listed twenty 50,000 gallon tanks as being the extent of the chemical's manufactured volume. But when the federal agents had checked the actual inventory, only seventeen of the tanks had been found on the company grounds.

Bud drove the sordid business from his mind and tried to concentrate on the work he had to do tomorrow. He was scheduled to give a few rabies and distemper shots in the morning, after which he would head to the Pittman farm to dehorn a couple of bad tempered bulls. Somehow, the simple practices of rural veterinary seemed downright tame compared to what he had been through the night before last.

Bud finished his beer while watching the local weather and sportscast. He was reaching for the remote control, intending to turn off the set and go to bed, when the news anchor appeared on the screen again with a special bulletin. Bud leaned forward and watched as the picture cut away to a live report.

A female reporter stood next to a train that had derailed a few miles north of Memphis, Tennessee. Firemen milled behind her and the wreckage was illuminated by the spinning blue and red lights of the emergency vehicles that been called to the scene. The lady reporter began to talk, informing the viewers of the time of the train derailment, as well as the cause and extent of the damage. But Bud Fulton's attention wasn't on the woman or the story that she had to tell.

Instead, his eyes shifted to the huge tanker car that lay over-

turned directly behind her. He prayed that he was mistaken, but his doubts faded when the TV camera moved in closer, bringing the details of the cylindrical car into focus.

Bud's heart began to pound as he noticed a wisp of yellow vapor drift, almost unnoticed, from a rip in one of the tanker's riveted seams. And, on the side of the ruptured car, were stenciled a series of simple letters and numbers. To those on the scene, and in the city beyond, they meant absolutely nothing. But to Bud Fulton they were like the bold signature of Death itself.

And its name that night was Tyrophex-14.

Torrent

Mark Rainey

I used to love to watch the rain. The gray veil that shrouded the hard edges of the city, the soothing patter against the rippling window panes, the white-capped rivers that overflowed the asphalt roads; these things carried me away from the intense crush of city living, if only for a short time. My living room window overlooks the tree-lined Kedzie parkway through Logan Square, with a full view of the eastern sky, which turns a tell-tale shade of gunmetal just before the violent autumn storms that blow in from Lake Michigan.

The rain reminds me of the life Lisa and I left behind in Aiken Mill, the small town where we'd both grown up, which we sometimes felt would be the only life we'd ever know. A small country town to a restless young couple could never be more than a dead end; at least, that was our perception in those days, only a couple of years ago. Here in Chicago, dreams waited to be fulfilled, all the experiences we knew we could never have at home dangled before us with tantalizing charm. So when Lisa's father died, the last of our respective parents, we decided to leave the familiar confines of the Appalachian Mountains and venture forth into life's uncharted territory.

My poor Lisa—how I miss her. She was beautiful, in every sense of the word. Physically, she could have been a goddess, tall, raven-haired, with clear blue eyes and a disarming, wide-mouthed smile. She was outwardly shy, yet inside, self-confident and wise beyond her years—no mere country girl that the city could victimize. When we first came here, our days and nights were hectic and invigorating;

it was tough while we looked for work, but the jobs were there. We found decent employment before our money ran out, and within a few weeks, we truly felt like we'd come to the place where we belonged.

In our spare time, Lisa and I loved to walk through the labyrinthine neighborhoods, the sprawling networks of streets and alleyways that were so much a part of Chicago's complex makeup. I think both of us have always been in tune with the *aura* of a location, the special traits that blend together to make a place what it is, in more than just the physical sense. It was like that in the mountains of Virginia, too. As a child, I spent many hours, day after day, roaming the woods and learning every inch of the terrain within several miles of my house. There was something romantic in growing close to the surrounding world, a feeling that was renewed as we became familiar with the city.

But it doesn't seem so long ago that the rains began and forced us indoors. They came in the spring, after several days of silver-gray skies and oppressively heavy air. I remember Lisa saying, "Look, John, it's the same kind of sky that we used to have in the mountains before a thunderstorm." And it was true, but now there was never any thunder. Just days of rain, great torrential downpours that virtually flooded the city. The street where we lived turned to tumultuous rapids, completely impassable by automobile. A few times, we lost our electricity, but Lisa and I never minded; we just lit candles when it got dark and fixed peanut butter sandwiches when we got hungry. We'd spend many evenings making love by candlelight, our passions made stronger by the sense of confinement the rains instilled in us.

Of course, the wet weather passed, and the summer began hot and arid. But by late July, the rains came again, this time with renewed fury, bringing fierce winds with them. I'd sit by the bay window of our flat and watch the gray sheets come down, soaking the trees that lined the street below. You seldom saw people out and about when it rained; I thought perhaps they might feel as Lisa and I did—warm, secure and happy, soothed by the sound of water thumping on the roof of the building and pattering on the windowpanes.

It seems the city people didn't share our feelings.

After a full week of the deluge, the news told stories about the good people of our town beginning to lose patience—sometimes in violent ways. Folks cooped up in their homes began to assault each other, some resulting in deaths. A number of par-

ents killed their children, and in one instance, a six-year-old girl set her parent's bed on fire while they were sleeping in it. I didn't understand what was happening—or looking back, I think I just didn't want to accept such ugliness from the place that I had idealized in my own mind. Lisa said the city people had no consideration for nature, and had not learned to live under harsh circumstances like we had in the mountains.

"They're weak," she told me with a cold, new-found cynicism. "If anything interrupts their lives, even something as simple as a lot of rain, they turn violent. People who live only for money really don't know how to live at all, do they?"

She was right. And yet, I sensed there was something deeper, more menacing in the violence that brewed around us. Six weeks ago, our power went out and stayed off. We got no more news, and even our battery-powered radio couldn't pick up any stations. The newspaper stopped coming after running a story that said, "Storm fronts crossing the midwest bring destruction and death." Even the small towns seemed to be suffering, and I could only wonder what it would have been like back in Aiken Mill. For the first time, I began to feel homesick.

Of course, I've been referring to Lisa in the past tense as if she were dead. That's not the case, though in a very sad way, it would seem better if she were. She's almost starved to death, and it's reached the point where I can no longer take care of her. I hear her crying so much of the time, and I think she wishes I had the nerve to end her misery.

You see, she lost her eyes in the blinding rain. One afternoon, she left for the store to buy us some food and to see if there might be some news about the storms. From our bay window I watched her walking into the downpour toward the grocery store down the block, but it only took a couple of minutes before she vanished altogether. When she came back, she was screaming, and she's never again spoken a rational word.

I do understand it now. I'm tired, and weak, and hungry, and I really do hate what the city people have done to the rain. The trees are all bare, even though it hasn't gotten cold yet—it will soon enough, I know. I saw a man yesterday going out into the torrent, and he hadn't gone far when he started screaming, just like Lisa had. He began to run, then fell in the street, thrashing in the deep water that flowed like a stream. Even through our closed windows, I could hear him crying and screaming like a tormented schoolgirl. I saw his face turn bright red and what I thought was water running down his cheeks. It wasn't—it

Mark Rainey

was his eyes, which had melted. Soon, his whole face had mostly dissolved, and there he lay, a wheezing skull-head who kicked for a couple of minutes and finally went limp.

I don't want to starve here, and I don't know how much longer I can take my poor wife's moans. The rains still don't show any signs of letting up, for the sky is just as leaden as it was on the day it all began. Perhaps it'll be best if she and I take one last walk outdoors, and enjoy our memories of the old days when the rain wasn't acid and Lisa could see the beauty of the earth and we could share our love, in our own special way.

I no longer like to watch the rain, because I see things moving out there, and I don't think they're human. Not any more.

Toxic Shock

Rick Hautala

1.

The police line could barely hold back the surging crowd as Sheila Dobson climbed out of the police van and started up the walkway toward the Pro-Choice Clinic. Hot, wind-blown rain misted in shimmering sheets against the glare of the sodium arc streetlights. Wooden barricades had been set up along the sidewalk with flashing red warning lights that illuminated the scores of angry faces, seen only dimly through the protective face masks that all of the protesters were wearing. The area looked like a vision straight out of Hell, rather than the quiet side street in downtown Philadelphia it had been…at least until the Pro-Choice Clinic opened.

Sheila sensed the anger in the eyes tracking her as she walked quickly up the stairs to the front door. With each step, her legs threatened to collapse underneath her. She kept telling herself to focus straight ahead but couldn't stop from glancing at the crowd. Handmade signs and posters were raised high in clenched fists, waving and bouncing in time with shouts and jeers.

MURDERER!

KILLER!

PROTECT THE RIGHT TO LIFE!

AB-SOLUTION IS THE ONLY SOLUTION!

Sheila couldn't tell if some of the words on the signs had purposely been drawn to look like splashes of blood, or if the burning rain was washing away the cheap red poster paint the protesters had

used. One of the ministers leading the group wore his vestments outside of his protective rubber coat. The cloth was pitted with small burn holes that smoldered as he waved his arms overhead, leading the group in a chanting song. The voices of the singers were drowned out by louder, random shouts directed at Sheila and the cordon of police, but all of their voices were muffled by the steady hiss of falling rain and the peoples' weather-proof face masks. Sheila caught only fragments of what they were yelling.

"Repent now, sister!"

"Respect the life that's been given to you!"

"It's not too late to save yourself!"

"Hell is for sinners—like *you*, you bitch!"

Sheila grew dizzy, trying to focus on the throng of glistening face masks that ringed her, looking like some horrible undersea invasion.

"Miss Dobson...?" a uniformed officer said.

Standing in the shelter of the doorway, he looked up from his plastic-encased clipboard. His voice was distorted by the clear plastic face mask and hood that covered his head.

Unable to tear her gaze away from the crowd, Sheila simply nodded. The impulse to rush to the policeman for protection was almost overwhelming, but she took a deep, steadying breath and squared her shoulders.

"Yes—"

"If you'll step right this way please, Miss Dobson—"

The officer stood to one side and reached for the door handle. He was just about to swing the door open when a fist-sized rock sailed over Sheila's head and shattered the glass. The crowd roared its approval as broken glass showered the steps like hundreds of diamonds. Sheila ducked behind the officer as he spun around and raised the riot-gun at his side. Hemmed in by the crowd, the line of policemen fell back closer to the building, their riot-guns poised and ready.

"Don't take it personally, mam," the officer said. "Most of these asshol—excuse me, most of these *people* don't even know what they're protesting."

Sheila nodded, telling herself there wasn't a tight quaver in the man's voice.

"I think they just ain't got anything better to do on a shitty— I mean, on a *lousy* night like this, you know?"

"Oh, really?" Sheila said. "I'd think they'd just as soon stay at home to get out of this horrible rain, if nothing else."

She glanced up at the night sky, which glowed with an eerie green haze of pollutants and neon light. Rainwater beaded up on her face mask and ran down the front of her rubber raincoat.

"Actually, I doubt if many of 'em even *have* a home, m'am," the officer said, narrowing his gaze as he looked at her steadily. Sheila squirmed, feeling as though it was written on her forehead in bright red letters that she, too, was one of the thousands of homeless people in the inner city. Even through the lights reflecting off his face mask, Sheila could read in his expression the thought that was most likely echoing in his mind—

You're so young, so pretty...What a pity that you've decided to do something like this!

But wasn't it obvious that she didn't care any more? Why else would she be coming here? Like a lot of the people out there in the crowd and most of the homeless people she knew, she was long past either caring or hoping that her life could improve.

She could have easily entered the building through the gaping hole in the glass door, but the officer unlocked the door, snapped the door latch, and held it open for her.

"You can leave your protective gear in the receptacle there on the right," he said mechanically. "Doctor Scott's office is straight down the hall, the last door to your left."

Sheila made momentary eye contact with him and smiled briefly, then lowered her gaze as she stepped into the brightly lit corridor. As soon as she was inside the building, another roar of outrage burst from the crowd. Several voices rose louder, and then a shrill scream filled the night, followed by a short, thumping burst of gunfire.

She shucked off her coat and face mask, and deposited them in the glass-lined barrel beside the door. Then, taking a shuddering breath, she started down the hall, past the row of nervous-looking armed guards.

2.

The bright fluorescent lights brought tears to her eyes. She willed herself not to think about what might be happening outside and reminded herself that the crowd wasn't there to protest her personally; it was just that she hadn't been ready to face such open, violent hostility. The doctor she had spoken with briefly at the Public Health Clinic yesterday had warned her about the Right-to-Lifers who gathered around the Pro-

Rick Hautala

Choice Clinic day and night to jeer and threaten anyone who entered. She knew she should have foreseen this when he had insisted on a police escort for her to the Clinic, but the most demanding thought tumbling around inside her head was, *How can these people say they respect life and want to protect it when they act like such animals themselves?*

Her footsteps faltered as she moved down the corridor, her heels clicking like hatchet chops on the linoleum. The harsh, white lighting and the stinging antiseptic smell frightened her even more than the hot, acid rain or the angry mob outside. She tried not to think about what she was doing but—obviously—couldn't. The only other clear thought she had was that the tiny life growing like a cancer inside her had to be terminated—now!

Tonight!

Before she could think and fret about it any longer.

She was almost nauseous with the thought of another human being—her child—being born into a world like this. If she had even a slender hope that the world would eventually get better, she might consider carrying her baby to term, but not now...not with the world going to hell the way it was!

"Miss...uh, Dobson?"

The voice caught her unawares, making her squeal and jump as she looked up. Lost in her own thoughts, she had arrived at the end of the corridor. An elderly man with thin wisps of white hair was looking at her from behind a desk stacked high with papers and folders. His eyeglasses reflected the bars of light overhead as he pushed himself to his feet and came around the desk to greet her.

Not knowing what to do, Sheila fumbled inside her tunic for the legal forms the doctor had told her she would have to present at the Pro-Choice Clinic. She hadn't read through them, as she had promised she would. She hadn't been able to. In the eighteen miserable years she had spent living on the streets, what use had she ever found for reading? Reading would never have kept her warm at night or gotten her a hot meal or stopped all those desperate, disease-ridden men from having their way with her in the back alleys. She knew what an "abortion" was, even if she didn't know the exact details of the procedure, and that was all she needed to know. The doctor at the pre-natal clinic had tried to counsel her, telling her over and over how precious life was, so much, in fact, that he had started sounding like one of those Right-to-Life protesters outside; but she had cut him off, insisting that she knew *exactly* what she was doing, and nothing was going to make her change her mind.

"Look, I don't need a sermon, all right?" she had told him before scrawling her mark on the necessary legal forms. "I'm happy just knowing there will be one less miserable person living in this horrible world, all right?"

He had finally agreed with her, witnessed her signature, and sent her on her way after making her promise that she would at least read through the papers so she would know what she was getting into.

But, of course, she hadn't. She hadn't even tried to find someone who could have read them to her, and now—here she was, ready to follow through on her decision.

"I'm Doctor Scott," the elderly man said, extending a frail-looking hand which Sheila took and shook gently. His hand was the first warm, dry thing she had felt in days, and the touch instantly brought tears to her eyes.

No! she told herself. *It's just the bright lights that are doing that!*

"There, there," Doctor Scott said, gently patting the back of her hand. Sheila felt an impulse to hug him but pushed it back as she squared her shoulders and handed him the legal papers.

"Yes…yes, everything seems to be in order," he whispered, nodding as he rifled through the pages. He walked back into his office, slipped the forms into the top envelope on his desk, then rejoined her in the hall.

"Would you like to take a moment or two for some coffee or a cigarette or something?"

"No," Sheila said, biting her lower lip and shaking her head. Her voice sounded almost like a dog, barking.

"If you'd like, you know, we have several ministers of different religious denominations on call who can counsel with you if you'd—"

"You mean like the man leading the chant outside?" She shook her head. "No thanks!" She studied Doctor Scott a moment, then said, "You know, I can see it in your eyes. You want to talk me out of this, don't you. You want to get me to reconsider my choice; but believe me, I know what I'm doing, okay? I've made up my mind, and I ain't gonna change it, so let's just do it and get it over with, all right?"

"Sure, sure," Doctor Scott said, smiling wanly. He hesitated a moment as if about to say more, then nodded and, taking her by the arm, directed her to the closed door across the hall from his office.

3.

Sheila almost fainted when he pushed open the door to reveal a vast array of medical equipment. She started to say something but cut herself off when Doctor Scott gently directed her over to the center of the room where there was a large, padded chair surrounded by banks of monitors and other medical equipment. She had no idea what any of this stuff was for.

"You can undress behind the screen there and put this on." Doctor Scott said, handing her a thin cotton hospital gown that opened in the back.

Sheila shivered as she walked behind the screen, hurriedly undressed, and slipped on the gown. It did nothing to cut the chill in the room. She smoothed the cloth down over her swollen abdomen, which stuck straight out, looking like she had swallowed a watermelon seed that had grown large inside her. Her teeth were chattering when she came out from behind the screen and, hugging her arms across her breasts, walked over beside the chair.

"Try to make yourself comfortable," Doctor Scott said, nodding toward the chair as he busied himself arranging some of the equipment. "I'll only be a moment."

He went to the sink and started scrubbing his hands with disinfectant soap while Sheila took a seat in the chair, settling her bare butt onto the cold, padded cushion. The gown flapped open on the sides as she slipped her feet into the leather stirrups of the footrests. There were also straps on the arms of the chair, but she kept her hands out of them, hoping that she wouldn't need to use them. There was a wide gap in the front of the seat that made it look a little like a toilet seat. An electric current of fear passed through her, and she found herself wishing that she had talked at least a little bit more with the doctor at the pre-natal clinic before coming over here. Not knowing exactly what to expect was making her stomach all tight and tingly with tension.

"I'm sorry, but I have to secure your arms, too," Doctor Scott said mildly.

"Do you really?" Sheila asked, her voice cracking.

"'Fraid so," Doctor Scott said, nodding as he flipped open the straps so she could place her arms inside the restraints. He pulled them snugly shut and buckled them, but not so tight

that it hurt. Then he pulled the belts on the footrests over her bare feet. The icy ripple of nervousness spread up from her stomach to her chest, but as if to convince herself that she was doing the right thing, she looked down at her swollen stomach and sneered.

"Say goodbye to a life of misery," she whispered.

"There, are you all set?" Doctor Scott asked as if he hadn't heard her comment. "Now, the first thing I have to do is give you an injection."

He produced a hypodermic needle, held it up to the light, and then pulled up Sheila's left sleeve, daubed her skin with alcohol, and slid the needle into an exposed vein. For a moment, there was a sharp sting like an insect bite; then a warm flooding sensation spread underneath her skin. It seemed to take only seconds before a wave of soft dizziness swept over her, making the lights in the room go softly out of focus.

"It's not too late now, is it—?"

"What, to change your mind?" Doctor Scott said, frowning with concern. "No, as long as you haven't had the second shot, we can still—"

"No, no—I mean for me to be doing this," Sheila said groggily. "Tin-pan Man, a friend of mine on the street, told me that— you know—that it was kinda dangerous to have an abortion this far along."

"Oh, no—certainly not," Doctor Scott said. "Actually, we prefer to wait until the third trimester. It makes it all that much easier, really."

He grabbed some electrode leads and, after smearing them with a thick, clear jelly, lifted the edge of her gown and taped them to her stomach. After adjusting the dials on some monitors until he was satisfied, he walked behind the chair. Sheila heard a clatter of glass and a high *squeak-squeaking* sound as he rolled a cart over beside the chair. Glancing out of the corner of her eyes, she saw a large bottle which was filled with a clear, yet heavy-looking liquid, like the fruit syrup they serve sometimes at the soup kitchen. Several metal bars were sticking out from the top lid and were connected by wires to some of the machinery.

"Whaz' that?" Sheila asked, surprised by the thick drag in her voice.

"Oh, just part of the preparations," Doctor Scott said. "You don't have to concern yourself with it." He covered one of her hands with both of his, squeezing almost desperately. "Tell me—

how are you feeling?"

Sheila shrugged but found the effort to be almost too much. The light in the room was growing dim and fuzzy around the edges, shattering into glowing splinters. Every sound she or the doctor made was oddly magnified. The sound of her own breathing was ragged and irritating, like ripping paper.

"If you're sure you want to continue..." Doctor Scott said.

Sheila barely reacted when he took another hypodermic needle from the cabinet, filled it with a clear liquid from a vial, and then slipped it into her arm. This time there was absolutely no pain, but within seconds, a strange leadenness embraced her body. She knew it was futile to try, but if she had, she was positive she wouldn't have been able to raise even her pinky finger. Her lower jaw felt like it was made of iron when she said, "This...won't...hurt...now...will...it?"

Doctor Scott smiled reassuringly and said, "Oh, no, not at all. The immediate pain is over. There's also a sedative in the first injection to calm you down."

He walked over to the intercom beside the door, pressed the button, and said into the speaker, "Nurse Morgan. Please report to O.R. 22." Then he went to one of the cabinets, pulled open a drawer, and withdrew a scalpel. After peeling off the protective plastic covering, he held it up to the light, turning it back and forth in his hand so the blade caught the light. The reflection hurt her eyes like a sudden bolt of lightning. Her throat felt like it was packed with sand when she asked, "What's...that...for?"

Doctor Scott looked at her, his bushy eyebrows rising with concern.

"Why, to cut the baby out, of course," he said.

His voice seemed to be coming from the far end of an echoing tube. It took several seconds for the meaning of what he'd said to penetrate Sheila's mind. Realization dawned slowly, rolling over her like the deep, steady growl of thunder.

"Didn't they review the entire procedure with you?" Doctor Scott asked.

Sheila wasn't sure if her head even moved, but she tried her damndest to shake it back and forth in denial.

"I—well, you see, that first shot I gave you was to relax you, for the operation, you see," he said. "The second needle was the suicide solution."

"Su...i...cide?"

"Yes...of course," Doctor Scott said. "Now, all that's left to

do, once Nurse Morgan gets here, is to cut open your uterus and take out your baby."

Sheila felt a distant rush of sadness and a dull stirring of fear as she stared up into the doctor's glistening eyes. She tried to lick her lips and speak but couldn't.

"But you don't have to worry," Doctor Scott went on. His voice had a deep, soothing buzz to it. "You're way past feeling much of anything now. You can die, assured that your baby will continue to develop and be maintained by the best life support systems available until he's ready to be 'born.' Then we'll find a suitable family for...was it him or her? Well, no matter." He shrugged and shook his head. "I'll see what it is in just a moment."

"But...I...don't..."

"What?" Doctor Scott said. He glared at her, his face an exaggerated mask of surprise. Sheila thought he looked a little like an enraged demon but attributed it the drugs. "Do you mean to tell me that you actually thought we were going to destroy your *fetus*?" His expression hardened into one of deepening concern. "When you first came in here, I asked you if you knew what you were getting into. Don't tell me you don't know about the government's changes in the abortion policy! It's been on the holovid news every night."

Sheila tried to speak, but she had completely lost the feeling throughout her body. Her eyes were wide open and staring, unblinking, up at the ceiling, which vibrated with subtle waves of light and shadow. She sensed motion behind her and wondered if the assisting nurse had entered the room.

"Surely, you must have heard about it on the news," Doctor Scott said. "Why, just two months ago, the government finally accepted the medical reports that showed that, because of an accumulation of environmental pollutants, pregnant mothers can no longer carry their babies to full term. Usually in the seventh month of gestation, all fetuses are removed from their mothers and put through a thorough detoxification in artificial wombs. You know—test tube babies. The government's policy on abortion has also been changed, so we're now required by law to save the baby and abort the mother."

Sheila was trying like hell to speak or move, but she could barely think. Her body felt as though it was encased in clear, solid plastic. She would have opened her mouth and screamed if she could have.

"Look, Miss...uh, Miss Dobson," Doctor Scott said. His voice

Toxic Shock

235

was edged with hopelessness, and his expression was one of deep regret. "I'm awfully sorry about this—this little misunderstanding, but it's absolutely too late now. That second injection I gave you is working quite fast. You'll be dead within minutes." He glanced at something behind her head and nodded. "I really must get to work now if I'm going to save your baby."

Then he began to cut.

Please

Stand By

Thomas F. Monteleone

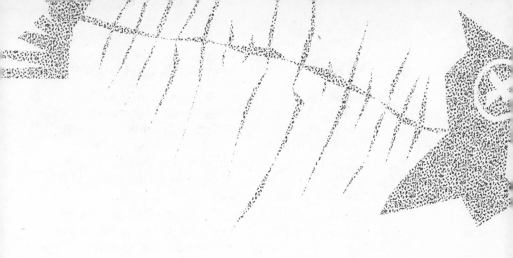

"**F**rank, what is it?" asked Lorenzo's wife, Marion.
She was sitting up in bed, as light from a half-moon filtered through curtained windows, staring at him. He had just replaced the phone to its receiver.

"That was John Wells...at the lab." Frank rubbed his eyes, trying to push the sleepiness from their corners.

"At this hour? It's almost four in the morning!"

"I know what time it is..."

"Well what did he want?"

"I don't know..." Frank slipped from the big platform bed and started to get dressed. "I've...I've got to go down there, honey."

"Now?" Marion's voice detailed her emotions. She was feeling hurt and rejected again, he could tell.

"Yes. Now. The latest results are up, and John is upset about something. He wants me to get down there right away."

"John's upset...! What about me? I'm upset too! God, Frank, that lab is like another woman in your life—worse than another woman!"

Frank smiled in the half-darkness as he pulled on his shoes. He wondered if she really meant that...

"Marion, listen—I'm sorry. But you know how important this project is. Something must really be wrong for John to call in the middle of the night."

There was only a huffy silence from the bed.

"I'll be back as soon as I can," he added as he leaned down to kiss her before running off into the night.

The November nightwind smacked his cheeks as he ran down the driveway to the new sedan—the car that was costing him more in payments each month than his first mortgage. As he climbed in behind the wheel and began the short drive through Bethesda to the National Institute of Health complex on Old Georgetown Road, he began thinking about how his life had gotten away from him.

As he approached the age of forty, he realized he was entangled in a social, economic, and cultural thicket from which the only escape would be death. His position as Assistant Director of Cancer Research at NIH sounded a hell of a lot better than it paid. There were hundreds of "assistant directors" running around the place, all struggling to pay the bills.

The bills. Jesus, he had never realized how fast a pay-check could be devoured by the financial machinery of running a family. Groceries, utilities, car payments, new shoes for the kids, new toys for the kids, tuition for the private schools, insurance premiums, doctor bills, orthodontics, credit cards, association dues, contributions, and a bunch of crap he didn't want to think about—not even mentioning the monstrous mortgage on the over-priced Montgomery County house. He couldn't save a dime if his life depended on it. They lived from check to lousy check, and he hated it.

It had been seven years since Marion had worked because they'd both agreed she should be there at home for the kids. Besides, he secretly believed that his wife didn't want to work, that she didn't want the responsibility of providing for the family. Hell, he didn't blame her...it was a sonuvabitch, that was for sure.

Money seemed like the only thing he and Marion ever argued about. His job bugged her, but she carped about the hours more or less out of duty than real concern. What really got them going was the money-fights. Frank had heard someone say that when you're poor, you only think about what money can buy you. But when you're rich, you only think about the things money can't buy you.

He laughed softly as he drove the empty suburban streets. I'd settle for those concerns for a change, he thought. I'm what they call a desperate man.

The guard waved him through to the staff parking lot and he entered the sprawling brick edifice which housed his particular lab. Frank felt torn. He needed a job that paid more money, but he knew that financial plums for medical research

were getting hard to find in the austerity-budget times of the present political regime. And of course he loved his work at NIH—he believed they would eventually make a difference, and that cancer would someday be talked about like cholera and polio.

Entering the lab, he was surprised to see his colleague, John Wells, standing by one of the desks with three other men. The strangers were dressed in dark, conservative suits. They had conventional, bland haircuts, and Frank didn't like the look of things.

"Doctor Lorenzo," said one of the Dark Suits. He smiled perfunctorily. "So good of you to come at such short notice."

"John, who are these guys?" Frank was confused, and more than a little pissed off that Wells didn't warn him about visitors in the lab.

"My name is Warren Travers," said the first man. "I'm with the FCC."

Frank nodded. He had figured as much, and he had a good idea why they were there. The bastards. "What do you want?" asked Frank.

"We've been monitoring the direction and intent of your research since its earliest stages," said Travers. "Now that you've reached definitive results, we thought it would be best to step in."

"What the hell does that mean?" Frank looked at John Wells, who only shrugged slightly. Wells appeared a bit frightened by the whole confrontation.

Travers smiled. "Believe it or not, Doctor, you're not the first people to have stumbled upon the significant relationship between radio and television broadcast signals and incipient carcinoma."

"What?" Frank couldn't believe what they were telling him. It was impossible! "That's ridiculous!"

"'Fraid not," said the second man, who had been holding several thick, bound typescripts. "Here's some of the most conclusive data from the last ten years."

He threw the reports on Frank's desk where they impacted with a heavy thud. Jesus, this was getting crazy! Impossible was the only word he could think of.

"Who're you?" asked Frank as he glared at the second man.

"Brunansky. I'm with the FBI."

Frank nodded. "Yeah, right. I should've figured that."

He looked at the third man, who remained silent. He seemed

Thomas F. Monteleone

to be dressed a bit more richly, more stylishly. He was, no doubt, the representative from the State Department, or maybe that quaint little farm in northern Virginia. That would make the triumvirate complete.

"We've got to shut this operation down, Doctor. I think you know that," said Travers.

"Really? I thought you guys were here to give me the Nobel Prize."

"I can understand your feelings, Doctor," said Travers. "But there's no other way. Radio and Television signals cause cancer. We now know it's an irrefutable fact. That's the only reason your project was allowed to continue—so we could confirm the earlier studies. Or, maybe, the outside chance your data could refute them…"

"But you didn't, so we've got to put a lid on it—now. The public will never know," said Brunansky, the FBI man.

"And of course, we certainly aren't going to stop broadcasting. Civilization would come to a halt," said Travers. "And there will be further studies—in secret of course—that will try to correct the problem…"

Frank looked at them and felt a terrible anger burning his guts. Those smug bastards! Who the fuck did they think they were? He looked from one to the other, then over at his colleague. "I don't know about you, John, but these guys aren't forcing me out!"

"Frank, what're you talking about?" Wells looked at his boss with confusion.

"I'm talking about these guys don't scare me, that's what!" He looked at all three government flunkies. "I'm going to sing, gentlemen! I'm going to tell the whole dirty story. I'm talking **Sixty Minutes** and **The Washington Post** time! And if you don't like it, you'll have to get one of your CIA animals to run me off the road one night and make it look like an accident…"

Travers smiled, looked at the third man. "I'm afraid he doesn't understand. Why don't you tell him, Mark."

"Tell me what?"

"I'm Mark Reuter," said the third man. "I represent a combine—the networks, the major independents, and the cable people. Obviously, we cannot allow the results of your study to become public knowledge. But we will not try to force you into silence."

Anger still coursed hotly through Frank. He had heard Reuter's words, but had not really understood them. He stared

dumbly at the man, then over to his colleague.

"For Christ's sake, Frank!" said John Wells. "They're going to buy us off! What's the matter with you?"

He suddenly felt very opaque, very stupid and silly. Of course! Was there any other way? And here he was making doing his crusader routine...

God, did he sound like an asshole, or what?

He knew that there'd have been a time in his life when he would have spit in their faces and walked out. Just thinking of all those millions of VHF and UHF wave-forms zapping through all those unborn fetuses would have been enough to make him do it. But now, he just nodded slowly and looked at Reuter.

There was a sour taste of defeat and self-loathing in his mouth as he spoke.

"How much?" he said.

Double-Edged Sword

Barry Hoffman

He sat up in bed, instantly awake. Heard the buzz of a fly. Reached out and snared it. Felt its wings beat furiously against his palm in an effort to escape. Squashed the fucker.

Once awake, Nicholas Cage found sleep impossible. It wasn't that he wasn't exhausted, but the sounds of the night—ones he'd taken for granted just a week before—assaulted him from all sides. The cricket's shrieks were like nails across a chalkboard. The gentle breeze was like an ocean crashing on shore. A falling breath, the imploding of a house in a tornado.

He looked at his watch. He'd managed twenty minutes. A cat nap, but all he'd get that night. Tonight he envied Baker, Charles, Stansfield and Washington and wished he were with them.

Cage effortlessly maneuvered the Chinook over the lush forest. The chopper released a fine spray of a new defoliant. A gust of wind blew some of the milky white goo on the windshield, obscuring his vision.

"Goddamn stuff looks like pigeon crap," Kyle Stansfield, the chopper's navigator said. He looked down at the forest. "Doesn't look like it's doing a hell of a lot of good."

"That's the whole point of this mission, schmuck," Cage said, a wide smile playing across his leathered face. "They get all this high-tech shit and we test it out. If it works as advertised the enemy's got no place to hide. If not," he shrugged, "we'll be trying something new next week. Got a problem with that?"

"Hell no. Long as the pay's good I'll do whatever they ask. Just wind me up and set me loose."

They both laughed.

Cage had been at war since being drafted in the mid-sixties. Instead of getting suspended for beating the crap out of some kid at school he was rewarded for his bravado. A grunt in Vietnam, he'd quickly caught the attention of superiors. He had no morals, no scruples, no humanity. He was a fighting machine; courageous, loyal and unfaltering. And his mama hadn't raised no fool. A borderline student in school, he'd nevertheless managed to master his enemy's native tongue within two months. It was simply a matter of survival and Nicholas Cage, if nothing else, was a born survivor. He'd also learned money was to be had—lots of money—if one was industrious enough.

His only problem, which had kept him from career advancement, had been his disdain for authority. It was the guys at the front who knew the enemy and given the chance to fight the war on his own terms he had no doubt of the outcome. But orders filtered down from pansies who considered Vietnam no different from Korea or Nazi Germany, or from the new breed who'd never set foot in a rice paddy. Asses one and all. So, he had no real allegiance other than to himself and his men. He was a warrior, and he had a job—with his resourcefulness a damn good paying one at that.

Twenty minutes into the mission the chopper began to lose power. It wasn't the first time. It got so he was surprised—even a bit disappointed—when everything went according to Hoyle. It had happened in Nam, in Angola and in half a dozen countries he'd waged war for money the past twenty years. Now, as then, he didn't panic. While he attempted to trace the cause of the trouble, Stansfield scoured the land below for a suitable place to land if the need arose.

"There's a lake at four o'clock," he shouted above the whir of the blades, just as they locked. They floated down through a fine mist of defoliant. Stansfield donned a pair of goggles as the syrupy glop pelted him.

"Tell the others we're going to ditch," Cage said, speaking as if this were an everyday occurrence. He banked right and a minute later they were down…all in one piece. All par for the course, Cage thought. A minor inconvenience. All in all a welcomed diversion from the routine.

As they scuttled out of the wreck Cage noted the two drums of defoliant had ruptured, spilling their contents into the lake.

He wondered idly if it would kill the fish or turn them into some weird mutation scientists would scratch their heads over years later.

As soon as they settled, Baker and Charles, without hesitation began lugging weapons and supplies out of the chopper. Washington, the last of the crew, rigged a charge to blow the downed copter so the enemy couldn't scavenge it for parts. Silent and efficient, just as they'd practiced dozens of times in case the worst came to pass.

Sloshing through the milky scum that spread across the water, Cage felt a thousand needles prick his skin and just for a second panic rose within him. He felt his pores intravenously absorbing the poison and wondered if his luck had finally run out. He stared into the sludge and saw a school of piranhas close in, make for his leg and nibble every last ounce of meat. In a frenzy they inched their way up and feasted on his genitals, then attacked the meat of his belly. He felt himself sucked under and they were at his face, ripping his left eye out of its socket; the teeth slicing through his ears as they made for his brain. With his one good eye he glimpsed himself in the reflection of the chopper and saw a skeleton—the kind they displayed in school when they made you memorize the names of all your bones.

"You all right, Nick?"

Cage started at Stansfield's voice and realized, with relief, he'd had some sort of hallucination. He forced himself forward and pulled himself out of the water onto the lush green carpet that bounded the lake. He looked at Stansfield and saw the terror in his eyes, and was certain they were a mirror image of his own. He heard Baker, Charles, then Washington scamp out of the water breathless and knew they hadn't been spared either. Now was not the time, though, to compare notes.

The soldier—the machine—took over; the instinct for survival that had served him so well before.

"Let's get the fuck out of here before she blows. Soon as she goes we'll have a lot of uninvited company on our tail. Baker, you take point. Move fast, but watch out for booby traps."

They moved silently into the forest, Cage checking his watch for the explosion, which never came. Six minutes…seven minutes…9…13…

"Hold it. Something's wrong. Washington, you didn't fuck up did you?"

The lanky black man smiled. "No mastuh," he said with mock

condescension. "I didn't fuck up. I *never* fuck up." The last words were tinged with pride and a bit of arrogance.

Cage knew if the chopper hadn't blown it wasn't Washington's fault. Knew, too, he didn't have to apologize. An apology would be an affront; give credence, in some perverse way, to the possibility the other man *had* indeed screwed up.

"Any idea what went wrong?"

Washington was all business now. No shucking and jiving; no phony Southern plantation accent. "Well, sir, I can't be certain without going back, but push come to shove I'd say that defoliant we were carrying ate away at the wires. The shit's like acid when it's released." He held up his hand. It was puckered and blistered, as if he'd dipped his hand in a pot of boiling coffee. "Burned right through my glove. Ate my hand till it got its fill and stopped all of a sudden. Reckon it did the same to the wires. You wanting me to go back, sir?"

Cage looked at Washington's hand and remembered the piranhas back at the lake. He saw Washington's eyes widen as he awaited his decision. He didn't think the man would go back even if ordered to, but he wasn't about to test the hypothesis. Something had happened to all of them back there and it was best to get as far away as possible.

"That chopper's not going to be much good to anyone. We've got about two hours of daylight left." He smiled, wanting to ease the tension. "Let's make like hockey players and get the puck out of here."

He could sense their relief. Instinct had served them all well or they wouldn't have survived as mercenaries this long. He knew their instincts were in tune with his. Flee. Vacate the premises. Make tracks *but* don't go back to the copter, they'd screamed at him in silence. And, dammit, he thought, they were right.

As they made their way through the lush foliage, backtracking the way they'd come in the chopper, they noticed a change— imperceptible at first, but more apparent with every step they took. The vegetation was dying before their eyes. No, not dying—being devoured from within. Leaves cascaded on their heads as if it were Fall in Pennsylvania. The forest floor was littered with dying leaves. They curled, as if they had cramps from eating something rotten, and turned to powder in a matter of seconds. It was like looking at the life cycle of fauna with time lapse photography. There was a rancid smell in the air, like rotting eggs.

A mile further the jungle resembled a petrified forest. Denuded trees stood glistening in the sunlight as if they were covered with varnish; stripped not only of leaves, but bark as well.

The insects, which they'd become accustomed to sharing space with, had perished or fled. Cage, taking in the sterility around him, thought this was how the Earth would look following a nuclear holocaust. He wanted to flee, but the carnage stretched as far as the eye could see.

"The defoliant," Stansfield said. "What in God's name have we done?"

"Our job, Kyle." It sounded like a cliche, even to him, but if the truth be told, they had done what they'd intended. No enemy could hide here now. They'd be spotted from above in seconds and slaughtered. The defoliant was a rousing success. So, he wondered, why did he feel like a butcher.

Half an hour later darkness began to steal the day. Cage decided they'd gone far enough. Even if the chopper had been found no one could sneak up on them without being seen or heard in the eerie stillness.

"Let's make camp here. Another day and we'll be at the river and clear sailing. Charles, you take first watch. Baker will relieve you as soon as he's eaten."

Stansfield dug into his C-rations and uttered a cry of disgust. "What the fuck is this?"

For the first time since the crash Cage looked closely at his friend—the only member of the team who'd been with him from Nam—and was startled by the transformation. Even at forty-five Stansfield's face had been baby smooth. Cage bought him a razor for this birthday each year, a running joke, as a blade could last a month with the peach fuzz he sprouted. Now his face was mottled and pitted; sores oozing sickly white pus. His close-cropped blond hair had fallen out in clumps. His raw scalp looked like he had a bad case of ringworm. His breath had the fetid odor of someone who'd just gotten out of bed. Was the defoliant eating at him from within? Cage wondered.

Stansfield held up the can for the rest to see. The top had been eaten away and whatever had been inside was dry powder.

Washington held up his canteen. "No water either. Damn metal's been eaten through."

Baker produced some beef jerky, wrapped in cellophane. "This looks okay. Think we can eat it, sir?" he asked, doubt heavy in his voice.

Cage wanted to ask him how the fuck he should know, but knew better. Individuals who abhorred authority one and all, they now looked to him, their superior in rank, for answers. He'd best provide some or they'd spook and be of no use at all. He took out his own beef jerky, checked the cellophane, looking for any sign of contamination. Whatever had eaten away at the metal seemingly had no effect on plastic. He tore his open and took a bite on the leathery contents.

The others looked at him, waiting for him to retch or go into spasms. When all he did was take a second bite they followed suit.

In the midst of their snack Ezra Charles came running. "Sir, I think we have a problem."

Cage waited for him to go on, but he just stared in space.

"Izzy, you think you could elaborate or should we play twenty questions?" Cage asked when the other man didn't go on.

"Sorry, but I thought I heard something."

Baker belched, then smiled, exposing teeth that resembled a crumbling picket fence. He had lost some teeth in the many barroom brawls he had; others had just rotted away from lack of care. "Maybe you heard my stomach rumbling. You wouldn't have anything to drink, would you, lad?"

Before he could answer Cage cut in.

"Izzy, you had something to tell us, or did you just have to take a whiz and want permission?"

The others laughed as Charles turned red.

"Sorry, sir." He upheld his rifle, or what had been his rifle, for the others to see; one piece in each hand. "I took up my post, took out my rifle and it…it broke in two." He looked about to cry.

Instinctively the others checked their weapons; the oaths they uttered let Cage know they indeed had a problem.

Fifteen minutes later Cage looked at their cache of weapons—two knives that hadn't gotten wet when they trudged through the lake and were only partially eaten away.

"A fine mess you've gotten us into now," Washington said, seemingly amused at their plight.

"What do you find so damn funny, asshole?" Baker said, still cradling his useless Uzi, like a sick child he was prepared to nurse back to health.

"No use moaning and groaning over something we have no control over," Washington responded, serious now. "I didn't

mean to make light of our lack of firepower, but we're all trained in the martial arts. Hell, this won't be the first time we've been stuck with no weapons. Ain't killed us yet, has it?"

"He's right," Cage said, taking Washington's initiative and using it to rally his troops. "We lay low, act like the trained soldiers we are and we'll be out of here tomorrow. Baker, you take watch. Wake me in two hours and I'll relieve you. I'm going to take a piss and hit the sack."

Cage awoke with a start, glanced at his watch and saw three hours had passed. Cursing under his breath, he sought out Baker. He came upon the man whimpering like a baby, scratching madly at his ankle.

"What's wrong, Baker?"

"Damn ants, sir. They was in the water when we got out of the chopper. Not in the water, exactly, but nesting on the leaves. Didn't you see them?" He went on without waiting for any confirmation from Cage. "They were on me as soon as I hit the water. Itching like crazy. Funny thing, though, after a minute or two they were gone. I thought I'd dreamed up the whole thing, but they're back. The fuckers planted eggs on my ankle and they're hatching. See for yourself."

Baker had scratched his ankle raw, trying to rid himself of something Cage couldn't make out in the dark. He held a piece of his skin in his fingers and showed it to Cage. "Big buggers, aren't they?" He squeezed, then smiled. "They die, though. Just as long as I can get at them." Ignoring Cage, he was back to scratching, pulling off skin and killing the phantom pests.

"Get some sleep, Baker," Cage said with exasperation. "I'll take over now."

Baker grunted and went back to work on his ankle.

When Cage woke Izzy Charles two hours later Baker was at work on his other ankle. Cage was thankful for the darkness, so he couldn't see what damage the man was doing to himself. Get out of this forest, he told himself. Things around here could get a lot worse before they got better.

Progress was slow the next day with Baker hardly able to walk. He'd done some job on his ankle the night before, Cage noted to himself, and had now begun working on his right calf. Exposed muscles twitched where he'd tore through the skin. Most unsettling, though, was the blood. He was bleeding steadily, but mixed with the all-too familiar red was a tinge of

white. He recalled Stansfield's comment about pigeon crap and it described aptly what he now saw. The same dirty white color he'd noticed in his urine when he'd taken a piss earlier. What's happening to us? he wondered.

They'd walk for ten minutes and then Baker would start ranting about the ants and dig at his calf. All four of them took turns cajoling and lugging him along, but it was slow going.

"Let's shoot the bugger and put him out of his misery," Izzy Charles said at one point, exasperation heavy in his voice.

"Cut it Izzy," Cage said, a part of him agreeing it would be the most humane thing to do. But Charles wasn't paying attention. He was staring in space again.

"What is it, Izzy?"

"I hear something again, sir, don't you? Plain as day. They found the chopper. Looking at it now. Two of them are arguing about what to do. One wants to track us down; the other's more interested in the chopper."

"They can't be at the chopper," Cage said. "Or if they are you *can't* hear them talking. We must be nine or ten miles from the wreckage."

He shrugged. "I hear them like they were next to me."

"Must be another side effect of exposure to the defoliant," Stansfield said in a strange monotone.

"Do you hear them, Kyle?" Cage asked. He noticed the skin on Stansfield's head and face had begun to flake and peel. He had to look down as it reminded him of the dying leaves they'd first seen the previous day.

"No...but, but I can see them."

"What the fuck?" Cage said.

"Look, Nick. I can't explain it," he said, his voice still flat. "But I can see what Izzy hears. Two men arguing; others checking out the copter. One's found the charge Washington set. The wire's eaten away. He's pulling his hand back like he's been burned."

Washington began to howl. He ripped off the bandages Cage had wrapped around his wound the day before and began sucking on his mangled limb. "Sweet Jesus, don't touch that wire!" he yelled. "Get your hand out of the water, man. Shit, it hurts bad."

"Let's take a break," Cage said, but it was like talking to himself. Izzy kept up a steady stream of dialogue, telling no one in particular the partisans at the river had split into two groups with one tracking them. Stansfield seconded him, in a detached

voice that made Cage squirm, giving a blow by blow description of their progress. Baker scratched and Washington praised the Lord as his counterpart's injured hand was tended to. Cage's bladder beckoned again—the fourth time in the last two hours—and he wondered if his curse was to piss milk every half an hour. They were dying, this he knew, though he kept the thought to himself. They *had* to get back, though, to alert the others so they'd destroy the defoliant. He dreaded the thought of a chopper crashing in a river and dispersing the poison to God knew how many others.

In another half an hour Charles and Stansfield were euphoric with their newly discovered powers.

"It's incredible, sir," Izzy said to Cage. "I'm like a satellite dish. Everything's so clear. We'll know their every move, every strategy, every secret. We don't need no weapons. We'll always be a step ahead of them. And to the North, I can hear General Ebersoll. He's sending a chopper out to look for us. Once he spots us he'll send a patrol and I'll know exactly where we should meet up with them," he said, his chest swelled with pride. "Imagine if there were another dozen…a hundred like me? We'd have this war over in a matter of days."

Stansfield was just as smug, though one wouldn't know by his lack of emotion. His words, though, conveyed his sense of awe.

"I can see everything Izzy hears. Think of the team we'd make. His ears and my eyes. They'd have no secrets. Every inventive strategy foiled. They'd be totally demoralized and constantly second-guessing themselves."

Cage wished he could share their fervor, but it all seemed too good to be true. There had to be a downside. All he had to do was look at Baker, now attacking his crotch, to know their bubble was bound to burst. A double-edged sword, he thought. A miracle, but also a curse.

They plodded on through the deathly silence of the denuded jungle until nightfall. They'd stopped to fashion a stretcher for Baker, who alternated between scratching his arms, chest and back. A sickly white froth covered his skin like a cocoon. His blood has turned the color of chalk, Cage noticed. Just like my urine.

Stansfield, monitoring the partisans, told Cage they'd decided to make camp for the night at dusk.

"They're spooked, sir," Izzy added. "Arguing among them-

Double-Edged Sword

selves. Some want to go back. A couple are sick, too."

"Yes," Stansfield said, his eyes a faithful companion to Charles' ear. "Those who went into the lake are slowing the rest down. One's scratching himself like Baker."

"Enough already," Cage said, unable to contain his irritation. "It's been non-stop with you two all day. Give it a rest. Now that they've stopped we might as well call it a day, too. We'll be at the river tomorrow by noon, even if we have to carry Baker the whole way. No more talking, though. We've got to conserve our strength."

While he knew this to be true, he had another reason for demanding silence. If the defoliant reacted the same way with their pursuers, sometime that night or the next morning he feared they'd acquire the same powers as Charles and Stansfield.

Izzy volunteered to take watch. "I can't sleep, sir. It's like a radio you can't turn off. As long as anyone's talking within five to ten miles I can hear. I tried plugging up my ears, but I hear it all inside my head. No sleeping, even if I wanted to."

He spoke with pride, but Cage wondered how long Izzy could go without rest. He himself slept fitfully, dreams of white blood and piss, Baker scratching and the dead forest plaguing him.

Izzy woke him at dawn. Looking at him, Cage saw he *hadn't* slept all night. He was hyper as if adrenaline alone was keeping him on his feet. But Cage could see the toll it was taking. His face had aged five years over the course of the night; his cheeks sunken, complexion sallow—turning to gray. A man on the verge of collapse.

"Anything wrong, Izzy?"

"Baker's gone."

"Fuck. Wake the others. We've got to find him." He hesitated, dreading to ask his next question, but knowing he must. "The partisans. Are they up yet?"

Izzy smiled. "They've had a busy night, they have. One got the power—*my* power—only with the rest of you asleep he didn't know who I was. I spoke to him half the night. Told him I was looking for him, waiting for him. Told him to flee this sanctified forest if he valued his life. He deserted. Took two others with him. There's three of them left. Been arguing with each other for the last thirty minutes or so. Thought I'd give you a little extra shut-eye and then I saw Baker was gone..."

"All right," Cage interrupted. A short squat man, with bawdy tattoos covering his head where he had gone bald, Charles spoke with actions not words...until now. He was more than making

up for it, though, and his high-pitched voice was grating on Cage's nerves like a woman filing her nails with an emery board. "Let's find Baker so we can get the hell out of here."

Ten minutes later Baker was found by Washington, impaled on the sharpened remains of a fallen tree. A knife lay by his side. It was clear it was no accident. It was also evident why. Baker had scratched every inch of his skin raw; had finally tore at his face with a vengeance. One of his eyes hung from its socket. A white blanket of blood covered him like a shroud. He'd taken the only way out.

A single fly buzzed around his corpse and Izzy clasped his ears. "Make it stop, sir! It's like a telephone ringing in my head."

Instinctively Cage reached out and with one swipe had the fly in his hand. He cradled the insect, let it go, then grasped it with his other hand before it had a chance to escape. For a second he felt the same exhilaration Izzy and Stansfield had experienced the day before. Superhuman instincts. But the downside. What was the downside? He squashed the fly and Izzy fell to his knees.

"That was a bad one Cap'n. My head was about ready to burst like an overripe tomato."

With no shovels, available, all they could do was cover Baker with the powdery reside of leaves that littered the forest floor.

While the others set to work, Washington sullenly distanced himself, cradling his injured hand. When they were about finished Cage joined him, offered the other man a cigarette and lit one for himself. "Something wrong, Carl?"

"Yeah, something's wrong. From the day I was born I've been dealt a short hand. A poor black in America could only go so far. An uneducated black in the army had little chance for advancement. But with you guys I was an equal. Didn't matter I was black. Till now, that is."

"What do you mean until now?"

"Even the defoliant's prejudiced," he said, then laughed. "Look at Stansfield and Charles. They got power. Even you, sir, I saw how you snapped up that fly. Your hand was a blur. Never seen nothing like it in my life. But me, shit, all I got is a bum hand."

"Everything's not what it seems, Carl. This power you talk of is not gift. It's a curse…"

"A curse I'd give my soul to possess," he interrupted. "Don't you see I'm no longer one of you. I'm an outsider again. Hell, I'd take the bad with the good just to be a part of it all." He

turned away from Cage. It was clear there was no convincing him how lucky he was. Cage joined the others and in five minutes they were ready to move on.

In the next half an hour the familiar green foliage of the jungle reappeared; a welcome sight to all but Charles. The multitude of insects that Cage almost greeted as long lost friends had Izzy in a frenzy.

With every step his complaints increased. He shouted to the others as if they wouldn't be able to hear him over the cacophony that surrounded him. "It's like rush hour in my head," he said, speaking to no one in particular. "I can hear every insect; each leaf rustling in the breeze."

Suddenly he fell to his knees and let out a howl. His eyes locked with Cages'. "Sir...I can hear the beating of your heart. Drums, like drums." His eyes glazed, he went silent, then convulsed, writhing on the ground. He vomited a frothy white liquid while more dripped from his nose.

"Blood," Cage said scarcely above a whisper. "He's hemorrhaging; bleeding to death."

"Do something!" Stansfield said, dull...flat, but clearly panicked. "For God's sake..."

Before he could finish Charles gagged, collapsed and was still. White liquid oozed from his ears, forming a pool on the ground. To Cage it smelled like rotten eggs. He felt for a pulse; found none.

"The ground's soft. We can bury..."

"Nick," Stansfield said, without emotion. "There's no time. They're closing in. I can see them, no more than half a mile behind. One of them is looking right at me. He has *the* power. We've got to get to the river."

Ten minutes later they broke through a clearing and the sun pierced through a smattering of trees. Stansfield pitched forward, his hands shielding his eyes.

"The sun. It's burning my eyes; frying my brain!" he bellowed. He began to burrow into the ground to escape the rays of the sun. Abruptly he stopped, sat up and was still; a wind-up doll wound down.

Cage bent down and stared into the man's haggard face. The corners of his eyes were singed, as if someone has poked him with a cigarette. Thin wisps of smoke drifted into the air. The smell of burnt flesh made him want to gag. Stansfield's eyelids were welded shut over his eyes. A look of serenity crossed his face.

"I've lost the power...I'm blind." A statement. A tinge of relief in the dull monotone.

The next few seconds were a blur.

"Behind you!" Washington shouted, pointing. Cage turned and a bullet struck Stansfield in the head. His skull exploded, white suds hitting Cage in the face, temporarily blinding him as he rolled to his left. A second volley cut down Washington. Red blood spurted from a half dozen wounds, like from an open fire hydrant. From behind Washington another volley; these aimed at their attackers. The three partisans who'd taken Stansfield and Washington out danced like marionettes before Cage, then fell—their strings cut. Two oozed white froth; the third, like Washington bled red. Silence permeated the air. Even the insects seemed entranced by the scene; too stupefied to keep up their incessant chatter.

A soldier Cage recognized as Duffy, another mercenary, slowly advanced towards him, while several others fanned out. Some checked the dead, others made sure there were no more enemy soldiers lurking about.

"Are you hit, Cage?" Duffy asked.

"No. I'm all right," he said and laughed at the irony. He'd pissed in his pants and a white stain spread over his crotch. He wasn't quite all right. Not all right at all, he thought, but it wasn't something Duffy would understand.

"What the hell happened?" Duffy asked, but didn't await an answer. "We thought you'd gone down with the chopper. A plane spotted it yesterday. Also saw the partisans. They said something about the jungle being bare and they stuck out like a sore thumb. We were hoping to capture them to find out if you were taken prisoner or dead. Never thought we'd run into you." He glanced at Stansfield, a look of bewilderment on his face at the lack of blood from his fragmented skull. "What's going on, Cage?" This time he waited for a response.

"You wouldn't believe it. Look, you've got to get me back to Ebersoll...now! I've got to warn him. I don't know how much time I've got left myself."

"Warn him about what?"

"Duffy, get me to Ebersoll. Don't be stupid and try to think for yourself."

The man looked hurt, which pleased Cage. Even if the man had saved his life, Duffy was a fool. He drank too much and cheated at cards. A good enough soldier, but not one to grasp the enormity of what Cage had to tell.

Double-Edged Sword

Duffy mumbled something under his breath, told two other men to tend to Cage and went to check out Stansfield, a barely audible, "Where's the fucking blood?" his only comment.

Cage was exhausted. He'd told his story three times, with General Ebersoll peppering him with questions each time. He tired with each telling; Ebersoll's excitement only grew.

"You've got to destroy whatever defoliant's left. And bomb the lake where we landed the chopper. God knows who'll come into contact with it and what it'll do to them."

"You can't see the forest from the trees, Cage," Ebersoll said, ignoring his pleas as he had before. "Can't you see we have the ultimate weapon? The defoliant makes napalm look like a match. There's no place to hide from the stuff. And just imagine what we'll have when we harness the side effects. Teams like Charles and Stansfield—the eyes and ears to put an end to this foolish uprising…and others like it."

"General, it can't be harnessed!"

"Look, Cage," he said with condescension. "You're a good soldier, but we have specialists who'll isolate whatever's causing the mutations, fiddle with it some and all your worries will be put to rest. You relax now. Get your strength back. We'll need your, uh, expertise when you're feeling better."

Right, thought Cage. Like always Ebersoll was like an open book. A guinea pig, that's what I am, he thought. A lab animal. Maybe a little experimentation. Tired. So tired. Too tired to even care, he dozed off.

He was poked and prodded the next three days; examined from head to toe. Blood—a sickly pink, getting whiter by the day—was drawn at regular intervals. Everything he'd feared.

All his senses were sharpened, though he kept this to himself. He'd developed Charles' uncanny ability to hear the slightest sound and Stansfield's unerring sight. His reflexes were refined to where he could throw five coins over his head and pluck them out of the air with his eyes closed. Even his sense of smell was accentuated. The doctors, psychiatrists and orderlies each had their own unique scent; Eversoll's was the most noxious. Cage had to contain himself so as not to puke.

Sleep became more difficult as his senses were assaulted by the sights, sounds and smells of the compound. His blood was turning progressively whiter. He knew it was only a matter of time before he'd be overwhelmed, like Charles and Stansfield, by his own body and self-destruct.

The fourth day he could read minds. Ebersoll would be ecstatic…if he ever found out.

At 7AM, as always, the General came in alone to brief Cage on the previous day's progress. Looking at the pudgy, short, middle-aged man with his jet black hair greased flat on his head and droopy mustache, Cage felt the man's disdain for him. The feeling was mutual. Cage was nauseated by the man's single-minded pursuit for the almighty dollar—whatever the cost.

With time to think the past few days Cage had come to grips with himself. He was no longer the callous youth who had no morals, and even less humanity, who'd killed with a vengeance in Vietnam. He had to admit he'd developed a grudging respect for the many enemies he's faced who fought for a cause, not money. And he wasn't loathe to acknowledge he'd developed a conscience of sorts. He'd never killed children in a bloodlust of revenge. And he'd come to realize most civilians, in whatever country he fought, could care less who won the petty wars. Whatever the outcome their lives would be largely unaffected.

He knew, too, that Ebersoll hated his disdain for authority and reveled in pointing out his failings, the few times a mission had been unsuccessful. Ebersoll could be blunt and cruel, just for spite. Just the other day he had held a mirror so Cage could see himself. "You look like shit," was all he said, a smirk betraying his delight.

Cage had to agree with the man's assessment. His thick shock of brown hair was dull and lackluster—like the leaves he thought, like the *dying* leaves in the forest. His blue eyes were bloodshot from lack of sleep. He'd lost twenty-two pounds from his already lean six-foot frame since he been found. Yeah, he looked like shit.

Today, though, Ebersoll was Nick's pal; his confidant.

"Nick, maybe you were right. It's going to take longer than we expected. The genetic ramifications are staggering. We're putting everything on hold for the time being. I won't lie to you, you're getting no better. No worse, but no better. We're going to fly you to the States and look for an antidote. We're mothballing the defoliant until we get some answers." He smiled paternally.

A lie. All a lie, Cage thought. They were done with him all right, but he wasn't being sent back to the States for an antidote. They wanted to be rid of him. Out of sight, out of mind. No one snooping around asking questions. He'd be under close supervision, all right, while they observed his final metamor-

phosis and inevitable self-destruction. Worst of all, the defoliant was to be tested again that afternoon. It was all could do to contain himself from strangling the smug bastard then and there.

Cage couldn't allow the new test to occur. He had to destroy the defoliant and the entire base with it, the scientists brought over to refine the poison and Ebersoll who planned to make a financial killing on its sale. And, he'd have to do it today.

A little before noon, he shed his lethargy, and made his way to a building which held the base's cache of weapons. He knocked out a guard before the man could utter a word; tied and gagged him. His hands a blur, he set a charge to go off in seven minutes, then fashioned a belt of plastique explosives which he draped over his shoulder. He made his way to three choppers, all loaded with drums of defoliant. Carruthers, a pilot he'd flown with in Angola, was doing a final check.

"How's it going, Sam?"

"Nick! I heard you were shot up pretty bad."

"A flesh wound, that's all. No worse for wear. Look, do me a favor. Tell Ebersoll I'm here waiting for him."

"Sorry, man, but we're taking off pretty soon and..."

Cage produced a gun. "Sam, don't argue. Do what I asked. You'll be a hero. Stand here and gawk at me, you'll be a dead man."

As Carruthers ran to get Ebersoll, Cage got into the lead chopper, set the charge he wore for 45-seconds and waited. He could hear the bewildered Carruthers telling the General what had ensued.

Just as he hoped Ebersoll came running, a whole posse in tow: guards, the scientists, a medic. "Come to Papa," he whispered aloud. Without warning the weapons shed exploded. Cage's finely honed senses were overwhelmed by the sound and he slumped forward; white froth dripping from his ears, nose and mouth. He never heard the plastique strapped to his shoulder detonate taking out Ebersoll and the others.

Five miles away Sean Elliott, piloting his chopper, heard the explosion. He and Mike Flanagan, sitting next to him, exchanged glances and shrugged. It wasn't their concern. They'd begun to disperse the defoliant as General Ebersoll had ordered. Duffy, sitting in the open doorway, machine gun ready in case they encountered unfriendlies, cursed as he was pelted by the fine white mist.

Without warning the chopper began to lose power. Flanagan pointed to a village at three o'clock and Elliott maneuvered as best he could...

General Estefan Cintron couldn't believe his eyes. A week before, when he'd been to the lake, an abandoned helicopter greeted him. Today, the husk he stared at could have been a rusted out car left at a junkyard. He really wasn't interested in the helicopter, though. He'd seen what the defoliant had done to three of his men—the enormous powers they'd possessed before they'd died. The Government, with their mercenaries, had made a fatal mistake in not destroying it when the chopper crashed, and they would pay dearly.

The General's men filled four drums with the white-scummed lake water. A thorn from a branch grazed Cintron's hand as he maneuvered towards his jeep. He was too deep in thought of victories that awaited him to notice the white liquid that dripped from the fresh wound.

The Fur Coat

Richard Laymon

anet wore her white ermine coat to the theater that night. The play was **Cats**. She went alone.

The evening was meant to signal a new beginning for her. She hadn't treated herself to a play since Harold's death. He had adored the stage. They'd seen **Cats** together many times during their eight years of marriage. He'd been dead, now, for more than two years. Janet knew that she had to quit mourning, quit feeling sorry for herself, and get on with her life.

She attended **Cats** as a final tribute to Harold.

She wore the ermine coat as a tribute to him, too.

It was a lovely coat, its fur as white as a drift of fresh snow as soft as down. A gift from Harold. She'd yelped with delight the morning she found it under the Christmas tree. Because they had no children and were celebrating the holiday alone, she had immediately thrown off her robe and nightgown. She'd caressed her naked body with the luscious fur coat, then slipped her arms into its sleeves and twirled around for Harold. In his arms, she thanked him for the coat. She kissed him. She hugged him. She stripped him. She urged him to the floor. There, kneeling over him in nothing but her wonderful new coat, she had stroked him, kissed him all over, licked and sucked him, and finally eased down onto him.

Afterward, he'd said, "My God. Wish I'd bought you this coat years ago."

"You couldn't have afforded it."

"So what? Debt, where is thy sting?"

During the next few months, she'd worn the coat every time Harold took her out to dinner or the theater. A few times, when their evening activities were such that she wouldn't need to remove her coat, she'd worn only a garter belt and stockings underneath it—which drove Harold crazy.

The coat never failed to make Janet feel special. Partly because Harold had blown a small fortune on it, she supposed. Partly because it looked so pure and beautiful, felt so soft and smooth against her skin. But mostly, she thought, because of how it had changed their marriage. The coat not only inspired its share of raw lust, but also tenderness, laughter, a fresh assortment of surprises and adventures.

Her first night alone in the house after Harold's accident, she took the coat to bed with her. She wept into its silken fur and fell asleep hugging it.

Soon, however, the coat ceased to give her comfort, became only a reminder of her loss. She couldn't stand to look at it, much less touch it, wear it.

And so she had put it in storage.

Left it there.

For over two years.

Until the day she was brushing her rich brown hair in front of the medicine cabinet mirror and spotted the silver thread.

Her first gray hair.

But I'm only thirty-six! Thirty-six isn't old!

Old enough to start going gray.

It was then that she decided to get on with her life. She phoned the Barkley Theater and made a single reservation for the Saturday night performance of **Cats**. Then she took her ermine coat out of storage.

At Bullocks, she bought an elegant black evening gown for the occasion.

On the day of the performance, she went to the beauty shop. She'd considered having her hair dyed. But she liked her natural color. Besides, the idea of masking the gray hair seemed cowardly. Better to accept it, to face the knowledge that her life was moving on, and make the most of each day ahead.

She had her hair trimmed very short. It made her look spritely. And quite a bit younger.

That evening, ready to leave, she stood in front of the full-length hall mirror for a while and gazed at herself.

The sleek, low-cut gown was brand new. The ermine coat *looked* brand new. And Janet *felt* brand new.

If only Harold could see me now, she thought.

Her eyes filled with tears.

She had to redo her mascara before leaving the house.

The drive into Hollywood took half an hour. Rather than hunt for street parking, she left her Mercedes in a brightly lighted pay lot four blocks from the theater.

The autumn wind had a chill to it. Janice was snug in her fur coat.

She picked up her ticket at the box office. In the warmth of the Barkley's lobby, she removed her coat and draped it over one arm. In her seat, she folded it and set it on her lap. She stroked it during the play. It was almost like having a cat on her lap. But no cat ever had such lovely, smooth fur.

She went nowhere during intermission. Instead, she stood in front of her seat and looked about. She saw no familiar faces, of course. But she noticed several women in furs. More in stoles than in coats, it seemed. Most of the women who wore furs were considerably older than Janet. Most, in fact, were very old.

Was she the only person under sixty, in the entire theater, who'd worn a fur to the play?

Sure looked that way.

Had it always been like that?

Janet didn't think so.

Could things have changed so much in such a short period of time? In less than three years?

Maybe it's because of those animal rights fanatics, she thought. Had they turned an entire generations away from wearing furs? Sure looked that way. *Something* had happened.

Unless it's the bad economy, and most people simply can't afford the luxury...

The lights dimmed.

Janet sat down.

At the end of the play, she wept and clapped. Then she wiped her eyes, pressed the coat to her belly and sidestepped to the aisle.

On her way to the lobby, she was aware of feeling proud.

She had taken such a large step, coming here tonight. She'd actually dressed up and come to the play all by herself. And she'd enjoyed the performance. In a way. If only Harold had been with her...

I'm on my own, she reminded herself. *And I got along just fine.*

Things would be easier from now on.

She would try a new play next week. Maybe, sooner or later, she would actually gather enough courage to dine alone in a fine restaurant.

Eventually, she might even meet a man as wonderful as Harold.

Fall in love.

God, wouldn't that be something!

Sighing, she slipped her arms into the sleeves of her coat. The lobby was hot, so she didn't fasten the buttons. Stuck in the mob waiting to exit, she wished she had left the coat off entirely. People pressed against her. The air seemed hot, heavy, suffocating.

Until finally she made her way through the door.

The chilly autumn night felt great.

She breathed deeply. The air beneath the theater marquee was fragrant with scents of myriad perfumes, with men's musky after-shave colognes, with liquor aromas, with smoke from cigarettes and cigars. Whether exotic or comforting or disgusting, the odors excited Janet. They were old, familiar friends. She filled her lungs and smiled.

This is so wonderful, she thought. *I'm really out in the world again.*

Look at me, Harold. I didn't wither up and die. I wanted to, but I didn't. I survived.

The crowd loosened as people headed off in different directions. Janet paused to recall where she had parked her car.

The parking lot. That way.

She turned to the right.

And took only three strides before a voice shouted, "Murderer!"

Janet was twisting around when a woman cried out, "No!"

She spotted her at the curb. Old, frail, silver-haired, wrapped in a mink stole, flinging up her arms as she was rushed by a pair of young women.

The two women looked vicious.

"Murderer!" the skinny one shouted into the old woman's face.

"Evil bitch!" shouted her partner, a tubby woman with stringy brown hair. "Those minks died for your sins!"

Both women dug into their handbags. Janet's heart thumped. She thought they were going for guns. But they came up with cans of spray paint.

"No, please!" the old woman whined.

Red paint sprayed her hands as she scuttled backward, trying to get away. Some got past her hands, misted her hair and forehead and glasses.

At least twenty people seemed to be frozen beneath the theater marquee, watching the attack.

Why was nobody trying to help?

Because the assailants were women? Or were all the spectators on their side, hating the old lady for wearing fur?

The old lady, sandwiched between the pair, whimpered and hugged her head as they sprayed her. Her hair dripped red paint. The fur of her stole was matted down, scarlet.

"Leave her alone, goddamn you!" Janet shouted.

The heads of both assailants snapped toward her. The chubby one squinted through glasses that were speckled with red paint. Round lenses in wire frames. Granny glasses.

"She didn't do anything to you!" Janet yelled. "Look what you've done to her! What's the matter with you?"

The one in the granny glassed grinned.

The skinny one raised her spray can high overhead. "Listen up, all you rich capitalist fucks! We're A.D.F. Hitters for the Animal Defense Front. What you've seen here is a lesson. It's what we do to assholes we catch wearing dead animals.

"You've been fucking Mother Earth long enough! Butchering her forests, poisoning her air and water, slaughtering her innocent creatures. *Murdering* her creatures! Bashing their heads. Slashing their throats. *Experimenting* on them! Eating their flesh! Clothing yourselves in their skins! No more! No more!"

"No more!" the chubby one joined in.

"A.D.F. forever!"

"A.D.F. forever!"

"Get *her*!" The skinny one hurled the old lady aside and rushed toward Janet.

The other grinned.

Janet whirled away.

The tight skirt of her evening gown bound her legs, but not for long. With her third stride, her knee punched through its front. A kick finished the job. The skirt split open from hem to waist, freeing her to run.

People nearby dodged clear, some yelping with alarm, others watching as if amused, none trying to help.

Janet glanced over her shoulder. Her pursuers were side by

side, no more than fifteen feet back.

What sort of range did the spray cans have?

I'll die if they ruin my coat!

But she knew that she couldn't outrun them—not in her heels.

The shoes, like the gown, could be replaced.

Without slowing, she kicked off her right shoe. The left gave her some trouble, but after a few strides she managed to fling it clear. Shoes gone, her feet felt light and quick.

She dashed along the sidewalk, silent except for her huffing breath and the slap of her feet and the whispery sounds that her pantyhose made as she whipped one leg after the other out through the split front of her skirt.

The girls behind her made a lot more noise. One seemed to be wheezing. One wore footwear, probably sandals, that smacked the concrete with harsh claps. One jingled with Christmas bells. From their spray cans came rattling sounds as if each contained nothing more than a ball-bearing.

The sounds of the pair didn't seem to be getting any closer. But not fading, either.

So far, Janet was keeping her lead.

Just ahead, her way was blocked by a knot of people standing at the corner. Waiting to cross the street.

"Help!"

Some looked around at her.

"What's the trouble?" asked a young man in a sweater. He looked innocent, collegiate.

"They're after me!" Janet cried out.

"What for?"

"Animal Defense Front!" shouted one of the gals. "Keep out of it!"

"Huh?" He wrinkled his nose.

And it was already too late. Janet had no time to stop and explain. Give the attackers two or three seconds, and her coat would be dripping crimson paint.

Just short of the group, she cut to the right.

"What's going on?" the kid called after her.

She didn't bother to answer. She poured on speed.

The sidewalk in front of her was deserted. Just as well, she thought. Nobody was likely to help her, anyway—not without an explanation. No explanation was possible. They'd be on her too quick.

If only someone would take out the two bitches on general

principles!

Isn't it obvious who's the victim here?

Apparently not.

Or people just don't care.

It'd all be different if guys were chasing me.

Men would be climbing all over each other to save me.

But these're gals after me. So I'm fucked.

Wonderful.

Her pursuers sounded farther away than before. Thinking that she was beginning to outdistance them, Janet risked a look back.

And gasped.

The skinny one was closer than ever before. No more than seven or eight feet separated her from Janet.

The heavy one was much farther back. She was the noisy one. The one with a wheeze. The one who wore sandals and sleighbells. The one who now carried both clinking canisters of paint.

Her friend in the lead was sprinting almost silent. Long blond hair streaming. Lips peeled away from teeth that looked very white in the streetlights. No earrings or necklace or bracelets or rings. No bra. No shoes or socks. Dressed in a white T-shirt and legless old jeans and apparently nothing else. Stripped for action, for silent running.

"Leave me alone!" Janet blurted.

"Butcher!"

"I'm *not!*"

"Gimme the coat!"

"No! Go away!"

"Yeah! After I've…ripped that fur…off your fucking back!"

Janet twisted sideways and hurled her clutch bag. Like the coat, it had been a gift from Harold. But she had nothing else to throw.

Inside the black satin bag were several odds and ends: some cash, tissues, a tampon, her parking lot ticket, the stub of her theater ticket, the folded playbill, and her driver's license. Also her key case, her compact and opera glasses—which gave the bag some weight.

Her pursuer saw the airborne bag. She flung up an arm to block it, but missed. She tried to jerk her head out of the way. The bag caught her in the right temple. Her face scrunched. She turned and tripped herself, hit the sidewalk shoulder first, and skidded.

Janet rushed back to her. She snatched up her purse.

"I warned you to leave me alone!" she said as the gal, moaning, tried to push herself up.

"Hey!" yelled the chubby one. "What'd you do to her! Leave her alone!"

"You leave *me* alone!" Janet snapped, backing away. While the big one chugged toward her, the other got to her knees. The fall had torn down the sleeve of her T-shirt. Teeth clenched, she took a quick look at her dark, scuffed shoulder.

"Are you hurt?" her friend asked, staggering to a halt.

"Get her!"

"No!" Janet yelled. "Quit it! She's already gotten hurt."

"Damn it, Glory, *spray the fuckin' coat!*"

Glory lurched past her, bells jingling.

"No," Janet said. "Come on. Please."

Glory kept coming, so she flung herself around. As she broke into a run, the cans hissed. She glanced back. Glory, firing with both barrels, was hidden from the chest up behind clouds of red mist. The paint didn't seem to shoot far enough to hit Janet.

But if Glory got much closer…

Janet rammed the clutch bag to her mouth. She bit it. The bag flopped, whapping her beneath the chin as she dashed along the sidewalk and struggled out of her coat. She brought the coat in front of her. Mashed it into a thick bundle. Clamped it to her chest with her left arm. Took the bag from her mouth with her right hand. And kept on running, hugging the coat.

They won't get you now, she thought.

The corner ahead looked deserted. Approaching it, she glanced both ways.

The parking lot.

If I can get to the parking lot…

Where the hell is it?

She had no idea.

But the traffic light was green for her and the intersection looked clear, so she leaped off the curb and raced into the street.

A horn blast stunned her.

She snapped her head to the left.

A cab running the red light sped straight at her. It swerved. She lurched to a stop, teetered backward. It rushed by, fanning her with a warm breeze.

Stunned by the near miss, Janet hardly noticed the sounds of smacking sandals and tinkling bells. The *sssssssss* took her by surprise.

She sprang forward.

But not fast enough.

Her evening gown was backless, so the cool paint plastered her bare skin from the nape of her neck and downward almost to her waist before she put on enough speed to leave Glory behind.

That would've been it for the coat, she thought.

Thank God! Got it off just in time.

At the other side of the street, she bounded over the curb. Then looked over her shoulder.

Glory, still pursuing her with a canister in each hand, had stopped spraying. Her hair was matted, her face slick with red paint. Janet wondered how she could possibly see through her glasses. The gal had obviously been racing into her own spray, soaking herself. Her sleeveless sweatshirt looked sodden. It was mostly red, only a hint of its original gray still visible low on the belly. Her plaid Bermuda shorts and heavy legs had caught some splatters. Janet noticed that the jingling came from a leather collar of bells around her left ankle.

Leather?

And what about those sandals?

Leather?

Maybe not. Maybe fake.

Or maybe the bitch is a hypocrite.

Fake?

Janet yelled over her shoulder, "My fur isn't real! It's simulated! You've got no reason to…"

Her voice went dead as the skinny one—the fast one—raced up behind Glory, overtook her and left her behind, charging toward Janet with shocking speed.

Janet bolted.

With the coat in her arms, she'd been able to stay ahead of Glory. But this one was so much quicker. Janet couldn't hope to outrun her—not without her arms free to pump.

Just a matter of time.

Janet began to weep.

I don't want them to ruin my coat! Please! Why do they want to do this?

She heard the girl's bare feet slapping the sidewalk, heard the girl's quick, sharp breaths.

"Please!" she yelled.

The word was still on its way out when a tackle took her down. Her arms, wrapped around the coat, were first to strike

the concrete. Then her knees. The coat cushioned her like a big pillow, saving her face and chest as she slammed the sidewalk.

The girl scurried up her body, squirming, sliding on Janet's painted skin, embracing her, reaching for the coat. Janet tried to elbow the hands away.

"All *right!*" Glory called, rushing closer.

Just as Glory halted, sandals and bells going silent, a sudden writhing tug by the other flipped Janet over. She found herself on top, the girl pinned beneath her back, Glory looming above her.

"Nail the bitch!"

Grinning, Glory squatted, stretched her arms toward Janet, and sprayed. Both canisters spat red paint.

Janet felt the spray on her arms.

On her arms, wrapped around the ermine coat.

And she knew that the coat was finished.

"You getting her?" asked the girl underneath Janet.

"You bet."

"Got the coat good?"

"Yep."

"Nail her in the face."

Janet let go of the fur. She squeezed her eyes shut, closed her mouth, and flung up her arms to protect her face. An instant later, the spray hissed at her.

While it showered her, she felt the coat being snatched off her chest.

She felt hands rip open the bodice of her gown. They plucked and tore, savaging her gown and undergarments.

"Nail her!"

The spray slathered her breasts, worked its way down her belly, burnt between her legs.

"Okay," Glory said.

The spraying stopped.

With a shove from below, Janet was sent rolling off the girl. She tumbled over the curb, dropped, and landed facedown in leaves and debris at the edge of the street. She lay there motionless. She didn't dare to breathe.

She heard quiet sounds of fabric being torn.

She knew they were ripping her coat to shreds.

Soon, the pieces of it fell softly onto her bare back and rump and legs.

"You think this was bad?" asked the nameless one.

Janet didn't answer.

"This wasn't bad. This was nothing. Imagine how the ermines felt."

"Ermines have feelings, too," Glory added.

"You had no right to slaughter them for your vanity," said the other.

She stepped on Janet's back, stepped down to the street beside her, knelt, grabbed Janet's painted hair and lifted her face off the pavement. "They were poor, innocent creatures. They only wanted to live, just like the rest of us. They didn't want to be made into a coat for a rich bitch like you."

"You had no right," said Glory.

The other one jerked Janet's hair down quick and hard. Janet's face crashed against the pavement. Her nose burst. Three teeth crumbled.

"Animals have feelings, too."

"Do you think they *enjoy* being skinned?" Glory asked.

"How do you think *you'd* like it, bitch?"

Janet began to struggle, but the girl bounced her face off the street again.

She was unconscious when they dragged her into the alley.

She woke up screaming when they started in with the razor blades.

Do Not Pass Go

Do Not

Collect $200

Chelsea Quinn Yarbro

If your Heels are Nimble and Light

Fred missed the ten-thirty meeting; he was still caught in traffic on the 460-A north freeway bypass. Somewhere up ahead there was a three-trailer in a double-jackknife across four lanes of traffic. Fred and eleven thousand other commuters inched along, trying to shrink down to one lane to get past the mess.

The State Department of Coastal Zoning, Harbors and Fisheries was under siege again and Fred had the crucial report in his briefcase—he set a good example with his recycled high-resistance woven plastic instead of leather—and his supervisor was counting on him. He had tried to use the car phone, but so many others were doing the same that the bleed-over made it impossible to hear anything clearly. Fred sighed, and hoped that his supervisor had contacted the State Department of Traffic, Road Engineering, and Urban Development. He did not want his supervisor to think he had been lax, especially since he had started out early with the express intention of having a few words with Tarlington before the meeting. Fred's supervisor might be the one the organizational structure said he had to satisfy, but Tarlington was the one he had to convince.

The traffic began to ease a little and Fred moved another ten feet forward. He had a produce truck behind him, a refrigerated behemoth driven by a fellow used to intimidating automobile drivers out of his way. He was still striving to do that now, though there was no way he could accomplish his goal and force Fred to change lanes: all

the lanes were packed.

A helicopter with the insignia of the Highway Safety Patrol and Vehicle Supervision Authority on its belly flapped toward the wreck, its public address system advising motorists to remain in their vehicles and to stay calm. The HSPVSA announcement informed everyone of what they had already heard on their radios—that the three-trailer rig had bent into three automobiles and a van. Ambulance helicopters, continued the bulletin, were in the air already.

Fred removed his glasses and pinched the bridge of his nose, his mind fixed on the meeting he was missing. He had developed his presentation so carefully in anticipation of this interdepartmental conference. It was so crucial, he thought. It could make a difference if a way could be found to implement the plan. That was the crux of it: implementation. As thorough as the bureaucracy was, Fred was not convinced that it could accommodate the proposals being made in his prospectus.

A new Bavarian-Benz with a plethora of foreign tags on its massive bumpers edged in front of Fred, and for an instant he had to fight the urge to press forward and ram the lavish automobile out of the way. "Fuel inefficient, showy, *vain* bastard," he muttered, as if he feared the driver might hear him through the metal and glass and over the racket around them. He would be lucky, he thought, if he arrived at the office by noon.

At the Tone, Please Leave

Tarlington glared at the five underlings gathered at the tremendous, oval-shaped table. There were supposed to be eighteen at this meeting, representing every department of the Bureau. He tapped his fingers on the tabletop—reconstituted paper bound with plastic and polished with reclaimed paint by-products, the very essence of recycling consciousness—and did his best to make light of this affront.

"I suppose the reasonable thing would be to postpone the meeting until this afternoon," he said, pitching his voice the way his speech coach had taught him, very resonant and deep and without a trace of the rustic twang he had had as a boy. "It will give the rest a chance to get here."

"They say that the freeways will be cleared in another hour," one of his minions said sycophantically.

"They'll still have to get here from wherever-they-are," Tarlington said in a manner designed to discourage presump-

tion. "We'll arrange it for one-thirty. Inform everyone of that fact." He stood up, and watched with secret relish as the five scrambled to their feet. He could see disappointment in all their faces, disappointment from a lost opportunity to enjoy a nearly private audience with Tarlington.

"This room will not be available this afternoon," his senior assistant announced anxiously. "I'll see if I can schedule one."

"A larger one," said Tarlington.

"Yes, of course," said the assistant, as keenly aware of the political implications in that request as Tarlington himself was. "Perhaps the conference room on 3H, the one with the two projection screens."

"That would be acceptable," said Tarlington. He longed to straighten his tie, but men in his position did not do such things; junior bureaucrats had such concerns, but Department Heads did not. He gave an ill-used sigh. "You may leave your proposals and prospectuses here with me, if you would. I'll try to look them over before we meet this afternoon."

The five exchanged looks, the first acknowledgment of potential advantage for the morning. Each opened their various cases and proffered bound documents of anything from twenty-five to three hundred pages; all this accompanied by murmurs of "Much appreciated", "So kind", "Thank you, Mister Tarlington", "How considerate", and "I hope this is useful, Sir."

This last was from Clara Martin, the only woman at the table. She was middle-aged and angular, looking more like a television version of a high school librarian than the ambitious creature she was. Her dress and grooming deliberately plain— greying hair in a no-nonsense French roll, mascara, a touch of lipstick; Prussian-blue suit, white blouse, low-heeled shoes— to disguise the complexity of her thinking.

"Ms Martin," said Tarlington, picking up her fifty-page report, "I would like you to bring your research files this afternoon."

The other four stared at her with blatant envy in their eyes.

"Of course, Mister Tarlington," she said meekly as if she were unaware of the honor of being singled out.

Tarlington realized it would be wise to diminish the impact of this a little. "And you, Mister Fedden. I'd like to have all your graph-data."

"Certainly," said Mister Fedden, doing his best not to be too smug. He opened his dispatch case at once and drew out well over a ream of computer paper. "Here, Mister Tarlington."

Chelsea Quinn Yarbro

There was a pause as Tarlington raised his eyebrow at the stack. "I hope that this doesn't indicate wastefulness in your department, Mister Fedden," he said in condescending accents. "I'd hate to think you were spending taxpayer's money on wasteful extravagance just to look impressive."

Bruno Fedden colored to the roots of his thinning hair. "Of course not, Mister Tarlington," he said, straining to get the words out. "I've introduced several economies in my department in the last six months, in response to your memo."

The others nodded, wanting to make the most of this opportunity. "I've left a standing order for recycled paper only," said Willie Monroe, wanting to seize what advantage he could.

"That was my order," said Tarlington at his most forbidding. "You were wise to heed it."

Monroe swallowed hard and nodded. "I think…" His words faded away as he gave up trying to impress his superior.

"One other thing," said Tarlington. "We will have to present our findings to the Federal Environment and Housing Control Agency when we have agreed on the program we will put forth. That is the final hurdle. Whatever we decide upon must accommodate their current programs and allocations. Otherwise we will have to try to get separate funding from Congress, and that would delay our actions for more than two years, and what we receive will not be adequate to the task."

The others nodded sagely; everyone was familiar with the way Congress whittled away at programs and filled their private allowances with siphoned moneys going to the pet causes and activities of the legislators. Everyone knew it was common practice. There was a long, thoughtful silence.

"Well, I assume that will take care of any questions until this afternoon?" Tarlington asked, not expecting anything but endorsement.

The others withdrew from the conference room; Tarlington watched them go with a half-smile. If he could persuade them all to follow his lead, the new plan could advance him up the ladder once again. At that he sighed. He would have to carry one or two of his underlings with him or risk being sabotaged by his support staff. It was a small enough price to pay, he reminded himself, and decided to devote his lunch hour to deciding which of the eighteen would come with him and which he would leave behind.

Fred found a parking place in the second over-flow lot, and reluctantly paid the outrageous day rate with his departmental credit union card. Another unexpected expense, and one that would cause Penny endless dismay. He straightened his tie before he gathered up his dispatch case, his recycled-wool jacket and his three authorization badges. Then he began the two-mile walk to his office; his pace was brisk though his back ached and his legs felt tight from the long hours in his car.

The first good news came from his assistant: the meeting he had missed was rescheduled. He jotted down the new time and location, all the while wondering if he would be able to speak to Tarlington before the meeting began. During his time in traffic, a few more notions had occurred to him and he wanted to make the most of them while they were fresh in his mind. He knew better than to suppose he would have the chance he sought, so he ducked into his office, logged onto his computer, used his private codes to get into his personal notebook and made an outline for himself, taking care to put extra guards on it so that no one could eavesdrop on his ideas. He smiled as he read the words appearing on the screen; the solution was so elegant, and it would not require much in the way of funding, making it exactly the sort of plan that Mister Tarlington sought.

Shortly before he was finished, his assistant buzzed him and told him that Clara Martin wanted to see if before the meeting. "She says it's important."

"She always says it's important," Fred declared, for once feeling secure against her. "And it always is, for her." He continued for another few minutes, and then filed his material. "All right. Where is she?"

"The lounge. She's working over lunch, she says." His assistant looked at Fred with conspiratorial amusement. "Very determined."

"Without doubt," said Fred, disliking the way his stomach clenched. "I'll go have a word with her." It seemed reasonable enough, he decided. He did not want to face her wrath at the meeting.

By the time he reached the lounge, Clara Martin was growing impatient. "Late again," she said, making it a reprimand.

"Hardly. I'm trying to catch up, is all. I want to be ready for the meeting this afternoon. I guess we all do." He sat down on one of the comfortless sofas and propped an ankle on his knee.

Do Not Pass Go Do Do Not Collect $200

"Sorry I kept you waiting. But I know I'm not the only one who was caught in traffic this morning."

"Everyone on the north and east side of town was caught in traffic," she said, as if it were his fault for living in the wrong place. "It's very inconvenient."

"That it is." He waited. "Is there something you wanted to tell me, Clara?"

She pursed her lips. "I've been informed you have a very good prospectus to present."

He was startled but strove to conceal it. "Oh?"

"It's not possible to keep secrets in the department, you ought to know that by now. People talk. The staff knows everything." She favored him with a pitying smile. "Your people are no exception. They talk."

He wondered who had blabbed, and what had been said, but all he offered in response was, "I don't pay much attention to gossip, Clara. You know that."

"Oh, Fred, Fred," said Clara with her best schoolmarm smile. "You're so naive in some ways. It's amazing you've progressed this far." She folded her hands and got down to business. "Tarlington took my report for his lunchtime reading. I have a very good outline of the trouble we face. It's probably the most complete study anyone has done in the department, and the best statistical projections." She made sure he understood how powerful her position was before she went on. "But word has it that you have the best series of recommendations and the most comprehensive solutions to the problem."

"That's flattering to know," said Fred. "I'd like to think it's true, too."

Clara Martin sat straighter, prepared to make her case. "The State Department of Coastal Zoning, Harbors and Fisheries has a mandate to preserve the oceans and police toxic containment facilities. And there have been fourteen complaints of beached whales in the last month. That's the Bureau of Fish, Game and Wildlife, but they try to foist it off on us. Water quality for a distance of twenty miles out to sea is our responsibility, as well as the protection of the coast itself, not the creatures in the water. As things are, we haven't the funds to do the tasks we're mandated to do, let alone the jobs other departments and agencies don't want to handle. Our authority is limited; in spite of our best efforts all our citations have resulted in prolonged court battles." She stared at Fred, daring him to contradict her. "Well, Mister Blue?"

"That's the way things have turned out," he agreed, wondering why she was belaboring the obvious.

"And we are supposed to find a way to increase our authority without interfering with other state or federal agencies, and to do it without any significant increase in our budget. That is what Mister Tarlington has asked us to do, isn't it?"

"What are you leading up to?" Fred asked.

"I am suggesting that we join forces, Mister Blue. That you and I pool our information and our results and offer them as a package to Tarlington. Otherwise he might not relate them, and that could mean that we do not get our chance to put some teeth into the SDCZHandF."

Fred felt his spine go cold, but he continued his most affable smile. "I suppose you have a point there," he declared as if Ms Martin's suggestion of co-operation was characteristic of her.

"Of course I have a point," she said with exasperation. "Think of what this could mean to the both of us a couple years down the line. Don't play the innocent with me, Fred Blue. I know you are as eager to improve your position as I am. So think about what we could do for each other."

"And what about the coast and the harbors and the fisheries?" Fred dared to ask. "What about them."

"Oh, we'd be able to protect them better, if the feds will get the FEHCA to go along with our program." She plainly thought this was of secondary importance. "But if we are allowed to run the program, we'll make quite a niche for ourselves."

Fred could not help frowning. "And what if the FEHCA people want to keep control of it for themselves? They've already opened up whole sections of coast to federal development, and there's nothing we can do about it, though it goes against all of our codes. If we try to get under their umbrella, won't that make it more likely that the feds will call the tune?"

She shook her head emphatically. "Not if we handle it right," she said with utter conviction. "We can arrange it so that all their programs have to pass our approval, and that should take care of it."

"Un-huh," said Fred, unconvinced.

"It could turn out very well, Fred," she said with what was for her a winning smile. "You mustn't forget that the feds are all playing their little political games in Washington. We're small potatoes for them, and that can help us very much." She smoothed her skirt then folded her hands again. "I've seen your

prospectus," she said blandly.

It was an effort for Fred not to lurch to his feet. "You didn't!" he protested.

"I didn't intend to, and I certainly didn't think my staff would," she said mendaciously. "But you know how the 'techs like to play with computers. Any time they find a locking code, they worry at it until they break it. It happened with your files, I regret to say. Though," she added as an afterthought, "Brian did say yours were about the best locks he'd found in the department."

"I see," said Fred. He wondered what he could do to salvage his position now. "And how do you intend to use the files, again?"

She shifted in the chair and made a show of thinking about it. "I can't believe that you would want to have your files used by someone like Willie Monroe, or any of the others. And it is ridiculous to think that others won't break into your files in time. So it seems to me that we ought to take half an hour or so and work out a scheme that incorporates your material and mine in a joint prospectus, with provisos that would keep us in strong positions. If you take my meaning."

Fred nodded. "Your project and mine combined."

"Yes. Since Mister Tarlington already has mine in hand, you would share in the advantage of his early attention. You know how important that first position can be, don't you? And if we tell him that we are dovetailing our work, he will be pleased because it goes along with his orders to economize and co-operate."

"In other words it helps all around," said Fred.

"Exactly," Clara Martin said, beaming at him, enjoying herself.

"I see." He looked down at his foot where it rested on his knee. "There isn't much I can say, is there?"

"Yes or no will do," said Ms Martin. "It would be foolish to say no, and from your prospectus it seems to me that you're not a foolish man, Fred. Too bad you weren't able to get here on time this morning. You might have had the upper hand, not me."

"Um-humm," said Fred.

"I'd give you time to think it over, but the meeting starts pretty soon, and so you'll have to make a snap decision." Her eyes glistened behind her tortoise-shell uncorrective glasses.

"It's only been cobbled together," Clara Martin said apologetically as she faced Mister Tarlington across the conference room. "We decided that it would be best to combine our efforts, since we seem to be moving in the same direction. Less redundancy that way."

"Really," said Tarlington. "That's in your favor already."

Fred sat beside Ms Martin and stared down at his shoes, disliking the bargain he had made. It was the only way to keep his proposed program under consideration, he reminded himself, but this pragmatic assessment did little to assuage the sense of prevailing failure that had come over him ever since he and Clara Martin had shaken hands an hour ago.

"I think you'll find that the project my department has undertaken fits right in with the projections that Mister Blue has detailed in his prospectus. Given the trouble we have had in the past in enforcing our rulings, I think that Mister Blue's suggestions are appropriate and apt." For her this was high praise, but it was given for a specific purpose. "I suspect Mister Blue and I will want to make some adjustment in his schematic once we have analyzed the current material in my report. But in large part I believe that we have the closest thing to a solution to our problems that keeps within our current budget." She was aware she was making a good impression so she went on. "We'd appreciate your thoughts on the fiscal implications of our program."

Tarlington looked from Clara Martin to the rest of the bureaucrats attending the meeting—there were a total of sixteen of them, two were missing; one was in critical condition in the hospital following a daylight mugging, and the other had been killed during the traffic crisis when a disgruntled fellow-motorist had blasted him with a twelve-gauge shotgun—and then glanced at the tower of prospectuses and reports that lay on the lectern. "I'll have to give the rest a chance," he said, but there was the sound of finality in his words that was heard by all of them.

"I understand that, Mister Tarlington," said Clara Martin, knowing she was secure as she sat down again.

"Yes," said Mister Tarlington with the uneasy feeling that Ms Martin had somehow manoeuvered him into this position. "Well, I do appreciate all the work every one of you has done, and I'm certain that once we've settled on a course, we'll all close ranks and support the work."

All sixteen of them nodded, and a few murmured assurances that they were ready to do whatever the department required of them.

Fred hated it all, and yet he could not pretend to be surprised, not after thirteen years in the State Department of Coastal Zoning, Harbors and Fisheries. He had always wanted to do something that would be useful, and taking care of the environment seemed to be the most useful thing he could think of. When he entered the SDCZHandF he had been shiny with purpose. The shine had been the first to go, but he still clung to his ideals against the constant onslaughts of political ploys and personal agendas. Now he condemned himself for succumbing to the same lures that the rest had. He noticed the rest of the department heads had risen and belatedly got to his feet.

"Is there something on your mind, Mister Blue?" asked Tarlington.

Clara Martin intervened. "I think we've both got our projects on our minds, Mister Tarlington."

"Actually," said Fred, getting slowly to his feet, "there is something on my mind." He shoved his hands into his pockets. "It's not projects, though, it's more than that."

"How is that, Mister Blue?" Tarlington did his best to be polite.

"It is...the whole thing, all of it." He looked at Mister Tarlington. "We make regulations, and the Governor backs us up, but nothing happens, and things get worse, or one of the big companies files suit and by the time the case works its way through the courts and appeals and the rest, it's out of our hands anyway, and..." He struggled to find the words. "We're supposed to take care of the coast, keep it safe. We're supposed to make sure our harbors are free from pollution and silt and overdevelopment. We're supposed to make sure the commercial fishermen have safe fish to catch, and that they don't catch too many of them. But if they take too many, they sell them at sea to one of the other countries out there, and if the fish aren't safe, they sell them to the fertilizer companies, and we still have to eat the poisons they contain. We're a sham, a fake." He looked at Tarlington. "We haven't the time, we haven't the personnel, we haven't the funds, and we haven't the clout. We're a bandage on a burst appendix. And people think that because we're around, they're safe."

All the department heads were staring at him, a few of them moving back to put the greatest possible distance between them

and Fred. Clara Martin glared at him in fury.

"That's a very interesting perspective, Mister Blue," said Tarlington after a short silence. "It's something we will have to talk about in future."

"That's what I mean!" Fred burst out, aware that he was only digging himself a deeper hole, but suddenly not caring. "You'll talk about it, and you'll make resolutions and everyone will agree and nothing—*nothing!*—will happen. If you try to assert your authority, the feds will step in and over-ride you, and you'll all start from scratch with another plan that doesn't step on federal toes, or the corporations the state protects. You'll all be doing projections and prospectuses and all the rest of it when the beaches are littered with dying sea lions and the whales are gone, when the harbors are quagmires and every little bay for a thousand miles has a cluster of factory-workers' condos on them, and the factory has inadequate screening for effluvia." He rounded on Ms Martin. "Sorry, Clara, but I can't adapt any more." Then he turned back to Mister Tarlington. "I'll fax you my resignation."

"Turn over all your codes before you leave," said Tarlington flatly.

"I'll fax them, too," said Fred, and picked up his dispatch case. "I hope you can figure a way out of this mess."

"It certainly won't be your way, Mister Blue," said Tarlington. "If you have a way."

"He's been under a great deal of stress, Mister Tarlington," said Clara Martin unexpectedly. "This outburst isn't like him at all. He's been doing excellent work in his department. Everyone knows that. Well, you can tell from how upset he is, that he is concerned for the welfare of this Bureau, and our effectiveness. If you review the material I've given you, you'll see how thorough his calculations are, and how well they fit into what my department has done. His ideas in his prospectus are quite well-considered, but—" She stopped as soon as Tarlington raised his hand. The look she shot toward Fred was vitriolic.

Fred's sense of relief vanished as soon as it came: Ms Martin was not defending him, she was trying to salvage her project and position for herself. Anger went through him, then vanished. If that was her desire, he was willing to let her have it. He no longer had an obligation to any of them, or to the SDCZHandF. At last his ties were severed. He hurried out of the conference room, glad that none of his former colleagues came after him. He could hear whispers start as he passed as

word spread through the secretarial pool. No one spoke to him. No one tried to reason with him, or stop him. There was, he decided, a certain liberty in being a pariah.

Won't Painted Jaguar Be Surprised

It was only a storefront, and the letters on the door had been painted by hand and not computer-etched. Inside the staff of six volunteers and two paid employees put on their last burst of speed to finish their new edition of **The Awful Truth**. The newsletter was considered chic in some circles, but for the most part it was regarded as raving and rambling from an excitable minority.

"The trouble is," said Cal Morgenstern who edited and published **The Awful Truth**, "no one wants to talk to us, no one on the inside."

"You can't blame them. If anything leaked, they'd lose their jobs and probably couldn't get another," said Sammy, a housewife-turned-activist of about forty-five.

"Right," agreed the slender, thirty-year-old Mark whose arms were badly scarred by acid.

Cal sighed and trimmed another hundred sheets. "No argument. And it's not as if **The Awful Truth** has prestige or grants to compensate for being out of work." He had said this before but everyone nodded commiseration.

"True enough," said his assistant Bernadette, a sloe-eyed exotic in blue jeans and an over-sized and shapeless shirt. "But you can dream." She handled the cranky, twelve-year-old-laser printer with care, coaxing pages out of it with patience as if caring for an ancient relative.

One of the volunteers, a wild-haired former college athlete known as Jumby, loaded another stack of collated pages for stapling. "It shouldn't take that. The facts ought to speak for themselves, no matter what the officials say. Besides, we've got good material on that spill last week, the one in Ventner's Harbor. You don't need an official to take samples of the water and get it analyzed."

"Perhaps not," said Bernadette fatalistically. "But everyone says we're fudging the findings. You know that." They had some variation on this discussion every two weeks as they readied the newsletter for distribution.

"And we know that the official agencies fudge on *their* figures." Cal shrugged. "All we can do is let the public know that

it ain't necessarily so." He whistled a few Gershwin bars. "Come on, let's get this done so we call get home."

For a time everyone worked quietly, concentrating on the repetitious tasks. There would be time to wrangle again when the work was done.

A little over half an hour later there was a sharp knock at the door, and for an moment there was stillness.

"What do you think?" Bernadette whispered to Cal.

"I don't know," he admitted, remembering with the rest of them the incident over a year ago when the place had been sacked by a group of angry young men.

The knock came again, a bit louder, and a call. "Is anyone there? I was told you'd still be here."

Jumby—by virtue of being the biggest of them—started toward the door. "Who told you?"

"Louisa Morgenstern," said the voice, naming Cal's sister. "She said you hadn't left yet."

Cal signaled Jumby to open the door. "Let's see who it is," he said, trying to be jaunty and failing. He was tense as the door swung open. "Good evening," he made himself tell the newcomer.

"To you, too," said Fred. He was beaming, holding out his hand with puppy-like eagerness. "May I come in?"

"Sure," said Cal dubiously, standing back. He glanced out into the street before he closed the door. "You alone?"

"Oh, yeah," said Fred. "No job, no place to stay since my wife kicked me out, no prospects."

Cal had seen his share of beggars, and steeled himself against the protracted tale of woe he knew was coming.

"But that gets me off the hook," Fred went on, much to the surprise of everyone at **The Awful Truth**. "I couldn't have come here while I was still with Penny, because it would have been bad for her career, you know—not that I wasn't embarrassment enough, but..." He cleared his throat and started again. "I want to help. I know you're a long shot, but you're the only place..."

Not a beggar, thought Cal in concealed annoyance. This one has a revealed truth to lay on us. Every now and then one of those came along, with prophesies and visions. He folded his arms, saying, "Mister...Uh, we have a newsletter to get out. It's late and we're all tired."

"I know, I know," said Fred. "And I know you want to get back to your work. I know that." He looked around with subdued excitement. "But don't you see, after being fired, I didn't think anyone would be willing to listen. I only found out about you by accident."

"I see," said Cal.

The rest of the staff was growing restive. Jumby shifted from one foot to the other, his face hardening.

"But when I found your newsletter," Fred went on, oblivious to the disapproval around him. "I knew that you'd be willing to hear me out. I tried other places, papers and news stations, but once they learned I'd been fired, they didn't want to talk to me. I think someone told them I'd had a breakdown."

"Fired from where, Mister...Erh?" asked Bernadette more to cut Fred's recital short than to gain any useful information.

"Oh, from the SDCZHandF," he said. "I thought you understood that."

"The SDCZ..." Cal's expression changed. "The State Department of Coastal Zoning, Harbor and Fisheries?"

"Yes," said Fred, and tried to begin again. "I was fired. Well, I guess actually I quit. You see, I...I had some trouble with policy. I thought maybe you'd want to know about it." He paused, and went on very quietly, "I hope you're interested. If you're not interested, I don't think anyone will want to listen to me."

"I'm *becoming* interested, Mister...Er?" said Cal, moving aside so that Fred could come farther into the vast, utilitarian room.

"Oh, Blue. I'm Fred Blue. Manfred Blue, really, but Manfred..." He stopped himself. "I was head of the Enforcement Projection Department, meaning I had to try to guess which of the lawsuits we were facing would be decided in our favor. It was a pretty thankless task." He hurried on. "Not that I minded that part; I wasn't doing it to be thanked. But it was hard to watch the other side win all the time. I got so I couldn't take it any more."

Cal's eyes were brightening. "And you'd like to tell me about it?"

"Yes," said Fred, and went on with care, "But not just that, the whole thing, the whole bureau and...and the rest of it." He hesitated again. "I think I might have to write a book, but I don't think anyone but someone like you would be willing to publish it. And I don't write very well."

"We can take care of that," said Cal.

"What about the bomb threats?" asked Jumby nervously.

"We haven't published yet," said Cal. "We'll worry about

them when we get them." He regarded Fred narrowly. "Do you mean this? Are you willing to talk to us?"

"That's what I came here for," said Fred.

Bernadette cocked her head on the side. "And you're not going to change your mind, or try to get into the Department's good graces again by using this as leverage? You really want to help us out?"

"Yes," said Fred. "Truly."

"All right," Cal decided. "If you mean it, come here tomorrow at noon and we'll get started. But I better warn you, I want the whole story. All of it."

"You'll get it," said Fred. "Tomorrow at noon. Great. I'll be here." He gestured to the half-filled boxes. "I know you have work to do. I won't get in your way any longer." He edged toward the door. "Thanks. Really. Thanks for everything." Before anyone could speak, he was gone.

For the next two hours as they trimmed and collated and stapled and stacked **The Awful Truth**, each of the eight people indulged in speculation about their unexpected visitor.

"I'll bet anyone twenty dollars that he doesn't show tomorrow," said Jumby.

"You're on," said Mark.

Cal, who had pulled on his jacket and was about to close down the office for the night, paused to turn on the radio for traffic bulletins.

"…and three cars are stopped in the west-bound center lane. Expect a ten minute delay. On State Alternate 54A South there is a high-speed chase in progress, cars and copters in pursuit of a high-speed all-terrain military transport. Motorists are requested to find other routes until the fleeing vehicle is stopped. On the north freeway bypass we're just getting reports of a series of drive-by shootings. Nine drivers reported killed, another ten seriously injured. Motorists are advised to avoid that part of the freeway. State Throughway #48 is backed up three miles due to an overturned chemical trailer." Cal snapped the radio off.

"Those poor drivers on north bypass," said Bernadette, preparing to drive one of their three step vans to the distributor's warehouse. "Hell of a thing."

"What a way to go," Cal agreed with a shake of his head. "Just random *pow* and that's it."

"Somebody should do something about it," said Bernadette as Cal turned out the lights.

Genesis II

Hugh B. Cave

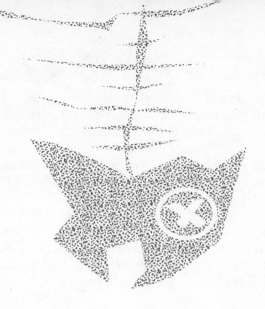

On the sixteenth day they came to a small lake that seemed to have possibilities. Heller, who by this time had assumed the role of expedition commander, first tested the water with one of the kits issued by the government, then cupped some in his hands and tasted it.

"This could be what we're looking for. I say we give it a try for a few days, anyway."

"It isn't going to be any different, you know," Lamont Pitman said. At 26 he was the youngest; he'd worked in a pharmacy. "Like I've been telling all of you from the start—"

"Lamont, shut up," Wade DaCosta said patiently. Wade was 30 and had managed an auto-parts store.

"Okay. But you know I'm right. All of you know I'm right." It was not defiance, only a quiet statement from a quiet man.

Heller, who at 32 was the oldest now and by far the most assertive—he'd owned a gun store—scowled at the women and said, "Well? You girls agree we should give it a try here?"

His overweight wife Sandy quickly said yes. Wade's pretty wife Dorita, wanting only to lie down somewhere, said without feeling, "Whatever you think is best, Heller. You'll do what you want to, anyway."

Blonde Kristina Strachen, Lamont's girl, said she agreed with Lamont. "Like he keeps telling us, it isn't going to make much difference unless we get rid of the rot that's in our hearts. Which I'm afraid"—and she looked straight at Heller—"some of us haven't."

At any other time Heller might have responded to that with an angry "Oh, shit." But they had done miles of portaging that day and were close to exhaustion. The canoes for which they had traded their cars in Burleson, at the end of their long drive from the city, were fine in the water but lead-heavy when carried. So heavy that the women had had to carry most of the gear and supplies.

"Lamont and I will try for some fish while the rest of you make camp," Heller said in his voice of command. "If the water's fit to drink like the kit says, then the fish should be okay to eat. Lamont, we'll need some live bait." He turned to glare. "Damn it, I wish to Christ you'd been more careful with that last lure of ours."

Kristina came to her man's defense, of course. They had planned to marry before people stopped doing that. "Now, Heller, it wasn't his fault. Anyone can snag bottom in a strange lake. You yourself lost some of the others."

"All right, all right. But it was our last fucking lure!"

"Heller, please," Dorita said.

"Please what?"

"Your language. If we're going to make a new world together in this wilderness—"

"What the hell has language got to do with it?" Heller flung back. Then to Lamont he said, "Well, are you coming? The bait won't come to us, for Christ's sake."

"You don't have to yell, Heller," Lamont said. "I'm coming."

As the two went along the shore, Lamont wondered which of the many new kinds of creepy-crawlies Heller might be looking for. They hadn't used live bait before. A little apprehensive, he began thinking of all that had happened since their flight from the city.

They had anticipated some monumental problems, of course. Everything was difficult these days, and an expedition of this magnitude cried out for careful planning. But there hadn't been time enough. When city officials suddenly announced a doubling of the weekly death toll in only one week, all had agreed it was imperative to leave at once.

"Any one of us could be mugged this very night on our way home, even in a respectable neighborhood like this," Mark Heller had said that evening at Professor Sadeo's house, where they and the three now dead had met as neighbors to discuss the situation. "Or we could die from drinking the water, or get cancer of the lungs from breathing this filthy air. I say if we want to

survive, we have to get the hell out of here right now and make a new life in an unspoiled wilderness somewhere. You agree?"

All had agreed.

"All right, then," Heller had continued. "I know a town on the north shore of Lake Huron where we can rent canoes and camping gear and hire guides. My dad and some pals of his did it once, back when people did that kind of thing for fun. We can head north toward Hudson's Bay, portaging between lakes. There are lots of lakes in there." A little drunk, Heller had walked around the room waving his hands while he talked. Then suddenly he stopped and grinned. "How about it, huh? A bunch of Adam-and-Eves looking for a new Eden. Only it'll be a damn sight colder than the first one. We sure as hell won't be running around naked."

He had been right about the town but wrong about the guides; none would have anything to do with such a venture. The outfitter, though, had been willing to give them canoes and camping gear in exchange for their cars, which they had planned to abandon there anyway. So with pup tents and supplies, but only a map to guide them, they had said goodbye to what was left of civilization.

Lamont still remembered a remark made that morning by the professor, the oldest among them. He had taught history at the university, and just before stepping into his canoe he had said, "I wonder what my father would say were he alive today to see us doing this. I was nine years old when he died in 1994, and he firmly believed the planet would perish in a nuclear war begun by some Arab state in the Middle East. Somehow I think this is worse because it is taking so much longer."

In the beginning there had been nine of them. Remembering the afternoon their number was reduced to six, Lamont felt sick all over again as he followed Heller along the shore. Professor Sadeo, his red-haired Irish wife Katy, and Terry Dirks, the one man in the group who didn't have a woman, had gone into the forest together to find wood for the fire. When they didn't return, Wade DaCosta and he, Lamont, had gone looking for them. What they found wasn't pretty. Just bits and pieces of bodies, and boots, and some bloody scraps of clothing. Even one of the boots had been half eaten.

Heller, when led to the scene, had wasted several minutes saying things like "God almighty!" and "Jesus Christ!" and "What the living hell could have done this?" Footprints around the remains indicated something very big had done it, but with

so many new mutations constantly appearing, not everything had a name these days. Heller shouted more of the blasphemies and obscenities they had learned by now to expect from him—outbursts none of them had ever heard him use back home—and at last he said they must break camp and leave.

"We have to bury them first," Lamont protested.

"Bury them!" Heller yelled. "Are you out of your fucking mind? Whatever did this could come back any minute and do it to the rest of us!"

Kristina Strachen stepped to Lamont's side and said, "No, no, Heller. Lamont is right. We can't go until—"

"Then you two idiots stay and bury them," Heller said, "and we'll leave a canoe for you. With three people dead, we only need two canoes now, anyhow. It'll be easier on those damned portages, too, thank God. The rest of you come on, let's go!"

It didn't happen that way, exactly. Lamont and Kristina had stayed to bury what was left of the three bodies and had even taken time to mark the graves with simple crosses made from dead tree-limbs. But they did it in a hurry and were back at camp before the others had finished loading the canoes, so they were not left behind after all.

But Lamont would never forget that day—especially how he had felt on seeing the huge footprints. Because they had been human footprints, he was certain. And months ago one of the professor's university colleagues had publicly warned that with so many mutants appearing in the animal world, there might soon be some among humans as well. "Anything mankind is capable of imagining is potentially possible" was the way he had put it.

Just ahead, Heller suddenly dropped to his knees and grabbed at something, then rose to his feet again and turned around. He had a strange-looking frog in his hands: more yellow than green, and with three eyes in a head that seemed to be too big for its body. For some reason—perhaps because of the extra eye—Lamont felt sorry for it.

"What do you think?" Heller asked.

"It's too big, Heller. Don't you think it's too big?"

"Well…oh, shit, I suppose so." Heller spat in the frog's face and hurled it full-force against a nearby boulder, where it hit with a sodden thud. Fragments flew back with such force that some of them splattered against Lamont's pants and one stuck to his neck.

He winced as he took a rag of handkerchief from his pocket

and rubbed his neck clean. "Did you have to do that, Heller?"

"Did I have to do what? What the hell are you talking about?"

"Kill it? It wasn't doing us any harm, Heller."

"Jesus Christ," Heller said. "What the hell's got into you? Here we are in a world gone stark raving mad, a world all poisoned and sick, and you worry about what I do with a dumb frog that's got too many eyes!"

Lamont looked away in silence, knowing no good could come of continuing such an argument.

Soon afterward, Heller found some smaller frogs and some crickets to use for bait, and the two men went out on the lake in one of the canoes. After fishing for an hour they returned with enough trout for all. Wade DaCosta by then had finished setting up the three pup tents and had a fire going among some boulders they could sit on while they ate. The three women did the cooking, as usual.

"If we decide to stay here, what's the plan?" Wade's wife asked when their first pangs of hunger had been satisfied and they were eating more slowly. The question took the others somewhat by surprise, because, though pretty, Dorita was a small, quiet woman who seldom initiated a conversation.

"What's the plan?" Heller echoed with a frown. "Why, each of us picks out a site and starts building a cabin." Presumably he meant each couple.

"Where?"

"Wherever we want to, for God's sake. The government owns this wilderness, and nobody's coming in here to charge us rent. You can be sure of that."

"Are you talking about cabins close together?" Dorita persisted. "Like in a group?"

Lamont Pitman answered that. "No, not too close," he said quickly.

Heller peered at him under lowered brows. "What's that supposed to mean? If we build our cabins in a cluster we can be like one family. The men can hunt and fish; the women can do the cooking and washing and maybe scrounge around for berries and such."

"And when the children start coming, as they will if we survive—what then?" Kristina asked, reaching for Lamont's hand as if for reassurance that he would stand by her if Heller became angry.

"What?"

"Each of us—each couple—will want to bring up our own

children in our own way. I know I will. That can't be a community thing."

"Good grief." Heller screwed his heavy-jowled face up as if the mere thought of children caused him intense pain. "Who the hell is thinking about kids at this stage of the game?"

"We are," said Lamont, clutching Kristina's hand. "And no matter what the rest of you decide, I plan to build our cabin where we can be alone when we want to be."

"Dorita and I, too," Wade DaCosta said.

"Okay, okay," Heller retorted. "But if you're half a mile from where I'm living, don't expect me to come running every time you holler for help." He finished eating and got to his feet, leaving his plastic plate on the ground for his wife to pick up. "See you later. You want meat tomorrow, I have to clean my gun."

The victim this time was not a three-eyed frog. In the morning, hoping to kill a deer and knowing he would need help in getting the animal back to camp, Heller again designated Lamont to accompany him. To be as quiet as possible, the former pharmacy worker walked a few steps behind him on the hunt.

When they had covered about a mile, Lamont carefully blazing trees with his knife to be sure they would be able to find their way back, Heller signaled his companion to halt. But the creature making the noise he had heard was not one they could use for food. It was only a porcupine waddling out of some underbrush, unaware that strangers had entered its domain.

A few minutes later it was a bird that caused the hunter to halt—one that Lamont did not recognize, but that appeared to be all legs and scrawny neck and was certainly nothing to feed six hungry persons. With a limited supply of shells, Heller could not afford to waste one on such a target.

He wanted to, though; Lamont could see that. First with the porcupine, then with the bird, the hunter had whipped the gun to his shoulder and taken aim, keeping a bead on the creatures until they disappeared.

He's the kind of man who enjoys killing things, Lamont thought, and remembered something his Kristina had said when they were alone together in their tent. In the quiet way she spoke when she had been thinking a lot, she had said, "You know something? I've decided it's silly for us to be praying to God to stop what's happening. He isn't the one poisoning this poor planet. He gave us a world that was pure. We're the ones who have loused it up—with the way we behave and think, and

even the way some of us talk."

Heller had stopped again, flapping a hand behind his back as a warning. Halting, Lamont peered past him into a clump of trees ahead. This time the forest creature that appeared was neither porcupine nor bird, but a skunk. At least, it had the black and white markings of a skunk. These days, you couldn't be certain. In any case it was a small one, perhaps a baby.

Heller, of course, had taken aim the moment he saw it. Now, with his legs spread wide and a finger on the trigger, he actually began to tremble. Lamont could see him tremble. This time the temptation was too great. His finger tightened. A thunderclap shattered the forest silence. The tiny black and white animal flew through the air to land in a small, quivering heap nearly twenty feet away.

Remembering the three-eyed frog, Lamont realized the futility of protesting and decided to remain silent.

Half an hour later the hunter killed a small deer and they carried it back to camp.

Kristina had been keeping a diary. On the twentieth of June, a week after their decision to stay at the lake, she wrote her longest entry since their flight from the city.

"Something terrible has happened. I can hardly find the words to describe it. In fact, though it happened several hours ago, my hand is still shaking as I write this.

"Heller said we should pick out our cabin sites, and of course we all wanted the pretty little spit of land that sticks out into the lake. So the men drew for it, using the pack of cards Heller brought along, and Heller won. He drew the king of spades, Wade the jack of diamonds, and my Lamont the two of hearts.

"Right away, Heller's Sandy said she was going for a swim in her front yard and proceeded to get undressed. Heller laughed and called her crazy, and the rest of us didn't feel like swimming after losing, so she went in alone. We don't have any swimsuits, of course. We had too many more important things to carry. But Sandy stripped to her bra and panties as we women have been doing —the men strip to their shorts—and ran into the lake laughing and shouting like a child.

"We all saw what happened because we were all standing there on the shore watching her. But afterward, when we talked about it, none of us could actually describe the creature. That's because Sandy, weighing over 200 pounds, made a big splash when she finished her run and fell forward in what she would

have said was a dive. It was like a geyser erupting, and in the midst of the eruption there was this yellow and green shape that looked to me, at least, like the head of a big frog, but it had three eyes. Lamont says it was a frog and he saw one like it when he and Heller were hunting for live bait the other day. But that was a small one, he says, and anyway Heller killed it.

"Wade and Dorita couldn't say what it was they saw, only that it had a huge mouth that opened up under Sandy and sucked her down into it, feet first. I saw her disappear screaming into the frog's mouth, then the mouth snapped shut, and a second or two later a great big bubble shot up from the depths and exploded, sending a kind of red froth in all directions. There are still smearings of red froth on the shore there.

"None of us was brave enough to go rushing into the water to investigate. I think even Heller was scared, although he began shouting his usual blasphemies and four-letter words. In fact, he kept it up so long that the rest of us decided he was out of his mind with grief. But now that the first shock has passed, he doesn't seem to be grieving much. Just before I began writing this, I saw him come out of the woods dragging a log for the cabin he's building. He'll live in it alone, he says.

"P.S. Lamont just came into the tent. After reading what I've written here, he told me how Heller killed the other three-eyed frog. Both of us are beginning to have some thoughts about what is happening in the world. Or, to be more precise, why it is happening."

Wade DaCosta had begun it. Now all of them called Heller Der Führer behind his back.

He had pitched his tent on the spit of land where he was building his cabin, and he kept one of the two canoes there. One day when he and Lamont returned from a morning of fishing, he stepped ashore and began to urinate on the sand.

Lamont, still in the canoe, watched in astonishment until he was finished, then said, "Heller, we drink this water!"

Heller looked up in disgust while zipping his fly. "Now what the hell are you bitching about?"

"We drink it! It's the only water we have!"

"Oh, for Christ's sake, shut up! All kinds of animals piss in it. The other day I even saw a moose crap in it."

Lamont gave up. But in tossing ashore the fish they had caught, he was careful not to throw them on the patch of sand darkened by Heller's urine. And on the way to the cluster of

boulders where the women still did the cooking for all, he ventured one last comment.

"Heller..."

"Yeah?"

"We did build a latrine, you know. We did agree not to relieve ourselves anywhere but there."

Heller stopped walking and turned to face him. "Lamont, for Christ's sake, I had to. Right there, right then, I had to. It wouldn't wait. So stop making such a lousy fuss about it, will you?"

With a sigh of surrender, Lamont walked on in silence.

With vegetable seeds brought from the city, Lamont had planted a garden, but nothing was up yet. The morning after the urination incident, Wade and his wife Dorita went into the forest to look for berries, mushrooms, and whatever other growing things they might find that were good to eat.

When the two did not return after the usual hour or so, the others were not immediately concerned. But when lunchtime passed and they were still absent, Lamont remembered what had happened to the Sadeos and said he would look for them.

"Wait," said Kristina quickly. "I'll go with you." Her glance at Heller clearly said that if left alone with Der Führer she would be afraid. Or at least uncomfortable.

Soon after leaving the campsite, she and Lamont began calling the names of those they sought, but they received no answer. An hour passed. Two. With no way of knowing which way the missing persons might have wandered, they were about to give up and go back. "They're lost," Lamont said. "The best thing we can do is return and light a fire, so they'll see the smoke."

Then suddenly the search ended.

This time the footprints did not appear to be human ones. When the first shock of finding the two mangled bodies had passed, Lamont examined the ground more carefully and settled on what he thought might be an answer.

The professor and his wife had been killed when the journey into the wilderness had only just begun. There had been people. Not the milling crowds they had left behind in the city, of course, but still people. Where there were people, there could have been mutations.

What had done this to Wade and Dorita was not human. Though as big as the others, these prints had been made by an

animal. The animal had left something else as well—a strong, unpleasant odor. So strong it burned Lamont's lungs and made Kristina's eyes water.

"A skunk?" Lamont speculated. "A skunk big enough to do this?" Because the two bodies had not been eaten—just ripped apart. Did skunks have claws? He didn't know. He had never been that close to one. Or had the maker of the footprints done this with its teeth?

Kristina had not answered him. On her knees, head bowed, she sobbed into her hands.

When recovered enough, they returned to the campsite and told Heller what they had found; then the three of them went back to bury the bodies. The digging was hard because the ground there was laced with tree roots and they had only a small camp spade. Heller, being the strongest, did most of the work. When finished, he returned to camp alone, leaving Lamont and Kristina to mark the mound with crosses.

As those two trudged back to camp, Lamont said in a low voice, thoughtfully, "There was something more to this than a mutation, Kris."

She looked at him. "What are you saying?"

"You saw how those two were torn to pieces. I think something wanted revenge."

"Revenge? On Wade and Dorita?"

"Not necessarily on them. When we're angry, do we always save our anger for the real culprit?" He stopped and turned to face her. "Heller killed a skunk there, Kris. He killed it the same way he killed the frog, for no reason except to satisfy some — hunger. I should have told you, but didn't want to upset you."

"A skunk?" Kristina looked back the way they had come, as if smelling the skunk odor and seeing the footprints again.

"More than ever, I think I know what's happening," Lamont said. "Not just to us, but everywhere. We have to talk about it."

"Yes." She looked at him. "And soon. While there's still time."

But when they reached the campsite, they found Heller on the spit, rolling up his tent. "We're leaving," he told them. "It was a mistake to think we could live here. We need to find a safer place."

"A safer place where?" Lamont said.

"How the hell do I know where? All I know is, if there's something around here tearing people to pieces, we have to get away from it!"

There by the beginnings of Heller's log cabin Lamont looked at Kristina, then back at the other man, and said very quietly, "Let's talk about this, shall we? Before we do something foolish?"

But Der Führer was angry. Or frightened. "We don't have time for talk, damn it!" he shouted. "I'm ready to leave now, so put your stuff in the canoe." He pointed to the canoe he always kept there on the spit. "With only the three of us left, we can't handle both, so we're using this one. And hurry up, will you, for Christ's sake! You saw what happened back there in the woods!"

With his tent over one shoulder he went striding down to the lake shore.

"Do you want to go with him, Kris?" Lamont asked.

Kristina shook her head.

"What if he tries to force us?"

She shrugged. "Why should he? He's never thought he needed anyone."

Heller strode onto the sand.

And stopped.

And yelled.

It happened so quickly that the two watching him had no time to help. When he dropped the tent and began shouting obscenities they began running, but the sand simply opened up and sucked him down. As they ran toward him they saw his expression change from rage to terror. Then the bulging eyes and screaming mouth were suddenly gone, the hole in the sand had closed, and it was as though nothing at all had happened there to shatter the quiet.

Lamont and Kristina could only stand there, side by side, staring in silence at the place where it had happened.

"It's where he did it," Lamont said at last.

"Did what?"

"Urinated."

That night, in their tent, Lamont and Kristina talked. They talked about what had happened to Heller. About whether they should leave or stay. About the future they now faced alone. In the moments when they were not talking, they were aware of a stillness profound enough to be a form of blessing.

"I think we brought the madness with us," Lamont said. "If you remember...from the third day out we kept thinking we had escaped and were safe. But always something spoiled it."

"But why the professor and his wife?" she asked. "Why Wade

and Dorita? Why even Sandy, for that matter? None of them did anything."

"Nature couldn't know who the offenders were," Lamont said. "When you stick a finger into a nest of hornets, they sting anyone they can reach."

"And in this case the finger was Heller..."

"In this case the finger was Heller. But not until today did the hornets sting the right one." Lamont looked at her. "Maybe that's what's going on everywhere. Nature is just trying to destroy the offenders."

After a long silence, Kristina spoke again. "You say 'nature.' Do you mean God?"

"I don't know. What do you mean when you say 'nature'?"

"I don't know either."

"In the morning I want to try something," Lamont said. "Then we'll know."

"Then we'll know what?"

"If we can stay here." He touched his lips to hers. "I love you. Do you think you can sleep?"

"So long as I have you beside me."

"I feel the same. So long as I have you."

She slept in his arms.

In the morning, after Lamont had told her what he proposed to do, they went to the spit together. Before approaching the spot where Heller had disappeared, Lamont picked up a heavy stone.

"Wait here, please," he said, and went the last few yards alone.

Just short of where Heller had sunk screaming into the sand, he braced himself and tossed the stone. It fell with a dull thud. Both of them, scarcely breathing, watched to see what would happen to it. The sand did not suck it down.

Lamont took a slow step forward.

"Be careful! Darling, be careful!" Kristina cried out.

He took another step. And another. The last one carried him to the stone.

To where Heller had perished.

The sand remained firm under his feet. He turned and looked at Kristina. "We can stay!" he shouted. "Kris, we can stay!"

April 3, 2061

"Dear Diary,

"We are still here at the lake. Lake Eden, we have named it. Little Janet is one month old today and beautiful.

"After making a pet of the fawn I mentioned, we have more or less become vegetarians. We still eat fish now and then, but it would be unthinkable to kill anything like our Bambi for food, and besides, our garden produces more of everything than we need. Also, we have enough warm clothing from the hides of the few animals we killed before.

"The winter was not nearly the problem we thought it would be. Our cabin is snug and warm, we caught fish through the ice, and we had all sorts of root vegetables stowed away. In the ten months we have been here, though, we have not seen another human being.

"Are we the only ones left? I don't believe that, nor does Lamont. Even if civilization as we knew it has been wiped out— or the slate wiped clean, as Lamont puts it—there must be others like us who have nature's blessing. The planet is renewing itself, that's all.

"But if we are the only ones left, so be it. Life is good and we are content."